W9-BYD-722

LAURA VAN WORMER
THE
BAD
WITNESS

MIRA®

ISBN 1-55166-739-8

THE BAD WITNESS

Copyright © 2002 by Laura Van Wormer.

All rights reserved. Except for use in any review, the reproduction or
utilization of this work in whole or in part in any form by any electronic,
mechanical or other means, now known or hereafter invented, including
xerography, photocopying and recording, or in any information storage or
retrieval system, is forbidden without the written permission of the publisher,
MIRA Books, 225 Duncan Mill Road, Don Mills, Ontario, Canada M3B 3K9.

All characters in this book have no existence outside the imagination of the
author and have no relation whatsoever to anyone bearing the same name
or names. They are not even distantly inspired by any individual known or
unknown to the author, and all incidents are pure invention.

MIRA and the Star Colophon are trademarks used under license and registered
in Australia, New Zealand, Philippines, United States Patent and Trademark
Office and in other countries.

Visit us at www.mirabooks.com

Printed in U.S.A.

For Marjorie Law Ault Van Wormer
Everyone who crosses her path
leaves a little bit better off in this world.

ACKNOWLEDGMENTS

My heartfelt thanks to my agent, Loretta Barrett, and my publisher, Dianne Moggy, and also to Nick Mullendore, Martha Keenan, Miranda Stecyk and Katherine Chamberlain.

I also owe a great deal of thanks to the Meriden contingent, Sharon Carabetta Jodon, Kerry McEntee, Bea O'Brien, Frank Ridley and Marcia Trotta.

And thank you, Chris Robinson, especially on this book.

I
Good Samaritan

CHAPTER | 1

"She can't be dying, Mother," I say quickly into my cell phone, before the light on Sunset Boulevard turns green and the cars start rumbling by again. "I just saw her at the garden center. She was screaming at everybody and looked perfectly healthy to me." We're speaking of Marion O'Hearn, a woman from my hometown who maintains a somewhat poisonous relationship with my family.

"No, it's true, darling," Mother tells me. "She's been diagnosed with a virulent form of liver cancer."

I swallow, changing the cell phone from my left hand to my right and rising from the table, covering my right ear against the noise that has resumed on Sunset. I'm not being rude, because my luncheon companion is sitting at another table trying to make up with his girlfriend, which is why I'm here for lunch in the first place.

Mother is saying something, but I can't make out what. I excuse myself as I slip around a waiter to step inside to a quiet corner of the restaurant, at the side of the bar. "I'm sorry, Mother, what did you say?"

"She really is dying."

"But why does she want to see *me?*" I ask incredulously.

"I don't know, darling." Mother pauses. "Phillip says she's dying and keeps asking to see you."

"Mother, this is SO screwed up!" I finally cry, prompting the bartender to look over in concern. I smile slightly, embarrassed, turn away and lower my voice. Outside I can see that my luncheon companion has just had a glass of water thrown in his face. "Phillip O'Hearn murdered *your* husband," I remind her, "and so now he's calling you to say Marion wants to see *me* on her deathbed?"

"Sally, please, just come home. See her and then you can fly right back out. I wouldn't ask you unless I thought it was very, very important."

If you knew my mother, you would understand how impossible it is to say no to her. She would never ask such a thing of me unless she considered it imperative.

"All right," I finally say. "I'll see what I can do. I'll call you back as soon as I know when I can get there."

I disconnect the phone, sighing. My father was killed twenty-two years ago last month in a collapsing building that, it turned out, had been rigged to fall in on him. The man responsible was Phillip O'Hearn, a friend, if you can believe, my father had set up in the construction business. Twenty-two years later, the evidence is long gone, O'Hearn Construction is a booming enterprise across seven states, the O'Hearns are filthy rich, my father's still dead, and my mother wants me to sit at the deathbed of Mrs. O'Hearn and make peace.

God help me.

I walk back outside to my table where Burton Kott is trying to blot water from his suit and shirt with cloth napkins. His girlfriend has fled the restaurant.

Burton is an associate attorney who has been assigned to baby-sit me until I am called into court to testify in the sensational "Mafia Boss Murder" trial currently unfolding at the Santa Monica courthouse.

"Didn't go so well, huh?" I ask, sliding back into my seat. I squint against the combination of sunlight and car exhaust. It is a typical November weekday in Los Angeles.

"She threw a glass of water at me," he says.

"I saw. So what did you say? It must have been something pretty bad."

He looks up from his suit to glare at me. "What makes you think I said anything?"

Inwardly I smile. I went to college in Los Angeles, at UCLA, and have lived among the Burton Kotts of this world. The trick to understanding these children of parents who hit it big in the entertainment business is to understand that they have been pampered as geniuses from day one and have had very little experience with people who might think otherwise. They have only known the best food, education, medical and dental care, toys, clothing, cultural experiences, charge accounts and credit cards. As a result, until they reach adulthood (if and when they reach adulthood), you have to make them think every good idea is their idea if you want to get anywhere with them, either personally or professionally. Otherwise they will reject it.

"It's a genetic trait women have," I say to Burton, explaining why I assume it was something he said that made his girlfriend lose her temper. "We always throw things when men hint they never found us sexually attractive, anyway."

He stares at me a moment. And then he frowns. "Do you think that's what she thought I meant?"

"I don't know what you said."

"I said—" He hesitates. "Well, she said I was too self-involved, and then I said so was she, like when we were— *Oh,*" he says despondently, sagging in his chair.

"Yeah," I say. I pick up a napkin and tell him to hand me his glasses so I can clean the water drops off.

"But you know?" he asks me a moment later. "When a man is not allowed to be man..." His voice trails off as he looks at me meaningfully. I think I am to understand there was not enough sex in his relationship. I hand him his glasses back.

"She's probably not good enough for you, anyway," I tell him.

His eyes settle on the table. "That's what my mom says." I smile.

My name, by the way, is Sally Harrington. I am a producer for DBS News in New York and as I mentioned before, I am here in L.A. waiting to testify in a murder trial. Burton's firm is defending Jonathan Small, former president of production at Monarch Studios. Jonathan is on trial for shooting Nick Arlcnetta, an organized-crime boss from the East Coast. The mainstay of Jonathan's defense is that Arlenetta was on a killing spree, and to kill him first was the only way to stop him. I'm a witness for the defense because Nick Arlenetta very nearly murdered me, too.

"Burton," I try to say gently, yet loudly enough to carry over the noise of a truck rattling by, "I hate to change the subject—"

"Change the subject," he begs, signaling to the waiter for a check, although neither one of us has finished our lunch.

"My mother needs me to go home to Connecticut for a day. Someone close to our family is dying."

He instantly appears deeply pained and slaps his hand down on the table, making the plates and silverware jump. "No way! You're going to be called to the stand any minute!"

"You've been saying that for two days," I point out. "And I'm still just sitting around." I soften my voice and lean forward. "Maybe you could at least check with the big boss and make sure that I am being called to the stand like today or tomorrow? Or ask him to reschedule me a day later so I can go home and get back?"

Burton absently touches his stomach while he considers this and I wonder if he's in the right line of business. (My on-again, off again boyfriend back in Connecticut, Doug Wrentham, is an assistant district attorney in New Haven and I know for a fact that a prerequisite for practicing criminal law is an iron stomach.) Burton stands up, pushing his chair back. Diners are looking at him, no doubt because his wet hair is every which way, and you can see his flesh through his wet white shirt. "We gotta get to the courthouse. I'll pay the check inside."

"I wouldn't ask," I add, "unless it was very important."

As Burton is shoving his chair under the table to get clear, I am astonished to see a car slowly driving over the sidewalk in our direction. I shout, "Watch out!" and all the diners react, except for a young man sitting directly in the car's path who can't hear me because he has a CD player headset on. I dash across the terrace to haul him backward out of his chair. The car, an old Toyota, crashes through the wrought-iron fencing, crushing it with ease, and comes to a stop on the terrace, the engine still running. The CD listener's table is decimated underneath. There is the smell of gasoline.

"Call 911," I yell, moving over to the driver's window. The diners are stumbling through overturned tables and chairs, fleeing to the street.

The driver is an older man who looks dazed and confused. When he doesn't respond to my question asking if he's all right, I ask him in Spanish and he says no. I look down inside the car and see that the front of the car has caved in around his left leg, trapping him. Gingerly I reach into the car, through the steering wheel, to turn off the ignition. "Don't touch him," I tell the waiter who has appeared at my side.

"We have to go!" someone whispers in my ear. I look back over my shoulder and Burton taps his watch. "Court!"

I send the waiter inside for tablecloths. When he returns, I gingerly cover the driver as best I can. He's in shock; he's starting to shiver. I hear sirens and relax a little, murmuring words I hope are comforting to the old man.

Two police officers appear and I back away from the car. An EMT vehicle pulls in.

"We've got to GO," Burton whispers urgently.

"But we're witnesses," I tell him.

"Shit!" he says. "I thought you wanted to go home!"

"Okay, okay," I say. A large, athletic-looking young fellow blocks my path. I recognize him as the CD listener I had pulled out of harm's way.

"Thank you," he says, squeezing my arm. "God, thank you. I would have been killed."

"You're welcome."

"Sally!" Burton whines with some urgency.

I write down the number of Lawrence Banks's law firm on the back of my card and give it to a waiter to offer to the police. The car valet is quick to retrieve Kott's BMW and soon we're on our way.

Sort of. The accident has brought Sunset Boulevard to a crawl. Burton calls into his firm to tell them we're on our way back to the courthouse.

"Tell them I have to go Connecticut," I whisper.

Burton dutifully relays that someone close to me is on their deathbed in Connecticut and I need a day to fly home and then back again. Whoever he's talking to wants to talk to me directly and Burton hands me the phone.

"Hello?"

"Your mother's dying?" a female voice asks.

"Not my mother, but someone else," I say. "But it's my mother who's begging me to come home to see this person before she dies." I hear the woman repeat this information to someone else.

"Oh, hell," a deep male voice then says into the phone, and I realize it's the big kahuna himself, Lawrence J. Banks, lead counsel for the defense of Jonathan Small. "Look, I'm sorry and everything," he says, "but how long do you think she'll last?"

"Maybe a week," I say as traffic stops again. As Lawrence (yes, the great attorney is only to be called Lawrence) talks with his office staff, Burton pulls a U-turn back the other way on Sunset, honks his way through traffic to turn onto Olive Drive, and then shoots west on Santa Monica Boulevard.

Lawrence comes back on the phone. "Get to the court-house," he says gruffly, and hangs up.

"What did he say?"

"He'll see us at the courthouse."

The prosecution finished presenting their witnesses last week, and on Friday the defense started calling theirs. As the third witness for the defense, I was supposed to be out of here by now, but instead have been waiting around since Monday. I've been sitting in a room drinking coffee and water and trying to get some work done until Burton comes to fetch me for breaks and for lunch. Then I am put back into the room and left until about four-thirty, at which time I am taken to the Shangri-la Hotel on Ocean Avenue. From there I spend at least four hours on the phone with DBS in New York, offering whatever assistance I can with the coverage of the trial since I know more about the background of this case than just about anyone.

The elements of "The Mafia Boss Murder," as it is known, make this trial a tremendous crowd pleaser: a slain organized-crime don, a Hollywood movie-studio execu-tive, an Oscar-nominated actress and tons of money. The entire area around the Santa Monica courthouse has be-come a media war zone. Entrances and exits have been sec-tioned off with concrete barricades and there are cops everywhere. We have a special plate in the windshield of Burton's car that gets us waved through the tight security. The perimeter of the courthouse complex is jammed with media. Since cameras are not allowed in the courtroom for this trial, five network news outfits have built scaffolding to the sky to accommodate cameras and shotgun micro-phones to see and hear all that they can outside. As a wit-ness, this includes me.

I have, to be honest, become somewhat of a sideline story to this trial in my own right. Nick Arlenetta, the "victim" in this case, nearly murdered me last March. At the time I had been covering a story for DBS News about the disappearance of actress Lilliana Martin and inadvertently stepped into the middle of the mob war that has resulted in this trial. Happily, nearly being killed with Lilliana Martin gave me the inside track on this multigenerational war between East Coast crime families—the Arlenettas and the Presarios—and the result was that I wrote and produced the recent DBS News documentary miniseries, *The Family*.

The first two hours of *The Family* ran on Sunday, September 9, and it won its time slot as the most-watched program on television. On Monday night, September 10, it came in second. Then the attack on the World Trade Center and the Pentagon horribly unfolded the next day and we turned to a twenty-four-hour all-news format for the next ten days. We put *The Family* on the shelf until the ratings sweeps in November (last week) and ran the series in its entirety. It did not win the number one spot on any night, but the ratings for DBS were excellent and I am sort of a hero.

I am still, however, very much the new kid on the TV block. I only joined DBS News full-time last summer from the world of print journalism, and although my title has been boosted from assistant producer to producer, my job is essentially to be the right hand of anchorwoman Alexandra Waring, uncontested queen of the airwaves. On good days, I am gratefully astonished at my rapid climb at DBS News. On bad days I dwell on the fact that no matter what anyone says, my job is still "Handmaiden to the Star," which is what I was way back, when at age twenty-one in this very town, Los Angeles, I began my career as an intern to the gossip editor at *Boulevard* magazine.

At any rate, my picture has been in the paper a lot lately, particularly as I am also a witness in the "Mafia Boss Murder" trial. "Don't kid yourself," Alexandra said to me. "If you weren't so pretty, the press wouldn't give you the time of day."

I don't know how pretty I am, but I do know that all of my life people have found my looks pleasing. I'm five foot seven, have light brown hair (streaked with blond at the moment, my concession to LaLa Land) and blue eyes. I've always gotten regular exercise and now that I'm in the world of TV, I hate to admit it, I watch what I eat. (You never know, they may let me on the air someday. You cannot imagine the tremendous jump in my salary if they do.... No, I am not greedy. *You* grow up with scarcely two nickels to rub together and then *you* tell me money's not important. Right... Only if you've been there do you know what I'm talking about.)

Where was I? Ah, yes, my alleged good looks. Well, let me tell you, it's nothing I've done, certainly, it's all in the genetics. My mother, Belle, is a genuine beauty, and my father, Dodge, was a very good-looking fellow. I'm afraid, though, that while my mother—like any genuine beauty—is truly beautiful on the inside (kind, gentle, gracious, patient), I am, like any genetically contrived good-looking person, chaotic and conflicted on the inside (nice, but a workaholic, alternately euphoric and cranky, dreadfully impulsive). At any rate, it's still very strange to see my face in the big newspapers, because I am from a small city in central Connecticut no one's ever heard of—Castleford—and I never dreamed I would end up at a TV network, much less be the focus of the press.

Interestingly, it is my mother who has taken all of these recent events in my life in stride, as if she always knew my life would evolve like this. Her only major worry seems to be that I remember to occasionally brush my hair. I usually wear it parted in the middle, and secure the two front pieces back with barrettes. This is what the *New York Post* insists on calling my "boarding school do," although I went to public school, thank you very much.

As Burton drives me into the courthouse compound, I think I should have brushed my hair because cameras, I know, are trying to zoom in on me for a close-up. As I walk from the secured parking area into the courthouse, I single out the DBS camera on the scaffolding and give a little wave.

Inside the courthouse it is cool and well lit. We walk down the corridor, where I am, once again, ushered into a small windowless room. I sit down at the plain oak table and look at the clock, wondering if there is time to begin testifying this afternoon so I can get out of here.

Let me tell you a little something about this trial. The case is essentially about two "normal" families, linked by marriage in the 1950s, whose patriarchs worked on the business side of organized crime. One branch, the Arlenettas, operated under the Gambino crime family out of New York City; the second family, the Presarios, operated under the Genovese crime family in New Jersey. The Arlenettas were in restaurant and hotel service; the Presarios, in unions, first construction and then office and hotel and telephone workers.

In the mid 1970s, the second generation of the New Jersey family, headed by Frank Presario, started cleaning up their act—and their unions—to go straight. The New York family, the Arlenettas, embodied by a bold young murderer named Nick Arlenetta, tried to push past the Presario unions to expand into Atlantic City. When Frank Presario blocked the Arlenettas, the Arlenettas put out a hit on him. Unfortunately, Frank's wife, Celia, was killed instead. Frank appealed to Celia's relative, Angelo Bruno, the don of Philadelphia, for revenge against the Arlenettas, but Bruno was murdered before he could act. And so, Frank Presario turned state's evidence to the federal government against the Arlenettas. Young Nick Arlenetta escaped the noose, but his father, Joe Arlenetta, was sent to prison, where he died. Frank Presario then took his two children, a girl and a boy, and disappeared into the witness protection program.

Fast forward to last March: Jonathan Small, president of production for Monarch Studios here in L.A., shot and killed Nick Arlenetta in his office. Jonathan Small, it turned out, was, in fact, Frank Presario's son, known as a child as Taylor Presario. Fortunately or unfortunately, depending on your point of view, that was shortly after the actress Lilliana Martin and I were nearly killed by Nick Arlenetta. Lilliana Martin, you see, was Frank Presario's daughter, known as a child as Lise Presario. It was the near murder of us—Lilliana and myself—which, the defense is maintaining, provoked Jonathan Small into killing Nick Arlenetta.

I sit at the table and look at a clock, wondering if anyone will really come to see me. The defense team always says this person or that one will drop in and see me, but nobody ever does, save Burton, who never seems to know what is going on.

I've been spending most of my time in this room looking over reams of confidential computer printouts that make up the DBS News network organizational system. Alexandra gave them to me with the vague instructions that I should know the personnel, budget numbers and organizational flow backward and forward, and be prepared to offer suggestions for improvement. Since DBS News encompasses more than three hundred part-time and full-time employees in twelve countries, and my management experience largely consists of being in charge of the milkshake machine at the Castleford McDonald's when I was sixteen, I am flying a bit blind. The only motivation I can attribute to Alexandra for giving me this assignment is that it is yet another attempt to test my skills.

Alexandra has been throwing all kinds of jobs at me ever since I arrived at DBS News: rewrite this, overhaul that, fly to Atlanta and produce this field report, rehearse this new on-air reporter, work with the techs on reediting the opening visuals of *DBS Magazine,* watch the new audio man to see if there might be a sexual harassment suit pending, fly to St. Louis and check the affiliate's field cameras, write and produce a documentary series on the Presario-Arlenetta families, visit showrooms in search of new chair models for the newsroom, set up an interview for Alexandra with Senator Clinton, find out which racehorse in America has the highest stud fees, create five detailed proposals for new programming out of the news division, change the story lineup for tonight, find out if the cafeteria has any avocados.

So now I'm supposed to assess the structure of the entire news organization.

I'm startled when the door to my room suddenly swings open. "We're going on," Burton announces a bit breathlessly. "Half an hour." He closes the door behind him and hastens across the room, grabbing a chair and swinging it around backward to straddle it. "Lawrence is putting you on next."

The great Lawrence J. Banks, Esquire, is one of the most expensive criminal defense attorneys in the country. Personally, I can't get past this thing Banks has with, er, big hair. I don't know how else to describe it. His gray hair is suddenly and rather startlingly fluffed up with hair spray in the middle of his head. He's pretty big, like six foot four, heavyset, around sixty years old, with immaculate Armani suits, perfect teeth, perfect tan (hey, we're in L.A.), but then he's got this big-hair thing going on in the middle of his head. Go figure.

There is another knock on the door before it swings open. It is Cecelie Blake. Cecelie is one of those good-looking twenty-first century women of some exotic unknown ethnic origin. She has a light brown skin, gorgeous long brown hair and slightly Oriental eyes. She wears a rock of a diamond on her hand with her wedding band; her husband, I understand, is a professional golfer.

Cecelie comes swooping in and stands across the table, squinting down at me with a critical eye. "The hair," she says, making her way around the table.

"I was just going to—" I say, rising.

She pushes me back down into the chair with surprising strength. "I was going to say the hair is good. You can comb it a little, but keep the strands falling out of the clips." She takes my jaw in her hand to turn my face toward her. "Take off the eyeliner. A little mascara, blush, but no lipstick, either, okay? We want you pretty but vulnerable. A little frightened-looking would be even better. Okay?"

"Scared hair, got it," I say, making motions to get up again, but waiting for her approval in case she's going to slam me back down in my chair again.

"Go on," she says.

"Relax," I hear Burton say behind me as I step into the bathroom. (Witnesses waiting to testify have their own powder rooms attached to their waiting rooms. It's probably to keep us from getting murdered or something.) I hold the bathroom door open a crack behind me to listen. "She'll be great," Burton says.

"She better be," Cecelie says.

Hmm. Things are not going as well as expected.

Of course, the prosecution did present sixteen straight witnesses whose testimony spelled out that the murder of Nick Arienetta had to have been premeditated by Jonathan Small.

I look in the mirror over the sink critically. I take the barrettes out and lean over to brush out my hair upside down. I straighten up, brush again, then secure my hair. Much better. Then I carefully pull out some strands and let them hang down, hoping they look scared.

Blue eyes are clear and admittedly pretty. I wipe off whatever smudges of eyeliner I had on. I wipe away a shadow of mascara under my right eye. I put on a little new mascara. Good. Nose is good. Cheekbones still high, but

I look a little pale. She said blush, right? A touch of contour stuff in the hollows. Voilà. Good. Look good. Brush off shoulders of blue suit. Button jacket. Smooth skirt. Yeah, I'm good. Good Samaritan. Ready to go, ready to testify.

CHAPTER | 2

Everybody is staring at me as I make my way to the witness stand and I pray that I do not trip. The courtroom is packed, and out of the corner of my eye I see the attention of the jury is fixed on me. Judge Horace Kahn, an older, eminently experienced criminal judge, is presiding. The clerk of the court meets me in front of the bench and asks me to raise my right hand, which I do.

There is some kind of disturbance outside the courtroom and we all turn to look. The double doors are open and a sheriff comes in, looking to the judge. Judge Kahn nods and the sheriff quickly moves down the side of the courtroom, through the bar and to the side of the bench, where the judge's clerk confers with him.

Meanwhile, the clerk of the court and I are still standing here, watching. (I feel like an abandoned bride.)

The clerk climbs up to the bench to whisper in the judge's ear. "Attorney Perez, Attorney Banks," Judge Kahn says, "will you please approach the bench."

I have to move out of the way. The clerk guides me to the side, where we stand there, awkwardly watching.

There is a furious exchange of whispers at the bench. Banks shrugs, then says, "I know absolutely nothing about it, Your Honor."

The judge sends the lawyers back to their tables, clears his throat and announces that court will be recessed until tomorrow morning at nine-thirty. As murmurs start in the courtroom, the judge adds, "Sheriff McDuff, you may escort the witness to—" He makes a waving motion with his hand. "Out."

Sheriff McDuff gestures for me to follow him. He leads me back to my witness room, where moments later Lawrence J. Banks and Cecelie Blake come in with a police officer. As soon as the door closes, Banks looks at me solemnly. "Officer Fitzwilliam of the West Hollywood Police has been instructed to pick you up, Sally, in connection with a hit-and-run accident."

The police officer is young, nice-looking and is standing there respectfully with his hat under his arm.

I shake my head, frowning. "I'm sorry, I have no idea what— I mean, I don't even have a car out here."

Banks turns to the cop. "Officer?"

"A hit-and-run occurred at 2211 Sunset Boulevard at 1:22 this afternoon," he reads from his notebook.

"Oh, the restaurant!" I cry. "Right." And I hastily explain that yes, I had been eating lunch at a restaurant on Sunset Boulevard with Burton when an older man crashed his car through the wall and drove right onto the terrace, right over the tables, and that I had left my name and the number of Mr. Banks's law firm where I could be reached if they needed more witnesses.

"You just took off?" Cecelie asks.

"No. First I checked on the driver, he was pinned in the car, and actually I covered him with some tablecloths because he was shaking—shock, you know—and then the police and the EMTs arrived." I look to Banks. "Burton said we had to get to the courthouse."

"Who's Burton?" the police officer asks.

"Burton Kott, one of my associates," Banks tells him. He turns to Cecelie. "Get Burton." He turns back around to address the cop. "It seems incredible you would interrupt a trial of this magnitude to locate a witness," Banks says in a low, for-whom-the-bell-tolls voice.

"As a criminal defense lawyer," the officer says easily, "I'm sure it does."

I smile slightly, impressed. He is young but well spoken, confident. And, well, cute.

To Banks and Sheriff McDuff the young officer explains, "We were told it was a hit-and-run accident, and there is an APB out on Miss Harrington."

My mouth parts in astonishment and I'm not so impressed anymore.

The officer turns to me. "I was told you were the driver in the hit-and-run."

"The driver was a Spanish man about seventy years old," I say. "And when I left, the car was still crushed around his left leg. He wasn't running anywhere."

Cecelie arrives with Burton and he backs up my story. And God bless him, despite the glaring eyes of his boss heavy upon him, Burton squares his shoulders and says, "I accept full responsibility. Sally didn't want to leave, but I told her she had to. She might have to testify."

"And you left your card with the waiter?" Banks asks me.

"I couldn't just leave," I say. The young officer nods slightly; he seems pleased by this answer.

"Well," Banks says, "court's recessed until tomorrow morning. You better go with Officer—"

"Fitzwilliam, sir."

"Officer Fitzwilliam and hopefully sort out your difficulties."

I sigh. "Okay."

"Lawrence," Burton says, "I think I should accompany our client."

"It would appear, Attorney Kott," the officer says, scanning his notebook and then looking up, "that you are a witness to the accident who fled the scene."

"Um," Burton says.

"Go with them," Banks tells him.

We are taken out the front door of the courthouse, where word has evidently reached the press that the police arrived to arrest someone in the courtroom where "The Mafia Boss Murder" trial was being held. I can only imagine the reaction of the DBS crew when they realize that it is me that is being ushered into the back seat of the West Hollywood police cruiser, along with a criminal defense lawyer. Within minutes, I know, my poor mother will be barraged with calls that I've been arrested.

By the time we reach the police station in West Hollywood, I have come to like Officer Paul Fitzwilliam. At this point he is being solicitous to me to the point of flattery, whereas with Burton, that no-good fleeing witness, he is being suitably short. When we reach the station, he allows me to call Mother immediately to forewarn her. "Do you understand, Mother? It's a misunderstanding, I've done absolutely nothing wrong, I'm absolutely fine, regardless of what you might hear."

"I understand, darling." A pause. "Does this mean you can't come home and see poor Marion?"

Oh, right. Mrs. O'Hearn is dying. Amazing how the O'Hearns always seem to steal the stage. Here I am on national television being taken away by the police from "The Mafia Boss Murder" trial and the priority is "poor Marion," whose husband killed my father.

"I'm doing the best I can, Mother."

"They've screwed everything up!" Burton announces when I return to the booking area of the precinct. "You were supposed to be picked up for assault, not a hit-and-run." He glares at Officer Fitzwilliam.

"They made a mistake," Officer Fitzwilliam admits to me.

"Assault?" I say. "I'm supposed to have assaulted somebody?"

The sergeant on duty reads from his desk register. "It says here a Mr. Rollo Sorrell claims you pulled him backward out of his chair, an action that resulted in the severe wrenching of his shoulder."

I blink.

The sergeant looks up from the book. "Do you have any response to this charge?"

"Uh, *yeah*," I say. "Like that Mr. Rollo was about to be squashed by an oncoming car."

The sergeant's interest picks up. "You're saying he was sitting in the path of an oncoming car?"

"Yes. And there were about twenty witnesses to the fact."

"Let's hope *they* didn't run away," Officer Fitzwilliam says, frowning at Burton.

"If he was so badly hurt, why didn't he say anything at the time?"

"Maybe he did and you didn't hear him," the sergeant suggests.

"I did hear him!" I nearly yell. "He said, 'Thank you. God, thank you. I would have been killed.' That's what he said, Sergeant. Write it down."

He does. And then, "According to the complaint, due to his injuries Mr. Sorrell's ability to work has been severely impaired and he is filing charges of assault against you."

I slam the desk in frustration, making everyone's eyes widen a little.

"He must have found a lawyer," Burton says.

"He's a massage therapist," the sergeant reads on with a hint of a smile, "and he is unable to work. He's gone to the hospital for X rays."

"I'll give him something to X ray," I mutter.

Officer Fitzwilliam gives me a warning look—*not cool to make threats.* He is most definitely on my side now. I can tell.

And he is cute. Dark hair, dark eyes, maybe five ten.

"Sergeant," Burton says, "my client stepped in to save the life of a man who was in the path of an oncoming car. Don't you find it the least bit odd that he would thank her, and then, within an hour, call the police to demand she be arrested for assault?"

"Yes, I do," he admits.

Burton whips around to me. "You're suing this clown. This is fraud, this is harassment, this is slander, libel—"

"Whatever it is, Burton," I say quietly, "you are *not* my lawyer. I'll get one of my own, thank you."

"You're the one who fled the scene of a terrible accident," Officer Fitzwilliam reminds Burton. He squints slightly. "When you take the oath of office, you become an officer of the court, you know."

While the boys fight it out, I leave to use the ladies' room. Inside there is a rather heavily weathered young woman trying to apply lipstick in the mirror. She's wearing a leather miniskirt, spike heels, fishnet stockings and a stretchy top with a plunging neckline. On her wrist I can see needle marks. She must have been a heavy user for a while to resort to using visible veins. She meets my eye in the mirror. "Don't you fuckin' hassle me, bitch," she growls.

"I won't," I promise, going into one of the stalls. Under the door, I look at how the woman's heels have worn on the outside. I wonder where she came from, where she started out. It always makes me sad. Who knows, maybe being slightly bowlegged made her turn to booze, later drugs? Oh, who knows.

What a mess this life can be.

When I emerge from the stall, the woman is still there, still trying to apply that lipstick that is by now grotesquely, redly thick. Her eyes are clouded over, her lids heavy, and this time she smiles wide at me, exposing a missing tooth and lipstick smeared over the others. "Oh, man," she laughs, letting her head fall forward.

She shot up, I realize, probably just before I came in. And now she's going into the nod.

Heroin, I bet.

In the police station. Heaven help us.

When I walk back outside to the booking area, Burton is nowhere to be found.

"I'm afraid you are going to have appear in court, Ms. Harrington," the sergeant informs me, writing out a form. "I know it's a pain, but we have to do it. If you'll just finish filling out the information on these forms and sign at the bottom, I'll give you a copy and you can go. Officer Fitzwilliam will give you a ride."

I accept the forms and a pen. "I live on the East Coast. When do you think this court appearance would be?"

"Couple months. Unless he should drop the charges."

I sigh, scribbling information, sign my name. When I'm done, I glance around. "Where's Burton?"

"He's talking to the captain about his situation," the sergeant says, smiling, taking my papers and making a tidy pile for his folder.

"I'll take you to wherever you want to go," Officer Fitzwilliam says to me, and for a fraction of a second I wonder if it is a double entendre.

Stop it. "I suppose I should wait for Burton." After a moment, I add, "Maybe." I look at Officer Fitzwilliam and we exchange smiles. "Maybe not," I say, and we both laugh.

The woman from the bathroom walks past us. The sound of her heels is loud, the scent of her perfume heavy. Officer Fitzwilliam barely glances at her, but I watch as she gives us the finger and makes her way down a corridor. The sergeant makes a photocopy of the forms for me and then I accompany Fitzwilliam outside to the precinct garage. "I could take a cab," I offer.

"It's the least we can do," he says, opening the front door of the squad car for me. He looks at his watch. "Besides, dropping you off will get me to the end of my shift and I'll just take the car home. I'm on again at midnight."

We make idle chat as we leave the garage. When we reach the street, I ask him if he noticed the woman who walked by us in the booking area.

"The one who flew the bird at us?" he chuckles, turning the wheel.

"I didn't know you saw her."

He glances over, flashing a smile. "That's my job. To see things."

I smile, too. He's awfully young. Clearly destined for good things, though. He's educated—or well read. I can tell by the way he speaks, by his easy good manners.

"Anyway," he says, "that was Sally."

"Sally? Her name's Sally?" I ask, pained.

"I think her real name is something like Madeline, or Mary Lynn—"

"And now it's Sally?"

"The johns must like it," he shrugs.

Well, this certainly gives me pause for thought.

And then Officer Fitzwilliam realizes what he has said and laughs. "That's not what I meant at all. Sally's a great name! But that's not her real name." He glances over. "Her father was some big shot in Beverly Hills, believe it or not. Maybe a producer or something? She got into drugs—the family moved away, won't have anything to do with her. She hangs out around Graumann's Chinese Theatre, where all the celebrity hand and footprints are. We have to pick her up occasionally."

"That's so sad," I murmur. "Was she ever clean?"

"I don't know."

Suddenly he snaps his fingers. "Now I know where I've

seen you!" He slaps his forehead. "I mean, I've seen stuff in the papers about the trial and everything, but I just saw you on something else. Recently." He looks over and drops his voice. "Was it a story about some guy who killed your father?"

I nod. "Could have been."

"I think I saw it on the Learning Channel," he says. "Maybe a week ago?"

It was very possible. *DBS News Magazine* recycles their "true crime" pieces to cable. ABC, NBC, we all do it now.

He glances over. "That was you, right? In Connecticut?"

I nod, suddenly feeling sad. I am reminded of my dead father, of my mother wanting me to come home to see Marion O'Hearn. "Yes."

"I'm sorry," he says. After a moment, "It seemed like your family got a rough deal."

"My mother certainly did," I say. "My brother and I were okay. We had her."

"Did she ever get any kind of compensation?"

"Some kind of stipend for me and my younger brother from social security, until we were eighteen."

"You never sued the guy civilly?"

I shake my head. "We wouldn't want anything from him," I say flatly, looking out my window.

We drive along for a bit. "Your mother is very beautiful, as I recall," he says. "Courageous, too."

"She is," I agree. This conversation is starting to give me a stomachache.

"Not that you aren't," he adds.

"Thank you," I murmur, eyes out the window.

A moment later, "My mom watches all the true-crime shows," he says. "Who do you work for again?"

"DBS News."

"Mom loves Alexandra Waring." He laughs to himself. "She says you can count on people from Kansas."

I look over at him. "Why's that, you suppose?"

"My mother's from Kansas," he laughs.

I smile politely, feeling dreadfully tired suddenly and not particularly like talking.

"So what is she like?" he asks.

I try to snap out of my lethargy. "I'm sorry, what did you say?"

"Alexandra Waring—what is she like?"

"Oh, well," I sigh, thinking a minute as we pass by a gigantic billboard featuring a young man, stark-naked save briefs. "She's—well, brilliant. At what she does. And she's..." I think about it. "Let's just say she can be focused in the extreme. A perfectionist. She's also extremely generous, and good to us all. She's actually good to just about anybody." I smile. "She writes thank-you notes that make you want to write a thank-you note back, you know?"

He laughs.

"She's really a terrific person." I yawn. "It's just hard to keep up with her."

We drive along for a minute. "I've heard things about her..." He glances over.

"I'm sure you've heard many things," I say diplomatically.

"Well, you know," he says. "A lot of people have seen her and Georgiana Hamilton-Ayres around here." He looks over. "She has a house out here."

I don't say anything.

"So, is she like, gay?" he asks, returning his attention to the wheel.

"Um," I say, as if just about everybody doesn't ask me this same question, "you certainly wouldn't assume so. What I mean is, Alexandra is just a very attractive woman—and attractive to everybody, you know? But she keeps her personal life private. I mean, everyone thinks they know what she is, or who she's with, but her ratings never seem to be affected one way or another."

He smiles. "So she is gay. I work in West Hollywood, remember?"

"Whatever." I shrug, looking out the window.

"You're protective," he says. "I like that."

I look over at him.

"And loyal. That's good. Not enough of it in this world."

"Well, what about you?" I ask. "Is your captain gay? I hear he's been hanging out with Dudley Do-Right. He has a house out here, you know."

He smiles. "Okay. Message received." He glances over. "I don't find anything wrong with being gay, you know. I just wondered."

"I know," I say. Of course I don't know, because I don't know him. I shift in my seat, turning to face him. "So where are you from? You said your mother's from Kansas."

"I'm from here, Pasadena." And he starts to tell me about his family. His father was in the air force, stationed in Kansas, met and married his mother, and then they were transferred to California. Father got out of the service and started working in a cardboard-manufacturing company, which he eventually bought. "He's done very well."

I'm studying his profile now. "So how did you get into law enforcement?"

"I'm pretty new still," he tells me, glancing over. "I was

in Montana for a while, after high school, working in the oil fields."

"That's kind of cool," I say.

He flashes a grin. "Well, I was going to be a great novelist. Instead I got drunk a lot—and really, really lonely. So occasionally a drunken story about a lonely novelist." He burst out laughing. "Oh, brother, it was pretty awful." He looks at me, still laughing. "Sally? May I call you Sally?"

"Yes, please do."

Still smiling, he looks at the road, shaking his head. "Oh, brother, I was a mess, Sally. I finally came back to California and started at USC. I worked, went to school, and then went through the academy." He glances over. "I finally just got my BA last summer."

"That's wonderful," I tell him sincerely. "Are you still writing?"

He shakes his head. "No." He lofts his eyebrows. "Don't have time." We drive along. "I'm toying around with the idea of law school. I see guys like that Burton Kott and I think somebody better counteract him. I'm sorry," he adds, looking over. "Is he a friend of yours? I shouldn't have said that."

"Don't worry. He just kind of looks after me. As a witness for the defense."

He nods. "Do you like lawyers?"

"I know a couple," I admit, thinking of Doug Wrentham back home and wondering why I have no feeling about him.

"My father hates that I'm a cop," he suddenly says.

"Why? I should think he would be proud."

"It's an Irish thing, I think. You know, all the Irish cops

in yesteryear, because it was the only profession they were allowed to pursue. Last thing a successful Irish-American family wants is a throwback to the police. My older brother? An orthodontist. My sister? A pilot. My younger brother? Getting his MBA from Wharton."

"But you were always different," I hazard a guess.

"I like the active nature of the job, you know? I like justice, I like seeing our system work to protect people."

As the police cruiser pulls up to the front doors of the hotel, I can see that the bellman is intrigued by the vehicle I'm arriving in. He hurries down the steps and I roll down the window. "Is everything all right, Ms. Harrington?"

"Fine, thank you," I tell him. I turn to Officer Fitzwilliam.

"I am so sorry about today," he tells me sincerely. "It was just one of those things."

"Yes," I say.

There is a funny little silence.

"Thank you for driving me," I say. "I've enjoyed talking to you. I wish you the best of luck in your career." I smile. "We need good people in law enforcement."

"Thanks," he tells me. He hesitates. "So, are you going to be all right while you're out here?" He swallows. "Is there something I can do for you?"

"No. Thank you, no."

Get out of the car, Sally.

"Well," he says, "I hope everything goes well."

"Thank you." I open the car door.

"Take care," he calls.

"Goodbye," I say, feeling inexplicably disappointed. I close the door and walk into the lobby of the hotel.

What was with me and that cop? I wonder, trying to shake it off.

He was adorable.

I check for messages at the front desk and am told that a FedEx package has already been delivered to my room.

I take the stairs up to my fourth-floor suite. I have a living room, bedroom, kitchenette and bath. I kick off my heels, slip off my jacket and skirt and hang them up. I am sifting through the pile of faxes in the living room that have come through the machine (and are spilled all over the floor) when the telephone rings.

"Hello?" I say, balancing the phone on my shoulder as I undo my pearls.

"Sally?"

"Yes?"

"It's Paul Fitzwilliam," he says.

I am astonished. "Hi."

"Well, Officer Fitzwilliam just went off duty two minutes ago, but Paul Fitzwilliam, the civilian, would like to know if maybe you'd like to have a hamburger or something."

"Where are you?" I laugh.

"In the lobby," he says.

I feel a question hanging in the air. I feel my heart racing.

"I was just getting changed," I finally say.

"Oh," he says softly. After a moment. "Would you like me to come up?"

Oh, my God, I think, taking a nervous breath. Why would he think— Why am I thinking—

My heart is pounding. "I—I don't know what to say."

"You could say you would like me to come up," he says quietly. A pause. "Sometimes it just happens this way."

I tell him the room number. As I hang up, I see that my hand is shaking. I find myself going into the bathroom to look in the mirror, where I find that I don't want to see myself right now, not when I'm planning to do what I'm afraid I am planning to do.

I go to the closet to pull out the skirt and put it back on.

There is a knock on the door.

I walk over and open it. Officer Paul Fitzwilliam, his hat tucked politely under his arm, shyly smiles.

I don't say anything and nor does he. He merely glides into the room, I close the door behind him, and when I turn around, it is to receive his hands around my waist, effortlessly pulling me into his arms. We kiss.

And kiss again.

He tastes of spearmint Tic Tacs, his breath is growing stronger, his grasp on me, too.

I feel the wall at my back and he moves closer, tighter, and I make a small sound in the back of my throat. In the next moment his mouth is breezing down the side of my neck, coming to rest in the hollow, his hands gently starting to roam.

So are mine. Fully around his back, down lower. There is a gun belt, bullets, below is his lower back. It is a marvelous fit between.

He smells wonderful. I remember this smell from long ago, back when the boys I dated did physical things during the day. It is so unlike adulthood, isn't it, I think, of men sitting in offices smelling only of expensive aftershave.

It is the smell of youth, of activity, of a strong, virile young man.

And my body is so into it, I cannot tell you.

We are moving toward the bedroom, and at this point I am resigned to my fate and don't care. About anything but enjoying this fate. We fall onto the bed, and the holster of his gun jabs me in the hip. I feel something else pressing hard on my thigh.

Wow. His mouth is back down onto my neck again, his hand sweeping over my breast, and I hear myself groan a little, and I feel him move against me, excited.

Suddenly he props himself up to look at me, narrowing his eyes, almost as if he were in pain.

"What?" I whisper.

He touches the side of my face a moment, his eyes searching mine. "Maybe..." His voice trails off.

Maybe what? Close the curtains? Take our clothes off? Maybe put that damn gun somewhere before it's permanently embedded in my hip?

Whatever it is, it's not good, I can tell that now. The desire is fading, rapidly, at least on my part. Something is wrong. I close my eyes a moment and then open them.

"Not like this," he whispers. Then he looks pained again.

"You're right," I say suddenly. I've got to say something, don't I? To save face? I don't know what the hell is the matter with Officer Paul Fitzwilliam, but I have compromised myself with him to no return. I swallow, shifting a little to offer a hint.

He slides off me and sits up on the edge of the bed, his back to me. I can't believe I'm sitting here looking at a set of handcuffs and the butt of a gun in the holster of a uniformed cop who is sitting on my bed. Wonder if this guy's a psycho? Wonder if he wants to handcuff me and do me with the gun or something?

What have I done? I wonder, an icy chill creeping up my spine.

I struggle to sit up, pull my skirt down and smooth my blouse. I slide over to the corner of the bed and sit there. "I don't know what got into me," I mutter. "I'm sorry."

"*You're* sorry?"

I look at him.

"Sally—" He moves over and reaches to take my hand. "I—" He stops again, looking at me. "I don't want this to happen and then you disappear."

I blink, not quite understanding.

He looks down at our hands, slowly squeezing mine. "It's weird, I know, but I—" He looks up. "I want to know you."

A number of replies come to mind, none of which seem appropriate.

When I don't say anything, he stands up. "Excuse me a minute, will you?" He walks manfully into the bathroom, his hardware making noise. I hear water running, the john flush. By the time he is out, I have pulled myself together and am out in the living room.

"I don't suppose you would consider having that hamburger with me?" he asks, eyes on the ground.

I smile. "Sure."

He raises his eyes and looks so vulnerable, so young and trusting, the panic in me begins to subside. I don't think he is a psycho. Maybe I am, though.

"Maybe now is not the best time, though," I add.

"Maybe tomorrow?" he asks.

"Sure," I say again. "Paul."

When I say his name, a flush appears on his neck. This pleases me. He is not unmoved. Nor am I.

He walks over to the door. "Tomorrow," he says, opening the door and turning around. "Six o'clock?"

"Six o'clock," I confirm.

In the next moment, he is leaving, the door closing softly behind him.

CHAPTER | 3

The telephone starts ringing while I'm in the shower, trying to wash off my embarrassment about my encounter with Officer Paul Fitzwilliam. I debate whether or not to answer it, because whoever it is might get my mind thinking straight and I'm not at all sure I would like it straightened. It may be preferable to stay out here in the zone where I continue to view my life from the third person.

I know I have to answer it, though, so I jump out of the shower and pick up the extension.

"Ms. Harrington?" a young woman's voice says. "It's Becky from the station? I'm supposed to take you to the studio? To be interviewed by Alexandra Waring? Live? For tonight's newscast?"

I am tempted to ask this child of LaLa Land if she's ever heard of a declarative sentence, but decide not to beat her up because of my own general mood of disagreeableness. "No one notified me," I tell her.

"You can call Will Rafferty? I mean, like, to make sure and everything?"

I wrap my wet hair in a towel and call Will, the executive producer of *DBS News America Tonight with Alexandra Waring,* in New York. "You know I'm not supposed to talk about the trial until I've testified," I begin, holding the phone under my chin while I apply moisturizer to my body. The stuff the hotel provides smells wonderful. It's pale green and smells vaguely of juniper.

"You're not going to talk about the trial," he tells me.

"They don't want me doing interviews," I add.

"They don't want you doing interviews about 'The Mafia Boss Murder' trial," Will counters. "You're talking about being arrested and taken away from the courthouse."

"I wasn't arrested!" I say.

"Not that you called in to tell us!" he yells.

I hold the phone away from my ear.

"Where the *hell* have you been, Sally?"

"I just got back to the hotel," I say. "I was with the police and couldn't call in."

"The cop dropped you off at the hotel an hour and a half ago!"

Spies, spies, everywhere spies. I suppose by being a member of the media I deserve this. And I suppose I should count myself lucky Will doesn't seem to know that the aforementioned police officer stuck around awhile.

"Look, I'm doing the best I can, Will," I say, using my fallback line, when what I really want to say is, *Be glad I'm here at all, because given the mood I'm in, I could otherwise be making love with this marvelous young officer for hours and hours, which would take me away from this idiot world where I have to testify at a trial you guys want me to cover, where you guys spy on me, while my mother is begging me to come home so I can hear what the wife of my father's murderer wants to say to me on her deathbed. Get a life, Will Rafferty,* I want to say. *Leave me alone for two minutes, will you?*

"Okay, look, Sally, we're going to talk about you being taken away from the courthouse by the West Hollywood Police. For this alleged hit-and-run."

"The whole thing was stupid," I tell him.

"Everybody's covering this story, Sally, so it might be nice if you said something about it. Like to the people you work for."

This stings. "All I am saying is, I'm a witness in an important murder trial and a man's life is at stake. What happened today was stupid and irrelevant."

"The guy shot a gangster in cold blood. What's the difference if you talk about a hit-and-run at a restaurant or not?"

"It was not a hit-and-run—"

"Alexandra said you have to do the interview. To set the record straight."

I roll my eyes. That's his fallback line—*Alexandra* said. "Fine, I'll be there," I say, hanging up.

I meet Becky in the lobby and we climb into her Honda. Getting to the affiliate studio in Burbank is a trip and a half during rush hour. We try to snake up the coast, and then east, over the Santa Monica Mountains on Mulholland Drive, and then north on Cold Water Canyon, easing us down into the Valley. This journey takes a while. After a few halfhearted questions, Becky gives up trying to make conversation and we listen to the all-news station.

I'm thinking about Paul Fitzwilliam again and what happened, and I'm feeling a little depressed.

I'm thirty-one years old and clearly not ready to get married. I mean, how can I get married if I can't—don't want to be—in any one relationship for any period of time?

I just don't know anymore.

"I don't want this to happen and then you disappear," he said.

My brother isn't very good marriage material, either, I don't think. Unlike me, Rob is quiet and on the shy side. On the other hand, he comes up with a new girlfriend like clockwork every year. His career, like mine, is chaotic. He blows up Colorado snowbanks to create avalanches for a living. In the off-season he's—well, let's see. He's been a cowboy, a bartender, a mountain guide, a lumberjack, and last year he helped build a new gondola at Snow Mass. Rob is twenty-nine. We *think* he has a college degree (Mother has yet to see it), and his major was in physical education or forestry or animal husbandry (or maybe something else, for we lost count of his majors and colleges).

So what's wrong with the Harrington kids that we can't seem to settle down? Anyone who meets our mother is utterly thrown by the question. Mother, in fact, is the one who is getting married next year. Will that influence Rob and me?

Paul Fitzwilliam.

I understand sexual attraction, and I understand my impulse to give in to it—but I don't understand why I *am* giving in to it! For years I was not terribly sexual, mostly because, I guess, my first two boyfriends weren't overly sexual. I mean, heaven knows, we had sex, but in high

school with Doug it was always over very quickly and per-
functorily, and then with Bill, an aspiring actor I met while
living out here, our sex life was more theatrical than sexual. (Bill always had these fantasies going and wanted to
do role-playing and by the time we ever actually did anything—with costumes and sets, practically—I was exhausted, both physically and mentally. Finally, I was just
sick of it.) But when he cheated on me with a working actress (notice the operative word *working*—she, like me,
earned a regular paycheck), you would have thought ours
had been the perfect, most fulfilling relationship in the
world, I was so shocked and hurt and indignant. "*How*
could he *do* this to me?" I wailed. While now I think, "*How*
could I have been such an *idiot?*"

Spencer Hawes was an entirely different matter. Spencer
is a, well, what would you call it? Sensualist? I don't know,
but whatever it is, it means hours of pleasure and sensation
that eventually is satiated by sex. In comparison to Officer
Paul, my introduction to Spencer seems like a long
courtship. I met him at a business luncheon, then met him
for dinner and walked around Fifth Avenue for at least an
hour before I fell into him like a sex-starved mariner.

But that is the point. I *was* starved. I see that now.
Spencer opened a whole vista to me about my own body,
about what it is capable of feeling if only I let go, if only I
trusted someone else to unlock its secrets. He was so patient. And so very, very good. And ever since I have felt
vaguely out of control, keenly aware of the potential my
body holds with another who intrigues it.

There are a number of problems with where I have been
left. Spencer is not the man for me. So I went back to
Doug, who is changing, but not into a man I can swear a

lasting bond to. I mean, look at what just happened this afternoon. It's still there, that hunger, that longing. Only now I know what it is, and now I find myself acting out on it with a stranger. A police officer!

So am I a sex addict now? Is that what happens? You just numbly function in everyday life waiting for, thinking about, savoring the opportunity to act out and let go in sexual abandon? Is that what happens to people who do not drink a lot or do drugs or overeat or undereat, or spend money they do not have? Do they become addicted to sex so that in the absence of it sometimes they feel as though they are next to dead?

I feel trapped with Doug. And I'm certain it is not about sex. Because we've had some good times. The truth is, I don't think I trust Doug and I'm not sure why.

With Spencer I felt as though he broke me down, took me apart sexually, found out what was wrong, and then started putting me back together. The only problem with Spencer is, I would never be convinced he was only "fixing" me.

What I've been feeling lately is a kind of panic, as if every opportunity to act out sexually may be my last. It could be my turning thirty-one that is making me feel this way. It could be my intent to buy my mother's house, although I live in Manhattan most of the time. (Talk about stress.) It could be my new career in TV news. Or it could be because Doug says he'll transfer to New York so we can be married.

Yeah, I'm feeling trapped all right.

Honest to God, I'm not completely immoral. I have principles, and I have loyalties, and I have been—and will be again—monogamous. But in this past year or two it's as if I moved through one door and can't find the next, and I'm stuck out here in the hallway, scared to move on in the dark, yet ready to lunge at the tiniest crack of light.

I just don't know what I'm looking for anymore.

I also have to wonder how often this kind of thing happens to Officer Paul Fitzwilliam, how often he drops a woman off and hangs around, "to make sure they're all right."

Don't be such a cynic, I tell myself.

Officer Paul Fitzwilliam, I think, is an essentially good man. I don't know why, but I do.

Becky and I finally reach the studio of KWRK, our modest L.A. affiliate, and I am hustled into their makeshift makeup room. (It consists of a mirror by the photocopy machine and a shelf with a bunch of slapdash cosmetics thrown all over it.) I am then whisked into the studio, where I am seated in a plain armchair. An earphone is placed in my right ear—held in place by a loop that discreetly fits behind my ear—and a microphone is hastily clipped on the lapel of my blazer. They have focused one klieg light and three fills on me. I face a single TV camera and listen into my earpiece for instructions and, later, the actual interview questions from Alexandra. I will never see the anchorwoman, who is in New York.

Soon the red light of the camera comes on and I know millions of people across America are looking at me.

Alexandra: It was reported today that just as you were being sworn in to testify in "The Mafia Boss Murder" trial, the West Hollywood police came to arrest you.

Me: No, they didn't actually arrest me.

Alexandra: But the trial was interrupted and recessed until tomorrow because the police took you away. In the back seat of a police cruiser. Is that part of the report correct?

Me: Yes.

Alexandra: And you were about to start testifying, were you not?

Me: I've been asked not to comment on any aspect of the trial until I've finished testifying.

Alexandra: Well, would you—can you (flirting with sarcasm) explain what happened? Why the West Hollywood police interrupted "The Mafia Boss Murder" trial to take you away in a police car?

Me: I was eating lunch today at a West Hollywood café on Sunset Boulevard. We were sitting at a table, outside, on the terrace. A driver, on Sunset, lost control of his vehicle and crashed through the fence and drove up onto the terrace of the restaurant. I saw that someone was sitting directly in the path of the oncoming car, so I grabbed him and pulled him backward out of his chair so he wouldn't get run over.

Alexandra: Was he hurt?

Me: No. He jumped right up and thanked me profusely for saving his life. But then an hour later—(I sigh). Evidently he called the police and told them I had assaulted him and he was going to sue me.

Alexandra: That's an odd way of thanking someone.

Me: Tell me about it! Popular opinion has it that maybe the guy's career isn't going so well—or maybe his lawyer's career isn't going so well—and someone has convinced him there is some money to be made in this.

Alexandra: And the police interrupted the proceedings of "The Mafia Boss Murder" trial because someone said you assaulted him?

Me: Well, Alexandra, the complaint got a bit twisted in the rendition, and the police had been under the impression that I was the one who had been driving the car. They thought I had crashed the car into this guy and then taken off.

Alexandra: But you were, in fact, the person who saved this guy's life.

Me: (I shrug.) Yep.

Alexandra: So do you testify tomorrow in "The Mafia Boss Murder" trial?

Me: I'm scheduled.

Alexandra: (Pause) Let me ask you this, Sally, have the police linked the car crash today with the fact that you are a witness in a sensational trial?

Me: (A little taken back) They didn't say anything to me.

Alexandra: The police made no mention of the extraordinary coincidence that you were waiting to testify and at lunch a car crashed through the fence of the restaurant where you were seated? A car that could have killed you? And that when you left the restaurant unhurt and reported to the courthouse, the minute you were ready to testify was the minute the police arrived to take you away? No one at the precinct noticed this extraordinary coincidence in the sequence of events?

Me: No.

Alexandra: How long have you been in the Los Angeles area waiting to testify?

Me: Since Sunday night.

Alexandra: Has anything else out of the ordinary happened to you in the past three days?

Me: No. (I think of Paul Fitzwilliam and wonder if my face is getting red.) It's been pretty quiet.

Alexandra: So only today, the day you were finally called to testify, have these strange events occurred.

Me: (Smile.) I need to just focus in on the fact that I'm here to testify.

Alexandra: Well, let's just hope the authorities do a good job of making sure you can. Sally Harrington, thank you for speaking with us tonight.

I jump off the set and charge into the control room to grab the hotline to New York. "Get Will," I say.

"Hang on," a voice says.

"What is it, Sally?"

"What the hell is she doing, Will? Trying to make me some sort of target?"

"You already are a target," he says. "That's why it's news."

"I am *NOT* a target," I say. "There was a stupid accident and greedy masseuse, that's it."

"No, Sally, that's not it," he says, sounding tired.

"I knew I shouldn't go along with this," I say loudly, well aware of those who are listening. "You're going to screw up Jonathan Small's trial and that's not fair."

"Except that it could be Jonathan Small's defense team who's behind this," Will says.

"Oh, don't be stupid," I say impatiently, but the next moment I wonder if there could be anything to this. That the defense might like to publicize how the Presario clan and their allies are constantly surrounded by would-be killers and assassins.

No, they wouldn't do it. Having lived in L.A., I am much

more of a believer in old men crashing cars into restaurants, and in masseuses who hire lawyers who convince them that they, too, can be one of those callers to financial radio shows who proudly say, "I am about to receive a large settlement. After I pay off my credit card debts, how should I invest it?"

"It's not stupid," Will says. "Particularly in light of the fact that no one can find this masseuse, Rollo Sorrell, tonight, and the driver of the car has disappeared from Cedars-Sinai hospital."

"Well he couldn't have gone far," I say, "his leg was crushed."

"Makes it all the more amazing, doesn't it?"

Another thought. "He's probably an illegal alien and his family got him out of there before he gets deported."

"Rationalize what you want, Sally," Will says wearily, "but Alexandra thinks the whole thing stinks to high heaven and I agree with her. So if people are going to play these kind of games, we want you to have protection while you're there and this story should see that it is given."

It is fruitless to argue. Alexandra and the whole West End Broadcasting Center executive staff is obsessed with security. And, to be honest, for good reason. TV is a personal medium and every wacko out there is waiting to form a personal attachment, which in more dire cases can end up in stalking. At one point in DBS history, talk show host Jessica Wright was kidnapped. A year before Alexandra came to DBS, when she covered Capitol Hill for another news network, a lovesick fan shot her. The moral of the story is, if you're on TV, you're a target.

Not long ago, Darenbrook Communications, the parent company of DBS, had an opportunity to buy studio space in Times Square. A trial balloon was sent up about doing the news downtown, where people could watch the broadcast from the street. Alexandra Waring's face in that meeting, I swear, went absolutely white. "You better talk to the next anchorperson in this job, because this one will not do it."

Alexandra is not a coward. She's merely careful because she's been shot once already, and her best friend at the network was kidnapped. On the other extreme, there is me, who has a tendency to deal with danger by simply denying that it exists. (It's a habit from childhood. When things are too uncomfortable or too overwhelmingly frightening, I latch on to distraction to shut it out.)

At any rate, the point is, my boss, Alexandra Waring, tends to deal with threats head-on, while I struggle to shove them quickly to somewhere I don't have to deal with them. The result is, she is the fixed point of power at DBS News and I am her careening employee, and if she thinks security is in order, it will happen.

It happens.

When Becky drives me back to the hotel, there is a Santa Monica police officer waiting in the lobby who has been assigned to keep an eye on me tonight. "I never quite understood this," I say to the officer as we walk up to my floor. "Doesn't having a police officer standing outside my hotel room door only bring attention to where I am?"

"It is a deterrent," she says gruffly.

So she stands outside my door. I fix some coffee and she accepts a cup. She gratefully takes today's newspapers from me. Finally, after forty-five minutes, she accepts a chair. The next watch, she explains, won't come on until seven.

At that point I climb into bed and try, unsuccessfully, to get a good night's sleep.

I miss my dog, Scotty boy.

CHAPTER | 4

All right, so here I am, it's Thursday morning and downstairs in front of the hotel Burton Kott's eyes fly wide open as I walk to his car with a fully armed policewoman at my side. I walk around to his window and lean over as it slides down. "I'm sorry, I would have called you, but she just told me she has to drive me to the courthouse."

"You may need her to protect you from Banks," Burton tells me. "What the hell was that interview about last night?"

"I didn't talk about the trial."

"Yeah, well, you're getting to be kind of a freaky sideshow to the trial," he observes.

"But it was your stupid girlfriend problems that started this mess," I say.

He brightens. "Hey, I talked to her last night. I reassured her about—you know, her sexual attractiveness. You were right about that. She's not so mad now."

"That's great, Burton," I say in sarcasm that escapes him, as I straighten up from his window. "See you at the courthouse."

"But why do you have this—this police *person?*" he wants to know.

I bend down again. "Because some people seem to think the car crash at lunch yesterday might have been an attempt on my life."

"But what about *my* life?" he says, eyes on me as he gropes for his cell phone.

With my new status as a possibly threatened witness, I am driven into a special underground garage and brought up into the courthouse by an elevator normally reserved for murderers and other notables. The guys at the press ropes must be furious, I think, not to get a shot of me walking in today of all days.

I am shown to my same little room, where the police officer first does a sweep of the bathroom before leaving me alone. I check my watch: nine-o-five. I take out the reams of DBS News organizational charts. What I am seeing in these lists and charts and budgets, if I am not mistaken, is an empire built piecemeal.

I make notes on areas of potential duplication and inconsistencies and remind myself I don't want to do *too* good a job. If I do, no doubt it will mean pushing myself deeper and deeper into administrative tasks, which, for the most part, I loathe. I'm kind of like young Paul Fitzwilliam: I like a more active job.

But, knowing myself as I do, I will do my best and work my derriere off because, well, that's just the way the Harringtons are. That is what we do. The best work we can, no matter what.

More notes.

I wish I had a better handle on what Alexandra is doing with me, or if she even thinks of me except as her handmaiden. I know what I'm doing here with these organizational charts is something Will Rafferty should be doing, and I suspect my work will be compared with his. His relationship with me is strained as it is, if only because I constantly work with him and yet am the only member of DBS News who does not report to him. That annoys him, I know.

It's funny how Alexandra is. She and Will have been working together for twelve years. She was a fledging reporter and he an assistant producer when they first met; when she anchored the news in New York for an independent station, Will went with her as a producer; when she covered Capitol Hill for one of the big three, Will became her field producer; when she came to DBS, he came with her as head of field operations, and then, three years ago, he was given the top job of executive producer. Will married Alexandra's best friend and DBS colleague, Jessica Wright, and yet, as close as they are, I know for a fact Will isn't quite sure what Alexandra wants to do with me. And as I said before, it annoys him. On the other hand, Alexandra makes it a practice to keep people working around her guessing a bit. I suppose she believes it staves off complacency.

Still, I wish I knew why she has me reviewing all this, what with all of my McDonald's milkshake-machine-management experience and all.

There is a quiet knock and the door opens and exotic Cecelie appears, carefully closing the door behind her. "You were certainly busy last night," she says quietly, walking over. "Going on the national news during the court's recess."

"I didn't talk about the trial." This is beginning to be my mantra.

"You spoke volumes about the trial," she says, looking at her watch. She looks up. And smiles. "But fortunately in a way that is not necessarily bad for us."

"Adding to the appearance that everyone connected with the Presario family is in constant danger from the Arlenettas," I say, borrowing from Will last night.

Cecelie cocks her head slightly, thinking this over. "Something like that." She walks around the table, critically examining my face. She pushes a piece of hair back off my shoulder and nods. "Good. You look good. Makeup is excellent." She takes a step back and gestures for me to stand, and when I do, Cecelie looks over my pale gray skirt and blazer, white silk blouse, pearls and quiet gold earrings. She steps forward again to reach into my blazer pocket. "This has to come out," she says, extracting my comb and tossing it on the table, "it looks like a weapon."

What a life.

"Okay, let's get to it," she says. "Banks might stray from the prep we gave you, but don't be disturbed by it. Just answer his questions. Okay? He knows what he's doing."

I frown, suspicious. Prepping me and then straying? What would be the point?

"Please state your full name for the record," the clerk prompts me.

"Sally Goodwin Harrington," I say clearly.

"Raise your right hand," she murmurs.

I wish I had gotten a manicure.

"Do you solemnly swear to speak the truth, the whole truth and nothing but the truth, so help you God?"

"I do."

"You may be seated," she says encouragingly.

I walk around to the witness box to step up into it, looking up to offer a shy smile at the judge. He looks back down at the papers in front of him.

Lawrence J. Banks, Esquire, rises dramatically from the defense table. Jonathan looks at me hopefully, and Cecelie, also sitting at the defense table, is looking very serious. The faces in the gallery are curious, eager. I recognize a reporter from the *Chicago Tribune* craning his neck; a contributing editor for *Vanity Fair* whispering something to the person next to her; I see a reporter from Fox; and I can see a writer famous for true-crime books almost standing in the back, for a moment, so he can survey the defense table.

Banks clears his throat and lumbers up to me. "Good morning, Ms. Harrington."

"Good morning," I say nervously.

He smiles. "Finally! You get to testify—"

"Objection, Your Honor!" cries the prosecutor, jumping out of his seat.

"Mr. Banks, Mr. Perez," the judge says, sounding tired already, "please approach the bench."

The lawyers walk to the far side of the judge's bench— Cecelie also hurries up to the bench, as does a balding young man who is the second to Prosecutor Perez—and the judge whispers something while his clerk leans over the judge's shoulder to listen. She is a somewhat heavyset woman of forty or so, and I've heard people talk about the changes in her appearance since the beginning of the trial. I made a note somewhere to see if we have film on her courthouse arrivals and departures to compare.

"Objection is sustained," the judge announces as everyone returns to their places. The judge's clerk, however, has pulled her chair up to sit almost next to him. I wonder why.

"Ms. Harrington," Banks begins again, "I'd like to ask you a few questions about your background for the benefit of the jury."

I nod once.

"Where are you from?"

"Central Connecticut, a city called Castleford. But I also live in New York City."

"You work in New York?"

"Yes."

"And what do you do?"

"I am a producer for DBS News."

"That's television news?"

"Yes, sir."

"And before that position? What did you do for a living?"

"I was a reporter for the Castleford *Herald-American,* a newspaper, and worked part time for DBS News out of New Haven."

"When you worked part-time for DBS News, in what capacity was that?"

"As a reporter. And I did some producing as well."

"What is producing?"

"Putting stories together for the network, but not appearing on camera as a reporter."

"Okay, very good," he says, taking a leisurely walk about the jury box. "Now, the defense has called you as a witness because of your past association with the deceased, Nicholas Arlenetta."

"Objection, Your Honor, no association has been established," Prosecutor Perez says.

"Withdrawn, I'll rephrase," Banks says. "Ms. Harrington, when did you first meet the deceased, Nicholas Arlenetta?"

"March 9 of this year."

"How is it you're so certain of the date?"

"I flew back from Los Angeles that day, and it's on my calendar."

"And where did you meet Nicholas Arlenetta?"

"At Newark," I say.

"Newark Airport in New Jersey," he clarifies.

"Yes."

"Would you share with the jury the circumstances under which you met him?"

"Sure. I had just arrived from Los Angeles and he approached me outside the airport. I was sitting in a car and he walked right up to me."

"Excuse me," Banks says, raising a finger in the air. "Let's go back a bit, to the time leading up to this first meeting with Nick Arlenetta."

The only meeting, I think to myself.

"Let's start with why you had been in Los Angeles."

I look at him.

"Mr. Banks, you should put it in the form of a question," Judge Kahn suggests.

"Yes, of course, Your Honor, thank you." Banks seems disturbed. He certainly is not asking questions in the order

I was prepped to answer them. "Why had you been to Los Angeles?"

"I had gone to look for Lilliana Martin."

"The defendant's sister?"

"Yes."

"Why were you looking for her?" he asks, walking away from me, looking at the jury.

"Well, um, she had disappeared. And that was big news. And my boss at DBS News sent me out to California to see if I could find her."

"Why were you sent, Ms. Harrington? You said you're a producer, not a reporter."

"It doesn't really matter who gets the story," I explain. "The reporter is just the one who goes on the air with it."

"Was there a special reason why you were sent? Rather than another producer or reporter?"

"Yes, there was. I had recently met Lilliana Martin and I had some leads to follow. Leads about how to find her."

"When did you first meet Lilliana Martin?"

"The last week of February."

"Of this year?"

"Yes."

"Where did you meet her?"

"In Beverly Hills."

"Tell the jury about this meeting."

I turn to the jury. Juror nine, an old lady in the back, is nodding, yes, and I haven't even said anything yet. "I met Lilliana at a party that was held to launch Malcolm Kieloff's autobiography. I was a guest. So was she. We were introduced and we chatted."

"And where was the party held?"

"Del Figlio's restaurant. In the banquet room."

"You chatted with Lilliana Martin. You didn't go anywhere with her?"

I cock my head slightly in question.

"At the party. Did you and Lilliana Martin go anywhere?"

"Yes, actually, we did. We went upstairs to the manager's office."

"Why?"

"She said she wanted to get away from the crowd for a few minutes."

"Ms. Harrington," he says, walking around again, "would you please tell the jury exactly what you did with Lilliana Martin in that office."

I don't understand the importance of this at all, but I try to think. "Lilliana called downstairs and had a waiter bring up two glasses of champagne. And some kind of cheese hors d'oeuvres. And a pack of cigarettes."

"Do you smoke?"

"No. I think she wanted to have a cigarette out of the public eye."

"Objection, Your Honor," Perez says. "Speculation."

"Noted," Banks says, waving his hand.

"Objection sustained," Judge Kahn says.

Banks smoothes his tie. "Did Lilliana Martin smoke a cigarette?"

"Yes."

"And what did you talk about?"

"We talked about the editor of Malcolm Kieloff's book, the man who had introduced us."

"What was his name?"

"Spencer Hawes."

There is a murmur in the courtroom and the judge

pounds the gavel once and orders silence. The murmur occurs because people remember Spencer's name and what happened to him.

"And what, specifically, did you and Ms. Martin discuss about Spencer Hawes?"

No one told me about this part. Interesting. I try to keep my answer honest and measured. After all, it only feels as though the eyes of the entire world are on me. "She wondered if he and I were in a committed relationship." I swallow nervously and reach for the glass of water. The courtroom is very quiet.

"Did Ms. Martin say why she was asking you this question?"

"Yes. She said she might be interested in dating him herself."

Murmurs again. The judge asks for quiet.

"Interested in dating him herself," Banks repeats, walking around to look at the jury again. Resting his hands on the jury box, without looking at me, he asks, "Did Ms. Martin say anything about having a boyfriend of her own?"

"Yes. She said she had just thrown him out of her house."

"Ah," he says, turning around. "And did she tell you, Ms. Harrington, at that time, who her boyfriend was?"

"No."

He walks back to the defense table to look at his notes and then comes back. "What condition was Lilliana Martin in that night?"

I can't resist. "Excellent. She's a movie star."

People chuckle.

Banks chuckles, too. "What I meant was, Ms. Harrington, was Ms. Martin drinking that night?"

"Yes."

"Was she drunk?"

"She had had several drinks," I say.

"Was she overtly drunk?"

"No."

"But she was, shall we say, very relaxed due to alcohol intake?" he suggests.

"Yes."

"After you and Ms. Martin talked upstairs, did you return to the party?"

"Yes."

"We have heard testimony that you both attended a dinner that night, in another part of the restaurant, also in honor of the publication of Mr. Kieloff's book."

"Yes."

"Would you tell the jury what happened after dinner?"

"We gave Lilliana a ride home."

"Who is we?"

"Spencer Hawes and myself."

He nods. "Okay, so you gave her a ride home. Where was that?"

"To a house on Cold Water Canyon."

"Do you know the number?"

I give it. He asks me to describe it and I do.

"And did you see anything unusual inside the house?"

"There was a pile of stuff in the foyer. She said it was her boyfriend's."

"Did she seem surprised it was there?"

"Yes. She said she thought he was going to pick it up while she was out."

"But he hadn't."

"No."

"Was he there, the boyfriend?"

"Not that I saw."

"Was anyone else there?"

"Not that I saw."

"Were there any phone calls while you were there?"

I stop to think. "Actually, there was one. Just as we were leaving, I heard the phone ringing."

"Did Ms. Martin answer it?"

"No."

"So when you left," Banks recaps, touring the jury again, "to the best of your knowledge, Lilliana Martin was alone in the house?"

"Yes."

"And then you and Spencer Hawes left together?"

"Yes."

"What happened then?"

There's no way I'm getting into *that* unless I'm hopelessly cornered. "I'm sorry," I say, "I don't know what you mean."

He looks at me. "The next morning, did anything unusual happen?"

"Lilliana Martin's agent called the hotel. He was looking for her. She had been scheduled for some kind of shoot and she had not shown up."

"And the agent's name?"

"Richie Benzler."

"And why did Richie Benzler call you?"

"Because he knew we had taken Lilliana home the night before."

"So Lilliana Martin was missing."

"Yes."

"So what did you do?"

"I told Mr. Benzler where and when we left her. Then I had to catch a flight back to Hartford. I had to get back to work at the paper."

Banks walks back to the defense table. Jonathan Small's eyes briefly meet mine. I feel sorry for him.

Banks reapproaches me. "You met Lilliana Martin in Beverly Hills and the next day you flew home to New York?"

"Connecticut," I say. "I was still working and living out there."

"You flew home to Connecticut. So this was not the return trip from Los Angeles when you met Nick Arlenetta?"

"No. That was my next trip to Los Angeles."

"When you returned this first time, did you know, before you left Los Angeles, that Lilliana Martin was missing?"

"Yes."

"And didn't it concern you?"

"No, not in the beginning. I knew she was upset about something. I just thought she may have taken a day or two for herself."

"Did you know what she was upset about?"

"Not specifically, no."

"Did you know what in general she was upset about?"

I shrug. "Just about her life in general, I think. She just seemed very sad."

"Did you, at some point, become more concerned about Ms. Martin's disappearance?"

"Yes. The first night I was home, in Castleford, the Los Angeles police called me and said an official missing person's report had been filed. And then, yes, I became concerned."

"And did anything unusual happen the following day? After the Los Angeles police called you?"

"Yes. A man showed up on my doorstep in Connecticut looking for Lilliana."

"What was his name?"

"Cliff Yarlen."

There is a buzz in the courtroom and the judge asks for quiet.

"Did Cliff Yarlen say why he was there?"

"Yes. He told me he was Lilliana's boyfriend and that he was worried about her. He wanted to know if I had any idea where she might be."

"Did Cliff Yarlen live in Connecticut?"

"No, Los Angeles."

"He flew all the way to Connecticut to ask you if you had seen Lilliana Martin?"

"He said he had business to conduct in New York," I explain. "So he just flew into Hartford and stopped in to see me on his way into Manhattan."

"And what did you tell him?"

"I told him I had no idea where Lilliana Martin was."

"So did he leave?"

"Yes. But actually, I went with him."

"Would you care to explain?"

"I had to go into New York myself, and he had a chauffeured car, and he offered me a ride, so I accepted."

"And you drove with him into Manhattan?"

"Yes."

"Was there a reason why?"

I am under oath. "Yes. Since I knew Lilliana had broken up with him, and now she was missing, I thought there might be a story. So I wanted to take him to the studio."

"For what purpose?"

"To set up my boss, Alexandra Waring, with an exclusive interview."

Banks takes a long walk in front of the jury box. "Ms. Harrington, did it ever cross your mind that Lilliana Martin might have been a victim of foul play?"

"Sure, it crossed my mind."

"But you rode into Manhattan with Cliff Yarlen, anyway?"

"Yes."

"And you didn't fear for your safety?"

"No."

"Why not?"

"I'm a pretty good judge of people," I say. "I didn't pick up any vibes about why I should fear Cliff Yarlen. In fact, I thought he was a lot more stable than Lilliana."

Banks looks at the jury as if this is news to him. "Did you find Lilliana Martin unstable?"

"Merely less stable than Cliff Yarlen," I insist. "She was an actress and he was a businessman." I shrug.

"What did you talk about with Cliff Yarlen during this ride?"

"We talked about his profession."

"Which was?"

"He said he was president of the American Federation of Technology Workers."

"What else did you talk about?"

I try to think. "That he was from Brooklyn. Went to NYU. Worked in New Jersey for a long time and then moved to L.A. with his union. He talked a lot about computers in movies and TV production, and why those workers needed a different union from the existing ones. He was very proud of the union he worked for."

"Very good." He's walking again. "What happened next?"

"He drove me to the West End Broadcasting Center—"

"This is where DBS News is located?"

"Yes. And he came inside with me. I took him to Alexandra Waring's office and went down to the newsroom to find her. When I got back, he was gone."

"Where had he gone?"

"One of the assistants said he made a phone call and then took off."

"Did you see Cliff Yarlen again that night?"

"Yes, I did."

"Where?"

"At JFK."

"How did you know he was there?"

"Someone from the news group had followed him when he left West End."

"Someone followed him?"

"Yes. They knew he was connected with Lilliana Martin, and so someone went to see where he was going so suddenly."

"Is this normal procedure?" he asks incredulously.

"Anything and everything's normal in TV news if it gets the story," I say, making everyone laugh.

"Tell the jury about when you next saw Cliff Yarlen," Banks directs me.

"I saw him later that night. It was sleeting out and JFK closed. I knew he was at the Admiral's Club and so I went there to see him. He was waiting for a flight to get out."

"What did you say to him?"

"I asked him if everything was all right. That he had disappeared so quickly and I knew how worried he had been about Lilliana, I was concerned."

"What did he say?"

"That he had heard from Lilliana, and she said she was fine, not to worry."

"And did he say why he was flying back to L.A. so suddenly?"

"No."

"Didn't you wonder why he was going back so suddenly? Didn't he tell you he had business in New York and that was why he came to see you?"

"By then I knew he was scared and upset by Lilliana's disappearance. And once he heard from her, he wanted to go home."

"He said this?"

"No. I surmised it."

"Objection, Your Honor," Perez says. "Conjecture on the part of the witness."

"Sustained. The jury will please disregard the witness's last remark."

Banks takes a stroll and then suddenly turns to me. "Didn't you find it odd, Ms. Harrington, that Cliff Yarlen would fly clear across the country to see you in Connecticut?"

I hesitate. "Yes, I did."

"He thought Lilliana Martin might be at your house, didn't he?"

"I believe he thought it was possible," I say, swallowing. *Don't go there,* I plead.

"Did you leave Mr. Yarlen in the Admiral's Club at JFK that night?"

Banks has just left yet another uncomfortable line of inquiry open for the cross-examination by the prosecution. There's got to be a method to his madness, but I don't see it yet. I simply resent it. "Yes, I did."

"After you left Cliff Yarlen at the Admiral's Club at JFK, what did you do next?"

"I went back to Manhattan."

"And did you ever see Cliff Yarlen again?"

"No."

"Why not?"

"Because he was murdered."

Murmurs in the courtroom. Judge Kahn asks for order.

"When was Cliff Yarlen murdered?"

"That same night. At least, that's what the police told me, that he was shot dead that night in a storage facility in a hangar."

The courtroom starts murmuring again, and Judge Kahn bangs his gavel. When the room has quieted down, he clears his throat and suggests this might be a good place to stop for lunch. Court, he pronounces, will resume at two.

CHAPTER | 5

"He has to prepare," Cecelie says with an air of patience that makes me want to slap her.

"But what is Banks *doing?*" I demand, pacing in my little room of the courthouse. "The cross-examination on this is going to throw mud on everybody in this trial."

Burton's ears perk up. "Well, it's not like you guys haven't led interesting lives, Sally."

"Shut up, Burton," Cecelie tells him. To me, "I apologize, Sally. I know it must be difficult, but you have to understand this is Jonathan's life on the line, and his family will go to any lengths to see him receive justice. I'm not even exactly sure what Banks is doing, but I do know he's the best in the business, and if he wants to open these doors, then there's a good reason why."

I drop into my chair, covering my face with my hands. "I just dread it."

"But you didn't do anything with anybody," Burton says. And then, a second too late, he says, "Did you?"

I drop my hands and look at him. "No, I didn't. But there was definitely an air of impropriety about that night."

"You mean Lilliana," Cecelie says knowingly.

"And Spencer Hawes," Burton adds. "Your ex. But he wasn't an ex, then. Right?"

"Shut *up,* Burton," Cecelie says.

"But she's been advising me on my love life," he adds, gesturing to me. "I should know something about hers."

I don't know if he's being serious or not.

Cecelie looks at me. "Don't waste your time, Sally. You think he listens. He doesn't. He whines and complains about his girlfriend of the month and then goes right out and does the same thing all over again."

"I listened to her yesterday," Burton says, "and it worked."

Cecelie edges to the door. "Burton, if I were with you, I'd kill you over the first breakfast." She winces slightly, realizing what she said.

"Nice, counselor," Burton says, laughing.

Cecelie rolls her eyes, moving to the door. "We've got work to do for Banks, Sally. I'll send the sheriff in about your lunch."

"Sorry about you having to stay in here," Sheriff Mc Duff says when he arrives, his courthouse keys jingling and jangling as he moves. "It's a beautiful day outside."

"Do you happen to know if I am *a* risk, or if I am *at* risk, Sheriff?"

He shrugs. "I guess you're just kinda risky, period."

I like Sheriff McDuff. Since I've been sitting around the courthouse, we've had a chance to talk. He was born on the wrong side of Chicago, was befriended by a firefighter who served as father figure and mentor, became a firefighter himself, married and had kids, moved to L.A. so his wife could be near her dying father, and when he retired from the LAFD, became a courthouse sheriff. He's studying computers at night school, in the context of security systems, which I think is very cool since I think Sheriff McDuff must be around sixty.

"I have some good news, though," he adds. "The State of California would be pleased to buy you lunch."

"There is no such thing as a free lunch," I say, quoting my mother.

"Well, today you're getting one. Sandwich or salad? And there's pretty good soup today."

I resist the urge for a grilled cheese and soup, your essential comfort foods. I ask for a green salad and crackers. Sheriff McDuff raises his eyebrows. "Rabbit food, girl? Are you sure about that? You're under some stress today."

"Make it a grilled cheese with bacon, vegetable soup and bag of potato chips, please. And water," I tell him.

"Water?" he says skeptically.

"No, really, water. I like it," I explain. "But a cup of coffee, too."

"Black?"

"Light. With sugar," I say. I laugh a little. "I've decided to go to hell in a handbasket, Sheriff."

"Aw, it's going to be all right," he tells me, walking to the door.

"I do need to make a phone call, though," I say quickly, rising from my chair.

"Hang on, I gotta get your gal," he informs me, referring to my escort from the Santa Monica Police Department.

I sit back down in my chair with a thump. I don't like being held in here. Moments later the officer arrives. She just stands there in the doorway, looking rather bored and asks, "Use the phone?" She kicks her head. "Well, come on, then."

We walk down the corridor to the pay phones. One might wonder at how members of the press seem so attached to these land phones during the trial. There is a reason why. Every call made from this courthouse on a cell phone will be scanned and heard by every media outlet covering the trial. So unless it is a newsbreak that will reach all, anyway, we use land phones. I punch in my credit card number and call Mother.

"Darling, how are you? I just walked in from school," she reports. I check my watch. It would be about three-thirty at home. Mother teaches sixth-grade English "Your dog, I'll have you know, Sally Goodwin Harrington, was on my couch in the living room."

"Did you actually see him on the couch, or do you merely suspect him?" I ask, being experienced in courtroom examination now.

My dog, Scotty, is a big love, an eighty-pound collie/German shepherd/golden retriever mix who is always initially feared by strangers because of his classic junkyard dog teeth. Mother has a small golden retriever, Abigail, who gets away with murder. It's not that she's smarter than Scotty; Abigail is simply less attached to the principles of right and wrong.

"I saw the imprint of an eighty-pound dog," Mother reports.

"He was framed," I insist. "The red dog did it."

"So how are you, dear?" Mother moves on and I can visualize her putting things away in the kitchen while she's talking to me. I see the two dogs playing in the backyard; I can see the meadow sloping down to the pond, the pine forest around it, the Connecticut mountains beyond. I love that house, that place. It's hard to believe I am the next in line to own it. (It's hard to believe I will ever get my finances in order to own it.)

"I'm finally testifying," I tell her.

"Oh, I know *that,* dear, it's all over the news," she says matter-of-factly.

"It could get a little—weird, Mother. The cross-examination. Be forewarned."

"Just tell the truth, Sally."

I smile a little.

"Phillip called me last night," Mother says, changing the topic again, back to the one I dread, the O'Hearns, "and Marion is not doing very well at all. She's still asking to see you and he's worried you might not get back—in time."

"Mother, why can't I just call her?"

Pause. "She's dying, Sally."

"Mother, I'm *trying,*" I say, feeling simultaneously angry and guilty. "As soon as I can be there, I will be. It's not like I don't have something important to finish here."

"I know," she says quietly. "It just seems to mean so much to Marion."

I resist saying, *Who cares, Mother? Her husband murdered Daddy. I hope it is hell on earth for them both.* "Did you explain the circumstances? Why I can't be there right now?"

"Darling heart, all anyone has to do is turn on the TV to

see what's going on! Your face is on every channel. By the way, everyone in the faculty lounge at lunch today liked your suit."

"Thanks."

"Sally, are you really in some kind of danger or is all of this hype for DBS?"

Possibly, I think. Though Alexandra is not one for crying wolf to the authorities.

"It's just hype," I say automatically, glancing at the SMPD officer.

"And darling, before I forget, the principal would like you to come in to school on career day to talk about TV news. Do you think you can come? It would be June 6."

Only my mother would to try to book me for career day while I'm under armed guard testifying in "The Mafia Boss Murder" trial. Clinging to the small normalities of life, I know, has always been Mother's way of maintaining her sanity during uncertain times.

"I will check and get back to you," I say, making a note, "though I think it's probably fine."

The police officer wanders over, tapping her watch. "You've got twenty minutes to eat," she says, which means, "*We've* got twenty minutes to eat." I get off the phone with Mother and return to my little room. I hate being confined. However, my sandwich and soup and chips are waiting on a brown plastic tray, so I wash my hands in the bathroom and sit down to eat.

It's really, really good.

After I finish, I neaten up the tray so it doesn't look quite so much like a wild animal has been here and move it to the side. There, on the table, where the tray had been, lay an envelope marked "Sally."

Thinking it might be instructions from Banks or something, I quickly break the seal and read the note that is inside.

Hi,
With all the excitement, I didn't know if you're still interested in having a bite to eat tonight. It's okay if you're not—I'll be disappointed, but I'll live.

There is a stick figure drawn lying on the ground, arm over face, saying, "Somehow I will go on." I smile.

We said six. When and if they give you a chance, you can reach me at this number. Again, if things are too crazy now, I understand. But I'm hoping against hope you'll still want to have dinner!

Paul Fitzwilliam

As I am wondering how Paul got this in here, Burton and Cecelie arrive to give me the once-over. "Hang on," I tell them, "let me just do my hair."

"You need to hustle," Cecelie tells me.

I use the facilities and wash my hands. Then I quickly brush my hair out, retouch my makeup, reach under my skirt to pull my blouse down so it is smooth in front (not that it will stay that way) and walk out for inspection. "Good. You look good," Cecelie says.

Burton, though, frowns slightly at me, cocking his head slightly.

"What?" I ask him.

"You are good-looking," he says, sounding surprised. "I was reading this thing in *Us,* and they're right, you are good-looking."

"As I said," Cecelie says, guiding me with a light hand toward the door, "I'd kill him at the first breakfast."

I feel strangely optimistic as I am brought back into the courtroom. I am directed back to the witness box, where I take my seat, and shortly thereafter the jury is brought in. I hazard a look out to the gallery, where I find that most eyes are focused on me.

"All rise," we are told.

CHAPTER | 6

"Earlier today," Lawrence J. Banks says, actually addressing the packed courtroom, though speaking to me, "you testified that you met first met Lilliana Martin at a book party in Beverly Hills in February."

"Yes."

"You testified that the day after the party, Lilliana Martin's agent, Richie Benzler, called you at your hotel because the actress, that morning, was missing."

"Yes."

"You testified you flew home to Connecticut that day."

"Yes."

"And the following day, Cliff Yarlen arrived at the front door of your home in Connecticut."

"Yes."

"You drove into Manhattan with Mr. Yarlen and he accompanied you to the West End Broadcasting Center."

"Yes."

"Then, according to your testimony, Mr. Yarlen suddenly departed from West End and you later found him at the Admiral's Club at JFK Airport."

"Yes."

"And the day after that, he was found murdered at JFK."

"No, it wasn't the next day. I believe they didn't find his body for three or four days." I look up at the judge. "I'm sorry, Your Honor, I'm trying to get the days straight."

"That's fine," he tells me.

"But the police told you—did they not?" Banks asks. "That Cliff Yarlen had been murdered the night you last saw him? At JFK?"

"Yes."

"Why did the police question you?"

"Because I was a suspect. I was one of the last people who saw him alive." I reach for my water and take a sip, not wanting to think about it. If Mother is good at focusing on the normalities of life in a horrible situation, I am, as they say, Cleopatra, the Queen of Denial.

"And where was Lilliana Martin at the time Cliff Yarlen was killed?"

"I don't know."

"You testified that Cliff Yarlen said he had heard from her—"

"Yes, Cliff said he had heard from Lilliana and she was all right."

"But isn't it true, that at the time Cliff Yarlen's body was discovered, Lilliana Martin was still missing?"

"Yes. Everyone was looking for her. It was a big story."

Banks walks over to look at some notes on the defense table. Jonathan Small looks to me and I imagine a flicker of support.

"So DBS News sent you to Los Angeles to look for Lilliana Martin?"

"Yes."

"And when did you go?"

"Wednesday night. As soon as the police in New York allowed me to leave."

He walks around and then turns to look at me. "Did you find Lilliana Martin?"

"Eventually, yes."

Banks takes a stroll around the jury box. "Tells us about your search for her in Los Angeles. What did you do?"

"First I went to Cliff's memorial service, but she wasn't there."

Banks is circling. "Then what did you do?"

"I called everywhere I could think of and left a message for Lilliana to call me."

"Did you go back to the house in Cold Water Canyon to look for her?"

"Oh, right. Yes, I did. After the memorial service I drove over to Cold Water Canyon to the house where we had dropped her off. After the book party, the night I met her."

"Which was also the night before Lilliana Martin disappeared," he reminds the jury. To me, "And what did you find at that house in Cold Water Canyon?"

"I found out that it was not Lilliana Martin's house," I say, snapping everyone out of their post-luncheon stupors.

"Whose house was it?"

"I can't remember the family's name. But I met the owners, a professor and his wife. They said they had been in Turkey for six weeks and had employed a young man as their house-sitter. They gave me his name and number and I went to see him."

"What was his name?"

"Jeremiah Sadler."

"And what did he have to say?"

"He said he had let a friend of his aunt's stay there."

"Was this friend of his aunt's Lilliana Martin?"

"No."

"Cliff Yarlen?"

"No."

"Who was it?"

"The defendant, Jonathan Small."

There are murmurs, but they quickly die.

"So Lilliana Martin and Cliff Yarlen had been staying in a house borrowed by Jonathan Small from a house-sitter?"

"Yes."

"Ms. Harrington, did you ever find Lilliana Martin?"

"Yes."

He pivots on his toes to look at me. "How?"

"She called me. She had gotten one of my messages and she called me."

"Was she still in hiding?"

"Yes."

"But she called you?"

"Yes."

"Why did she call you?"

"Objection," Perez says, standing up. "The witness does not know what Lilliana Martin was thinking."

"Withdrawn." Banks takes a step closer. "Did Lilliana Martin tell you where she was?"

"Yes."

"Where was that?"

"At 126 Skyview Drive in Bel Air."

"Did you go to see her?"

"Yes."

"When?"

"Right after she called."

"When you saw Ms. Martin, did she offer any explanation as to why she was hiding?"

"No."

"What did you talk about while you were there?"

"I told her about Cliff's memorial service—"

"And how did she react?"

"She appeared very sad, on the verge of crying."

"Did you tell her anything else?"

"Yes. I told her Spencer Hawes was missing and I asked her if she knew anything about it."

There is a buzz in the courtroom.

"Spencer Hawes the book editor? Your friend with whom you gave Lilliana Martin a ride home? After the Malcolm Kieloff book party?"

"Yes."

"When did he go missing?"

"The day after the book party."

"Is that the same day Lilliana Martin disappeared?"

"Yes. But Lilliana was missing in the morning. I saw Spencer that morning. He disappeared later, toward noon."

"He disappeared here, in Los Angeles?"

"Yes, sir."

"And what was Lilliana Martin's reaction when you told her he was still missing?"

"She was very upset."

"And what did she do?"

"She immediately left the kitchen, where we were sitting, and made a phone call."

"Could you hear any of her conversation?"

"Objection, Your Honor!" Perez cries. "Hearsay!"

"It's not being offered for the truths of the matters asserted," Banks counters, "but merely to show why Ms. Harrington did what she did subsequent to hearing that conversation."

Judge Kahn thinks a minute and then says, "Objection overruled."

"Ms. Harrington," Banks resumes, "what did you hear Lilliana Martin say during her telephone conversation?"

"I heard her tell someone, 'Spencer Hawes is missing.' And then she yelled, 'He's Malcolm Kieloff's editor! He hasn't been seen since!' And then she said something like, 'Cliff saw him standing in the driveway, looking for me.' And then she yelled at whoever she was talking to that they better do something. And then she hung up."

"Was it your opinion Lilliana Martin knew something about Spencer Hawes's disappearance?"

"Yes. Definitely."

"Did you believe she knew who was responsible for Spencer Hawes's disappearance?"

"Yes."

"You just said that you overheard Lilliana Martin say, on the telephone, that Cliff saw him in the driveway, looking for her."

Perez jumps up. "I renew my objection, Your Honor."

"Overruled." Judge Kahn tells him.

"Yes."

"How did she know Cliff saw him, if you know?"

"Because I told her."

"You told her?"

"Yes."

"You and Cliff Yarlen had discussed the fact that Spencer Hawes had disappeared?"

"Yes."

"When was this?"

"The day I met him."

"How did you know Spencer Hawes had disappeared?"

"His boss had called me to ask if I had any idea where he was."

"And did you?"

"No."

"Let's get this sequence of events clear for the jury, Ms. Harrington," Banks says, using his hands to count each event.

"You met Lilliana Martin at the Kieloff party?"

"Yes."

"You and Spencer Hawes gave her a ride home to Cold Water Canyon?"

"Yes."

"You both left the house, you and Spencer Hawes?"

"Yes."

"Lilliana Martin's agent called you the next morning to say she had failed to appear somewhere? Correct?"

"Yes."

"She was missing?"

"Yes."

"You saw Spencer Hawes the morning Lilliana Martin went missing?"

"Yes."

"You flew back to Connecticut."

"Yes."

"That night, the police called you to say Lilliana Martin was officially missing?"

"Yes."

"Then Spencer Hawes's boss called you?"

I nod. "The next day."

"And was it the next day that Cliff Yarlen also appeared on your doorstep in Connecticut?"

"Yes."

"And you told Cliff Yarlen that Spencer Hawes was missing also?"

"Yes."

He stands there and looks at me, frowning heavily. "Why didn't you say this before? When I asked you what you and Cliff Yarlen had discussed?"

I shrug. "I forgot."

Banks looks at the jury, as much as to apologize for me being such a cruddy witness. He circles, then, "Cliff Yarlen told you he had seen Spencer Hawes?"

"Yes. The day after the party. Around noon. Cliff said he had gone to Lilliana's house—the house on Cold Water Canyon—and he said he saw Spencer there in the driveway. That's when Cliff discovered Lilliana had disappeared."

"And did he say what happened then?"

"He left, and Spencer was still there in the driveway."

Banks circles again. "Let me ask you something, Ms. Harrington, when you found out Lilliana Martin was missing, and the next day Spencer Hawes was missing, did you have an opinion of what had happened?"

"Yes. I thought perhaps they had gone away together for a few days."

A buzz in the courtroom.

"But weren't you dating Spencer Hawes?"

I hesitate. "We broke up the morning after the party."

Damn him, I think. The door is wide open for the prosecutor.

"As far as you know, did Spencer Hawes and Lilliana Martin go away together?"

"No, sir."

"Did you ever find out what happened to Spencer Hawes?"

"Eventually."

"What happened to him?"

"He had been kidnapped the day after the party and kept on an ocean-going garbage barge."

More murmurs. Irritated, Judge Kahn raps his gavel several times.

"When did Spencer Hawes turn up?"

"The day after I told Lilliana he was missing."

"After you heard her make that phone call?"

"The next day after that, yes."

"When did you next see Spencer Hawes?"

"Two days later, the day after he was found. I went down to Long Beach to see him in the hospital."

"He was hospitalized?"

"Yes. He had been beaten, suffered severe dehydration, a number of things. He was in pretty bad shape."

"Did you meet anyone else at the hospital in Long Beach that day?"

"Yes. A man introduced himself to me as Schyler Preston."

"Who is Schyler Preston?"

"He said he was a special federal prosecutor."

"And what did Mr. Preston want to talk to you about?"

"He wanted to know what my connection with Cliff Yarlen was."

"Anything else?"

"He wanted to know what I knew about Cliff Yarlen."

"What did you tell him?"

"That Cliff's union was connected to organized crime, and that his brother, Nick Arlenetta, a mob boss from New Jersey, was trying to muscle in."

"What else did he ask you about?"

"He wanted to know how I found Lilliana."

"And what did you say?"

"I told him the truth. I told him I had left messages everywhere for her and that she had called me."

"Did he ask you anything else?"

"Yes. He wanted to know what my connection was with Jonathan Small."

"The defendant?"

"Yes."

"What did you say?"

"I said the only connection I had with him was that he had asked me on a date." I look at the jury. "I didn't go."

Banks cruises back to the defense table to look at his notes. "Did Special Federal Prosecutor Schyler Preston explain anything to you? About what he was doing there?"

"Eventually I learned that Spencer Hawes had been mistaken for an associate of Cliff Yarlen's. That's why he had been kidnapped. But he wouldn't explain anything more than that."

"Did he ask you anything else?"

I nod. "He wanted to know what I talked about with Lilliana Martin when I saw her."

"Did you tell him?"

"Yes."

"Then what happened?"

"I drove back to Los Angeles. I came back down to Long Beach the next morning, to see how Spencer was doing, but he was getting a bunch of tests done and so I didn't see him. So I drove back to Los Angeles."

"Why?"

"I wanted to see Lilliana again. I knew there was some connection between the phone call she made the last time I was there and Spencer Hawes being found. I wanted to know what it was."

"So what did you do?"

"I stopped in Torrance and called for a private car to pick me up."

"Why?"

"Because Sky—that's his nickname—Preston made me nervous about being followed. To Lilliana's. I didn't understand what was going on, but he did make it clear that Lilliana was in some kind of danger."

Banks nods and takes his stroll, letting this sink in with the jury. "So what happened then?"

"A car and driver picked me up in Torrance and drove me to Lilliana's house on Skyview Drive in Bel Air."

"Could you describe for the jury what the scene was like?"

"Yes. There were several large men walking around the property and they didn't want to let me in the gate, but I threatened to call 911 and then Lilliana told them to let me come up to the house."

"Who came to the door?"

"Lilliana."

"What happened then?"

"She told me to go away, I said I wouldn't, not until I knew what she knew about Spencer's kidnapping, and so finally she said, 'Okay, you win, you're in.' Then she took hold of my arm and pulled me into the house."

"What did you see inside the house?"

"There was this huge, wrestler-type guy standing behind the front door. And then Lilliana said we had to go downstairs to the basement."

"Did she say why?"

"She said she was in danger and she wished I had not come."

"What happened then?"

"We went downstairs into the basement and we were sitting there on old lawn furniture and then we heard this horribly loud helicopter noise. Do you know the opening of the movie *Apocalypse Now?* It was like that. You heard it, but you also felt the reverberation in your chest. It was that loud, that close."

"What happened then?"

"Lilliana said, 'Oh, no,' or something and then there was this really loud whistling sound. A second later, it sounded like the whole house had blown up and plaster was flying everywhere. A second later there was another explosion and I was blown out of my chair. The whole basement staircase came crashing down—part of the kitchen floor had fallen through. And then the refrigerator fell into the basement right after that."

"Where was Lilliana Martin?"

"She was thrown on the floor as well. Then she got up and ran over to the cellar doors, slid the bolt over and threw them open. Then she ran back, grabbed my arm and pulled me under this worktable in the corner, and it was good thing she did. The smoke and fire had started, and steam—because all the water pipes were broken—and this stuff kept falling in from the main floor of the house. Then we heard a commotion outside."

"What did you hear?"

"Men yelling. Gunshots. But then things kept crashing upstairs. The whole side of the house was falling in."

"What did you do?"

"Lilliana ripped up her T-shirt so we could both cover our noses and mouths against the smoke. She led me behind the water heater, into a kind of crawl space. And then we heard men's voices getting closer. Lilliana told me, no matter what, to be quiet and keep down."

"What happened next?"

"I heard men's voices outside of the house."

"What did you hear, exactly?"

"I heard one man say, 'Cellar doors are open, she's gone!' Then another man yelled, 'Check the pool house!'"

"What did you do?"

"We just hid and tried not to cough."

"What happened next?"

"I saw a man standing in the cellar doorway. He yelled—" I turn to the judge. "He yelled an expletive, Your Honor." To the jury, "He yelled the expletive and then, 'Where is she?' and the other man yelled an expletive."

"And what was your condition at this point?"

"We were about to succumb to the smoke. I knew I was going to have to run for it or I'd never get out."

"So what happened?"

"Luckily, there were sirens. The fire department, I think. The man in the doorway said they needed to get out of

there. So they took off. Lilliana was just about uncon-
scious, but we managed to stagger out. I was sick, I think—
no, I know I was sick to my stomach, and Lilliana was out
cold, but the EMT workers gave us oxygen and stuff and
so then we were okay. Relatively okay."

A hush has fallen over the courtroom. Banks takes a
very long time to ask his next question. Finally, very quietly, he asks, "You say you saw a man in the doorway to
the cellar, Ms. Harrington?"

"Yes. He was the one yelling, 'Where is she?' And he
was the one who said they needed to get out of there."

"Did you get a good look at this man?"

"Yes."

"Did you recognize him?"

"No."

"You had never seen him before?"

"No."

"When the EMT workers arrived, was this man still
there?"

"No. At least, I didn't see him."

"Did you subsequently ever see this man again?"

I nod. "Yes."

"How long after the firebombing attack did you see him?"

"Objection, Your Honor," Perez says. "The People request a sidebar."

They go up and do their thing at the bench. I glance at
my watch. It's after four.

The attorneys return to their places.

"The objection is overruled," Judge Kahn announces.

"The man whom you saw," Bank resumes, "standing in
the doorway of the firebombed mansion, who yelled
'Where is she?'—when did you next see him?"

"Three months later."

"Where?"

"In Fort Lee, New Jersey."

"Would you please explain to the jury what the circumstances were."

"Sure. I was working for DBS News and Alexandra Waring was going to interview Michael Arlenetta about the death of his older brother, Nick."

"This is the younger brother of Nick Arlenetta, the alleged victim in this case?"

"Yes."

"What happened?"

"When Michael Arlenetta came outside to do his interview, I recognized him immediately as the man I saw in the cellar doorway after the firebombing of Lilliana's house."

A murmur through the court.

The judge asks for order and then notes it's getting late, could Mr. Banks find a good stopping point in the next ten minutes? Banks assures him he can. Still, however, Banks walks for a bit, looking at his notes at the defense table, nodding solemnly to the jury as if they must be thinking the same thing as he. Then he turns to me. "How long after the firebombing attack did you return to New York?"

"Two days later."

"All right," Banks says. "Let's recap this sequence for the jurors." He glances over at Perez as if he is expecting him to object. He doesn't and so Banks continues. "You were very nearly murdered, Ms. Harrington?"

"Yes."

"And your friend, Spencer Hawes, was kidnapped and very badly hurt?"

"Yes."

"Lilliana Martin was very nearly murdered with you?"

"Yes."

"And Cliff Yarlen had been murdered?"

"Yes."

He rests a hand on the jury box. "And what happened when your plane landed at Newark?"

"A man approached my car as I was leaving the airport. I rolled down my window. He said he had seen me on TV, and he congratulated me on my work. He shook my hand and introduced himself as Nick Arlenetta."

Gasps.

"Did he say anything else?"

"Yes. He said, 'I believe you knew my brother, Cliff Yarlen.'"

More gasps. The judge asks for quiet.

Banks walks over to me. "Do you believe this was an accidental meeting with Nick Arlenetta?"

"No. It was very obvious to me he wanted me to know he was watching me."

"Objection, Your Honor! There's no way the witness—"

"Withdrawn, Your Honor," Banks says, holding up a hand. He pauses and then asks me, "Were you scared?"

"Very."

"Why?"

"Because by this point I knew a lot about him."

"What had you learned?"

"His long criminal record, his participation in organized crime, how he murdered Lilliana Martin's mother—"

"Objection, Your Honor!" Perez cries. "There is no established connection between the victim and—"

"Objection, Your Honor!" Banks thunders, indignant. "It remains to be seen if Nick Arlenetta *was* a victim."

"Counsel will approach the bench," the judge says sternly.

I hazard a look at Jonathan, who is looking tired and vulnerable behind the defense table.

When the sidebar is finished, the judge announces court will be recessed for the day and will resume at ten o'clock tomorrow morning.

CHAPTER | 7

Sheriff McDuff escorts me from court to my little room to pick up my stuff. Cecelie Blake swings in shortly behind us. "Listen, Sally, Burton is going to take you back to the hotel."

I look over at her. "What about the policewoman?"

"The order of protection's been called off," she explains.

"Is that good or bad?" I want to know, gathering my stuff.

"All I know is you're to go with Burton," she says, "and you need to hurry."

Sheriff McDuff shrugs. "Officer Defano left."

"Is she ready?" Burton says, appearing in the doorway. "We need to get through these crowds."

Dutifully I follow him out into the corridor and through the throngs of people milling in the courthouse lobby. Cecelie brings up the rear. At the doors leading outside, Lawrence Banks is waiting for me, smiling. "Good job today," he murmurs, holding the door open for me.

Burton looks over his shoulder to make sure I'm behind him. Beyond him are the media towers, and I realize how much Banks wants me in front of the cameras this afternoon.

As we cross the front sidewalk, I hear it. A helicopter. Coming from the west. Given the testimony I have just given, about a helicopter swooping down to firebomb Lilliana Martin's house in Bel Air, I have to admit that my first instinct is to duck. But I know it's got to be a news helicopter, or at this time of the day a traffic helicopter, cutting over the Pacific Coast Highway to check out Route 10.

And then Burton yells, "Get down!"

I don't need much encouragement. There's no way I'm going to be a sitting duck out here, surrounded with a bunch of gasoline-fueled cars, so I whirl around and yell to people, "Get back to the building!" and I run, dropping my briefcase and grabbing Cecelie with one hand, and pulling a matronly lady along with me with the other.

The sound of the helicopter has become a roar, and it suddenly appears, hovering over the courthouse, barely fifty feet above. Papers and dust fly everywhere, people are screaming and diving for cover. I head into the shrubbery, dragging the matronly lady with me, and we softly fall into a flower bed next to the building. The helicopter spins, bobbing slightly; its windows are dark and impenetrable. I cover my eyes against the dirt, trying to take in the registration number.

There is a gunshot. Then another. I look over and through the shrubbery I see three police officers standing in classic position, hats blown off by the wind of the blades, handguns bravely trained on the helicopter. The helicopter suddenly soars upward, swinging round and sailing south. Moments later, it is comparatively quiet. Sirens screaming and people yelling, yes, but no threatening dark helicopter bearing down on us all.

"Are you all right?" I ask the matronly lady, as I pull down her skirt a little and help her up.

"My glasses," she says.

I see them, lying at the base of a hibiscus, and retrieve them for her. While she carefully cleans them off and puts them back on, I wonder what the chances are of this one suing me, too. She is in her early sixties; her serviceable blue suit, her sensible pumps and matching purse seem undamaged.

Suddenly she smiles, eyes twinkling. "Did you save me because I looked like I needed help, or because you knew I'm with National Public Radio?"

Radio people. You never know what they'll look like.

"I didn't save you, I just dragged you along for company," I joke, offering a hand as we step out of the garden.

"Sally, are you all right?" Banks says breathlessly, but carefully standing on the edge of the garden so as not to muss up his thousand-dollar shoes.

"I'm fine," I say. I turn to my companion, "Do you know Lawrence Banks?"

"No, I don't," she says, rising to the occasion.

"Lawrence, this is—"

"Mary Beaton Darlington," she supplies, holding out her hand. "Stringing for National Public Radio."

"I'm very pleased to meet you," he says.

I spot Burton. "Get me out of here," I beg.

"I don't know if I can," he says, craning his neck. "The police have sealed the area."

"Oh, God," I groan. Then I get an idea. While everyone's busy scanning the skies for helicopters, I hustle across the parking lot to the media barricades. Someone hails me and I wave to the cameras. I look around—no cops around—so I hike up my skirt and scale the barricade, receiving help from the other side to lift me over the fence and safely down on the other side. I am swarmed by reporters and I want to give DBS first dibs, but I can't move. I repeat over and over how I can't talk about the trial, but I can talk about the helicopter. I describe how it approached, how it behaved, the three cops standing bravely beneath it, firing the warning shots that sent it on its way. I describe how people screamed and ran for cover, and, *and,* I recite the serial number on the helicopter. Now, that's a scoop.

Someone is asking me about the accident at the restaurant yesterday when a bullhorn is turned on and horrible feedback screeches (on purpose, I'm sure), making all the press (including me) cover our ears. Then a commanding voice booms, "Back away, please, police business, back away, please, police business," and I find myself being spirited through the crowd by two police officers.

I think I hear someone coming. I have been left alone in a small courtroom conference room for nearly twenty minutes. The door finally opens and an official-looking man walks in and introduces himself as the chief clerk of the courthouse. Coming in behind him is Prosecutor Perez, Lawrence Banks, a Beverly Hills police captain, the policewoman who had been watching over me earlier today, and a nervous-looking Sheriff McDuff.

Nobody looks at me as the courthouse clerk takes a

chair opposite from me and tells everyone else to sit or stand. Since there are only two vacant chairs left, only Perez and Banks take a seat.

The clerk fusses with some papers, an obvious delay to give us all time to worry. Finally he settles back in his chair and with his elbows resting on the chair arms, clasps his hands in front of him and narrows his eyes. "Ms. Harrington, were you or were you not told that you were being provided with police protection today?"

"Yes, sir, I was."

"Then why did you leave the witness room without your police escort?"

"I was told that Burton Kott was going to drive me back to the hotel."

"Who told you that?"

"Attorney Blake told me."

The chief clerk turns to Sheriff McDuff. "Tell someone to go find Attorneys Kott and Blake, will you?"

McDuff does as he's instructed, poking his head out the door and then coming back in.

"Officer Defano—" the clerk begins, refocusing his attention.

The female officer snaps to attention, her legs parted, hands clasped behind her back. "Yes, sir."

"Who instructed you to leave your post?"

"I received a message from Captain Bhuvan, sir, that the order of protection for Ms. Harrington had been dropped."

"Who delivered this message?"

"He said he was an assistant clerk, Your Honor. From the administration office."

"Who was it?"

Officer Defano's mouth presses into a line and the captain speaks up. "It appears that it was someone posing as a clerk from the administration office."

The chief clerk frowns and looks at Sheriff McDuff, who nods. "It wasn't any of our people. We're looking for this guy now. The courthouse grounds are secure and if we need to, we will walk every single person past Officer Defano until we find him."

The chief clerk sighs and sits forward, running a hand through his hair. His eyes come to rest on me. "And you climbed over the barricades to talk to the press?"

"Not about the trial," I say.

There is a quiet knock and then Cecelie and Burton come in.

"Attorney Blake," the chief clerk says. "Who told you the order of protection for Ms. Harrington had been dropped?"

Cecelie blinks. "A clerk from your office."

"He was not from my office," the chief clerk tells her. "Where did this impostor tell you this?"

"Outside the defense council's conference room. He knocked and I answered the door, and he said, 'The clerk's office wanted you to know the order of protection for Sally Harrington has been dropped and you're responsible for transporting her after court ends today.'"

"And you didn't recognize him?"

She shakes her head. "No." She reaches up to touch her shoulder. "He had a courthouse badge, though. With his picture. It read 'J. Finley,' I think."

"What did he look like?"

"Five-eight, nine. Youngish, maybe thirty. Heavyset, dark hair, brown eyes. Uneven teeth."

"That is a very good description of the man who delivered the message he said was from Captain Bhuvan," Officer Defano says. "Although I believe the name on the badge was Finely—f-i-n-e-l-y."

"It could have been Finely," Cecelie acknowledges.

The chief clerk looks at Sheriff McDuff. "We need to find out where this man came from." He looks at Burton. "Attorney Kott, who told you that you were to take Ms. Harrington from the courthouse today?"

"Attorney Banks."

"Yes, I did," Banks said. "As soon as Cecelie—Attorney Blake—told me the order of protection had been dropped."

The chief clerk sits back in his chair then, eyes squarely focused on Banks. "And you made no attempt to find out why?"

"I assumed the police had determined there was no longer a threat to Ms. Harrington's safety," Banks says smoothly.

"After having this witness testify that Michael Arlenetta was trying to kill her," Perez says angrily, "you assumed there was no threat to Ms. Harrington's safety? Come on, Banks," he adds scornfully.

"I only assumed the police had determined there was no threat to Ms. Harrington's safety," he says firmly. "Then I assigned Attorney Kott to remove her from the courthouse as soon as possible, at which time we could—and would review the issue of her safety."

The chief clerk's eyes remain on Banks for quite some time. Then, quietly, he says, "Sheriff McDuff, Officer Defano, you may return to the investigation. Attorneys Kott and Blake, you're free to leave. Captain Bhuvan, I would suggest you take over on the matter of Ms. Harrington's safety. And Ms. Harrington, I suggest you go with Captain Bhuvan and listen very carefully to what he has to say." He frowns at Banks and Perez. "I wish you would stay behind for a few minutes."

There is an uncomfortable silence. Captain Bhuvan murmurs something and I stand up. McDuff, Defano, Bhuvan and I silently file out, Cecelie and Burton behind me. When we are in the corridor, I turn around to get a good look at Cecelie. She is stone-faced, which means, I know by now, she's worried.

And I should think she should be. This whole hostile helicopter escapade outside the courthouse stinks to high heaven.

CHAPTER | 8

Paul is standing across the lobby of the Shangri-la when my police escort and I come downstairs. He is even younger-looking than I remember, but then, he is not in uniform. He is wearing khakis, a red-and-white pinstripe shirt, blue blazer and highly shined loafers. He does not look like a cop; he looks like an escapee from a Ralph Lauren ad.

Interesting.

He smiles, showing his white, even teeth, and extends a hand as he walks toward me. I take his hand, we sort of shake, and then he moves closer, murmuring, "You're bringing a cop with us on our date?"

"There's nothing I can do," I tell him, shrugging.

"That was really something today," he murmurs, nodding. He looks at me. "Are you all right? You sure you want to go out?"

"Positive," I tell him, thinking I better find out how old he is. I mean, with Montana and college and the academy and everything, he's got to be in his mid twenties at least. Right?

He smiles. "You look absolutely wonderful," he tells me. "I guess testifying suits you, huh?"

I'm just in jeans and a blouse and blue flats, gold hoop earrings, a bracelet. You know, getting-a-hamburger clothes. "Thank you," I say, pleased to be with him. Very pleased we're having dinner.

He's freshly shaven. He got a haircut since yesterday, too.

"Well, these are our choices, Sally," he says, looking at my escort. "We can either ride in his police car to the restaurant, or we can give him a ride in mine. Or, he can follow us in the squad car, which I should add will probably make it look like we're about to be arrested."

"He rides with us," I vote. Actually, for me, this comes as an added relief, for having the police officer ride with us eliminates a lot of elements of choice in this date. With a cop in the back seat, we can't do anything in the car, and we can't go anywhere terribly romantic. We can't—I mean, *I* can't—let myself get into trouble tonight. It means I can't even entertain certain possibilities about tonight. And since I am already acutely aware of how attractive I find this young man, it alleviates a great burden.

A chaperone. I should have tried one of these years ago.

"All right," Paul says to the cop, "you heard the lady, you're riding with us."

"Do you eat with us, too?" I ask the cop as we walk out.

"I just need to maintain visual contact," he tells me.

We zip over to Colorado and park at a place called Hamburger & How. I can't tell you how many times I've eaten here over the years. It's a lot of fun because the hamburgers are very good, in about one hundred varieties, including all kinds of vegetarian ones, but there never fails to be someone famous in here. Usually someone younger and fairly hip.

How surprised am I when I discover the famous person tonight appears to be me. When we walk in there is a hush, which in LaLa Land means people recognize you.

Of course, I've been all over the TV news for the past twenty-four hours. I saw myself on a couple of networks as I was getting ready to meet Paul.

"So what really happened over there today?" Paul asks me, after we're seated.

I briefly recap what happened with the helicopter.

"You think the Arlenettas have put out a hit on you?"

His eyes are very nice. Brown. Earnest. Young. "No," I say. "I think it is a sensational trial with all kinds of sensational things occurring."

He leans his head to the side slightly, considering this. "You think Banks arranged it? To scare the jurors? Give them a taste of paranoia?"

I shrug, picking up my menu. "It's not for me to say." But I know he gets the message, that yes, I do think Banks arranged the charade today. But I'm not allowed to talk about the trial, right? So we order our hamburgers. Mine with Monterey Jack cheese and avocado, Paul's with cheddar, crisp bacon, lettuce, tomato, onion and blue cheese dressing.

I love men who eat things I like to eat.

So we talk. And laugh a lot. Maybe we're nervous, I don't know, but we keep laughing at things. I am talking like I don't know what, amusing him, and telling him about Castleford, about the house I grew up in, and, of course, I spend about ten minutes talking about Scotty, my dog, and am reassured when I find out he loves animals, too. "Scotty is my most successful relationship to date," I tell him.

He smiles as he cuts his cheeseburger in half. "Tell me about the fellow you've been seeing. You said you were seeing someone."

Oh, boy, I think, *got a year to listen?* But I try valiantly to describe my relationship with Doug without dragging in all of my more neurotic baggage. (It is not polite, on a first date, to spill your guts about everything that is wrong with you.) I tell him about Doug and I dating in high school, about breaking up in college, his marrying and divorcing and reappearing in Connecticut almost three years ago. I explain how we saw each other, stopped seeing each other for a while (I don't mention throwing myself into Spencer Hawes's arms for six months), and then took up again this summer.

"So you like people in law enforcement," he observes, resting the end of his fork on his lower lip a moment.

Oh, boy, I sigh to myself, looking at that mouth and then looking back down at my plate. "Yes, I guess you could say that." I look up briefly to smile encouragingly at him. "Okay, your turn."

So Paul tells me about who he is seeing, a young woman he met at his parents' country club. She's working as an assistant at a talent agency.

I'm thinking, *beautiful, with rich parents to subsidize her existence.* If *Boulevard* paid the fledglings badly, talent agencies are the worst. I bartended on weekends to make ends meet; it doesn't sound like this girl moonlights anywhere but at her parents' country club as a guest.

"How long have you been going out?"

He thinks. "Not long. Five months."

I nod, taking another bite of my burger. As if he hears what I'm thinking, Paul says, "We're at that uncomfortable place where I need to make a decision."

"Uncomfortable?" I say, reaching for my Amstel Light beer. I see the officer sitting tragically alone in the corner and give him a little wave. He doesn't wave back.

"Yes. It's uncomfortable because one of us wants to get married, and one of us doesn't."

I meet his eyes. "Same here."

"In your case," Paul says quietly, "I'm hopeful it's you who doesn't want to get married."

I smile slightly. "Yes."

He looks down, fingering the base of his glass. "I have to be honest, in the beginning I thought maybe I would want to marry this girl."

I pat my mouth with my napkin, waiting for the rest.

"But then I knew she wasn't the one. Very soon, actually." He brings his eyes up. "Can you understand if I tell you I can't seem to get out of it? That every time I try to—" He shrugs. "You know, end it, I feel more pulled into it than ever."

"Oh, yes I can," I tell him, laughing.

Encouraged, he says quietly, "I shouldn't be sleeping with her."

I choose not to respond to this, but ask, "How old is she?"

"Twenty-three."

I want to ask him how old he is.

"I'm twenty-five," he tells me.

I look off to the side, at the people next to us, and say,

"I just turned thirty-one." I bring my eyes back to his. "You guys have a lot of time to sort it out."

"And you don't?" He's teasing me.

"Well, I am older."

"Yes, very, very old," he says in mock seriousness.

I avert my eyes. "But I am," I tell him, picking up my fork to eat some French fries. "In comparison to where you are in your life."

"And where is that?" he wants to know. "Where do you see me in my life?"

"Starting out. Finding your way. Looking for someone to build a life with."

"And you're not?"

I sigh. "I don't know anymore, Paul. Honestly, I don't." Abruptly I drop my fork in favor of sipping my beer.

"I think you want to get married," he says. "But not to him." He waits a moment. "Right? You don't want to marry Doug."

I look out the restaurant window at the traffic. "I don't think so. It's funny—" I return my eyes to him. "I know you're supposed to be best friends when you're married. Lovers and everything, but best friends, too. And the romantic part evolved pretty well—"

This is shorthand for our sex life has improved over time.

"But he's not my best friend, and I can't imagine Doug ever being my best friend. Because, I don't know, I just don't like him that way. As a close friend, yes, but..." I let my voice trail off because I don't really know where I'm going with this.

"Who is your best friend?" Paul asks.

I widen my eyes and then shrug. "Golly, I don't know."

"Do you have a lot of friends? You seem like someone who would have a lot of friends."

I think about it. "I have a lot of friends, but I don't have many close friends. My roommate in college—but she's in South America and I never see her or talk to her anymore. My mother, I guess. I don't know," I say uncomfortably. "I think because I've always worked such long hours, my close friends tend to be whoever I'm working with." And then I think of Alexandra Waring, Miss Privacy Plus, and have to laugh out loud.

Paul smiles, wondering what the joke is.

"I'm thinking that if my colleagues at DBS News are my close friends, then I'm in big trouble. I scarcely know them."

"Oh, I don't know," Paul says. "My partner on the night shift and I aren't really friends—but because of our long hours together, we're more like family. We're stuck with each other and so we have a kind of loyalty code."

He's right. It is like a version of family.

The waitress comes for our plates and we both order coffee. When it arrives, we both reach for the cream and smile when our hands touch. "Sorry," I say.

He covers my hand with his for a moment. Then he murmurs, "Please," and pushes the creamer toward me. As I prepare my coffee, he says, "So how are you going to tell him?"

This gives me a stomachache. Obviously I don't know how to tell Doug I don't want to go on, because if I had, I would have told him by now. "I think I have to tell him he would be happier with someone else."

Paul is shaking his head. "No, that's no good. He'll just say he's happiest with you. That's what Mindy always says."

"I could say I just don't want to get married and I think he should see women who do want to get married."

Paul's shaking his head. "He'll just say fine, we'll just be together, we don't have to get married."

I look at him. "So what do you suggest?"

"That you love him as a friend, but you don't love him the way a girlfriend or wife should and you have to stop seeing him for a while."

My eyes lower to the table. "He'll think there's someone else."

"God, I hope so," Paul declares.

I quickly look at him, startled.

"The point is," he says quietly, "you're not marrying him because you don't want to marry him and for that reason alone, the relationship shouldn't go any further."

I swallow coffee and say over the top of my cup, "Then there you go, that's what you should tell what's-her-name."

"Mindy," he says, lowering his cup with a clatter in the saucer. "It's not going to be easy."

"I know," I say softly.

Now we are both depressed, thinking about what we need to do in our private lives. Paul is right, I do have to end it with Doug, but I'm not sure I can bear to hurt him again. It would almost be easier to marry him. I think about all of our high school classmates who have been married and are divorced—Doug included—and I wonder how many of them had been in this situation, too, where they got married because it was easier than breaking up.

The check arrives and Paul reaches for it. I offer to pay half, but he shakes his head. "Not this time. Maybe next time," and while I am pleased he would like to see me again, he must realize that after I finish testifying, probably tomorrow, I'll be returning to the East Coast.

We hook up with our cop at the door and walk to Paul's car, an older blue LeBaron convertible with gray interior. We drive back to the Shangri-la and the guys talk about football. At the hotel, the cop gets out so we have a moment alone. "I really enjoyed this," I tell him.

"I'm afraid we both got a little depressed," he says, looking down at the wheel.

We're silent a minute, each with our own thoughts. Then his hand moves over to take mine. We turn to each other and my heart starts to pound.

"We'll take it as we can take it," he murmurs.

I think he's going to kiss me. I want him to kiss me.

But he does not kiss me on the mouth. He simply leans over and kisses me softly on the cheek, hesitates, and then sharply pulls back. Then he lets go of my hand and looks down at the wheel again. I take the cue and undo my seat belt. His hand shoots across again suddenly, to touch my arm. His eyes are earnest. "I want to see you tomorrow, Sally. Please. I've got a shift tonight, but I want to see you." He smiles, trying to appear less intense, but I can tell how much he means it. It is affecting me, his sincerity.

I want very much to see him again, too.

"I'd love to see you tomorrow," I tell him.

He swallows. I swallow. Slowly he leans over to kiss me. Then he pulls back, murmuring, "Great." He looks at me, letting out an exaggerated breath. "You better get going."

"Good night," I say, opening the door and getting out. I lean back down. "I get out of court around four. Call me and we'll figure out when and where."

He smiles, broadly. "Great."

I close the door and walk a few steps before turning around to wave. He waves back, puts the car into Drive and slowly pulls away.

My cop is waiting for me in the lobby.

His uniform, I notice, does nothing for me.

CHAPTER | 9

Upstairs in my suite, I find an urgent message from Will Rafferty on the voice mail system. I call him.

"Where have you been?" he demands to know.

"Eating dinner," I sigh, tired, resentful of being snapped out of my pleasant evening with Paul.

"Why is the trial suspended?" he says next.

I blink. "Nobody told me it was suspended."

"How could anybody tell you if nobody can find you?"

I take a breath. "Let's start this again. The trial has been suspended?"

"Until Monday," Will says. "Nobody knows why and since you are there, supposedly, we wondered if you knew why."

"I would imagine it has to do with the helicopter business," I say. "And/or security in the courthouse."

"Why? What was wrong with the security?"

I sigh. I'm not supposed to talk about the trial. Does this include people masquerading as clerks? I would imagine it does. "The helicopter business," I say. I look at my watch, having another thought. It's only ten to nine. If the trial really is suspended until Monday, maybe I can catch a red-eye to New York tonight. I really would like to get this Marion O'Hearn business over with. "So the trial's really postponed?"

"You're serious," he says. "You really don't know."

"No. No one's called."

"It's postponed until Monday. The *press* was notified. Maybe if you hadn't been so busy talking to the other networks today, Sally, you would have been notified, too."

"I was stuck, Will. I couldn't get to the DBS camera."

"Alexandra had a stroke when she saw you on ABC. And what happened in that meeting with Perez and Banks? Somebody said the chief of the Santa Monica Police was in there."

"Not the chief. A captain. Captain Bhuvan," I say. "How do you know about that?"

"Because not everybody talked to the other networks and then went out to dinner," he says sarcastically.

Huh. So DBS has someone on the inside of the courthouse.

"I can't talk about anything connected to the trial until I'm through testifying," I tell him.

"You certainly talked in front of the cameras."

"I wanted the helicopter to be found."

"Fat chance of that," Will growls.

"*What* is the matter, Will?" I say loudly. I feel like there's a second agenda to this conversation I know nothing about.

"Fucking everything is the matter," he says, hanging up.

I call Burton Kott's cell phone, which he answers immediately. "Court's in recess until Monday," I say.

"I know. I was about to call you."

"Well I need to go home. Tonight."

"Sorry, Sally, no can do. You've got the order of protection on you."

"Then buy the protection a plane ticket, will you?"

"Forget it, Sally."

I get off with him and think about this. Well, if all else fails, there is always the truth. I throw a pair of underpants and some deodorant and a toothbrush into my briefcase and walk outside, where a new officer is sitting. "Hi," I say.

"Hi," he says.

"I've got to go to the airport. My mother needs me in Connecticut."

He starts blinking, clearly thrown by this.

"Could you take me to the airport and put me on a plane? At least, could we start for the airport and you can check with your supervisor on the way to see if it's okay? My mother needs me to come home immediately, because someone very close to me is dying."

I've got him standing up now, at least.

"I just learned the trial has been recessed until Monday, so this is the first opportunity I've had to get home. And I'll call my mother, Officer, you can talk to her. Marion's dying and I need to be there." I try to evoke a tear, but the thought of the O'Hearns only leaves me feeling cold inside. So I think of Daddy, and the tears come easily. "I'm so scared I'll miss the last plane and she'll be dead before I get there."

He's following me to the stairs now. "I can't promise

anything, Ms. Harrington," he says kindly, "but at least we can start toward the airport until I find out."

"Thank you, thank you," I say, meaning it.

I am mad at Burton Kott. He didn't even try to help me. So while we're in the squad car, sailing to LAX, and the officer is on his radio with his precinct, I call Will back in New York. "If I were you," I tell him, "I'd get someone who sounds like me to call this number." I give him Burton's cell phone number. "And she should say, 'Burton? Sally. Why are we in recess?' If he doesn't start explaining, she should say, 'Do you want me available to testify or not?' That will get him talking. And from there you'll have to wing it. Best if she calls on a crappy cell phone, or get the Nerd Brigade—" a group of techno-wizards in the DBS electronics lab "—to jury-rig some noise."

"This is Burton Kott?" Will asks.

"Yeah. That's his top-secret cell phone number. I can't talk about the trial, so I'll let him. Don't forget to tell me what he says, so I'll know." After I hang up, I sit back with satisfaction.

"You're right," the officer tells me, glancing over, "the trial is in recess until Monday. Captain Bhuvan is going to call me. An unplanned flight might be okayed, though we might have to arrange for an escort on the other end."

I call Mother. "Hi, it's Sally. I'm sorry to awaken you."

"It's all right, darling," Mother says. "What's wrong?"

"Nothing. I just wanted to tell you court's in recess until Monday and a nice police officer is trying to help me get home. Before poor Mrs. O'Hearn dies."

"That's wonderful, dear. Thank you."

"It's the police officer you should thank," I say, looking over at him. "He's the one trying to make it happen for us."

I hold out the phone. "Do you want to speak with my mother?"

He looks nervous. "No, that's okay."

"She just wants to thank you."

He smiles. "Tell her I'm waiting to hear from my boss. And I'm trying my best."

"Did you hear that, Mother?"

"You sound very odd, Sally," Mother says, "but I'm very glad you're coming home."

"Maybe, Mother, the officer can't make any promises. It's out of his control. But someone in greater authority may have to call you, to make sure this is a legitimate emergency."

"Why on earth...?" she begins, but then she simply plays along, not quite understanding fully what's going on. "Certainly, darling, I will be prepared."

I get off with Mother and call American Airlines. There is a seat open on the 11:00 p.m. The question is, can I get through security? At this time of night, I might. I reserve the seat. We're making excellent time and are nearing the exit for LAX.

The officer's cell phone rings and he picks it up. "Yes, Captain Bhuvan." He listens, glancing over at me. "Yes, sir. Yes, sir." Pause. "Her mother. It is a family emergency. She only just received word the trial's postponed until Monday." Pause. "Very anxious, sir." He lowers his voice. "Someone's dying." The latter is said with such sincerity I am in love with this man. "Yes, sir." He glances over and holds the phone out to me. "Captain Bhuvan wants to talk to you."

"Captain," I say.

"I'd like to speak to your mother about this so-called family emergency," he tells me.

"Of course, sir." I give him Mother's name and number, and add, "You'll like her. She's a schoolteacher." Why I think cops get along with schoolteachers I have no idea, but it's all I can think to say. He asks to speak to his officer again.

"He's going to call us back," he reports, putting the phone down. "Which airline?"

"American." I give him the flight number.

Captain Bhuvan calls back. The officer says, yes, yes, and then gives him the American flight number, and says yes, yes, yes. "Okay, you're in business," he reports happily, hanging up. "The Captain is alerting airport personnel we're bringing you through."

"That's terrific," I murmur. I am very moved. I didn't think they would really go for this, but I guess they all have their own family emergencies. I suppose if it didn't involve the O'Hearns I would feel more sympathetic toward my own case.

We pull up to the departure gate, where an airport cop and national guard reservist meet us. The officer gets out and confers with them, showing his badge, and then I am asked to get out. They examine my driver's license and I explain I have to pay for my ticket. The police car is left with the reservist, and the officers accompany me to the AA ticket counter, where a brief conference with a supervisor sails me to the head of the line. The next available agent checks me in, issues a ticket and hands me a boarding pass. "Luggage?"

"No, luggage," I say. "No time to get it."

She nods as if this is normal and hands my boarding pass to the airport cop. So we're off again and shortly I am put at the front of the security line. I take off my bracelet and walk through the detectors unmolested. Then we're off again, very quickly, for it is a long walk out to the gate and we have, at this point, about twelve minutes.

We end up jogging to the gate, where the cop hands my boarding pass and license to the attendant. The attendant tells him I have to go over and get searched at the security table. I walk over and quickly empty my pockets and they take everything out of my briefcase, including my clean underpants. Fortunately I have no other questionable items and am waved onto the plane.

At the door, I turn to the officer who helped me. "I will never forget your kindness," I tell him. And I kiss him on the cheek.

The flight attendants are looking a little strangely at me as I enter the plane (heaven knows what they've been told about my status) and I am seated in first class, although my boarding pass is for a seat in tourist. I guess they want to keep an eye on me.

Whatever. I am so grateful to be here. I only wonder, as I begin to relax, what it is I am flying home for.

CHAPTER | 10

We make a lovely landing at JFK at 5:30 a.m. Eastern Standard Time and I dash to the Budget phone to request the shuttle. I am assured one is already nearby and I walk outside to wait. I am freezing. I didn't even bring a sweater and the November chill is deep, the gray skies shifting in the wind. A shuttle drives up and a couple of us board and rattle out to the Budget satellite. I am first in line to get my car assigned and after glancing briefly at the exterior of the car, I open the trunk to make sure it's empty before I drive away. (Don't ask.)

It is now six-thirty and a good time to call Mother, just a few minutes after her usual morning shower. "Darling, where are you?"

"On my way. I'm just leaving the airport."

"JFK?"

"Yes."

"That's great, dear."

She sounds funny. "Are you okay?"

"Honey?" I hear a male voice call. "Where are the drops for Abigail's ears?"

Ah-ha. That's why Mother sounds funny. Mack Cleary, her fiancé, slept over last night, on a school night.

I smile to myself. Mother is so funny. I remember the first time I realized she and Mack were having sex, and yes, I felt very weird about it. But then, like everything else in life, I got used to the idea. What was more weird was when they announced they were going to get married, and Mother announced she was retiring early and leaving Castleford to build a house on the water in Essex with Mack. (They share a love of sailing, something my landlubber father did not.)

Mack and Mother were originally supposed to marry in September, but Mother found she just couldn't walk away from her job. "I just can't do it," she told me this summer, sitting with a calculator, pencil and a bunch of papers at the kitchen table. "If I retire now, I receive fifty percent of the three highest years of my base salary. If I wait and retire in two years, I receive seventy percent." She looked at me. "There's no way. I don't care if Mack has a mountain of gold, I'm not walking away from that money." Blink. "I've worked too hard for too many years."

My heart nearly broke. Let me tell you how hard my Mother worked after Daddy died. She taught school, she tutored, taught summer school, sold jams and jellies and flowers, she did everything she could to hang on to the house my father built for us. So we were, well, "house rich," I guess you would call it. With zippo in the bank. But as I learned from Mother, and boy is it true, there is a big difference between being poor and being without money. Being without money, according to Mother, is a period a family goes through until they work their way into a better situation; being poor is a tragic family without hope of ever changing their situation.

So we were never poor, just without money. For a long, long time.

At any rate, Mother and Mack are supposed to marry in June, and now, I guess, Mack is sneaking over during the week and Mother doesn't want me to know.

My smile expands. I just love her. "Oh, I'm glad Mack's there," I say. "I think the dogs are too much when you're teaching. You can't talk him into staying until lunch, can you, so I can see him?"

There is a pause and then Mother says, "I love you, Sally." Her voice breaks a little on the last and I realize how guilty she's been feeling. Mothers are so funny.

I promise her I will call the O'Hearns at a decent hour and make arrangements to see Marion today. (My spirits simply plummet at the thought, I am so dreading this.)

After hanging up with Mother (and thus no longer violating the New York no-handheld-cell-phones-while-driving law) I fairly fly across the Van Wyck, which usually threatens traffic at the slightest provocation, but this morning is simply offering a lovely drive along the inside waterways of Queens. Then the landscape turns heavily urban as I take the Whitestone Bridge to the Bronx. I pick up the Hutchinson River Parkway north, which, a half an hour later, crosses into Connecticut at Greenwich and becomes the Merritt Parkway. Sixty-three miles to home, I know.

The rising sun is trying to shine bright, but blustery winds keep clouds rolling by. From the top of the great hill in Stratford, just before the Sikorsky Bridge, shadows can be seen racing over the land.

I don't want to see Marion O'Hearn. I really don't want to see Phillip O'Hearn.

Someday this property will be mine. A four-bedroom house, a small greenhouse and gardening shed on five acres. The house looks like it's two hundred years old rather than thirty, because Daddy was an architect and adapted colonial blueprints and built it with modern materials. Modern materials, that is, with the exception of stone, largely granite, which was quarried from the ground beneath the house. (In case you've never gardened in New England, granite is our greatest crop.)

This five-acre parcel is all the Harringtons retained from the estate next door, now a Franciscan convent, which was my father's boyhood home. Daddy's father, my grandfather, blew the family fortune on ill-advised investments (read, he was a gambler) and blew his brains out in the playhouse.

I don't think—I *know*—I've bitten off more than I can handle by declaring my intention of buying this house from Mother. At best I can be here on weekends. As I get out of the car, I notice there is a crack in the chimney mortar. I see that the outside windowpanes need painting. I know the deck in the back needs sanding and resealing, and that two boards need to be replaced. The lawn takes four hours to mow on a tractor. The long driveway becomes nearly impassible with more than three inches of snow. (Ah, another great New England crop.)

Mack's not here. No one's here.

I unlock the front door and my heart lurches when I see my Scotty boy, eyes shining bright, his mouth open in delight, his tail wagging and whole body twitching down the desire to jump. Zooming in next to him and having no such qualms, Mother's Abigail simply leaps up on me. I kneel to the floor and hug them both, burying my face in the fall fur of Scotty's neck. He squirms, frantic to lick my face. So I draw back slightly and let him, as Abigail slips behind me and bounds through the door to the outside. Scotty stays, nuzzling me, making whining noises, and now I hug him with both arms, falling back to sit on the floor and drawing all eighty pounds of him into my lap as if he's still a puppy.

It's not right to love a dog this much, but what can I do? I give him one more kiss on the nose and shoo him outside. He gives one last loud bark hello to make me wince, and charges outside after Abigail. I close the front door.

The house is quiet. I walk into the kitchen, where we all always live in this house, with its large windows and sliding glass doors looking out over the lawn, the meadow, the woods, the pond and, finally, the Connecticut Mountains.

I look at the phone and then the clock. I've got to call. I start some coffee and use the powder room off the kitchen first, delaying.

Driving over to the O'Hearns' house, I cannot for the life of me imagine what Marion wants with me. It's so weird that she's dying. Since Daddy died, I've always thought of the O'Hearns as indestructible. Kind of like how Parisians must have felt about the Panzer tanks that patrolled their streets during World War II. We, the Harrington widow and kids, were without money and freedom, and the O'Hearns, whom my father set up in business, increasingly seemed to own everything in Castleford. They were getting all the money, all the respect, everything.

From the two-bedroom the O'Hearns used to rent, they moved into a five-bedroom house. And then, about ten years ago, they built a seven-bedroom mansion on the hill of what used to be the Erickson Farm. Mrs. O'Hearn receives a new Cadillac on her birthday every year; he drives any one of the three other cars he keeps in their detached four-bay garage: the Lexus four-by-four, the Ferrari and the Rolls-Royce.

I didn't know until relatively recently that Phillip O'Hearn had anything to do with the death of my father. Until that time all I knew was that Daddy had been a very good architect, had set up his friend Mr. O'Hearn in the construction business, and the more successful Mr. O'Hearn got, the less we socialized with them. Then Daddy was killed and Mother seemed to avoid Phillip O'Hearn, which in retrospect I believe had more to do with how great-looking Mother was and how Phillip turned out to be anything but faithful to Marion.

Mr. O'Hearn has always had a girlfriend.

Anyway, by the time I learned that Phillip O'Hearn was connected to the murder of my father, the evidence to prove it was long gone. Still, courtesy of Alexandra and DBS News, I was able to publicly air the circumstantial evidence that pointed to O'Hearn as my father's killer. Naively I thought the townsfolk of Castleford would turn their backs on him. Stupid. Turn their backs on the largest employer in town? No way. The town of Castleford recoiled from *me*, loudly resenting that Harrington girl for "causing trouble," and "stirring up the past" for no good reason.

And I still want to live in this town. Go figure.

Remembering how important this errand is to Mother, I drive through the brick pillars that mark the beginning of the O'Hearn driveway. They like to call it an estate. (I like to call it nouveau riche.) Actually, it's in pretty good taste, kind of Martha Stewart-by-numbers, although everything is carefully placed right out there for every visitor to see and be intimidated by. Many wealthy people prefer houses that are modestly viewed from the front (à la real Martha Stewart). Do you know what I mean? That it is only when you're lost inside that you begin to realize how big the house really is? Well, the O'Hearns built their house so you can see everything from the front. It sprawls sideways across the top of the hill, often only one-room deep, two floors high, and in some places three. Then there is that four-bay garage on the right of the drive, with the entire house sprawling left of that.

We are rich! the property screams. *We will bury you with our money!*

I park the rental and walk to the massive front door. The house is painted white, which of course, makes it loom even larger. I ring the doorbell and hear loud chimes inside, the real thing, rhythmically clanging against one another in a melody.

Phillip answers the door himself. He is about five foot eleven, balding and getting a bit of a paunch. Except for his immaculately tailored clothes, he really is rather non-descript. The last time I saw him, I knocked him into the wall outside the country club rest rooms. (He had leered at me and I had had a few too many glasses of wine.)

Now he only looks small, grayer and deeply sad. "Thank God you came," he whispers. "Thank you for coming."

"It was important to Mother," I say quietly.

He nods, stepping back to let me in.

I've never been in this house. The front hall is enormous, with black-and-white linoleum, a huge chandelier, what looks to be a walnut staircase winding up to the second floor. I can't help myself. "Is that staircase...?"

"It's from the Old Soldiers Home in New Haven," he says automatically. He holds a hand out to direct me. "She's in the sunroom," he whispers. "Where we've set up a hospice."

Hospice. Where, I assume he means, Marion is to die.

It is a beautiful room, three walls of glass, looking out over terraced gardens, and lawn, woods and then the mountains, of course. (Mother's view is better, I note.)

In the middle of the room is a hospital bed, raised so its patient may look straight out. A nurse stands up from the chair where she has been reading a Nancy Thayer novel. She gently smiles, stepping back to make room for us.

I cannot believe this small wizened person is Marion O'Hearn. A month ago I saw her at Agway, loudly berating the garden staff, her face red with anger and her hair money perfect. (I remember this because at the time I thought how strange it was her hair didn't move as she shook her head.) She's lost at least thirty pounds. She's tiny, frail. Her hair looks good, though.

O'Hearn clears his throat and whispers something to her. Marion's eyes struggle to open, as if she is exhausted, and for a moment her eyes remain unfocused. It's hard to believe even cancer can do this so quickly.

Slowly her eyes look at me. I move closer. "It's Sally Harrington, Mrs. O'Hearn."

The lady's clearly dying. It's not going to hurt me to be polite.

When she doesn't respond, O'Hearn says, "It's Sally,

darling. She's come. Sally Harrington. You wanted to talk to her. Do you remember?"

Her lips scarcely move. "I remember."

Mr. O'Hearn pats his wife's lips with a damp washcloth.

"Go," Mrs. O'Hearn suddenly says.

Mr. O'Hearn and I look at each other.

"Phil. Leave us," she says.

I look at him. "I'll call you if she needs anything," I promise. He and the nurse leave.

I look down at Mrs. O'Hearn. Then I pull up a chair, close. Her eyes meet mine. "I'm sorry, Sally," she whispers.

I don't know why, but I start to cry. I can't help it. She's dying and the whole thing, everything between the O'Hearns and the Harringtons, has gone on so long. I can remember this woman bandaging my scraped knee at their tiny house when I was little, when we went to a barbecue there. I can remember Mr. O'Hearn tapping a keg and my father and he reenacting great football moments at Castleford High. I remember the four O'Hearn kids, loud and noisy kids, but fun to play with.

Death is horrible. I don't care what anybody says, I hate it. No one should die like this.

Her hand moves toward me and I take it. I don't know what the hell is the matter with me—this woman hates me, I hate her, what the hell is going on.

I look up, sniffing, trying to stop the tears.

"I didn't know," Marion whispers. She takes a breath, trying to gain strength. "I didn't know what he'd do."

I assume she is talking about her husband. If this is to be a conversation to alleviate her conscience in some way, it is a good way to start, by saying she didn't know Phillip would have my father killed to keep him silent. But who did? Who knew Daddy would find out that O'Hearn had deliberately used faulty building materials in the high school gym and that's why it collapsed?

"I know you didn't," I whisper back, squeezing her hand. "Mother knows that, too. It wasn't your fault."

"But it was," she whispers, closing her eyes. A tear squeezes out from under one lid and down her sallow cheek.

I don't say anything, but wait.

"He had a girlfriend," she whispers.

"Mr. O'Hearn?" I have got to get this straight.

"Yes." Her eyes open. "I was so hurt." She swallows with difficulty. "I had four children, Sally. I had nowhere to go."

"I understand," I say. "You couldn't leave. You wanted your children to have a good home."

She nods slightly. "I wanted to hurt him."

I nod. "That's understandable."

"I told him—" Her eyes clamp shut; now there are two tears falling. "Oh, Sally," she moans, clearly wanting to sob but not having the strength to. Instead, she starts to drool. I grab a tissue and wipe her mouth and chin. I wipe her nose. Her red-rimmed eyes look at me, miserable. "I couldn't face Belle. I couldn't tell her."

"Tell her what?" I whisper.

"He—" she breathes. "I told Phillip I loved Dodge."

Dodge, my father's nickname.

Color is coming into Mrs. O'Hearn's face and suddenly she seems stronger. "I told Phillip I didn't care about his girl. I loved Dodge." Pause. "I told him I was sleeping with Dodge."

For a moment, my mind reels and I cannot catch my breath.

We always assumed O'Hearn had arranged my father's death because he was afraid of being exposed, afraid of being ruined. But if what Marion is saying is true, that he believed my father was sleeping with his wife—

"Can you forgive me?" Marion says in a tiny, faint voice.

"Yes, of course," I automatically whisper back. "You didn't know," I say, starting to cry again. "You didn't know what he'd do."

"He still thinks—" She tries to swallow but can't. She takes a jagged breath. "I never told Phillip it was a lie. I couldn't. Not after..."

"It's all right," I whisper, sniffing.

Marion's eyes widen a little and then she begins sinking away before my eyes. I utter a cry of alarm and run to the door. "Mr. O'Hearn, Nurse! She's in trouble!"

They rush in and I wipe my eyes, watching as Phillip O'Hearn falls to his knees, grasping his wife's hand and pressing it to his mouth as the nurse checks her pulse and lifts the lids of her eyes.

Then the nurse puts her hand on Mr. O'Hearn's shoulder. "She's gone. She's at peace now."

He lets out a howl of anguish and drops his head on the side of the bed, sobbing. I am sobbing, too, and rush out of the room.

CHAPTER | 11

It's really rather hopeless trying to rake leaves at my cottage in Castleford, mainly because there is one third of an acre of lawn and ten acres of woods around it. I've been renting the 1920s caretaker's cottage on the old Brackleton Farm for a couple of years now, and I have yet to clear all the leaves out of the yard even once.

I brought Scotty home from Mother's and have numbly gone about doing chores, unable—unwilling—still, to think clearly.

So, Scotty and I are outside raking leaves. It is ridiculous. With two sweeps of the rake I've got leaves higher than my knees. But I do it, anyway. Scotty and I are going to make the biggest pile of leaves in the history of the world, I decide.

It is starting to get dark when Mother's forest-green

Outback wagon comes around the bend of the drive. Scotty bounds over to greet her. In moments Abigail is streaking around the yard with him—the two tear through the piles of leaves, and then jump around, looking like wacko kangaroos.

I glance over, continuing to rake. "Hi."

"Hi," she says, walking across the yard, her hands deep in the pockets of the fleece-lined leather coat Mack bought her. She stands by the pile, watching the dogs. The attention only spurs them on and Abigail leaps into the air, doing a very impressive reverse, falling on her back in the leaves so that Scotty can quickly pounce on her. The two of them sound like Cujo. "So you went to see Marion," she finally says.

"Yes." Rake, rake, rake. I bend over to pick up a branch and toss it into the pile of branches that I've accumulated on the other side. "And I'm not absolutely certain what to do with what she said to me."

Mother absently touches her forehead and steps closer. "You mean how much to tell me."

Finally I stop raking. I hold on to the top of the rake handle and lean on it, looking at her. "She said she told Mr. O'Hearn she was having an affair with Daddy. She told him she was in love with Daddy."

It hasn't sunk in yet.

"She said it was a lie, but that's what Mr. O'Hearn has thought all these years. She never told him. And she said she couldn't face you."

Mother simply stands there. And then her hand involuntarily comes up to cover her mouth and she turns away.

"Then she asked me if I could forgive her."

Mother wheels around. She is not crying. In fact, she looks angry.

"Then she died, Mother." I pause. "She's dead."

As the words register, that Marion O'Hearn is dead, the anger in my mother's face leaves. "Did you forgive her, Sally? Before she died?"

I nod. "I told her I forgave her," I say, swallowing. "And then she died. I called Mr. O'Hearn in, and there was this nurse, and then I left."

I don't know what I expect Mother to do, but it is not what she does. She comes over to kiss me softly on the cheek and quietly says, "You're my good girl, darling, I love you." She walks back to her car, calls Abigail, and a minute later, they are gone.

No questions. No discussion. She, like me, only wants to be alone.

II
Worker Among Workers

CHAPTER | 12

"You didn't even *watch* the news yesterday?" a voice asks from the doorway of my office.

"No," I say, holding the telephone between my chin and shoulder while I continue to type into my computer. I swivel my chair to see my boss, Alexandra Waring, standing there. Today being Saturday, when she is not supposed to be here, she is wearing jeans, a turtleneck and barn boots. Understand that this is a TV anchorwoman (read thin), so even on her day off she tends to look like something out of *Town & Country.* "I'm on hold for L.A.," I tell her.

"Ah, yes, L.A.," she says, slipping into a seat in front of my desk, "the last to know of your sudden departure. It was merely your assigned field office."

I study her a moment, trying to figure out if she's really

mad or not, but all I can think of is *Town & Country*. The anchorwoman's shoulder-length dark hair is a bit wild today, giving her a slightly tempestuous look; her trademark blue-gray eyes are killers since the turtleneck she is wearing is, of course, the same blue-gray. I am particularly glad to see that she is wearing the turtleneck because it signals to me she is no longer self-conscious about her health status. After a lumpectomy and radiation treatments for breast cancer, Alexandra has been given a new lease on life. Does it make a difference with Alexandra? Who can ever tell with her for sure?

All in all, looking at the healthy glow of her face and eyes, I think she is excellent.

But is she mad at me?

L.A.—which means Glen, the news producer out there—comes back on the line and I briefly outline the situation for him. I'm flying back tomorrow I tell him, and then I get off the phone to face the music.

"So how come you're in today?" I ask cheerfully, hanging up the telephone.

She doesn't answer, but merely continues to look at me.

"Am I to guess?"

She sighs. "You're running around the country without protection."

"Oh, that," I say. "There's no real threat."

"So now you know more than the police?" she says levelly. "Your testimony on Thursday, you know, sealed the deal on an arrest warrant for Michael Arlenctta."

"Fine," I say, "I'll meet a cop at the airport tomorrow when I get there."

She crosses her legs. "By the way, the trial was postponed for courthouse security reasons."

"Did someone call Burton Kott?"

"I did."

"Pretending to be me?"

She doesn't answer but just sort of shrugs. (This must tread some fine line in her mind, I suppose.) "I didn't quite understand what he was talking about," she says. "The courthouse is looking for an impostor of some kind?"

I don't say anything, but just offer her the same sort of shrug. I am not supposed to talk about matters concerning the trial. Whatever I tell her will no doubt end up on the news today.

The anchorwoman lifts one eyebrow. "And Paul Fitzwilliam. How interesting is that?"

I settle back in my chair. "What about him?"

"He's been looking for you," she tells me. "Evidently you were supposed to have dinner with him last night."

"Oh, my God," I say, clapping my hands over my mouth. "Oh, my God," I say again, now moving to cover my eyes. "I completely forgot."

"So he called the hotel yesterday and found out you weren't there, that you'd left no message for him and no forwarding number...." She lets her voice trail off.

"Did he call here?"

"He called the L.A. station, but they didn't know where you were, either. So he got really worried."

I'm fumbling for my purse. "I've got his number here somewhere—"

Alexandra stands up to toss an index card on my desk. "That's his cell phone number. I already talked to him, though, and told him you were all right—but had a bit of an emergency. Thank God he didn't ask what it was."

I look up. "Thank you."

"His mother's apparently a big fan of mine," she says, smiling, then turning away.

"Yeah, she is, he mentioned that."

While walking to the door, she says over her shoulder, "Twenty-five years old, huh?"

I hate working for this woman. If she doesn't know everything already, she goes over to Dr. Kessler and the Nerd Brigade in the electronic reference division of DBS and finds out what she doesn't. "We had a hamburger together," I tell her.

"In your hotel room that first day?" she says, turning around. "Or was that the next night at Hamburger & How?"

I slam my fist down on my desk and stand up. "You know, Waring, you don't friggin' own me. You have absolutely no business spying on me."

"A threat was made on your life, Sally. And if some cop makes a bogus pickup on you and then goes back to your hotel room, we need to know if he might be killing you or something."

I am floored. "So what did you do? Have someone listen at my door?"

"Yes," she says boldly. "And he was prepared to go into that room and shoot that cop if he was hurting you."

"God, Alexandra!" I cry, rubbing my face hard with both hands in frustration. I drop them. "What kind of place is this? It's like a cross between the Gestapo and the Snoop Sisters around here." I give the open bottom drawer of my desk a shove with my foot, making it slam.

Alexandra comes back to my desk and offers a genuine smile, one of those long, dazzling and disarming smiles. "The Gestapo and the Snoop Sisters, I like that." The smile disappears. "The fact remains, Sally, there is something completely messed up with your sense of self-preservation. This isn't the first time. It's like you go into denial or something and take these stupid risks."

"I have to function," I grumble.

"You have to be careful," my thirty-eight-year-old boss says.

"Let me get this straight. Are you telling me something's not right with Paul Fitzwilliam?"

"No."

I cut the air with my hand. "Then stop it. He's a police officer. He's a nice guy. I like him."

The look Alexandra gives me makes me want to smack her.

"You'll be careful," she says, turning to go, "and you'll pick up an escort at LAX. And tell Security today what flight you're taking."

"Fine."

She turns around. "Listen, before I forget, we have a seat in the courtroom now. When you finish testifying, I want you to take it."

I brighten. "Oh, yeah?"

"Oh, yeah," she confirms, walking out.

Huh. I wonder if this means I might be going on the air as a reporter. If I do, it activates all kinds of clauses in my contract with DBS News. I may be able to afford buying Mother's house yet.

Suddenly I feel scared, though, anxious. Marion O'Hearn. I wish I hadn't thought of that. Dead. Daddy's death. Mother's leaving.

Do I really want to live in Castleford anymore?

I sit down, feeling weird.

Alexandra chooses that moment to reappear in my doorway. "Sally? I wanted—" She comes in. "What's wrong?" Her radar is excellent.

"I don't want to talk about it," I say abruptly.

She draws closer to my desk, circling halfway around it, her expression sympathetic. "It's not your mother, is it? That's not why you came home?"

"Sort of," I sigh, rubbing my eyes again and dropping down into my chair.

After a moment, Alexandra lowers herself down next to my chair. Reluctantly I drop my hand and look over at her.

I tell her. Damn it, I tell her all about it. I need to talk to somebody. About Mrs. O'Hearn and Mr. O'Hearn and my father. And poor Mother.

CHAPTER | 13

After my bout with True Confessions, I finish reading through the mail accumulated in my office and walk down to the dog run located in the square of the DBS complex. Scotty is alone this Saturday afternoon. During the week there is usually a full house. He jumps up against the chain-link fence, waiting, his bushy tail sweeping back and forth, and showing those teeth that always scare strangers.

"Hey, babe," I greet him, opening the door to the run. He trots over happily and I bend to pet him and clip on his leash. "Want to go for a car ride?" I ask him. *Hooray!* shines in his eyes, no doubt in anticipation of a lowered rear window through which he can stretch his face into freezing November winds.

"Sally?"

I turn around. It's Alexandra again.

"Your young police officer called again," she says. She's wearing a navy parka and has a large leather bag slung over her shoulder. Clearly she's ready to head out. "I told him you had a family emergency."

Scotty jerks his leash. I let it go so he can walk to Alexandra, who kneels on one knee to say hi to him. She pets him with both hands, rubbing behind his ears, and looks up. "He said he thought it must have been something like that." She smiles. "He said he wanted to make sure you didn't run off and get married."

"No," I say, smiling and embarrassed, but nonetheless pleased.

She raises her eyebrows in merriment. "Oh, boy, Scotty," she says to my dog, "Sally's got another one."

"Yeah, right," I mutter.

Alexandra finishes with Scotty and stands up. "He asked if you could just call him when you get a chance."

At this point I am too embarrassed to respond. Alexandra has known too much for too long about my personal life. I guess the same could be said about me and her personal life. Scotty comes walking back over, circling to drag the handle of the leash in front of me. I pick it up and we all start walking to the West End garage.

Alexandra starts talking about a story unfolding in Houston and I realize she's merely filling the air. There is no meaningful reason for her to relay this information to me, so I relax a little. After we walk out through the gate of the park, making our way around the Darenbrook I building to reach the garage, out of the blue she says, "Will is upset with me and I think you should know why." She looks at me and adds, "Although you may be very upset with me, too. Still, you should know."

By now we've come to a stop.

"This is still confidential information...."

I nod, acknowledging this.

"Jessica is pregnant." Jessica Wright, the talk show host, is married to Will Rafferty.

I smile. "That's wonderful. I understand she and Will have been trying for quite some time."

"Yes, yes, it is wonderful," she agrees. Then she winces slightly. "It's going to be difficult for her to hang on, though, medically, and she may only be able to safely work for maybe one more month."

"How far along is she?"

"Only ten weeks."

I frown. "So there's a real problem."

Alexandra nods. "Yes. So quite rightfully Will wants her out of here like yesterday."

I shrug. "If I were them I'd feel the same way."

"Well, it's not quite so simple. Jessica knows there are an awful lot of people whose employment depends on the ratings of her show." She meets my eyes. "Like all of us at DBS News."

"I thought we were doing great."

"We are, but every time she has a rerun, our overall ratings slip."

"I noticed that," I say. "Last time it was almost eighteen percent."

"Exactly. There's never been any question about *The Jessica Wright Show* being the heart of the schedule. I mean, there is no question but that the show is critical to our success. So if Jessica is not able to do the show," she sighs, "who or what could possibly replace her?"

I am getting the strangest feeling of butterflies in my

stomach. "So why can't we weather it with 'best of' shows, or maybe a series of celebrity hosts? Until we find one who pulls?"

"That's what I said," Alexandra says quietly. She looks away briefly and then back to me. "Jessica thought you should have a shot at hosting her show."

My heart skips and my mind races. *Cool.* Me? Host a national talk show? And I know, deep down inside, that Jessica might be on to something. We are not terribly unalike, she and I. Stylistically, perhaps, but—dare I say it—we're both compulsive personalities. Having a compulsive personality is one of the traits good hosts seem to share. And I'm outgoing, good at getting people to talk...

But for the sake of a show of modesty and loyalty to the news group, I say, "How on earth did she come up with that idea?"

Alexandra looks disgusted with me. "Come off it, Sally. So listen to me—I'm the bad guy. I told Cassy to forget it, I'm not letting you go. Will is furious and I can't say that I blame him. But you have a contract with the news division and I am determined to see that you honor it."

For a moment, I don't know what to say. Yet once again I feel as though I've been promoted and demoted by Alexandra in the space of a minute. And I can't believe the discussion got as far as reaching Cassy Cochran, president of DBS.

"You host one talk show for the entertainment division, Sally, and your journalistic credibility is gone. One show and you can't come back to news."

I feel Scotty edging closer to me, pressing against my thigh. He knows something's up and he is going to protect me, he thinks. I reach down to absently touch his fur. "It's not as if I'm doing much for the news division," I finally say. "The series I produced for you could have come out of the entertainment division."

"No, it came from the news division. It may get recycled on entertainment networks down the road, and it did have a high entertainment factor—there's no question about it—but that was news, covering it, reporting it and relating it to current events that affect the lives and well-being of the general public. That's news."

"All right," I say. "But why is it so critical to you that I stay in the news division? I mean, what if *I* don't feel that way?"

She studies me critically. "You have no idea why I think it is important you stay in the news division?"

"I don't, Alexandra. I honest to God don't know *what* you have in mind for me down the road, if anything. Nothing adds up in this job. One week you've got me creating, writing and producing a documentary series, the next week you've got me figuring out the dry cleaning procedures for the friggin' clothes in your dressing room!"

At the last part, Alexandra starts to laugh, and it pisses me off. But it's true. A couple of weeks ago she asked me to find out why her dry cleaning was always late. I couldn't believe it. I was furious, but I knew better than to complain.

A security guard appears around the corner from the garage. "Everything all right, Ms. Waring?" he calls.

"Fine, thank you," she calls back, turning to me. "So, you are honestly telling me you have no idea why I have you do all that I do?"

"Not a clue," I say firmly. "I don't even know what my job is. Handmaiden to the star, that's all I can come up with."

"For a very smart young woman, you certainly aren't very bright," she says, amused.

"Well, so what is it?" I say, exasperated, holding out my hands. "What the hell is my future here?"

"Pretty much whatever you want to make it," she tells me.

I swing my weight to my other foot. "Now, what's that supposed to mean? You never give me a straight answer about anything, Alexandra."

"It means you're good at a number of things. Writing, reporting, producing, editing and your TV-Q is high. People like to watch you." She looks behind me. "That was my stupid mistake, sharing your scores with the people here. Now they want you to fill in over in the entertainment division." Her eyes sweep back to mine. "But do you understand the risk, Sally? One show—you tape one show in Studio B and you're out of straight news forever. And chances are—you know what the business is like—you won't get a job out of it. Or if you do, it will be for ten weeks, at which time Jessica or someone with a big name like Jessica's will be hired to replace you. And then where will you be?"

"Rich and able to do whatever I want?" I ask hopefully.

"You're not going to get rich in ten weeks," she says.

"I bet that money could last a long time in a town like Castleford," I say defiantly.

"I bet it will. Too bad you won't be finding out, because I'm holding you to your contract, Sally."

"But it's not for you to decide!" I blurt out. "It's *my* career. If I want to gamble—"

"It is *NOT* for you to decide," she says, eyes flashing with anger. "You decided to sign that contract, and that contract says *I* decide what is best for DBS News, and what is best for *you*. And it is *not*, by any stretch of the imagination, in the best interest of DBS News to have my protégée stolen away by the entertainment division. Not for such an uncertain future."

Protégée! I think. Highly trained, highly experienced, highly controlled Alexandra Waring is claiming that all-or-nothing me, who in her short career has bounced all over the journalism walls, is some kind of apprentice studying under her? *Ha!* So then I say it out loud. "Protégée? *Ha!* I'm your protégée?"

"Yes, you jackass," she says, walking away.

After one stunned moment, Scotty and I hurry to catch up with her. "Great," I tell her, "so are you saying I'm going to get your job? I'd like to know when so I can plan on it." I know I'm being obnoxious but I don't care. How dare she make all the decisions regarding my career future!

"Sometimes you are such a jackass, Sally, I just want to throttle you," she says, whirling around with a spark of menace in her eye. "Why the hell do you think I spend so much time on you?" Before I can answer she continues, "I'll tell you why. Because we need you. You may end up on the magazine, you may end up in the field, you may end up on the newscast in New York, I don't know, but there are tremendous—" She pauses. "*Tremendous* opportunities coming your way and I'm doing my best to prepare you so that you will be ready. I am not happy with the organization of the news division as it is. I am not happy with our ranks, I am not happy with the overall quality of the newscast, I am not happy with the magazine show yet, either—and I am sick of feeling as though the sun must always rise and fall on me and me alone."

"Oh," I say, feeling rather unsettled.

"So I will not sacrifice you and your career to the entertainment division and that's it. I don't care what Will and Jessica say, it puts your career at risk and the future of DBS News at risk and that's completely unacceptable to me."

She walks off and this time I let her.

In the garage, though, as Scotty and I go over to my old secondhand Jeep, I call to her, "Thanks. I think."

She gives me a wave, signaling she's heard me. Then she pulls up next to us a moment later, in a marvelous two-seater Mercedes. I roll down my window. "Good luck in L.A.," she says, leaning across the passenger seat to look up at us. "And don't forget to call your policeman."

I offer a brief smile. "I won't."

She looks at me a moment longer. "Trust me?"

After a moment, I nod. "Yes," I tell her.

"Good." And then she is gone.

CHAPTER | 14

I may well have been the first person to be ticketed for yakking on a cell phone while driving a motor vehicle in New York. The law was enacted last November 1 at midnight and I got nailed on the 72nd Street entrance ramp of the Henry Hudson Parkway at 12:03 a.m. There was no prize, only a hundred-dollar fine. So I have a hands-free system in the car, which means now when you see me driving by in my 1993 blue-gray Jeep (with Scotty's nose out a rear window), you can see me alternating between yelling and cringing as the same problems I experience in private are now magnified over the car's audio system. Driving to central Connecticut from New York on Route 15, you see, involves a great deal of hilly terrain, which means at certain junctures I am suddenly talking to no one, or thinking I am talking to no one, and then they yell, "I can't hear you!" over the speakers.

At any rate, I reach Paul Fitzwilliam on his cell phone. Paul, it turns out, is in search of waves near San Diego.

"We're just driving around, looking for some surf," he says cheerfully.

At thirty-one, I know it sounds ridiculous to say that I feel old, but when I hear Paul say this, I do. At twenty-five I think I used to drive around with friends looking for things to do, too; by twenty-six, however, I'm pretty sure I didn't have time anymore. Or the inclination. "Looking for some waves," I translate to mean, is checking out the beaches and the bodies hanging out there, eating French fries, drinking a couple of beers and simply being the cute young adventurer I think Paul probably is. I imagine he is wearing sunglasses today, with perhaps a touch of white zinc oxide on his nose. Loose bathing trunks. The T-shirt? Possibly Nike. Possibly no shirt at all.

"May I ask what you're wearing?" I say, smiling, glancing in the rearview mirror at a car coming up quickly behind me.

"What am I wearing?" he says, sounding surprised. "Jack, it's *GQ*. They want to know what we're wearing."

"Fashion-conscious sweats" comes the answer from his friend.

"Sweats?" I say, changing lanes to let the speeder behind me get by. "I imagined bathing trunks and T-shirts and zinc on your nose."

"Icicles are more like it," Paul says. "It's barely sixty today. And the waves stink. We tried Long Beach this morning, but it stunk. So we're heading south. Hey, so where are you?"

"Driving home from New York to Connecticut," I tell him. Pause. "How is everything?"

"Uh, okay. Someone close to our family died yesterday. Actually, while I was there visiting her."

"I'm sorry."

"She was very ill. I'm just glad I got here in time to see her. It meant a lot to my mother."

"Do you stay for the funeral, or do you—"

"Oh, no, I'm coming back to California tomorrow. Early. I should be in around two."

"Really? That's great. Any chance I can buy you dinner? I have tomorrow night off."

"I'd love to, but you're not buying. You just bought me dinner and I just messed up last night. So dinner's on me."

"We'll see about that," he says, sounding happy. "Well this is great. This really gives me something to look forward to. What?" he says to his companion. A laugh. "Jack wants to know why I never offer to buy him dinner."

I smile.

"I know it's kind of crazy for you right now," he says, "but if you can't do tomorrow for some reason, you'll give me a call? Or leave a number where I can find you?"

I give him the number of my cell phone. We agree on a time for tomorrow night and get off.

As I sail past the Darien/New Canaan exit, I know I can't postpone it anymore, I need to call Doug and let him know I'm here. In our better periods, we talk every day, in our strange periods, which is what we've been in lately, we talk a couple times a week. Doug doesn't like talking a whole lot unless he's going to see me. "Going to see me," I guess, means whether or not we'll be spending the night together.

Interestingly, we once took it for granted that we would sleep over at each other's houses every weekend, but in this last go-round between us we have kept the sexual part and done away with the sleepover part.

I reach him at home, at his apartment in New Haven. He's just returned from playing a freezing nine holes of golf. "Why don't you stop by?" he suggests. "Quick bite, whatever."

Right. I know what the "whatever" is. I don't dread sex with Doug the way I once did, it's that I'm afraid I pretty much really do know, at long last, that Doug and I are not going to get married, and that the whole exercise is empty and pointless. But then this has only been lately and my relationship with Doug has been through so many incarnations over so many years I've lost count of how many ways I've felt about it.

He lives in a terrific apartment in downtown New Haven, not far from the courthouse where he practices law as an assistant state's attorney. He's a prosecutor, and to Doug's credit this is a second career, for he began in lucrative tax law (zzzzzz...) in Boston. At the time he had been married to another corporate attorney, and the career, like the marriage, looked great and was truly awful. He loves his work now, and once he shed the social-climbing wife (can you tell how much I liked her?), he enjoys a sense of purpose and satisfaction in his life.

I park in the underground garage and walk Scotty outside to take a brief whiz—yes, on a fire hydrant—say hello to the concierge at the front desk and take the elevator up to Doug's apartment. When we get off the elevator, I let go of the leash and Scotty trots down the carpeted hallway to sit in front of Doug's door. Doug opens it and Scotty offers his paw (a ritual) and Doug bends to shake it and say how do you do, Mr. Scotty?

"Hi, famous person," he says to me, kissing me on the cheek and giving me a hug.

"Hi," I sigh, hugging him back.

We go inside and I slide onto a seat at the breakfast bar, while Doug automatically walks into the kitchen and pours me a glass of seltzer. He has showered and changed, and is wearing corduroys and a long-sleeved shirt and moccasins. He is a nice-looking man, with dark hair and dark eyes and a kind face. Once upon a time he was terribly shy. Not anymore. And sometimes I wonder if that is part of the problem, that he has changed so much and I don't feel as though I have.

The first hint I receive that things with Doug may not be what I think they are comes as he opens the refrigerator. Inside, I see, are two bottles of wine spritzers. I instantly get a hollow feeling in my stomach.

A woman has been here drinking.

We used to laugh at people who drank wine spritzers, I want to say to him.

But I try to think this through to another explanation. Maybe his mother was here. (His mother drinking wine spritzers? Never!) Maybe it was another prosecutor. (Drinking while working? Never!) Maybe it was left over from a party. (Doug having a party? Never!)

My face shows everything, I'm afraid, and when Doug hands me my glass of seltzer he asks me what's wrong. The fact that he has noticed my expression also implies that things may not be the way I thought.

He's jumpy and I know this behavior. As a matter of fact, Doug and I would have been married had not that same behavior occurred two years ago, when I found out he was smitten with a new colleague at work. That was what started this whole rock and roll in our relationship, when I thought we were a permanent thing and he strayed. But then he came back. And then I strayed. But I came back. And now...

And now what?

I feel that icky feeling of anxiety in the back of my neck. I can't stand this feeling and will do almost anything to push it into anger or tears or anything that will stop it. "Someone's been here," I say, sipping from my glass. Scotty, who had followed Doug hopefully into the kitchen, senses something and comes quickly back out to sit at my feet.

Doug frowns, walking into the living room. "What are you talking about?"

I turn on the stool to watch him. "I'm talking about whoever drinks wine spritzers."

He throws an angry glance at the refrigerator, as if it's all the refrigerator's fault. "Some guys came over after work," he says, dropping down onto the couch. He puts one arm up along the back of it, as if to illustrate his openness.

"Some *guys?*" I say. "Drinking wine spritzers? Oscar Wilde and Liberace are dead, Doug."

He laughs a little and I know he's nervous.

I can't stand this. "Just tell me," I say.

"There's nothing to tell," he says.

"What's her name?"

He looks over at me and meets my eye. *"Who?"*

"I don't mean are you sleeping with her yet," I say, sliding off the stool, feeling the anger starting to rise.

"Stop it, Sally," he warns.

"Look, I know it hasn't been the best lately," I begin.

"You said you'd go to therapy," he reminds me.

"Yeah, well, I don't think therapy's going to fix what's wrong with us."

"If we leave it to you," he says smoothly, "we're certainly not going to find out, are we?"

He's right. I did say I would go see a therapist, but I haven't because, well, I have this horrible feeling this therapist is going to talk me into marrying Doug, is going to tell me that this is as good as it gets, that I'm immature to believe in a different kind of relationship, and that after the passion is over, this is what a lasting relationship is like: boredom, mistrust, idle fantasies.

"I can't do this by myself, Sally."

"I didn't say I expect you to."

"The fact you haven't seen a therapist says it all."

I look at him.

"That you expect not to be with me. Otherwise, you'd be working on it."

I walk over to the window to look down at the city. People are standing in front of the church below, waiting for a bus. I feel a wet nose gently touch my hand. Scotty. He knows.

"I don't know what you expect me to do," he says. "We can't go on like this."

"No, we can't," I say, feeling my hand tremble slightly. This is like tearing a family apart. The thought of a life without Doug is frightening to me. We've known each other so long. We've spent half our lives knowing each other. "I don't know how to let go," I say quietly. "I love you. I need you."

"You don't need me, Sally. And that is part of the problem. You don't want to need me."

I don't say anything but simply stand there, looking down at the people at the bus stop.

"You do everything in your power not to rely on me,"

he continues. "Oh, yeah, there have been times you've let down your guard, you've let me in, let me be a part of your life—when you were absolutely down and out for the count. But most of the time—"

I breathe in, I breathe out, the wind blows the people below.

"I'm like a rest stop. You pull in, get what you need so you can leave again and be on your way."

"I don't think that's quite right," I say quietly.

"That's right, it's not," he says.

"No," I say, turning around, "I mean, you make it sound as though I use you for something. I haven't. My only sin is that I love you in a way that isn't working out to be what you want. Which is settling down with a woman who puts her home life first and the rest of her life second. And that's not happening with me."

"I'll say," he mutters, looking down at his hands.

"But let's suppose I played it the way you want me to," I say, gaining strength. "We move in together to Mother's house. You'd be there seven days a week, I'd come out on weekends. How would you feel then? Like a caretaker? Like the house-sitter?" When he doesn't say anything, I say, "Of course you would. My house, you're taking care of it—that's why I had no intentions of letting you move in. I know I'm not ready to make the kind of commitment you need to be happy, and, Doug, you can't tell me I haven't been honest with you about it."

"Oh, yeah, honest," he says sarcastically. "Stupid me for thinking I would come first in your life over your fucking career."

"Yeah, my career," I say, walking back to the window. "Like you've put yours on hold."

"I offered to transfer to New York—"

"Yeah, you offered, all right," I say, "and what would have happened if I had taken you up on that and then it didn't work out? It was just a little pressure on me."

"So what the hell am I supposed to do, Sally?" he yells, jumping up. "I'm damned if I do, damned if I don't."

"You do exactly what you've always done and are doing now," I mutter, eyes down on the square. "Start buying wine spritzers and look around for a better offer."

There is a horrendous crash and I whirl around, shocked to see that Doug has hurled the coffee table into the wall. This is a first. "I am not cheating on you!" he roars.

Scotty gives him a warning bark, backing up against me. "It's not working, Doug." I look down. "Scotty, shut up!" I look back at Doug. "Surely your shrink has told you, I am not the woman for you. I will only continue to make your life miserable."

"But you love me," he says.

"I will always love you," I say honestly. "But I will never be the woman you want to marry. And I think you've known that for a while. And I think both of us have been scared to say or do anything, because it's so painful. It is always so painful with us," I say, starting to cry. "We're always hurting each other, letting each other down."

"How have I let you down?" he says, still angry.

"You tell me what I want to hear, but not what you really feel. Oh, you started to, at one point, remember? When you wanted us to move in together? But then we started to argue, didn't we? And so you backed down and started telling me what I wanted to hear, that we shouldn't live together, that you should transfer to New York and we should get married—"

"I meant it."

"You loathe and despise New York!" I cry. "And I would be the one responsible for making you live there!"

"So you're saying if I had insisted on living together, I wouldn't have let you down."

"You wouldn't have misled me about what you really wanted, about what you need."

"Maybe I didn't know. For sure."

I sigh. "You're probably right." I cover my face with my hands and rub my eyes, wondering how to get out of here. I just want to go home and lock the door and have a good cry.

Doug makes it easy for me. "Her name is Robin," he says. "I don't know her very well, but I like her. And she likes me."

I drop my hands and look at his angry face. I resist making another crack about spritzers and opt simply to leave. "Of course she likes you," I say quietly. And then I walk out the door, Scotty obediently following.

I park the Jeep and let Scotty out, who promptly goes charging off into the darkness. Something must be wrong with the motion detector on the front porch because the light doesn't come on.

I hesitate. Then I call Scotty while I climb back in the car. He finally comes and I let him climb over me into the front seat. I lock the doors and start the car. Then I put on the brights. Everything looks quiet and locked up and undisturbed. But still.

I drive the Jeep over the side lawn and around to the back. There the motion detector does work and the back-door light comes on. Okay, now what? Go in? Call the police and ask them to come in with me? But there's no sign of entry, just a motion detector that's out.

Boy, am I jumpy. I leave the car running and call Scotty to come with me to the back door. It's locked. I slip in the key, take a breath and then open it. Ready to race back out to the car, I turn on the light. "Go on, boy," I whisper to Scotty. If anybody's here, he'll know. But he just stands at my side, looking up at me, wondering what the heck is going on. So I let go of the door and slowly move forward into the cottage, turning the lights on as I go.

Nothing.

I walk into the bedroom, turn on the light, slowly approach the closet—

The telephone rings and I scream. Then I swear and move over to answer it.

"You're there," a man's voice says. "I've called several times, Sally, I need to talk to you."

"Who is this?" I ask.

"Phillip O'Hearn."

"Oh," I say. "I was in New York today, I just got home this minute."

"Could I come over? Just for a few minutes? Please?"

He murdered my father and wants to come over. Of course, his wife died yesterday, and no doubt I have the unpleasant task ahead of me of discussing what she told me.

"Certainly," I say, thinking better he talk to me rather than Mother. "I'll put some coffee on."

I make some coffee, though at seven o'clock on a Saturday night I think something else might be in order. I'm not drinking with him, though. He sounds like he's had a few already, anyway. Then I go outside and move the Jeep to its regular parking spot, and turn the front lights on by hand.

O'Hearn arrives minutes later in Mrs. O'Hearn's Cadillac, and when I see the chalky, haggard paleness of his face, my heart almost goes out to him. The last few weeks have taken their toll and now, I suppose, I might finish him off.

It's interesting how I could so hate someone—and so fear someone—and yet, in this moment, feel so badly for him. I suppose its like the Articles of War. It would be fair for me to kill him in cold blood after what he did to my father and to my family, but it doesn't seem quite fair to tell him he killed my father because his wife lied to him, not right after that same loyal spouse of thirty-two years has died so torturously in front of his own eyes. It doesn't seem cricket somehow.

We sit down and he gratefully accepts the offer of coffee from the tray I've brought out from the kitchen. He takes it black and ignores the cookies. I, on the other hand, put sugar and milk in my coffee and nervously reach for a cookie.

He rambles for a while about funeral arrangements, where Marion's body is now, contacting various members of their far-flung family (not one of the four kids stayed within five hundred miles of Castleford), who's conducting the service. All the while I nod sympathetically, wondering why I am, and nibbling on one Milano cookie after another.

Then he's silent, lowering his head to press his mouth against a fist. Then he looks up at me, swallowing. "I'd like to know what Marion said." His eyes are red-rimmed, exhausted, and I am amazed at how old he has gotten so fast.

It could break him permanently with what I know, and I wonder why I am not gloating over the prospect. Instead, I feel sick with dread.

Bizarre.

He's waiting for me to say something. So finally I get

up and move to the corner of my living room that serves as my office and retrieve my pocket recorder. I come back and sit down, placing it on the table between us.

His eyes are glued to it. Then slowly his eyes come up. "It's on there?"

"Yes. I taped her so there would be no question. I didn't want anyone thinking I made up what she said."

For a moment there is a glint of steel in his eyes and he says, "You mean you wanted evidence."

I shake my head. "No. The tape is for you. I told Mother what she said. I didn't play it for her."

The steel has left his eyes and the old man remains, scared to death, I realize, not wanting to hear that tape, but having to know what she said. So I reach forward and hit Play.

Marion: I didn't know. I didn't know what he'd do.
Me: I know you didn't. Mother knows that, too. It wasn't your fault.

O'Hearn's eyes are glued to the coffee table.
Marion: But it was. (Pause) He had a girlfriend.
Me: Mr. O'Hearn?
Marion: Yes. I was so hurt. (Long pause) I had four children, Sally. I had nowhere to go.

O'Hearn's head falls into his hands.

Me: I understand. You couldn't leave. You wanted your children to have a good home.
Marion: I wanted to hurt him.
Me: That's understandable.
Marion: I told him. Oh, Sally. (There is the sound of

moaning. I say something about tissues.) I couldn't
face Belle. I couldn't tell her.

Me: (Whisper) Tell her what?

Marion: He— I told Phillip I loved Dodge. (Pause)
I told Phillip I didn't care about his girl. I loved
Dodge. I told him I was sleeping with Dodge. (Long
pause, I can hear me sniffing.) Can you forgive me?

Me: Yes, of course. You didn't know. (Sob) You didn't
know what he'd do.

Marion: He still thinks— (A jagged intake of breath.)
I never told Phillip it was a lie. I couldn't. Not after...

Me: (Whisper) It's all right. (Pause) Mr. O'Hearn!
Nurse! She's in trouble!

I turn off the tape recorder and look at what remains of
my archenemy. He's sobbing now like a child.

Now he knows he killed his friend, my father, for no reason. Now he has to live with that.

CHAPTER | 15

"Yes, I'm back," I say on my cell phone as I trudge up the stairs of the Shangri-la, with Dino from the front desk following me with cleaning I left on Thursday.

"Good, I'll tell Banks," Cecelie Blake says. "Burton will pick you up in the morning."

"I'm not sure about that," I say. "I'm supposed to call the police for protection, I think."

"Oh, no," Dino groans, "not more cops out on the land ing. It gives the other guests the creeps."

"I'm not going to call until the morning," I whisper to him.

"Did you watch any of the trial coverage over the weekend?" Cecelie asks.

"The masked helicopter, yes," I say, walking down the outside hall, admiring the gardens, thinking how lovely

November is out here. "Very dramatic." Over and over the media showed the helicopter swooping in over the courthouse parking lot and witnesses recounting how in the courtroom Sally Harrington had just described a similar firebombing at the Presario mansion in Bel Air. "I was at DBS on Saturday and Alexandra told me the feds will probably find the pilot and the bird by tomorrow." I stand there, offering a pause of significance, as Dino unlocks the door of the suite for me. "So what happens when lead counsel is arrested? Who conducts the trial, you?"

"Why would Banks be arrested?" Cecelie says, unruffled.

I only laugh and walk past Dino into the suite. "I'll see you tomorrow," I promise, and hang up.

It is absolutely gorgeous out this afternoon, and I decide to go for a run to rid myself of the airplane-itis I always get on longer flights. I change into sweats, leave the hotel, cross Ocean Boulevard and descend the cliffside stairs, cross the pedestrian walkway over Route 1, and take that staircase down to the vast beach. It is too cold to swim, but this afternoon has drawn a lot of kite flyers. Dogs aren't supposed to be on the beach, but they are, running with their owners, fetching sticks in the saltwater, playing Frisbee. There is a couple wrapped in blankets on the sand, not leaving much to the imagination about what they're doing.

I stretch a bit and then start to run on the hard-packed sand. Oh, boy, I'm going to feel this in my calves tomorrow. It's been a while. The wind has picked up, but the sun, low in the horizon, is warm on the side of my face. Up ahead I see the Santa Monica Pier and decide I don't want to continue in this direction and turn around to jog the other way. Beyond the Santa Monica Pier is the hotel, Shutters, a wonderful, wonderful place if only it hadn't been the place I had last been with Spencer. It's not that I miss Spencer, but I do miss the excitement and happiness I felt when I first met him. I really thought that he might have been the *one*. A journalist and a book editor? Not a far stretch, is it? He lived in New York, he knew so much about everything—

Poor Spencer is not very happy these days, either. He went back to the woman he had been having an affair with for some time, Verity Rhodes, the editor of *Expectations* magazine. The only problem is, a very, very rich and powerful business tycoon is still married to her, and the divorce proceedings have been a nightmare, with custody of their young son first being awarded to her, then to the husband, then back to Verity. I'm sure the situation is not one Spencer envisioned. I think he thought they would live quietly in her vast Central Park West apartment and in a smaller house in Litchfield, Connecticut, have a nanny for the boy and continue the first-class social whirl that has been Verity's professional life. But what Spencer has is a vindictive old man making their lives miserable, whose latest ploy was having Verity evicted from the Central Park West flat as he threatened to pull the financial plug on *Expectations*, thus cutting off Verity's means of support. Certainly Spencer has no money.

It will be interesting to see how it plays out. Do I feel sorry for Spencer? Not on your life. He chose Verity. The only person involved who deserves any concern and help is that poor little boy being shuffled from the West Side to the East Side and across the social pages.

So I run the other way down the beach, trying to think good thoughts.

I have a date tonight, which is nice. I smile. Very nice. (I push myself to pick up my pace.)

I think about Mother a little. I was surprised how wonderful she looked when I dropped Scotty off at her house this morning. I thought she would be a basket case, but no. Clearly something in her welcomed Marion's revelation. Something must have fallen in place for her. A finality to Daddy's death, perhaps.

Age is supposed to be the enemy of us all, but it is interesting how Mother has embraced it. She doesn't fight the aging process. But then, she never fights life either, but merely takes it a day at a time, making the best of things, and always—*always*—trying to maintain a good outlook. She will tell you this is no virtue of hers, but simply the best way she's found to celebrate this world and all that is right with it. She claims she *likes* growing older, because it means she doesn't have to make so many mistakes. The only exception about aging she admits to is, for Mack Cleary's sake, she wishes she had the body of a twenty-year-old again. (Mack is totally gaga over her the way she is, and I can scarcely imagine how he could handle any more.)

I don't want to think about Mother having sex. But she does. And I bet she's very—

Oh, stop!

All right, what else can I think about? My date tonight. I have a date. I'm not thinking about Doug, I'm not, I'm not, I'm not thinking about spritzer-drinking Robin who likes him—I ask you, why does that sting?

By the time I finish my run and climb the stairs to Ocean Boulevard, I am absolutely exhausted. I am drenched with perspiration and have used my T-shirt to wipe my face along the way so that it looks as charming as I do, with smudges of old mascara and sweat all over it. And it is like this that I enter the lobby of the Shangri-la and find my date standing there, smiling, looking me over like an amused parent at a sandbox.

"I'm early," he says.

"Yes you are," I say, standing there. I put my hand behind my head and pose. "So what do you think? Should I go to court like this tomorrow?"

He grins. "Sure. You look great." His eyes make an appreciative sweep that makes me shy.

"She looks like low tide," Dino opines from behind the desk, making me laugh.

"I've got a bike," Paul says, "so I came early in case you'd like to change."

"A bike?"

"A motorcycle. I borrowed a friend's Harley. It's a road bike, a Fat Boy, very comfortable. I thought we could ride up the coast and have dinner. I know a little clam bar up there—I don't know if you like clams. It's not really ritzy or anything, but I think it might be fun." He pauses, and I think he colors slightly.

Gosh, he's young.

And appealing.

"I was trying to think of something you couldn't do this time of year back East. I brought you a jacket to wear. And a helmet." He gestures to the chair behind me.

I smile. He's so anxious to please. I'm touched. "It sounds absolutely wonderful," I tell him, and he breaks out in smiles.

"You really do need to shower first," Dino reminds me.

"Wise guy," I tell him. "I'm going to shower right now. Um, I have a suite, if you   "

"I'm okay," Paul says quickly.

"Right," I say, moving toward the stairs. "You wait down here and I'll be ready in fifteen minutes."

* * *

I shower and change into jeans and a blouse and cotton sweater, but I don't know what to do about footwear. I call downstairs and Paul says he's brought some kind of guards for me to slip over my ankles.

A man who thinks of everything.

When I come downstairs, Paul holds a black leather jacket for me to slip on. He puts one on, too, explaining we may be hot now, but in a few minutes, along the coastal waters, we'll be glad of them. "Besides," he adds, handing me a helmet to carry, "you should always keep your body covered in case..." His voice trails off and he waves good-bye to Dino and opens the front door for me.

"In case what?" I want to know. "Bye, Dino."

"If you fall, you don't want to get scraped up. I know a guy who can't ride very well yet and he started to wobble while he was starting up from a red light. He just fell over at five miles an hour. His whole arm is scraped."

"Hmm," I say. I must confess, I am not a wild fan of motorcycles, probably because I do not know how to drive one. (No control issues here!) None of my boyfriends ever had one.

"We'll be very careful, Sally," Paul says to me, winking and lightly touching my back to guide me over to the bike.

Wow. This *is* a big Harley road bike. The seat has a back to it, so I can lean back, he explains. We put on our helmets and he draws close to secure mine properly. He smiles, glancing down at my mouth as if he might kiss me and then flips my visor down. Then he flips his own visor down, hauls the bike upright, kicks back the kickstand and swings his leg over to straddle the bike. He turns the key, does something with the gears, and suddenly the electric starter hits and the motorcycle rumbles to life. It is not terribly loud. (I don't know why, but back home in Castleford all the motorcycle guys deliberately make theirs louder.)

"Okay, swing your leg over," Paul calls, "and slide into that seat."

Awkwardly I do. The back seat is higher than Paul's. I lean against the back, testing it, not wanting to cling to him for dear life quite yet. The bike moves a bit and Paul shifts his legs to keep the bike upright. Then he points down to where my feet go, craning his neck around to shout for me to watch out for the muffler, that's where it gets burning hot. "That's your job, to make sure you're not pressing in on it. But if you do, that's what the shields are for."

Then he reaches back for my hands and pulls them around his waist, a movement that brings my chest forward against his back. We bump helmets. Without further ado, we move out onto Ocean Boulevard and navigate the surface streets until we reach the ramp for Route 1 north. Minutes later, we're sailing along the ocean at the legal speed of 40 mph. The sun is setting over the water, the steady hum of the motorcycle is hypnotic, and I wonder at the vibration I feel between my legs from the bike. Is that why girls are always riding on the back? Or is this why guys always have them on the back? Because they know that vibration might subtly get them into a more, shall we say, romantic mood?

Golly.

Since we're doing nothing but going comparatively straight along at the same speed, I am not clinging to Paul. Still, it is a warm, lovely feeling to hold him as we move through the evening. The air is chilly, but marvelously so.

We only ride for maybe twenty minutes before he turns off near Pacific Palisades. Soon, too soon, I almost think, he navigates us into the dirt parking lot of a whitewashed building called Harper's Clam Cove. We take off our helmets and walk into the building, and while I feel alien in this gear, I'm fast warming to the novelty of the experience. Gear. Motorcycle gear. Rushing air, moving through the world unshielded. I wonder if I should learn how to ride.

The Clam Cove is old and worn, but fastidiously clean. A lovely older woman, hair falling from her bun, greets Paul by name and leads us over to a table for two in the corner, where the fishnets on the wall aren't quite so droopy. "He said he was bringing someone special, tonight," she says under her breath while handing me a menu.

"What's that, Maude?" Paul asks.

"Scallops are excellent tonight," she says. "Would you like a drink?"

"I'm going to have a beer, Sally," Paul says, "what about you?"

"Actually, I may just have a seltzer, if you don't mind. I've got a big day tomorrow and I'm dehydrated from the plane."

"Make it a seltzer and a Diet Coke," Paul tells her.

"Paul, you have your beer—"

"I don't really want one. I was just saying that to make you feel comfortable. I'm not a big drinker." Then he chuckles, putting his napkin in his lap. "Corrcction. I could have been a big drinker and now I save it for special occasions."

"Because you're a police officer?"

"Because my father's an alcoholic," he says.

"Oh." I mean, what do you say to that?

"He's gotten better, in that he only drinks at home at night now," he says, scanning the menu, "but I don't know why or how my mother puts up with it. He's just an ass-hole when he drinks."

"Has he ever gotten any help? A rehab? AA or something?" I ask.

He rolls his eyes. "My father going to AA? Never. It would be 'beneath him.'"

"I know someone in AA," I say, thinking of Jessica Wright, the DBS talk show host. "She says all you have to do is meet one person in AA who's more successful than you and your thinking about AA will turn around."

"He won't go," Paul says. "He'll just drop dead of a heart attack or stroke or liver cancer or something and everyone will pretend to be surprised." His eyes meet mine. "I used to think he might get fired and then would go to a rehab or something, but then he became president of his company, which only adds to the self-delusion that everything's fine now—now that he doesn't drink at lunch anymore."

"What kind of work does he do?"

"They create and manufacture cardboard point-of-sales materials. You know, like at Halloween? You see a cardboard display with all the candy in it? Or a shelf card on a counter, selling stuff? They do a ton of stuff. Dad started the company, but then he got into a bind and sold stock to raise some money, and then later he bought it back." He shrugs. "He's done very well. I can't complain. He paid for most of my college." Pause. "I just hate the drinking, you know? He just sits there at night, half in the bag, snarling insults at my mother." He shrugs. "But as I say, it's supposedly better than before, when he got tanked up at lunch and spent the afternoon chasing secretaries. That's why he stopped drinking at lunch, because of a sexual harassment suit." He drops the menu and looks around for Maude. "They settled."

I am very surprised at Paul for volunteering all this information about his father so soon. Maude comes over with our drinks and takes our order. We're starting with some clams on the half shell and then I'm having the scallops and Paul is going for crab cakes.

"I apologize for dumping all that stuff about my father on you, Sally," Paul says after Maude leaves. "Just before I left to meet you, my mother called. Dad got picked up for a DUI last night and she wants to know if I can fix it." He falls back into his chair, shaking his head. "She's as sick as he is. 'No problem here,'" he mimics. "'He hasn't killed anybody yet!'"

He is angry and I don't blame him. I'm so lucky on that score. That's one problem my family seems to have escaped, although there is some question about Daddy's father, the one who shot himself.

"Sometimes," I say, leaning forward slightly, "all we can do, in the quieter moments, is reassure the people we care about that we love them. I mean," I add, lowering my eyes as it seems Paul is very close to glowering at me, "if we do love our parents, for example, then they need to know that that's why we're upset." I raise my eyes. "We're upset because we love them, not because we hate them. There's a big difference. Certainly in living with ourselves. Because when we make that distinction to them, we don't help them make excuses. Do you know what I mean?"

He doesn't answer, but his expression has somewhat softened.

"I got drunk," I sneer in imitation, thumping my glass, "because you upset your mother." I thump my glass again. "I got drunk because you told me you hated me." I raise my eyebrows. "If you tell him you love him and he gets drunk, then he got drunk with no help from you. So you don't have to carry any of this guilt around."

Maude brings the clams. "This is really a hot date," Paul says dully, eyes surveying the food. "Sitting around talking about my screwed-up father and whether I love or hate my parents."

I smile. "It's what people do while they get to know each other."

He looks at me and I can almost hear him struggling with whether or not he is going to snap out of his sudden bad mood or not. I see the anger that is simmering beneath the easy facade of this young man and I am glad to spot it now so that I have some idea from where it comes. To be honest, I feel somewhat reassured about it, because otherwise I haven't been able to see anything wrong with Paul.

He has principles. I know he works hard. I know he's healthy and strong and young and...

Gorgeous. Not handsome, really. Just gorgeous.

He smiles. "What are you thinking about?"

"You," I say honestly. "I'm thinking how glad I am you shared that with me. Because I'm scared you're the perfect person and I am a bundle of neuroses."

He laughs. "You?"

"Remember," I say, reaching for the lemon wedge, "I am the older woman. I have six more years of baggage to bring along on the trip."

"As long as you're willing to take the trip with me, I don't care," he says.

I feel a little flip-flop in my stomach. His eyes are still on me and mine are still on the lemon wedge. Finally I look up. The attraction is so strong, I feel overwhelmed by it. Neither of us says anything—we merely sit there, looking at each other over the table, locked in the sensation.

Finally he lowers his eyes and lets out an exaggerated breath. "Whoa." He takes another breath and then looks up. "This is really something, Sally." He reaches for his soda. "But," he says, sipping, "I really want us to take our time." He swallows and puts down his glass. "I have this feeling about you. About us." He slowly closes his eyes and then reopens them. "Just so you know, I think you are the single most attractive woman I have ever met in my life."

I blush, looking down, embarrassed at this exaggeration.

"But I don't want to act on it. I don't want to wreck things with moving too fast. You know?"

I raise my eyes. "I know."

"And you live on the East Coast," he points out, sounding almost cheerfully relieved, as if three thousand miles is going to be what it takes to keep us out of bed. "So look," he declares, bringing a fist down softly on the table, "let's just decide to have a great dinner and a great ride and we'll just—" His fist wavers in the air as his eyes lock with mine again and we get pulled into that vortex of desire.

"What's wrong with the clams?" Maude demands, startling us both.

"Nothing!" Paul cries.

"Nothing!" I say, blinking rapidly and finally squeezing that lemon I've been holding all this time.

"I've got your entrees coming!" Maude says, panicked. "They're nice and hot."

"Bring them," I tell her, pushing my plate of iced clams to the side. "We'll eat these for dessert."

And that's what she does, and that's what we do. We have finally snapped out of it. When I excuse myself to use the ladies' room, however, I find that I am an absolute mess and wonder what is going on with us. The guy lives in L.A., I tell myself. He's twenty-five years old. Next month it will be another woman. Who knows? Maybe this is his whole method of operation with women.

I return to the table to find he has paid the check. When I object, he tells me I can get the next dinner.

"Tomorrow?" I hear myself say.

He grimaces. "I have to work. But we could have breakfast, maybe."

I debate. "I really shouldn't tomorrow. I've got a big day."

"Just a half an hour," he says. "Coffee and a muffin."

"I'm probably going to have a cop again."

"I don't care," he laughs. "They're my people."

"Okay," I say. I am amazed how happy it makes me to know I'll see him in the morning. "But I'm paying."

We zip up our jackets and walk outside with our helmets. It is dark, finally, though there is still a glimmer of twilight over the water. Paul straddles the bike and brings it roaring to life. I get on, holding him around the waist more comfortably. I am absolutely convinced now that the vibration of the bike is a babe trap.

We sail off onto Route 1 and I wonder if I am really going to be able to let Paul leave tonight. There is no reason, I tell myself, that he cannot simply come upstairs with me and make love and spend the night. I won't be in L.A. much longer, and we need to find out all that we can.

No. No. No.

But why not? I want to know. I can visualize it all right now, the only question being how much time will elapse between parking the motorcycle and feeling him inside of me, finally and once and for all satiating this incredible longing of the last three hours.

He's not attached, nor am I. Why not?

Because he is taking this seriously, I hear myself think. *He wants to stay a gentleman and he wants to make you his lady.*

It's at the first light on Route 1 when the car hits us.

CHAPTER | 16

"Oh my God," Burton says when I step down into the lobby Monday morning. He looks down at the cast and sling on my left arm. "Is that real?"

"Yes," I say wearily.

"Oh, my God, your hand," he says then, eyes growing larger at the bandages wrapped around the palm of my right hand.

"It's not so bad," I say, walking past him toward the door. "I just have to keep it on a day or two and then it will need open air." A California state trooper appears at the head of the stairs and looks at Burton. "He's one of the lawyers on the defense team," I explain. To Burton, I explain, "I have to go with him to the courthouse."

"But what the hell happened to you?"

Burton walks me out to the trooper's car as I give him

a brief rundown of events. That while sitting on a motorcycle at a red light on Route 1 last night, a car hit us from the rear, sending me flying forward and relatively out of harm's way. I suffered a clean break in my left arm and scraped out my right palm on the asphalt. Poor Paul, however, badly bashed his right elbow on the pavement and then the bike came down on top of it and smashed it.

"And then the car left," I add matter-of-factly.

"Oh, my God," he says yet again. And then he beams, moving closer to whisper, "Banks will be pleased. One look at you and the jury's going to know someone—" He stops.

"Is really trying to kill me?" I say. "Thanks, Burton." I turn to the trooper. "I'm ready, thank you."

Burton runs over to his car to follow us and I climb into the cruiser. I am in such trouble with Alexandra, I can't tell you. First of all, I didn't call the Santa Monica police before I got back last night, which I promised I would do, and then after the accident, I didn't call DBS News to give them the scoop. I didn't want my date with Paul Fitzwilliam broadcast across the country, all right? Well, the APB that went out on the hit-and-run driver—who struck an off-duty cop—took care of broadcasting that information, as well as Paul's name and, of course, mine.

Alexandra is going to kill me.

I look at my watch, which is now on my right wrist. Paul should be out of surgery soon; they're operating on his shattered elbow, the first operation of what the orthopedic surgeon said last night might be at least two surgeries. He was in blinding pain after the accident, but he still managed to drag himself over to me and then stand up in between me and the traffic that was careening to a stop. He stood there, blood pouring from the leather sleeve of his dangling, useless arm, and holding up his other as if he could physically stop another car from hitting me.

We swing into the courthouse lot and I keep my eyes lowered until the trooper has pulled up to the entrance. I get out, trying to dismiss the dizziness I feel. I had passed out for three hours to call sleep and am now functioning on Percosets, which I hate but are the only reason I can move. My whole body hurts. I don't have my briefcase or even a purse; everything I need is in the pockets of the blazer I'm wearing. (Half wearing, for it is only draped over my left shoulder, pinned on the inside to my sling.)

I hear people murmuring around me as I wait in line at the metal detector. Soon Sheriff McDuff is at my side, saying, "Lord have mercy, girl, who did this?"

"Can we just get to the room?" I whisper. "I don't feel so hot."

He pushes us to the head of the line and I walk through the detector with no problems. In the waiting room, Sheriff McDuff holds out a chair for me and dashes, unasked, to fill a water pitcher and pour me a glass, for which I thank him.

"I can't believe I have to testify," I say, sipping the water. "I can't even find the end of my nose."

"You just sit there and take it easy," Sheriff McDuff says nervously, backing out of the room.

A moment later, Cecelie Blake comes flying in. "Holy shit!" she says, looking at me.

There is a brief knock and then Sheriff McDuff reappears with the chief clerk of the court. "Dear God," the latter says quietly, looking at me.

"Hello," I say, wanting to rub my eye, but the bandages on my right hand prevent me from doing so. I use the back of my wrist instead.

"What is with your hair?" Cecelie wants to know.

I look down at my cast and hold up my bandaged hand. "The maid at the hotel did it for me," I say, not being able to help but laugh. Between the shock, my exhaustion and the drugs, I'm on shaky ground. "She washed it for me. Kind of a jailhouse-do, don't you think?" Now I start laughing for real, feeling utterly zonked.

Cecelie takes the comb and makeup from my pockets and starts to work on me as the clerk of the court edges a little closer. "How do you feel, Ms. Harrington?"

"Horrible," I tell him honestly.

"Are you woozy?"

"Sometimes."

"Do you think you are fit to testify?"

Cecelie freezes, looking down at me with such a menacing look I don't dare say anything but "I am quite able to testify. Thank you for asking."

The clerk and Sheriff McDuff exchange uneasy looks and file out.

"She's *teased* your hair back here," Cecelie says incredulously, mercilessly yanking my hair with the comb.

"She used her own rattail comb," I say, laughing again. "I'd never seen one before."

The door flies open and Lawrence J. Banks strides in with Burton on his heels. He takes one look at me and bursts into a huge smile. "Thank heavens you're all right," he says, although I know full well he would have liked it even better had I been murdered and could never be cross-examined. "The police say they have leads on the car." He pulls out a chair and sits forward on it, elbows resting on his knees, clasping his hands in front. "You were with a police officer? Was he your protection?"

"He was her date," Burton snitches. "It's the same cop who came here to court that day about the accident at the restaurant."

Banks looks at me with new admiration. "You're dating a cop while under police protection?"

"There was no police protection," Burton says. "She never called in yesterday."

"Hmm," Banks says, cinching the side of his mouth to the side slightly, studying my condition.

"Excuse me, Lawrence," Cecelie says, leaning between us, "I need to put mascara on her."

I angle my face toward her and close my eyes. I'm seeing about a million different colored dots.

"Are you all right to take the stand?" Banks asks.

"Whatever you want," I tell him.

"The jury needs to see you," he says gravely. "They need to understand the lengths organized crime is prepared to go."

"We know it is organized crime that hit us?" I ask while Cecelie works on my eyelashes.

I hear Banks's chair scoot back. Evidently he's choosing to ignore my question, and says, "We'll have brief testimony and then it will be time for cross-examination. If at that time you are feeling unwell, or worse, I hope you will speak up."

I hear him. Let Banks finish and then feel free to be sick. Well, this will not be too hard because I am already sick and shouldn't be here to begin with.

"Ten minutes, Cecelie," he says, and I hear the door open. And close.

"Okay, you can open your eyes," she says.

I do and the dots are still there. I reach for the water glass. Maybe I'm just dehydrated as opposed to dying.

"I don't think there's enough makeup in the world to make you look better this morning," she tells me.

As the jury is led into the courtroom, every set of eyes travels to me in the witness box. One woman covers her mouth with her hand.

I am used to people staring at me by now. Jonathan Small hasn't taken his eyes off me. I like to think he is concerned about my well-being.

I am reminded by the judge that I am still under oath, and then Banks is instructed to continue his examination of me.

The defense lawyer wastes no time in charging up to the witness box to somewhat breathlessly ask, "Are you all right, Ms. Harrington?"

"Objection!" roars Prosecutor Perez. "The People request a sidebar, Your Honor."

The lawyers approach the bench and a lot of hissing starts and the judge says something that shuts everybody up, and Banks and Perez, both stony faced, return to their places.

"When we recessed last week, Ms. Harrington," Banks begins, "you had explained to the jury how you met Nick Arlenetta at Newark airport."

I nod. Even with the painkillers the motion hurts.

"You stated on Thursday that you believed the meeting was intentional."

"Yes."

"You also stated you believed it was a warning from Nick Arlenetta, that he was watching you."

"Yes."

"Can you tell the jury what happened after that? After Nick Arlenetta approached you at the airport?"

"I went to the West End Broadcasting Center, where DBS News is."

"How did you get there?"

"A DBS intern met me inside the airport. There was a New York police detective, undercover, driving one of the DBS cars. They drove me to West End."

"Did you tell them about Nick Arlenetta approaching you?"

"No, sir."

"Why not?"

"At that point, I had been instructed by the federal authorities not to discuss anything in connection with the Arlenetta crime family to anyone."

"Why?"

"Because they were still in the throes of a major investigation."

"And who was this? That told you not to speak to anyone?"

"Sky Preston, the special federal prosecutor."

"I see," Banks says, walking over to look at the jury. "And what did you do when you reached West End?"

"I went to see Will Rafferty, the executive producer of DBS News. To check in. I also met briefly with the head of DBS security at West End, Wendy Mitchell."

"Did you discuss anything with Wendy Mitchell?"

"Yes. I told her that Nick Arlenetta had been as close to me as she was. I didn't elaborate on the details, or tell her why I thought he approached me, but as she was the person in charge of my safety at West End I knew I had to say something."

"Did you tell her anything else?"

"Yes, I said I felt as though there was nothing to prevent Nick Arlenetta from getting to me."

"How did Ms. Mitchell respond?"

"She agreed."

"What happened then?"

"Um, a friend, Doug Wrentham, gave me a ride home to Connecticut."

"What does Mr. Wrentham do?"

"He is an assistant district attorney for New Haven County."

"In what division?"

"Criminal."

"Did you say anything to Mr. Wrentham about what had happened?"

"I warned him that there was someone who might want to kill me."

"Ms. Harrington, this is important, do you remember your exact words?"

I think for a second. "I said, 'I have to warn you, a Mafia guy may want to kill me.'"

"And how did Assistant District Attorney Wrentham react when you told him this?" Banks asks.

"He said, 'Welcome to the club.'"

There is some laughter in the courtroom.

"Has Assistant District Attorney Wrentham ever been threatened?"

"Many times."

"Does he carry a gun?"

"Objection," Perez says. "Relevance?"

"Defense is trying to establish the seriousness of the threat against Ms. Harrington by the Arlenetta crime family."

"Objection, Your Honor! There was no threat, it was merely the witness's opinion that it was."

"Your Honor, defense counsel respectfully submits that

this line of questioning will clarify Ms. Harrington's ability to determine if such a threat was real."

Judge Kahn thinks a moment. "Objection overruled. You may continue, Mr. Banks."

"Ms. Harrington," Banks says, wheeling around, "Does Assistant District Attorney Wrentham carry a gun?"

"Yes, sir."

"And had he ever told you about a threat made against him?"

"Yes."

"More than once?"

"Yes."

"More than five times?"

"Yes."

"Why did he tell you about the threats?"

"Because he and I were spending time together, and he thought it was only fair that I knew."

"That you knew what?"

"The possibility of danger."

"Given your past experiences with Assistant District Attorney Wrentham, did you take Nick Arlenetta's warning seriously?"

"Objection, Your Honor," Perez says. "There was no warning."

"Withdrawn." Banks circles. "Did your past experiences with Assistant District Attorney Wrentham contribute to your interpretation of the motive behind Nick Arlenetta seeking you out at Newark?"

"Yes."

"And what was your interpretation of Nick Arlenetta tracking you down at Newark airport?"

"That he was warning for me to back off or—"

"Or what?"

"Or something bad would happen, like what happened to Cliff Yarlen."

"Objection, Your Honor!" Perez cries. "This is speculation on the part of the witness."

"Your Honor, it's the sensible conclusion reached by the witness, based on her personal experience in such matters and situations."

"Objection is sustained." Judge Kahn rules. "The jury will disregard the witness's last statement and it will be stricken from the record."

Banks circles slowly. "Do you believe Nick Arlenetta was warning you to back off?"

"Yes."

"Were you frightened by your encounter with him?"

"Yes."

Banks goes for a walk again, back to the defense table to look at his notes. I glance at Jonathan. He's looking sadly at me, as if to apologize for all this.

"Do you remember when you heard that Nick Arlenetta was dead?"

"Yes."

"Where were you?"

"In Castleford, Connecticut, my hometown."

"How did you hear about it?"

"It was on a television news bulletin."

"What was your reaction?"

"Shock. At first. And then a sense of relief."

"Did the same news bulletin mention the defendant's name?"

"Yes, sir. It said he had been arrested for the murder."

"And what was your reaction to that?"

"Well, it was all at the same time. I heard Arlenetta was dead and that Jonathan had been arrested for his murder."

"Could you please tell the jury what you thought and felt at that moment."

"As I said," I tell them, "at first I was shocked. And then, when I heard that Arlenetta was dead, I was relieved. I mean, I don't want anyone to die prematurely or anything, but I was relieved I wouldn't have to worry about him, and be looking over my shoulder every minute, worrying about being killed."

"And what was your reaction to Jonathan Small being arrested?"

"I felt badly, very badly, because I knew Jonathan and his father and Lilliana and her cousin, Cliff, had been working with the feds to put Nick Arlenetta behind bars. So when I heard that Jonathan had been accused of killing him, I knew that if it were true, then he must not have had any other choice."

Banks pauses, as if waiting for the prosecutor to object, and even looks over at the People's table. But Perez is frantically scribbling notes on a legal pad.

Banks looks back at me and says, "Thank you, Ms. Harrington, for all you have endured. Your Honor, I have no further questions for this witness."

The judge swings his head in Perez's direction. "Assistant District Attorney Perez?"

"Your Honor," he says, scribbling one last thing and then standing, "the People respectfully request a short recess before beginning our cross-examination of this witness."

It's a good thing Perez says that, because shortly thereafter everything starts turning yellow, and then kind of gray, and moments later, black.

C H A P T E R | 1 7

I come to moments later, finding myself wedged between the seat and the front of the witness box. Banks is holding me up by the nape of my blazer, as if I'm an overgrown kitten or something. Shakily I grasp the top of the witness box and with Banks's help, I slide back into my chair. My face is covered in cold sweat. Court has been dismissed but nobody's moving; even the jury is still standing in their box, craning their necks to look at me, ignoring their sheriff who is urging them to file out.

"Ms. Harrington needs to go to the hospital, Your Honor," Banks says.

"No, no," I say.

"Shut up," Cecelie says quietly but firmly in my ear.

"An EMS team is coming in now," the judge reports.

"She needs an ambulance, Your Honor," Banks says.

I can see Perez standing to the side, watching angrily. I catch his attention, meet his eye and miserably shake my head, trying to convey I did not fake this. There is no change in his expression.

"No, Your Honor, I don't need an ambulance," I say firmly.

"She needs a Coke," a familiar voice says. "Here. I apologize, Your Honor, for bringing a drink into the courtroom, but knowing Ms. Harrington as I do, I believe her blood sugar may have plummeted."

An icy can of Coke is pushed into my hand and I look up to see Alexandra Waring.

"What are you doing on this side of the bar?" the judge demands. "Return to the gallery immediately."

"Yes, Your Honor," the anchorwoman says respectfully, quickly withdrawing.

The jury is finally moving out of the courtroom; the EMS workers have reached me, taking my vitals, but after a couple gulps of Coke I feel amazingly better. I suppose I should have tried to have eaten something this morning, but when you're zonked out on pain, painkillers, no sleep and jailhouse hair, you consider yourself lucky to get out the door.

The EMS techs question me a bit and recommend that I be allowed to rest. That's what I need more than anything.

"Ms. Harrington needs to go to the hospital," Banks says yet again.

"Ms. Harrington needs one good night's sleep, Your Honor," I say.

"Oh, God," Cecelie groans quietly.

"Ms. Harrington," Judge Kahn says gently, looking at me, "do you think you will be up to testifying tomorrow?"

"Yes, Your Honor."

"Very well," he says, "then court will resume tomorrow morning at nine-thirty."

Burton helps me out of the courtroom and in the hall I find my boss squaring off with Banks. At first I think it's a serious disagreement, but I quickly catch on to the fact that Alexandra is placating Banks in front of the ineffable number of spies floating around the courthouse. "You obviously cannot protect the witness *you've* called for the defense," she is saying loudly, "so somebody has to. I will personally make sure that no one else has another chance to make an attempt on her life!"

"Your employee is in great danger," Banks says in his deep voice, supposedly trying to be quiet but easily heard by all.

"Tell me about it," Alexandra says, looking around. "The wheelchair's over here!" she calls to someone.

The clerk of the court is escorting Sheriff McDuff as he rolls a wheelchair toward us from the security-checkpoint area. Alexandra turns to me and points. *"In."*

I don't argue; I welcome it. I'm feeling airy-fairy again. The clerk, Alexandra, Burton and I roll out into the parking lot. Burton theatrically scans the skies for enemy aircraft and I cover my eyes with my hand. The whole defense team is making me sick. A black Lincoln Town Car with darkened windows drives up. A very large fellow jumps out to help me into the back seat; Alexandra slides in on the other side; and the wheelchair is collapsed and put in the trunk.

As we swing out of the parking lot, I reach feebly for the window button. I want to wave to the press guys to let them know I'm all right, but the window won't go down. When I look at Alexandra, I realize there is no point in asking why it won't go down. I am a prisoner.

Instead of turning left at the intersection, we turn right. "Where are we going?"

"Don't worry, we have all your stuff already."

I'm so tired it's hard to think. "But where are we going?"

"A friend of mine's. I've got a doctor coming over to check you out. You'll be safe there." She pauses. "You need a little—care, I think."

I let my head roll back against the seat and close my eyes. I am too weak to argue. "How did you get into the courthouse?"

"I told you, we bought a seat."

"Oh, right," I remember. I open one eye. "How much?"

She smiles. "We're not saying." Pause. "You didn't see me in the gallery?"

"I couldn't see the end of my nose," I admit, closing my eyes again. This time I don't even try to open them anymore.

"I need to know how Paul's doing," I tell Alexandra when I come to. We're driving over some beige gravel through wrought-iron gates that have metal sheeting over them. Huh. Serious security.

"He's doing very well," Alexandra says. "He's probably going to have more surgery on that elbow, but today's procedure went very well and he's resting comfortably." She's leaning forward, looking around the outside of the car. "We can call him in a bit."

"We?" I repeat, suspicious. I look around, too. We're in

front of a modern two-story timber-and-sandstone house with a lot of reflective glass. When my door is opened, the smell of ocean meets me, and I can hear it. I smile. I think I'm going to like it here.

"Any news about who hit us?" I ask as the driver helps me out. I look up into his large but kindly face.

"I'm Louis," he tells me.

"Sally."

"I know," he smiles, offering his arm.

"Nothing anyone's admitting to," Alexandra says from the other side of the car. "The police are still asking people to come forward with information."

I am unsteady on my feet. My whole shoulder is throbbing at this point. I'm also very thirsty.

The driver walks me up to the house. Alexandra unlocks the front door and pushes it open for me. As I step in I have to smile, because right there is the most marvelous panoramic view of the Pacific Ocean. We are in a great room, of sorts, with a vast sunken sitting area, a dining area one step up, and then a large kitchen yet another step higher. To the left, I am told, is a guest suite, which is where I will be staying; to the right there is a staircase upstairs to the master bedroom. For the moment, however, I am ushered out the sliding glass doors onto the wood deck and am gently assisted into a heavenly lounge chair. A moment later, Alexandra has covered me with a blanket. "This is really nice," I say.

A minute or two later, I open my eyes and see Alexandra placing a tray next to me. On it is a glass of orange juice; an open bottle of Perrier—with condensation dripping down the green sides—and a glass; a bowl of fruit salad; a small basket with a crescent roll, a Danish and a doughnut of some kind in it; a bowl of baby carrots and short celery stalks; and a small bowl of some kind of dip. "I'd like to see you eat a little of everything here," she says, sitting beside me and reaching for a carrot. She looks at her watch. "A good doctor is coming by in about twenty minutes to check you out. I wish you wouldn't take any more medication until he sees you." She crunches on the carrot, studying me as I survey the tray. I reach for the Perrier with my bandaged hand first and thirstily drink some of it down, suppressing a burp at the end. I glance over. Alexandra's smiling. I reach for the cheese Danish and sink my teeth into it. Very, very good.

"I have no idea where my medication is," I admit, putting the Danish down and picking up the cloth napkin to wipe my fingers.

"You left it on the radiator in your hotel bathroom," she says, reaching for celery this time.

"You packed my stuff?" I try to remember if I had anything embarrassing with me.

"Hastily," she admits.

"I can't believe they let you in my room."

"Put yourself in their place. I walk in and say DBS is taking you to a secure location, I need to get your stuff." A smile. "It's not as if they don't know where they can find me."

"On the nine o'clock news," I say, reaching this time for the orange juice. "I don't think I can eat the carrots or celery. For some reason my teeth are really sore."

"Probably from clenching them as you went down on the bike," she says. She leans forward a little more. "Listen, Sally, we've got tonight's newscast." She looks at her watch again. "In three hours."

I look at her. "I'm not sure I can do it."

"Oh, I don't expect you to," she says quickly. "You're still testifying and everything. I just wondered if you could ask Paul if I could interview him in his hospital bed today for a minute or two. With a camera present."

I suppose I should be annoyed, but I've been in this business too long not to understand making the most of an opportunity. But how will Paul feel about it? "I don't know how he's going to feel about it, but I'll ask him."

"On one condition," Paul says forty minutes later over the telephone, sounding groggy but okay. "Alexandra Waring has to call my mother and tell her about it. Before. Okay? And she's got to let my Mom be here to meet her."

I laugh. "Okay." Pause. "I wish I could visit you tonight, but I'm—"

"I know," he says, interrupting me. "It's all over CNN. They keep showing you in a wheelchair. Your hair looks different."

I laugh again, feeling better partly because this doctor of Alexandra's gave me some kind of *wunderbar* shot, but mostly because Paul does sound okay and isn't angry about my request. I'm not sure why I thought he might be. *(Because you're exploiting your relationship?* asks my conscience. Well, come on, who ever got involved with someone in TV news who didn't have to negotiate some touchy areas regarding privacy? He might as well know the score up front.)

Alexandra takes off shortly thereafter, leaving me under the protection of the big guy, Louis. I retire to my bedroom—a lovely harmony of beiges, with marvelous windows—intending only to take a nap. I open one of the smaller Andersen windows and smile at the sound of the ocean. I take off my sling and slip under the duvet, curling up on my right side and carefully elevating my cast on another pillow. As a wave of exhaustion rolls over me heavily, I know I may well be out for the count. It is heavenly to know I can sleep. Digging deeper under the duvet, I do.

CHAPTER | 18

I open my eyes. It is dark outside, but there is a very faint light. This light flickers and I wonder if it is a candle. I'm wondering if I left a lit candle in the living room, but then I think, no, I'm in New York, not Castleford, because those windows look out onto the street. I squint, then grimace at the pain shooting across my left deltoid muscle.

"I don't know," I hear Alexandra's voice say softly, "it's hard to tell."

Oh, right, I think focusing, *Santa Monica. California. Broken arm.*

"Is she good?" another woman's voice says, a voice with a British echo. Upper-class British; it is an eloquent, educated voice. "It's rather difficult to ascertain with all the fuss."

I move my head slightly. The door is closed. Alexandra

must be on the deck. My eyes travel to the nightstand. There is the tiniest kind of night-light there, along with a glass of water and a vial of pills. One pill is laid out on a napkin. I have to haul myself up to sitting position to reach it.

"Very good," Alexandra says. Pause. "You think I'd hire someone who wasn't?"

The vial is a new pain medication, prescribed by the doctor who looked me over. Alexandra must have had it filled and put it here next to my bed in case I, as I have, awakened with a new wave of aches. I'm taking one.

"Think about it," the low voice of Great Britain says, floating through my open window. I think it must be the new executive producer of the ITN News Channel in London, with whom we are affiliated. "This woman comes out of relatively nowhere, and the moment she appears anywhere in connection with DBS News, events of such an extraordinary nature—"

Extrorrrdinary nay-churrr reverberates in my mind.

"One can't—"

Cahnt.

"—help but wonder if she isn't a one-woman publicity campaign for DBS. First you did that story about her father being murdered by his friend and then she started working for you. It seems like someone's been trying to blow her up ever since."

They laugh. *They laugh!*

"Now she's a witness in a Mafia trial," the voice continues, "and she's forever being chased by cars, like in that dreadful James Brolin movie. I mean, honestly, Alexandra, one would think she works for Fox."

They both laugh (I almost do, too) and Alexandra

shushes her. "No," she whispers and then she says something I can't hear. Damn it, now I'm interested, for obvious reasons. I gingerly creak out of bed and walk across the room to the window. There is nowhere to sit, but I must, so I sink cross-legged on the floor.

"I've seen it in journalists during war and disasters," Alexandra is saying. "It's not that they don't realize the danger they're in, it's more that they thrive on the rush they get when they realize what danger they're in."

"Marvelous," the other woman says. "She's addicted to almost getting murdered."

Mehrrr-dehrd.

"No. It's just her way of dealing with depression, I think. Going for the highs. She does it in her personal life, too."

Depression? I think. *I'm depressed?*

"And you see nothing wrong with encouraging her and banking on the publicity?"

Pause.

"I don't encourage Sally to put herself at risk," Alexandra says. "And no, I see nothing wrong with DBS benefiting. It's no different than when Jessica was kidnapped. You think any of us even for a moment wanted that to happen? But it did and the fact our ratings shot up—well, that's just the way it goes. Remember when that nutcase in Detroit tried to shoot me on the DBS Across America tour? The ratings soared. And do you think I wanted someone to shoot me at the Capitol?"

"Of course not."

An ironic laugh. "Yeah, but that single gunshot is probably what made DBS News possible. And the thing is," the anchorwoman adds, "you don't know even *half* of what

Sally's gotten into while for she's been working for us. Half the stuff that's happened to her will never see the light of day. It's all under sealed records and federal indictments." Pause. "She's got a real nose for things in the wind. It's nothing you can learn; it's something people develop as kids. It's as though Sally can sense stuff before it happens, and it distracts her, pulls her off the path. We're all running one way, and she's out drifting along in a field somewhere." She laughs and I don't know why, but it hurts. I sound like a freak.

There is the clink of ice in a glass. "I thought she was supposed to be your assistant."

"She's supposed to be whatever she evolves to be. We have something special here, we're just not sure exactly what."

"But Alexandra," the woman says.

AlexZANdrah.

"Does she listen to you?"

"Not particularly," Alexandra admits. "I mean, she does. About work. She soaks information up like a sponge. But in terms of the way she works, or how she approaches things, she plays her hand pretty close to her chest."

Look who's talking, I think.

"We're not close," Alexandra says. "Even with everything I know about her, sometimes I feel as though I scarcely know her."

If I had any backbone at all, I'd call out, "Yeah, right, so says the woman *TV Guide* calls 'The Mona Lisa of TV News'!"

"Did something happen between her and Lilliana?"

"No. Sally's not like that."

"No?"

"No."

"I see." Pause. "I only ask because it has been suggested to me," the British woman says, "that perhaps I have been replaced."

My stomach flip-flops as I realize who is out there. This isn't the London news producer for ITN, this is Georgiana Hamilton-Ayres, Alexandra's ex. Actually, Alexandra's rumored ex, since neither ever acknowledged a relationship in the five years they were seen together.

I'm trembling against the damp cold that is rolling in off the ocean, or maybe my body's simply giving up on me. Whatever, I know I should get back into bed.

"Nobody could replace you," Alexandra says quietly.

Pause. A theatrical sigh. "You were always very good at that."

"It's the truth."

Pause. "So you haven't...?"

"No, Georgiana."

Pause.

"Aren't you going to ask me if—"

"No."

Silence. I heard the waves and continue to shiver. I also need to whiz.

"I just don't know what to do." This from Georgiana.

"About what?"

"About us."

"What makes you think there is anything to do?" Alexandra says. "You find my life impossible, I'm not ready to change it—"

"But I love you," she says. "You know I do. How much I do. But I feel as though we're set up to fail."

"You keep saying that." Alexandra sounds annoyed now.

"Because it's true. You're always at a fixed point in New York when I'm working everywhere else but New York. And you can never come, and weeks go by and I get so lonely—"

"I know. Remember, I know."

Pause. "I don't know why I ever even told you about that! It was nothing. I swear, it was nothing."

"It was something," Alexandra says.

"I only told you because I was scared it would happen again."

"So you *left*." The last is said with such bitterness, I am taken aback.

"Yes," Georgiana Hamilton-Ayres finally says. Clinking of ice. "But that wasn't why. And you know it."

"Do I?" Cold as ice.

Alexandra must have been very badly hurt, I think, shivering. Somehow it seems impossible that she could be. If you met Alexandra you would know what I mean. She seems perfect, unflappable, eminently desirable. Everybody is in love with her.

"You've never loved me as much as I love you," the actress says.

No response.

"There's always that ghost around us," Georgiana continues. "And every time you refuse to bend, or compromise, or alter anything about your life, I can always see that ghost standing on the sidelines, waving at me." Pause. "I wish I knew who she was."

I have a very good idea who it is.

"I think," Alexandra says, "you're an actress, Georgiana. A drama queen, to be more exact. And I think you know how much and how deeply I love you, and certainly by now you must know how devastated I've been. After you left. It's been an absolute nightmare."

I can't believe it. Alexandra is crying. Alexandra NEVER cries.

"Oh, God," Georgiana sighs.

"And I don't know why I'm here," Alexandra says. "Yes, I do, because I knew Sally would be safe here, but I know I took you up on the offer because I wanted to see you. I've wanted to see you for so long." She is crying. Muffled. "So much has happened, Georgiana. I've missed you so much."

Scrape of a chair or something. A whisper, "I'm here, love, I'm here."

Crying.

"I'm not going away." Silence. "What happened, darling? Something very bad has happened, hasn't it? And you didn't call me?"

Silence.

"What happened, darling?"

Sniff. "It doesn't matter now."

"Of course it matters. If we're to be together, we have to tell each other."

Pause. And then, in her normal tone of voice, Alexandra says, "Tell each other what? What else did you do?"

"Nothing. I've been miserable, darling. Crying my eyes out, if you must know. Honestly, I'm so relieved that you even cared that I left—"

"What is the matter with you?" Alexandra says, voice rising. "How could you possibly think I would be anything other than destroyed? Everywhere I went, I was reminded of you. It was horrible. I kept waiting for the day you'd send for Savannah and I thought I would just die. You'd take her away and leave Hunter all by himself in the stable and I thought, *God,* doesn't that just about sum it all up?" Pause. "I was thinking I would have to move into the barn. Hunter and I could keep each other company."

Quiet laughter. "Oh, darling."

A long silence.

I have got to take a whiz and stiffly manage to get up and pad across the room to the bathroom. I turn on the light, hoping it will fall out on the deck to alert them that I'm around. I happen to glance in the bathroom mirror and cringe. I look like—I don't know what. But it's not attractive.

I come out, flicking the light out on the way, and head straight for bed and climb in.

"Did you hear that?" comes a whisper.

"I should peek in and see if she's all right," Alexandra says.

"I don't want you to move."

"But—" Sounds of moving furniture again.

I nestle down on my right side. Soon the door opens and a head appears. "Hi," I whisper. "I found the pills, thank you."

"You okay?"

"Can't keep my eyes open," I say, trying to sound dead to the world.

"Good night," she whispers.

"Night."

I close my eyes and will myself to sleep. Then I think maybe I should close that window on the deck so that

Alexandra doesn't notice it in the morning. So I suck in my breath against the pain, getting out of bed yet again, and move silently to the window. I don't close it, however. I dare not do anything but retreat, for in the candlelight outside I see the back of Alexandra's head and the open blouse of Georgiana Hamilton-Ayres.

CHAPTER | 19

A nice lady named Hazel greets me with a glass of fresh-squeezed orange juice as I stagger out of the bathroom Tuesday morning. She explains she is here to help me bathe and dress for court. "Miss Georgiana has a good breakfast waiting for you," she adds, walking past me to start a bath.

"So this is her house?" I ask the lady when she comes back out. I'm trying to figure out her accent. It is a well-spoken Spanish dialect, but I don't think it's Mexican, or Puerto Rican, or Cuban or Spanish. It's more exotic, I have a feeling.

"Yes," she replies, drawing a plastic bag from her apron pocket and slipping it over my cast as I drink my orange juice.

"And you work for her?"

"I work for the Monarch Studios, miss," Hazel tells me.

"Oh, I get it," I say. "The defense team thinks I look horrible."

Hazel looks at me a moment and smiles. "No, miss. Miss Georgiana is making a film for Monarch and I am her dresser. This is a little side job this morning. She believed you may need assistance in the bath."

"No, actually, I'm fine," I say. "There's a handheld sprayer in there, I can do it myself, thank you."

"Perhaps I may assist you with drying your hair?"

"Yes, actually, that would be very helpful, thank you." I look around. "Where are my suitcases?"

"I believe everything has been put away, miss. If you tell me what you would like to wear, perhaps I could lay the clothes out for you."

"Um, sure," I say, wanting a pill in the worst way. If yesterday morning was horrible, at least I was half out of it to begin with. This morning I am just aching, period. Head, eyes, arms, legs.

There is a knock on the door. "Come in!" I call.

The door opens and Alexandra's head pops in. She's already dressed. "Good morning." She holds out a banana. "If you take a few bites of this first, you can take your medication. After your bath, we have breakfast ready."

Hazel is already traveling across the bedroom to get the banana for me. I start for the vial, the side of my mouth hitching up in pain.

"Just lie in the bath for a while," Alexandra advises. "Keep the water good and hot, and just soak, and wait until the medication sinks in before getting out. All right?"

"All right." Actually, I know all this stuff, because I looked after my mother when she was very ill a few years ago.

The bath helps, big time. For some reason I start thinking about Romans and hot springs.

"Miss?" Hazel says from far away. "Miss?"

I am startled awake, blinking. "I fell asleep," I admit, the sound echoing over the tile.

Hazel ends up coming in to get me going, shampooing my hair and drying it after I get out of the bath. It is a long way up out of that bath with one arm and a screwed up back, and Hazel has to pull me out of it.

Soon I am dressed in a suit and heels and pleased with the way I look. Damaged but clean and recognizable. Then I slip off the heels because they're killing my back and walk out into the great room.

I have seen at least seven or eight Georgiana Hamilton-Ayres movies and I am frankly surprised at how comparatively normal she looks in real life. Don't get me wrong, she is beautiful in her own way, but she suffers from the same comparison I do with my mother. Hamilton-Ayres's mother, actress Lillian Bartlett, was the drop-dead gorgeous poster girl of the fifties and sixties, never to be mistaken for a highly accomplished actress, but always revered for her sheer voluptuous beauty. A former sales assistant from Brooklyn, Lillian Rosenblatt was discovered by agent Swifty Lazar, launched in a series of hit drive-in movies and quickly found herself in the papers over an extremely interesting but messy personal life. She suddenly married Lord Hamilton-Ayres of Scotland and disappeared from public view during the one pregnancy she went to term with. The baby was born, Georgiana, and a raging custody battled ensued after Bartlett ran back to Hollywood. Lord Hamilton-Ayres, teetering through the halls of his ancestral castle, became notorious for his two obsessions: his daughter and how the Corn Laws had destroyed Great Britain.

How the forever calm and collected Georgiana Hamilton-Ayres emerged from this union is anyone's guess. She was taller and thinner than her mother, but had inherited many of the famous Bartlett-Rosenblatt curves; Georgiana had also inherited the patrician beauty of her paternal grandmother, whose portrait hangs in the British Portrait Gallery in London. Georgiana has spent her entire life in the public eye, from a new little actress and writer (she published a storybook when she was a child), to an accomplished movie star in her own right. Last summer she played Viola in New York's Shakespeare in the Park series, and has performed in several plays, between movies, in London's West End.

She was married some time ago, and then there was some kind of brief scandal about some woman writer on the set of a movie. And then, in an interview, she admitted she was bisexual but was never really linked with anyone in particular.

Then, about five years ago, she started hanging out with Alexandra.

"Gal Pals" the *Inquiring Eye* called them.

Very close friends, Alexandra and Georgiana would say.

No incriminating photos or anything, but everybody knew. Or thought they knew. It was a rather strange situation, actually, kind of a public relationship with no acknowledgement of it.

"Sally!" the actress says brightly, coming across the great room to meet me. She is in blue jeans, a tank top and loose white Oxford shirt, and no makeup. Her hair is blond, long and flowing, her smile broad and engaging, her blue eyes sparkling. She is very white—you know, U.K. pasty white—and maybe that is what takes me back a little, the absence of the glamour, of the makeup that transforms her into such a stunning silver-screen star. I think I like this version better, though. "So very glad to meet you," she says in that upper-class Brit accent, her handshake firm. "And so very glad to see you up and about."

I smile, a little self-conscious. "Thank you."

"We have scrambled eggs and bacon and soft bread—" she says, leading the way to the dining table. "Alexandra said you were having difficulty chewing."

This is so bizarre, being fed by Georgiana Hamilton-Ayres. I'm also, to be honest, very embarrassed. After what I heard and saw last night, I feel, well, awkward to say the least.

"Alexandra's making some calls," she continues, pointing to a chair for me to sit. "She's supposed to take you somewhere to meet someone from Banks's office to take you to the courthouse."

"I can't just go with her?"

"I think they want to see you before court." She glances over the counter at me. "Alexandra doesn't want them to know where you are, so..."

I nod.

After the banging of a few pots and pans, the actress brings me a plate of scrambled eggs, toast and four strips of crisp bacon. She returns to the kitchen and comes back with what looks like a silver dollar of scrambled eggs, one piece of bacon and, I kid you not, plain popcorn and a bunch of raw baby carrots.

I meet her eyes as she sits and then she glances down at her plate and laughs. "I'm working," she says. "I've been fitted for costumes in a Renaissance film and they will kill me if we have to alter them a stitch."

"It's just that you're so generous with my food," I say quietly, beginning to eat.

"You need to get your strength back," she says. "Oh." She jumps up, grabs some newspapers in the kitchen and brings them back to the table. *Los Angeles Times, New York Times* and the *Wall Street Journal*. "I have yesterday's *Times of London* if you would like," she adds, starting to eat.

"No, that's fine, thank you," I say, pulling the *Los Angeles Times* over.

"I'm sorry," the actress says suddenly, "I'm being very rude. I just assumed you were like Alexandra and would want to look over the papers rather than talk. Particularly since you're in most of them."

"I'm even ruder," I tell her. "I wonder if we could see what's on the morning shows?"

"Oh." She looks startled. "Surely." She jumps up and turns on the TV in the living room. "Which?"

"Good Morning America," I say. "Thank you very much. It's just that I'm curious—" And then I see it in the paper, a picture of Paul sitting in a hospital bed with his arm in traction, and a photograph of me being wheeled across the courthouse parking lot yesterday. L.A. Cop Victim of Hit-and-Run: Or Is It Attempted Murder of Defense Witness in "The Mafia Boss Murder" trial?

Oh, my.

"Hey," Alexandra says brightly, swinging into the kitchen, "good morning. How are you?"

"Alive, thanks to you," I say. I'm starting to feel embarrassed and guilty again as I try to shake the image of these two last night.

"Do you want some coffee, Sally?"

Georgiana looks up from her paper. "Oh, so sorry, I forgot. I don't drink it myself, so I forgot."

"That would be great, thank you," I say. "Well, you drink tea, right?"

"Decaffeinated, but you mustn't ever tell my father. He thinks it's unholy."

I laugh. Alexandra brings me a mug of coffee that is fixed just the way I like it. Over the rim of her coffee cup, Alexandra is struggling to say something. She swallows. "Look—"

On the TV screen it's Paul in his hospital bed. Without even looking, Georgiana picks up the remote and aims it behind her, raising the volume so we can hear it. Evidently she has eaten breakfast with Alexandra many times.

"We don't know," Paul is saying. He looks very banged-up, but surprisingly good. He's telegenic. Some people are a disaster, others meet the distortion of the lens with success. He's clearly the latter.

On the bottom of the screen it reads, "Courtesy of DBS News."

"You gave it to them," I say.

"This morning, after we ran it a million times over the course of the night."

On the screen, they've cut to a long shot of me being wheeled across the courthouse parking lot yesterday, with a voice-over of Paul saying, "Yes, Sally Harrington was with me, and sure, it's possible it was on purpose, but as I say, we don't know. I do know—" the visual comes back to him "—the force will find the driver." He looks into the camera. "So whoever you are, I urge you to give yourself up now."

The visual cuts to a helicopter view of Route 1 where we were hit, as Paul explains what happened.

"Look at that!" Alexandra cries, laughing, "they've cut me out of every shot! Look at that! They edited me and my voice and all my questions out. They've strung Paul's answers together—and see that? How they drop the DBS News credit when they cut away to the courthouse and the road?" She's laughing, shaking her head. "That's hysterical." She looks at me happily. "Just confirms what we already know—right, Sally? Everybody's nervous about our growing market share."

I smile. It's true.

I eat every bit of my breakfast and then Georgiana walks me and Alexandra out the front door to where the car is waiting. "Good luck today, Sally," Georgiana calls as the driver holds the door open for me.

"Thank you."

Alexandra says something to her I can't hear and the actress says, "I'm just going to be working on my lines. I got this great book on customs of the period, too, which I want to study."

Alexandra murmurs something and Georgiana laughs, happy, and kisses the actress on the cheek. Alexandra gets in and we're on our way. The very air around my boss seems light with the sunshine.

"She's lovely," I say.

Alexandra looks over at me carefully. Then she smiles slightly. "Yes."

I reach for the telephone in the car. "I'd like to call Paul and tell him I saw him."

III
Whore of Babylon

CHAPTER | 20

I am transferred to Banks's limousine in the parking lot of a Wendy's. "So where are you staying?" is his first question to me.

"I'm not at liberty to say."

He grunts, looking at Ceeclic. "Okay, let's get down to it. Perez is going to try and tear you apart today. He'll start by accusing you of trading testimony with the Presarios in exchange for help on the TV series. He's going to question your credentials as a journalist—in short, he'll do anything to discredit you in the eyes of the jury as a bad witness."

"You warned me before."

"If it gets too hard to handle, faint."

I look at him.

"Just be sick, you know. If you don't know what to say,

you look like shit and nobody will blame you. Say you're ill and then we'll help you with your responses."

I think I must be sneering at him or something because he gets irritated. "This is a murder trial, Sally. A man's life is at stake. A man who probably saved your life."

"Yeah, I know, but I'm not doing anything sleazy."

"Well that's exactly what Perez is going to make you out to be today. Sleazy, unprofessional, a real media whore."

I loft my eyebrows. "Nice."

"I warned you."

"You warned me," I confirm. Thankfully, these new pills of mine have given me a personality that's somewhere between gentle and nice at the moment. (I took an extra half before leaving the house.)

"Remember, Sally, simply answer the questions he asks, don't offer any more," Cecelie coaches. "And take your time. You don't have to fire those answers back. You can take your time. But know the more time you take, the more emphasis you put on the answer. I know it's hard, but you have to be cautious, even though you will be honest. And the jury needs to know that. That you're being honest. And if Perez gets very rough, go ahead and get upset. Don't lose your temper, go for tears. You know. Make the jury feel that you've been nothing but physically and mentally and emotionally assaulted since you agreed to testify. Make them know you are a good person who showed up because you think it is wrong to punish Jonathan for protecting his family from a mass murderer."

Cecelie is good. Very good. By the time I enter the courtroom, she's got me feeling like a cross between Joan of Arc and the new Messiah.

* * *

"The People will now conduct their cross-examination of this witness," Judge Kahn announces. "Ms. Harrington, you realize you are still under oath?"

"Yes, Your Honor." I sip water. These pills make me thirsty. Or was it the bacon?

In the gallery I can see Alexandra toward the back on the right side. Jonathan is in his seat, of course, looking somber and sincere. For some reason he looks tiny today. Probably the suit. Probably some instruction from Banks's team, to make him look defenseless.

"Good morning, Ms. Harrington," Prosecutor Perez says nicely.

"Good morning."

"For the benefit of the jury, Ms. Harrington, could you please explain how you sustained these recent injuries?"

I turn to the jury. "I was riding on the back of a motorcycle, the night before last, and we stopped at a red light. While we were sitting there, a car hit us from behind. I was thrown to the street and the car—"

"Thank you," Perez interrupts me.

"Objection, Your Honor," Banks says, rising from his chair, "Ms. Harrington hadn't finished her sentence. I think the jury should hear the rest of answer."

"Ms. Harrington answered my question, Your Honor," Prosecutor Perez says.

A moment of silence as the judge thinks this over. Clearly Perez does not want me to say it was a hit-and-run, opening the possibility of witness tampering, and clearly Banks would be delighted if I did, which is why I said it. I've got to remember, though, I'm not supposed to be thinking. I'm just supposed to be answering the questions.

I don't want to be a bad witness. Really I don't.

(Man, are these painkillers great.)

"Objection overruled, you may continue, Attorney Perez."

Perez is standing in front of me, scratching the side of his neck, as if wondering how to broach the next topic. "All right, Ms. Harrington," he says finally, dropping his hand and taking a step toward the jury box, "I want to take you through your testimony, step by step, and try to clarify several points." He glances over and I nod, trying to look willing.

"By the way, are you on any medication today?"

"Um, yes," I say.

"What kind?"

"I'm sorry, I don't know what the name of it is." I send an apologetic look to the jury. "It's very long. The vial is in the waiting room, if you want it."

"What is the medication for?"

"To numb the pain."

"So it's a painkiller?"

"Yes, sir."

"Were you on these painkillers yesterday when you testified?"

"Yesterday I was taking Percosets. Also a painkiller."

"But your medication was changed?"

"Yes."

"When?"

"Last night."

"By a medical doctor?"

"Yes, sir."

"And why was it changed?"

"He said this new medication was more effective."

"In killing the pain?"

"Yes."

Perez thinks about this a moment and then asks. "Did your medication yesterday affect your ability to recall information or testify accurately in this case, Ms. Harrington?"

"I don't believe so."

"But your medication was changed last night?"

"Yes."

"Does the medication you're taking today affect your ability to recall information or testify accurately in this case?"

"I don't believe so," I say.

Perez nods, glancing over at the jury before continuing. "Ms. Harrington, you testified that you are an employee of DBS News in New York."

"Yes."

"How long have you been a full-time employee?"

"Full-time?" I think. "Since May 1, so that's six and a half months. About."

"Six and a half months," he repeats. "And what was your job title when you were hired?"

"Associate—golly, what was it?" I say out loud, trying to think. My brain feels so sluggish.

"You don't know what your job title was?"

Wrong question, buddy, don't annoy me. "Since I was hit by that car, Prosecutor, I'm not thinking as quickly as I would normally. I'm sorry." I drop my eyes to appear humble instead of angry.

In a gentle voice, Perez says, "Take your time."

"My job title was assistant producer," I say, looking up.

"And your duties were what?"

"To assist Alexandra Waring with all facets of her job as managing editor of the news division."

"So you would—" Perez is walking around "—do what, exactly?"

"It would depend on the needs of the day," I say. "Sometimes it would be working on the story lineup for the nightly news. Sometimes there would be a problem in the field somewhere and I would work with the producers and reporters to iron it out. Sometimes I worked with the writers, or the tape editors. Many times I simply assisted the affiliates in their story assignments."

"How many assistant producers are there at DBS News?"

I think a moment. "Six."

"And, on the average, how long have those other assistant producers worked there?"

I think. "A year." I shrug. "It's an entry-level job. I mean, it's higher than a secretary, where a lot of people start."

"And what is your title at DBS News today?"

"Producer."

"What was your salary when you began full-time at DBS News? Six and a half months ago?"

"Objection, Your Honor," Banks says. "Relevance?"

"I'm establishing the credibility of the defense's witness, Your Honor."

"Objection overruled."

Perez. "What was your starting salary at DBS News six and a half months ago?"

"Eighty thousand dollars a year."

"Bonuses?"

"Possibility of bonuses, yes."

"What is the average starting salary of an assistant producer at DBS News?"

Damn, I've been looking at all the charts, so I know this. "Thirty to forty thousand dollars a year."

"But you were paid twice as much than the other assistant producers?"

"Because I had—"

"Yes or no, Ms. Harrington," Perez says, smiling as he cuts me off. "Were you hired at DBS News at twice the salary level of the other assistant producers?"

I want to explain that the others are almost all twenty-three years old with a year's experience at best, and I came with almost nine solid years of professional journalism experience, but clearly he is not going to let me.

I don't like this.

"Yes," I say.

"And you were made producer after how long?"

"Three months."

"And you received a raise?"

"Yes."

"To what salary level?" he says, pretending to try to contain his envy.

"One twenty-five."

"One hundred twenty-five thousand dollars," Perez repeats, walking over to the jury. "That's a great deal of money, Ms. Harrington." He turns around. "What did you do to earn it?"

"I'm sorry, I don't understand the question."

"Why were you promoted after three months and given another forty-five thousand dollars a year?"

"Because my work was excellent and they wanted to keep me."

"Isn't it true, Ms. Harrington, that you were hired in the first place because of your friendship with members of the Presario crime family?"

"Objection!" Banks roars. "There is no Presario crime family, Your Honor, there is only the Arlenetta crime family."

"Objection, Your Honor!"

"Counsel will approach the bench," Judge Kahn says.

I sit there while the lawyers argue and do as Cecelie suggested, which is to sag in my chair a bit as if I'm trying my best to do what the court wishes me to do, although the prosecutor may kill me in the process. I hazard a look to the gallery. I can't see Alexandra.

"Objections are sustained," Judge Kahn announces.

Finally the lawyers return to their places. "Now, Ms. Harrington," Perez says, "I want to better understand your soaring career climb at DBS News."

"If it was soaring, I'd have Alexandra's job," I say.

The courtroom bursts into laughter and the judge bangs his gavel. Perez is beside himself.

Judge Kahn turns to me. "The court recognizes your efforts to continue testifying, Ms. Harrington. Please just listen to the People's questions and respond accordingly."

"Yes, Your Honor," I say solemnly. Innocently, I turn my eyes up to Perez.

"Were you hired by DBS News on the condition you would work on the news coverage of the Arlenetta murder? Yes or no, Ms. Harrington."

"Yes."

"And did you work on the news coverage of the Arlenetta murder?"

"Yes."

"Did you use personal contacts to enhance DBS News's coverage on the murder?"

"Yes."

"Were you instructed by your employers to produce a series of special reports on the Arlenetta murder?"

"No."

He wheels around, clearly surprised.

"Could you explain?"

"I'm sorry, what do you want me to explain?" I say politely.

His neck is getting red. He pauses and then says, lowering his tone of voice slightly, "Were you instructed to produce a series of special programs that *related* to the Arlenetta murder?"

"Yes."

"Was that series of special programs called *The Family?*"

"Yes."

"Was *The Family* run on DBS two weeks ago?"

"Yes."

"Your Honor," Perez says, walking to his table to pick up a pamphlet, "the People wish to enter into evidence a Nielsen's ratings report for the first week of November." He hands the document to the clerk, who then has him give it to Banks to examine. Banks poses no objection and Perez brings the report to me, asking me to identify it. I explain that it is a Nielsen's Ratings Report, the standard by which the television industry gauges the popularity of shows. The report is then entered into evidence and, once again, is brought back to me to review.

"What category is *The Family* listed under?"

"Program with the highest number of viewers."

"*The Family* was a tremendous hit, wasn't it?"

A titter breaks out in the jury box, which spreads to the gallery. I think it is because he used the phrase *The Family* and *hit* in the same sentence.

"Yes," I say with a straight face.

"And who is listed as the producer?"

"I am."

"And who is listed as the writer?"

"I am."

He takes a break, walking the document to the clerk to file into evidence. He walks back and looks hard at me. "Did you ask a member of the Presario family to work on this project with you?"

"Yes."

"Who?"

"Lilliana Martin."

"Lilliana Martin, the sister of the defendant."

"Yes."

"And what contribution did Ms. Martin make to the series?"

"She loaned us family pictures to use. She agreed to be interviewed for it."

He waits, but I have nothing more to say.

"That's all? She gave you pictures and agreed to be interviewed?"

"Yes."

He pauses, walking over to the jury box. "Did you and Ms. Martin ever live together in a suite at the Bernier Hotel in Manhattan?"

"Objection, Your Honor," Banks says, sounding disgusted. "The prosecutor is deliberately distorting the facts of the case."

"Sustained. The People will rephrase the question," the judge directs.

Perez hesitates and then shakes his head. "There is no other way to phrase the question, Your Honor. Did the witness or did she not live with Lilliana Martin in a suite at the—"

"Objection, Your Honor!" Banks roars. "Attorney Perez is off his rocker!"

The courtroom erupts.

"Attorney Banks," scolds the judge, as the laughter dies down.

"I apologize, Your Honor."

"Counsel, approach the bench," Judge Kahn says wearily.

This sidebar lasts awhile and there is a lot of hissing. Meanwhile, I sit here trying to look innocent and abused.

Finally the trial lawyers return to their places. "Ms. Harrington—"

I wait.

"Did DBS News pay for Lilliana Martin to stay in a suite at the Hotel Bernier in Manhattan?"

"Yes."

"Why?"

"She was helping to identify family photographs and had nowhere to stay."

"But she was kept in a suite?"

"Yes."

"Did you yourself ever stay in that suite?"

"In the second bedroom, yes," I say. "There was an attempt on—"

"A simple answer yes or no, Ms. Harrington," Perez says.

I look at Banks, whose face is unreadable.

"Ms. Harrington?" I look at Perez. "Do you understand? Simply answer yes or no?"

"Yes, sir."

"Did Lilliana Martin set up an interview between Alexandra Waring and Rocky Presario?"

"No."

"No? Who did?"

"Alexandra Waring did."

"But did Lilliana Martin ask her grandfather to do an interview with Ms. Waring?"

"Yes."

"And did you ask Lilliana Martin to ask her grandfather to do the interview?"

"Yes."

"Did you ask Lilliana Martin to ask her father to do an interview with Alexandra Waring?"

"Yes."

"Did you ask Lilliana Martin to ask her brother to do an interview with Alexandra Waring?"

"Yes."

"Did you ask Lilliana Martin to ask other relatives to do interviews with Alexandra Waring?"

"Yes."

Perez lets this sink in as he walks over to stand next to the jury. "Would the special series of programs, called *The Family,* have been possible to produce without the cooperation of Lilliana Martin?"

"Yes."

"Yes? Would you care to explain your rationale? If Lilliana Martin had not provided the family photographs and all of the interviews, how would it have been possible to produce this series?"

"The same way we put together any news special," I say. "We would have used other sources. I would have, for example, more aggressively pursued members of the Arlenetta crime family—"

"Your Honor—" Perez says.

"You opened the door, Mr. Perez," Judge Kahn says irritably. "You must let the witness finish answering your question." He looks to me. "You may continue."

"I would have aggressively pursued members of the Arlenetta crime family," I say, "because I knew they were anxious to convict the defendant and sway public opinion so they could continue their illegal activities."

The judge clears his throat and then says, "I think this is a good stopping place for lunch. Court will recess until one-thirty. I would like to see counsel in my chambers now before you go to lunch. Thank you." He raps his gavel.

"All rise," calls the clerk of the court.

The jury is led out and Sheriff McDuff delivers me to Burton Kott. "You did great," he murmurs, leading me through the people.

"I've got to lie down," I tell him.

"Banks wants to talk to you."

"Fine, he can talk to me while I'm lying down," I say. "Burton..." I grab his arm with my right hand; everything's starting to turn yellow.

"Here," Sheriff McDuff says, hurriedly unlocking a door marked Staff. I lunge forward through it, hanging on to Kott, and sink to the floor, quickly flopping onto my back. Immediately I feel better, and the swimming stops. The only problem is, I'm lying in the middle of a linoleum hallway with a bunch of people staring down at me. "Just give me a minute," I plead, closing my eyes.

"Did anyone call the EMTs?"

"No," Burton says. "She's fine." What he means is, we want her like this in court.

I open my eyes. "Screw you," I tell him, reaching for Sheriff McDuff. "I just need to lie down for half an hour."

"We've got a lounge," the Sheriff says, helping me up. "But I don't know, girl, maybe you should call it a day."

"She can't," Burton says.

"I'll be fine," I assure Sheriff McDuff, slinging my arm around his neck because I think I might faint again.

"That news babe, Alexandra Waring," a voice calls from down the corridor, "says to get the witness some Gatorade."

CHAPTER | 21

I return to the courtroom fortified with Gatorade, another banana and painkillers. Perez is looking positively hostile now and Banks is looking smug. We all stand as the judge enters and the proceedings resume.

Perez looks at me a moment before sauntering over to the jury box. "Ms. Harrington, the jury has heard about your first meeting with the defendant's sister, Lilliana Martin, at a party in Beverly Hills."

I nod. "Yes."

"It was a party in celebration of the publication of Malcolm Kieloff's autobiography?"

"Yes."

"May I ask how you came to be at that party?"

"A friend of mine, Spencer Hawes, was Mr. Kieloff's editor and he invited me."

"Is it not true that at the time of the party, Spencer Hawes was, in fact, your boyfriend?"

I hesitate a moment and then say, "Yes."

"And that you and Mr. Hawes were staying together at a hotel in Santa Monica together? Shutters?"

"Objection, Your Honor," Banks says. "I don't see how grilling Ms. Harrington about her personal life will shed any light on this case."

"Your Honor, Ms. Harrington's personal life has a direct bearing on the course of events that led to the murder of Nicholas Arlenetta."

"Your Honor, the prosecutor—"

The judge hammers his gavel and focuses on Perez. "A direct bearing on the course of events?"

"Yes, Your Honor."

"Objection overruled, the People may continue."

He looks at me, a glint of gleeful merriment in his eyes. "Were you and Mr. Hawes staying together in the same room at Shutters?"

"Yes."

"So this was a very serious relationship?"

What am I going to say to *that?* "Yes."

"Was the defendant, Jonathan Small, also present at the party held in Malcolm Kieloff's honor?"

"Yes."

"Were you introduced to him?"

"Yes."

"Did the defendant seem scared or upset in any way?"

"No."

"Did the defendant seem in fear of his life?"

"No."

"Did he appear afraid or concerned about the safety of Lilliana Martin in any way?"

"No."

"Isn't it true the defendant, Jonathan Small, asked you out on a date when you met him at Malcolm Kieloff's party?"

I hesitate. "Yes."

"I see," Perez says, taking a leisurely walk over to the prosecution's table to look at some notes. He walks back to me. "After meeting Lilliana Martin the night of the Kieloff party, was your relationship with Mr. Hawes in any way compromised?"

I hesitate. "I don't quite understand the question." Actually, I think I do understand and I'm getting mad.

"After meeting Lilliana Martin the night of the Kieloff party," Perez repeats, as if I'm a child, "did your relationship with Mr. Hawes change?"

I don't say anything.

"Ms. Harrington," the judge says quietly. "You must answer yes or no."

I swallow. "Yes."

"Why?"

"We had an argument."

"You had an argument with Mr. Hawes about what?"

"About our relationship."

"What about your relationship, Ms. Harrington?"

"About whether or not I wanted to continue it."

"Ms. Harrington, isn't it true that Mr. Hawes did something that night that upset you?"

I don't know where to look, so I just continue looking at Perez. "Yes."

"What was it?"

Banks rises. "Objection, Your Honor. The prosecutor is badgering the witness. And the defense still fails to see the relevance of this line of questioning."

"Your Honor, I repeat, Ms. Harrington's personal relationships have a direct bearing upon the course of events leading up to the murder of Nicholas Arlenetta."

The judge pauses and then calls the lawyers up for a sidebar.

I take a deep breath, feeling my face burn. I knew Perez would get into this at some point, about the night we met Lilliana, which started the whole chain of events. But it never occurred to me that Perez would somehow know something of what happened. Then I wonder how does he know, who told him. It wasn't me, and the only other people there had been Lilliana and Spencer.

I glance over at Jonathan Small and see that is he is staring down at his folded hands on the table in front of him.

I am getting the decided feeling I may have been set up.

The entire jury is looking at me. I try to smile a little, sipping my Gatorade, and shift a bit in my chair to get my cast in a more comfortable position.

Finally, the boys are back in their place.

"Ms. Harrington, isn't it true that you and Spencer Hawes drove Lilliana Martin to a house in Cold Water Canyon after the party?"

"Yes."

"And that you and Mr. Hawes went inside that house with Lilliana Martin?"

"Yes."

"And Ms. Harrington, isn't it true that *that* night—the night you met Lilliana Martin—you knew that your boyfriend, Spencer Hawes, was sexually attracted to her?"

"Half the planet is sexually attracted to Lilliana Martin," I say, prompting the courtroom to erupt into laughter.

Perez doesn't get ticked off. He smiles and laughs along with everyone as the judge calls for order. "Very true, Ms. Harrington, she is a very beautiful actress." He pauses, turning toward the jury. "And isn't it true, Ms. Harrington, that Lilliana Martin told you, at the house in Cold Water Canyon, after the party, that she was, in fact, sexually attracted to you?"

There is an audible gasp in the courtroom and I look dumbly ahead at Perez, as he turns around to look at me.

"Yes," I say.

There is a buzz in the courtroom and the judge asks for order.

"You and Mr. Hawes had a terrible argument that night. Is that correct?"

"Yes."

"And you and Mr. Hawes, for all intents and purposes, broke up after that, didn't you?"

"Yes."

He takes a walk. "You testified that Mr. Hawes disappeared the next day."

"Yes."

"He was kidnapped, was he not?"

"Yes."

"Do you know by whom?"

"No."

"Isn't it true, Ms. Harrington, that Spencer Hawes was kidnapped by associates of Lilliana Martin's?"

"I have no idea if they were associates of hers."

"But in your testimony, Ms. Harrington—" he goes back to the table to flip through his notes "—you said that when you told Lilliana Martin that Spencer Hawes had disappeared, Lilliana made a phone call and by the end of the next day, Spencer Hawes had been found."

"Objection," Banks says unenthusiastically, "Prosecutor is leading the witness."

"I'll gladly have the witness's testimony read back to the court, Your Honor."

"Objection sustained. The People will please focus their questions."

Perez is really getting me mad now. He's twisting everything around, I realize, to make the jury think Lilliana and I had something going on and so she got Spencer out of the way. "All right, Ms. Harrington, let's get absolutely clear on this. Were you aware that Lilliana Martin was sexually attracted to you?"

"Yes."

"And she told you this?"

"Yes."

"And she made a pass at you, didn't she?"

"Yes, but I—"

"Simply yes or no—" Perez taunts me, walking away.

"You're misleading the jury," I tell him.

"Objection, Your Honor," Perez says to the judge. "The witness's last statement is unresponsive and I ask that it be stricken from the record."

The judge gives me a vaguely disgusted look. "The objection is sustained and that last remark will be stricken."

Perez whips around. "Permission to treat this as a hostile witness, Your Honor."

The judge sighs and then nods. "Granted."

Perez whips around practically in my face. "You flew

home to Connecticut and the very next day, Cliff Yarlen appeared at your home. Yes or no?"

"Yes."

"He was there because he thought Lilliana Martin had run off with you. Yes or no?"

"That's not how—"

"He thought Lilliana Martin, after meeting you only once, had flown to Connecticut to be with you, yes or no?"

I sigh. "Yes." I look up at the judge. "This isn't fair, Your Honor."

"Ms. Harrington, answer the People's questions. Attorney Banks will have the opportunity to clarify your testimony later."

Miserable, I turn back to Perez.

"You testified that you drove out to JFK Airport to see Cliff Yarlen before he was killed," the prosecutor says.

I turn to the judge. "Is that a question, Your Honor?"

He nods.

"Yes," I say.

"And you met him in the Admiral's Club?"

"Yes."

"And while you were there, isn't it true you started making out with him?"

"No!" I cry, creating a buzz in the courtroom. "I think you've got sex on the brain, Prosecutor Perez," I tell him.

The courtroom erupts and the judge slams the gavel and tells me to simply answer the questions. "I have to warn you, Ms. Harrington. Comments such as that may be considered in contempt of court."

"I'm sorry, Your Honor," I say, raising my bandaged hand briefly to the side of my face. "It may be my physical condition."

"Are you able to continue?" he asks seriously.

"Yes, sir. I'll do better," I promise, thinking, *Man, no amount of drugs can make this bearable.* I have half a mind to swoon. But this is a court of law, and believe it or not, I have the utmost respect for the law.

Well, most times.

"Did you kiss Cliff Yarlen at JFK?"

"Cliff Yarlen kissed me."

"And you resisted?"

"I did not participate."

"Did you slap him?"

"No."

"Did you push him away?"

"No, I didn't have to. The kiss was very brief."

I drink my Gatorade and wonder why on earth I ever agreed to testify, and why on earth the Presario family would want me to.

Perez is back at his table, flipping through that legal pad again. "Let us move on to your second trip to Los Angeles. You attended the memorial service for Cliff Yarlen."

"Yes."

"And you saw the defendant there?"

"Yes."

"And at this time, the time of Cliff Yarlen's memorial service, were you aware that the defendant, Jonathan Small, was in fact the brother of Lilliana Martin?"

"No, I was not."

"At the memorial service, Ms. Harrington, did you tell Jonathan Small where you were staying?"

"Yes."

"That night, did the defendant come up to your hotel room?"

I glare at Banks. "You should be objecting," I tell him.

Murmurs in the courtroom and Judge Kahn bangs the gavel. He sighs theatrically and then frowns at me. "Ms. Harrington, one more unsolicited comment, and I am going to fine you for contempt of court."

"I apologize, Your Honor," I say sincerely. "Truly, I will not let it happen again." I look up at Perez and wait.

He's looking at me, assessing my mood, I bet. "Did Jonathan Small visit you in your hotel room?"

"Yes."

"Did he make sexual advances toward you?"

"Yes." I'm waiting for the follow-up, but of course, it never comes, Perez is simply leaving me twisting in the wind as the Whore of Babylon.

"So, you went out to L.A. with a boyfriend, Spencer Hawes, and broke up with him on that trip. Yes or no."

"Yes."

"The sister of the defendant, Lilliana Martin, made sexual advances toward you. Yes or no?"

"Yes."

"The cousin of the defendant, Cliff Yarlen, also made a sexual advance toward you, yes or no?"

"No."

He looks surprised. "You do not consider kissing you on the mouth a sexual advance?"

"No." I blink. "Well, yes, I guess, in a way."

He nods, biting his lower lip, studying me. "Okay." He takes a step toward the jury. "And then, finally, the defendant himself, Jonathan Small, made sexual advances toward you as well. Yes or no?"

I take a breath. "Yes."

"Isn't it true, Ms. Harrington, that you have used your

sexual attractiveness in the pursuit of getting a news story?"

"Objection!" Banks roars from the defense table. "Irrelevant! The prosecutor is badgering the witness, Your Honor. And it's argumentative!"

"Objection sustained," Judge Kahn rules.

Perez nods slightly, raising a hand as if acquiescing. But he is not, for his next question is "Ms. Harrington, did you play upon Ms. Martin's attraction to you in order to gain her confidence?"

"No."

"No?"

"No."

"What did you use to gain Ms. Martin's confidence?"

"My genuine concern and interest in her."

He nods slowly and walks over to the jury. "Did you know Lilliana Martin well?"

"No."

"But you felt genuine concern about her?"

"Yes."

"Why?"

"I liked her. And I knew something was terribly wrong in her life. But I didn't know what."

"Ms. Harrington, isn't it true that DBS News ordered you back to Los Angeles to find Lilliana Martin and gain her confidence?"

"They sent me to find her."

"And you were not told to gain her confidence?"

I'm trying to think. I remember Alexandra saying something about Lilliana liking me was helpful. I shake my head. "No. I was simply assigned to the story."

"You were simply assigned to the story. You were a reporter for DBS News in New York, assigned to find Lilliana Martin, the famous actress who coincidentally had made sexual advances toward you the very first night you met her. Is that correct?"

"It is a version of the truth," I say.

"Yes or no, Ms. Harrington?"

"I'm sorry," I sigh, bringing a hand to my face. "Could you please repeat the question?"

"Out of all the reporters at their disposal, isn't it true DBS News chose you to cover the story of Lilliana Martin's disappearance?"

"Yes."

"And was your employer aware of the sexual advances Ms. Martin had made toward you, yes or no?"

"Yes."

Perez retreats to his table to that infernal pad of notes.

My back is starting to throb. I look over miserably to the jury as I sip my Gatorade. Juror number three looks as though he wants to ask me out.

"Ms. Harrington, I want to ask you about the television series you produced for DBS News, called *The Family*."

I wait.

"You wrote and produced this series with the assistance of Lilliana Martin. Yes or no?"

"Yes."

"And you stayed in the same hotel with her while working on it?"

"For about a week, yes."

He turns to me. "Was Lilliana Martin still sexually attracted to you?"

"Objection, Your Honor." Banks says. "Perhaps this question should be saved for Ms. Martin?"

"I will rephrase, Your Honor," Perez says, holding up a hand. He looks at me. "Did you ever have any sexual contact with Lilliana Martin while staying with her in the Hotel Bernier?"

I am about to say no, but remember the night Lilliana kissed me—and simultaneously drew my hand to her breast. I withdrew immediately and she retreated, hurt, and that had been it. Still, this court wants a yes or no, and whether I like it or not, I have to wait for Banks to straighten it out in his redirect.

"Ms. Harrington?" Perez says. "I asked you, did you have any sexual contact with Lilliana Martin while staying with her at the Hotel Bernier?"

"Yes," I say, and I see two reporters flying for the doors as the courtroom is abuzz.

"I have no further questions of this witness, Your Honor," Perez announces.

CHAPTER | 22

"That son of a bitch!" I yell in the witness waiting room, pushing a chair over on its side, which shoots a searing pain through my hand.

"Don't worry," Burton assures me, "Banks will clear it all up on the redirect."

"I'm *talking* about that prick Banks!" I yell.

Burton looks to Cecelie and she starts edging toward the door. I point at her. "You guys set me up. You've been feeding this crap to the prosecutor and you're using me for something that's going to come down and I am not doing it! I am going on the news tonight—"

"You can't talk about the trial—"

"When I finish testifying I can say what I damn well please!" I cry.

"But you won't," a deep voice says. Banks. At the door. "Sit down, Sally."

"To hell with *you*," I tell him, walking away to face the wall, like a child. I feel like one. An abused one, waking up in a house of crazy people.

"You wanted to help," he said quietly. "You're helping."

"You're destroying my life," I point out.

He laughs a little and I have a half a mind to whack him over the head with my cast. "When this is over, the sky's the limit for your career and you know it."

He's right, of course. In the sometimes perverse universe of media, my fifteen minutes is probably permanent. "That's not why I offered to testify."

"I know that. And everyone else will know that, too, in the end, Sally. But if you want to see justice done for Jonathan and his family, you need to let me do my job."

I turn around. "Why didn't you warn me what was going to happen?"

"Because we needed you to be who you are. We needed you to be—sincere. On the stand. There are enough actors and aliases in this trial, we needed naked emotion up there and you gave it."

I fall into a chair, feeling weak, rubbing my eyes with the back of my bandaged hand. "How long will the redirect take?"

"About an hour."

I look up at him. "Are you going to clarify all the sexual stuff?"

"Oh, yes, I will. Certainly." He pauses. "And as I say, in the end, all will become clear. But if you want to help the Presarios, I've got to ask you to stick with it. Just for a while longer."

I sigh, rolling my eyes. Then I look at Burton. "Grilled cheese and soup, please. Like now."

Cecelie helps me with my makeup for the afternoon session of court. If I am to be transformed into Helen of Troy from the Whore of Babylon, I've got to look better than I do. Alexandra sent a note into me, but I told Burton to tell her I'm lying down and can't come out, I'll see her when court's over for the day.

New pills have me pain free and the food has done me good. I take the stand with a sense of hope that I will soon be free to collapse and then hide for the rest of my life.

The judge enters and court resumes, Judge Kahn explaining to the jury that the defense attorney now has the opportunity to redirect the examination of this witness.

The Bad Witness, I think.

Banks walks up to the box. "Are you feeling well enough to continue testifying, Ms. Harrington?"

"Objection, Your Honor. Theatrics," Perez says.

"Objection overruled, but Attorney Banks, you'll begin the redirect, please."

"Yes, Your Honor." He walks over to me. "I want to clarify a few points to the jury," he says quietly. "First, your salary at DBS News. Could you explain to the jury what hours you work at DBS?"

I look over. "Generally speaking, I am at work by noon and leave after we break the set down after the nightly news, usually eleven-thirty or so. I work Monday through Friday and usually take work home on the weekend."

"So all told, Ms. Harrington, how many hours do you work in an average week?"

"Seventy to seventy-five."

He nods. "And you mentioned that you travel?"

I nod. "I'm usually in the field six or seven days a month."

"Where do you live?"

"I have a cottage I rent in Castleford, Connecticut."

"But you did not always live there?"

"I grew up there. But then I went to college here at UCLA."

"What kind of work did you do after college?"

"I first worked at *Boulevard* magazine as an editorial assistant."

"Did you have any other jobs?"

"I bartended on weekends."

"Why?"

"To pay my rent and pay off student loans."

"Your parents didn't pay for college?"

"Objection, Your Honor," Perez says. "The People fail to see the relevance of this line of questioning."

"The defense wishes to clarify the character of the witness for the jury, Your Honor," Banks says. "After the prosecution has done their best to smear her good name in this courtroom."

"Your Honor!" cries Perez.

Judge Kahn calls counsel up to the bench for a brief sidebar. After the attorneys return to their places, the judge whispers to his clerk for a moment. She whispers something back and the judge addresses the court. "The objection is overruled. Mr. Banks, you may continue."

"I was asking you, Ms. Harrington," Banks says, "if your parents paid for your college education?"

"My father died when I was nine. And I had a younger brother my mother also supported by herself."

"So your parents did pay for your college education?"

"No."

"So how were you able to go?"

"I was lucky to get several scholarships, some from UCLA and some from organizations in the town where I grew up."

"For how many years?"

"All four."

"And how much of your tuition expenses did these scholarships cover?"

"About eighty percent."

"And how did you pay for the rest?"

"I worked all through school and I took out student loans."

"Did you ever finish paying off your student loans?"

I can't help but smile. "Yes. About six weeks ago."

He nods. "Congratulations."

"Thank you."

"You were able to accomplish this by your increased salary at DBS News?"

"Yes."

"Describe for the jury, if you will, Ms. Harrington, the work experience you had before joining DBS?"

"I had six years at *Boulevard*—"

"What was your job title when you left?"

"Editor."

"Why did you leave?"

"Um, well, my mother had been diagnosed with cancer and I wanted to be with her while she was undergoing treatment. So I came back to Connecticut—and I ended up staying."

He smiles. "Did your mother recover?"

"Yes, indeed, thank you. She's a hundred percent."

"So what did you do when you stayed on?"

"I joined the staff of the tri-town newspaper, as a features reporter, and I rented a cottage in Castleford."

"And that is the cottage you still rent?"

"Yes."

"Have you ever won any awards for your work?"

"Yes."

"Could you name them?"

I do. It takes a while, because each has a long classification in its title, like "Best Investigative Reporting for a Newspaper with a Circulation of 50-100,000 Readers."

"What other work have you done?"

"I did a major freelance piece for *Expectations* magazine in New York, which brought me to the attention of DBS News. They hired me to work part-time as an investigative reporter at their Connecticut affiliate."

"What happened to that affiliate?"

"DBS cut ties with them, but they offered me a full-time position as Alexandra Waring's assistant."

"So you made a lot more money."

"Yes," I agree, nodding.

"And what do you spend it on?"

"Well, as I said, I've been paying off my student loans. Because of my hours, I have to have an apartment in Manhattan. I'm subletting, but it's still expensive."

"What kind of an apartment?"

"A studio apartment."

"And how much is your rent?"

"Nineteen hundred dollars a month."

A murmur in the courtroom.

Banks walks over to the jury box. "Any plans for your new income?"

"Yes. I'd like to buy the house I grew up in."

"Why?"

"My father designed and built it. And it's on a piece of property that has been in his family for over a hundred fifty years."

"What happened to your father, Sally?"

"Objection, Your Honor," Perez says. "Relevance."

"The prosecutor has attacked every aspect of the witness's character, Your Honor, I'm merely trying to show the jury what kind of person she is."

"Objection overruled," Judge Kahn says.

"Thank you, Your Honor." He looks at the jury. "What happened to your father, Sally?"

"He was murdered." Murmurs in the court.

"How old were you?"

"Nine."

"And you said your mother raised you and your brother by herself?"

"Yes."

He walks over to the defense table. "Let's move on to some of the questions Prosecutor Perez asked you," he says, picking up an index card. "I'd like to clarify a few points for the jury."

I wait.

"Could you explain to the jury what exactly happened between you and Cliff Yaalen in the Admiral's Club at JFK?"

"We had spent the afternoon together, driving into the city, talking, getting to know each other. And later that night, when I went out to JFK to find out why he was leaving so suddenly, he thought I was taking the same plane to Los Angeles."

"And he was happy about that?"

"Well, not happy exactly, just pleased, I guess. He thought we'd have a chance to get to know each other better."

"He liked you?"

"Yes. And I liked him, frankly. I thought he was a nice man."

"Did you think about him romantically?"

I squint a little. "No. Well, it crossed my mind that he was single, sure. Because he was very well spoken, bright, personable." I shrug, which instantly makes me flinch. "Ouch," I say, touching my shoulder to let the jury know what the face was about.

"So how did this kiss come about?"

"Because the weather was so bad, I offered to give him a ride back into town, into Manhattan, but he declined, saying he was going to wait until a plane could get out, he needed to get back. And then he just sort of kissed me and said goodbye."

"So it wasn't some sort of passionate, sexually charged gesture?"

"No," I say honestly. "It was a surprise to me, frankly. But he just kissed me and said goodbye and I knew it meant he liked me and would like to know me better."

"But then he was murdered."

I nod, lowering my eyes. "Yes."

"The defendant, Jonathan Small," Banks says loudly, walking across the courtroom, "came up to your hotel room after the memorial service for Cliff Yarlen."

"Yes."

"Did you invite him up?"

"No."

"How is it that he was in your room?"

"I had ordered room service, and I thought it was the waiter and I opened the door and Jonathan rushed in."

"Did he make a sexual advance?"

"Oh, yes," I say in such a voice as to make the courtroom laugh.

"And what did you do?"

"I basically ran around the room," I said, making people laugh again.

"Now, this is important, Sally, did you do anything to encourage this behavior from him?"

I sigh. And nod. "Yes."

"What did you do?"

"At the memorial service, I pretended to be interested in him."

"Why?"

"I wanted to talk to him about his connection to Cliff Yarlen."

"Why?"

"I thought he might be connected to his murder."

"But he surprised you by coming to your room?"

"Yes."

"And he made sexual advances?"

"Several."

"What did you do?"

"I threw him out."

"You physically threw him out?"

"He was stronger than I was, but yes, in effect, I did."

"And what was his reaction?"

"He was amused."

"And how did you feel?"

"Furious. And stupid, for thinking I was going to find out much that way."

"Later on, when you found out that the defendant was Lilliana Martin's brother, did his behavior make sense to you?"

"Yes. Oh, yes. I realized at once he had been doing the same thing with me, trying to find out what I knew about Cliff Yarlen's death."

"So he was pretending to be sexually attracted to you?"

I smile. "You'll have to ask him." Laughter.

"But this is an important distinction, Ms. Harrington, so please be careful in your answer. Did you use your sexual attractiveness to win the confidence of Cliff Yarlen?"

"Yes."

"Were you attracted to him?"

"Yes."

"Did you use your sexual attractiveness to win the confidence of the defendant, Jonathan Small?"

"Yes."

"Were you attracted to him?"

"No."

"Did you use your sexual attractiveness to win the confidence of Lilliana Martin?"

"No."

"No?"

"No."

"What did you use to win Lilliana Martin's confidence?"

"Friendship."

"Friendship."

I nod.

"Do you care about Lilliana Martin?"

"Yes."

"Very much?"

I nod.

"Are you in love with Lilliana Martin?"

"No."

"Do you love her as a friend?"

"Yes. And I love her as extended family, in a way. We've been through a lot."

"Would you care to explain to the jury about your relationship with Ms. Martin while staying at the three-bedroom suite at the Hotel Bernier?"

"No, I wouldn't. It's nobody's business."

"But when the prosecutor asked you if you had any sexual contact with Lilliana Martin while working on the television series, you answered yes."

I don't say anything.

"Did the prosecutor's question upset you?"

"Yes."

"Why?"

"Because he was trying to infer that Lilliana and I had some sort of sexual affair, and the truth is," I say to the jury, "we didn't, we haven't and we won't. She is my friend and I care deeply about her and if that compromises me as a witness in this trial, it's only because the prosecutor has twisted everything around to make me sound like some sort of whore. The truth is, life is complicated, and everyone we've been talking about is single, and I defy anybody in this courtroom to define their every thought, action and statement in terms of it being sexual or not—*ANSWER YES OR NO!*"

I drop my face in my hand. "I'm sorry, Your Honor."

"Attorney Banks, are you just about finished?" the judge asks quietly.

Wearily, I raise my head, blinking back tears. I can't see a damn thing at this point, my head's so cloudy.

"Sally—Ms. Harrington—could you tell the jury why you agreed to testify?"

"Because I believe in our justice system. And if I could help shed some light on what happened, then I wanted to do that."

"Do you think the defendant murdered Nick Arlenetta?"

"I don't know," I say. "That's for the jury to decide."

"When DBS News asked you to work on the series that turned out to be *The Family,* what was your reaction?"

"My first reaction was that I couldn't do it."

"And what changed your mind?"

"My boss, Alexandra Waring."

"How did she change your mind?"

"She pointed out that the more information available about the Presario and Arlenetta families, the more likely justice was to be carried out. And as it stood, very few people understood how far back Nick Arlenetta had been trying—and succeeding—to hurt the Presario family."

"So she convinced you the right thing was to write and produce the series?"

"She convinced me I could do both, and what I learned while working on it wouldn't—and couldn't—affect my testimony about the events that occurred to me."

"For example?"

"How the fact that the Presarios and the Arlenettas used to celebrate Aunt Rose's birthday in the 1950s wouldn't affect the fact I was nearly blown up in Lilliana's house in Bel Air."

"Very good, Ms. Harrington. And I thank you for enduring all that you have in order to testify in this trial."

Judge Kahn turns toward Perez. "Do the People have any further questions of this witness?"

"Yes, Your Honor," Perez says, rising and walking over. "We are all very moved by your declaration of friendship with Lilliana Martin, Ms. Harrington, but you are not amending your testimony, is that correct? You stand by your testimony that you did have sexual contact with Lilliana Martin while staying with her in the Hotel Bernier?"

Overtly disgusted (I hope), I look up at the judge. No help there, though. I look back at the prosecutor. "I am not amending my testimony."

"And you acknowledge that Lilliana Martin's participation in the series made it much better than it would have been otherwise?"

"Yes."

"And you acknowledge receiving a large promotion and salary increase from DBS News because of the television series Lilliana Martin helped you with?"

"Yes."

"Who paid for your airline tickets to come here to testify?"

"The defense attorneys sent them to me."

"So they were paid for by the Presario family."

"I don't know," I say honestly.

"Who is paying your hotel bills?"

"They were sent to the defense counsel's office. I'm no longer in a hotel."

He is tempted to ask me about this, but refrains. He doesn't know the story and doesn't want to risk opening the door to something else.

"Who has been paying for your meals during your stay in California?"

"The defense counsel's firm. With exceptions."

"Very good. Thank you, Ms. Harrington." He nearly skips back to his table. "No further questions, Your Honor."

"Thank you, Ms. Harrington," Judge Kahn says. "You may step down now."

Suddenly, it is over. I am no longer a witness.

CHAPTER | 23

Hazel was instructed to allow me one hour and twenty minutes of rest at Georgiana Hamilton-Ayres's house before preparing me for national TV.

"Alexandra went ahead to the studio in my car," Georgiana informs me from the doorway of my room. "I have been instructed to do your makeup. Alexandra says the lighting is horrendous."

"You mean she said *I* was horrendous and begged you to make something of me before airtime," I say, watching helplessly as Hazel maneuvers a blouse over my cast. I better not get used to this; I *like* someone else making all the decisions about my appearance. (You cannot imagine how Hazel washed my hair. She set up this portable massage table thing, slapped me down on it and wheeled me over the side of the tub.)

When I am dressed, I follow Georgiana through the great room and to the stairs. What I find on the second floor is breathtaking. Her bedroom is huge, with an old four-poster bed. Tremendous windows make up the far wall, looking out over the cliffs, down over the Pacific. From here I can see a rickety wooden staircase leading down to the beach. There are French doors opening onto a small, low-walled terrace, where a table and chairs for two sit. I glance over at the bed (I have to), and fleetingly admire the light and soft-looking linens and pillows. I follow the actress into an adjoining dressing room. Let me tell you about this dressing room. There is a large, well-lit vanity table and at the end of the room is a mahogany wardrobe. (I swear it looks about four hundred years old.) Instead of clothes or linens or something inside the wardrobe, the doors are wide open to reveal three long mirrors and a system of strange-looking lightbulbs to illuminate them. To the left there is an open closet, which has nothing in it but shelves of shoes; to the right there is a much larger walk-in closet—a room, really—of clothes. Long dresses and slacks hang on the left, blouses, blazers, skirts and shorts hang in a double row on the right.

"Have a seat, Sally," she says easily, opening a drawer of the vanity to reveal an array of tools.

I sit on the luxuriously padded bench and wince a little when I see myself in the mirror. I look absolutely horrible, with purple circles under my eyes, a swollen cheek, bruising along my right chinbone and dreadfully chapped lips.

Yech.

"Okay," she says on a slight intake of breath, watching me. "In my profession, we quickly learn how to undo a multitude of sins." She slides her hand around my chin and gently turns my face toward her. She is elegant, regal, and I find her presence a bit unnerving. How can I explain? With Lilliana Martin, you know you're with an actress. As attractive as she is, to me, there is too much—well—*pretend* about her to be, well, alarming, I guess. Lilliana's hair I know is really dark, dark, dark, but is bleached nearly platinum; she grew up in suburban New Jersey in a mob family; and she frankly changes personalities at the drop of a hat. Understand, that is the American Way of self-improvement, to make the most of what you have, and I think that is very attractive.

But Georgiana Hamilton-Ayres has something else. Class. I know her mother was this poor Jewish girl from Brooklyn, and I know her father's Church of Scotland bloodline in Scotland has been inbred too many times over too many generations to avoid producing a lot of kooks, but Georgiana nonetheless possesses a natural air of refinement and polite intelligence, and also a gracious manner that is utterly attractive in anyone.

Alexandra has a version of this aura, too, but her dynamism can be intimidating. I cannot imagine anyone being intimidated by this woman's warmth and kind eyes.

And now those large blue eyes are bent close to mine, looking over the terrain of my face, surveying what needs to be done. They move to meet mine and she smiles, and I feel awkward and shy. She looks down into the drawer, selects some sort of pad and a compact. "I don't know which would be more nerve-racking," she says, reaching for an atomizer and spraying the pad in her hand, "being chased by the Mafia or working for Alexandra." Her eyes crinkle in a laugh as she glances at me, and then she returns her attention to rubbing the damp pad over the compact.

I smile, lifting my eyebrows. "No comment."

She laughs and turns to me, telling me to close my eyes. I feel her hand under my chin, guiding my face. I feel the pad competently sweeping over my face. Pause. The pad comes back to give particular attention to the area under my eyes. "Just keep them closed a moment longer," she says, the touch of the pad disappearing.

I take a breath. I feel strange.

"I gather they gave you a rather difficult time in court today," she says, and I notice again the grace of her accent—you know, the kind that makes you want to speak that way.

"Yes, they did."

"You can open your eyes," she says, and I find her right there, examining my face. I glance down and then look away.

She's looking at me with a slightly puzzled expression. "Are you all right?"

"Yes, I'm fine, thank you. Just a little—" I gesture vaguely. "Airy-fairy."

"Close your eyes then, and I'll just be as quick as I can."

"I appreciate your efforts," I tell her, "but at this point I don't think much can help."

"Nonsense," she says.

NAHN-sense.

"You're a beautiful girl, you've got lots to work with."

A moment too late, I say, "Thank you."

Georgiana laughs and I open my eyes.

"You're a funny kind of a person," the actress tells me. "Close." I do. And she continues, both talking and working on my makeup. "Alexandra thinks the world of you, you know."

"I think pretty highly of her, too."

"She can be a handful, I know. But evidently you can keep up with her, which is more than anyone else has been able to do, not for years." She is holding my chin again, the unbruised side, and I feel eye shadow being applied. "She used to have this wonderful woman working with her, Kate Benedict—"

"I've heard about her," I say.

"She started—"

Stahhhrted.

"As Alexandra's secretary and became a producer. But then she moved on to Paris, to work for ITC." She laughs to herself. "My life became utter hell after that. Alexandra was simply off the wall and went through about nineteen assistant producers." Pause. "Open."

I open my eyes and find hers about ten inches away from mine. She smiles. I swallow.

"What do you know about us?" she asks quietly.

"I know you mean a great deal to her," I say, swallowing again and wishing for a glass of water.

She sighs, reaching for an eyeliner pencil. "It's very difficult, Sally."

"I imagine it is," I say. Thinking what the hell, she brought it up, I add, "I think it's wonderful you guys found each other. I'm not sure many other people in your position could manage it."

"Jessica introduced us. Close. Now, try and hold very still." I feel her tugging my eyelid tight and drawing on it. "Lilliana's rather a mess, isn't she?" she murmurs. "Don't answer that yet, I want to finish." Pause, drawing on me. "The thing is, she's genuinely got talent. And if she ever gets through this unpleasantness, she could have a brilliant career. I think. With or without Jonathan at the studio. Did you see that last movie she made?"

"Yes."

"She deserved that Oscar nomination. She was remarkably good." Pause. "Okay," she says, touching my shoulder. "Relax."

I open my eyes and watch her sort through blushes, holding up various containers against my complexion.

"Alexandra thinks she really fell for you," she says matter-of-factly, glancing at me for a reaction.

"I think she's just very lonely and—" I can't help but smile. "And I think Lilliana has a very high libido and pretty much considers anything—or any*one*—who happens to be handy."

"You underestimate yourself," Georgiana tells me.

Wordlessly now, Georgiana proceeds to brush on blush in the hollows of my cheeks, on the end of my chin, on my temples and—yes—even on the end of my nose! When she's finished, she urges me to look and I am amazed at the illusion. I look really, really good. She brings out a tray of lipsticks and a small brush and hands them to me. "You can do this part," she says, but when she sees my bandages, she makes a small sound and takes them back. She turns my head toward her with her pinkie and begins painting my mouth. Concentrating on layering a second color on my lips, Georgiana says, "Are you in love with Alexandra?"

"Good heavens, no," I blurt out, making the brush skid off my mouth and onto my cheek.

She looks at me, a little surprised.

"And I'm shocked you would ask such a thing," I add. "I admire her enormously—I can't tell you how much—

and I feel intensely loyal to her—personally and professionally. But golly, no, no way."

"Most everyone does fall in love with her, you know that," she says quietly, reaching for a cotton ball and dabbing at the lipstick smear. "Hold still." She finishes what's she doing and lowers her hand to hear my response.

"Oh, I know," I assure her. "You see people around Alexandra, they're like gaga."

"Exactly."

"I imagine you have the same problem," I say. "That everyone falls in love with you."

She genuinely laughs. "Oh, my." She colors slightly, backing away.

Good, finally she's embarrassed.

Sitting back now, she studies me a moment. "I only learned about her breast cancer last night. And I thank you from the bottom of my heart for being there for her." Her eyes well up slightly. "I only wish I had known." She turns away abruptly, starting to put things away. "And the other... I'm sorry I asked about—well, when she told me you helped her, I wondered..." She looks at me helplessly. And sadly.

"I don't know if this helps," I say quietly, "but the woman I saw here this morning—the Alexandra who came to breakfast—is a woman I've never seen before." There is a flicker of something in Georgiana's eyes.

"She's obviously so very happy when she's with you," I continue. "The transformation in her is unreal." I smile. "Oh, yeah, she's always Alexandra Waring, you know how that goes—old Alexandra Eyes, sweeping into the studio, mesmerizing America, educating the masses, expanding the horizons of narrow-minded jackasses everywhere—"

The actress starts to laugh and I feel relieved.

I lower my voice. "But until I saw her with you, Georgiana, I had no idea how dreadfully unhappy she's been. And I mean it, the woman I saw this morning is a woman I've never seen before."

She sighs, looking down at the ground. Then she shyly looks back up at me. "Thank you."

I smile a little. "Go for it," I tell her.

CHAPTER | 24

I am delivered to the Burbank studio in time to make the news. Alexandra is already on the air and I am led silently across the studio floor to a second set, arranged for a two-person interview. Some guy I've never seen in all my life is sitting in the seat across from me, leaning forward to shake my hand and thank me for coming, as if I am the stranger.

He is getting miked. He is around forty and has those boyish good looks NBC news anchor Brian Williams has made popular. For the life of me, I don't know who he is.

"Hey, kid, how are you?" a voice I recognize whispers from behind me. I turn around as Will Rafferty squats down next to my chair.

"Hi," I whisper. "When did you get here?"

"Today," he whispers back. "So listen, we've got

changes." He glances over at the main set, where Alexandra is reading a story and back to me. "We're keeping you here in L.A. for the rest of the trial. You're going to be working on something we're calling *DBS Late Edition,* a half-hour recap of the trial with this guy—" his eyes indicate the Brian Williams look-alike "—Emmett Phelps—"

"I thought guys named Emmett played dominoes at the general store," I whisper.

Will smiles. "Alexandra dug him up out of some law school. Supposedly he's pretty good, although I've never seen him. You just rehash the trial every night for a half hour with this guy until it's over."

"You mean I'm on-air talent?" I say, thinking of the union clauses this activates in my contract and the new money that will be flowing in my direction.

"Starting tomorrow," he says. "But tonight you're just an interviewee." He looks at his watch. "Emmett's going to do a quick interview with you during the newscast as a promo." He waddles over on his haunches between the two chairs and motions for Emmett to lean forward. Will whispers an introduction between us and then waddles off our little set.

"Okay, now, don't be nervous," the law school professor tells me, his voice aquiver. "I will ask you a question and you just look at me and answer it, okay?"

I realize he has little or no clue as to what he is doing, but is simply repeating the instructions given to him. More than that, I don't think he understands I work at DBS News.

"Now, don't be nervous," he says again with false bravado, his papers sliding off his lap into a mess on the floor. As he drops to the floor with a thump, scrambling to pick them up, I slide down next to him and gently place my bandaged right hand over his. He looks at me with startled eyes behind those glasses. "Focus only on what you, personally, want to ask me," I tell him. "What you want to know about the trial today. If you forget something, don't worry, I will remember and fit it in. What's our time on this segment?"

"Four minutes, um—something..."

"Four minutes ten," I tell him, quoting our usual segment length.

He squints at me. "Are you...?"

"Yeah," I tell him, "one of us. I'm the one who works for Alexandra. I'm a producer. This is what I do for a living, helping you guys do this stuff."

Immediately his face brightens. "Oh!"

"I think this was kind of hastily put together," I whisper to him confidentially, guiding him back up into his chair and straightening his tie. "Pull the back of your jacket down and try not to move your hands, okay?" When he complies, I add, "Let me look at you."

I look around the studio and motion to a production assistant to come over. "His mike should be lower, and aim it up. I can't do it myself," I explain, showing my bandages.

The newscast has cut to a commercial and Alexandra yells across the studio, "Sally, Emmett teaches criminal law at UCLA and will be covering the rest of the trial with you."

"Great," I yell back. As the assistant fixes his microphone, I watch Emmett's nervous fidgets, listen to his series of terrified little sighs (gasps for breath?) and decide I better get him talking, engage his attention.

"I went to UCLA," I whisper.

"Really? What degree?"

"Bachelor's. Dual. Journalism and English."

The floor manager sails over. "We're coming to you in three on two."

"Three minutes," I translate to Emmett, "and on the second camera over there. The second and third one will be moving over here in a minute." I smile. "So how long have you taught there?"

"Um..." he says nervously, almost dropping his papers again.

"Get rid of those," I tell him. "You've got your intro and questions on the monitor there, right?"

"Right," he says, closing his eyes a moment.

"Get rid of them!" I whisper.

He swallows and leans over to toss the papers. Then he sits back up, looking at me. Perspiration has started to appear on his forehead. I get up and carefully blot his forehead with my bandages. Then I linger a moment, smiling down at him, lean close to his ear and whisper, "You will be fantastic. You just have to talk to me as if we're in front of the class, and you've brought me in to use as an example. Forget the camera, forget everything but me and the class."

I withdraw and sit down. "Do you have a class tomorrow?"

He nods.

"Show the tape of tonight to them."

Immediately (finally!) I see in his eyes that he is thinking.

"One minute," the floor manager signals.

I use my bandaged hand to straighten my clothes, smooth my hair. Emmett's looking at me. "Maybe we can bring some of your better students to the studio one night," I whisper.

Again, the flicker in his eyes that he has forgotten to be terrified.

Very faintly we can hear Alexandra starting into the segment introduction. I don't dare say anything at this point, for the sound on our microphones has surely been brought up. Two cameras have dollied over to our set and now the floor manager has arrived, kneeling under the lens of the camera focused over my right shoulder on Emmett. The floor manager signals five, four, three, two, one and then he points at Emmett.

"Thank you, Alexandra," Emmett says, his voice strained. There is an awkward moment as he swallows and clears his throat.

Come on, Emmett, speak! I scream in my mind as his vacant eyes stare at me.

"Sally Harrington..." he begins. And ends.

I don't know what Emmett's problem is, but I do know that TV is comprised of both sight and sound, so I laugh and say, "I can't tell you how many times in the last few days, Emmett, how I've wished I was anyone else *but* Sally Harrington!"

He looks startled, knowing this is not on any of those notes, but it doesn't matter because the camera is now on me.

"And I'll tell you something," I say, slightly raising my bandaged hand, "I was this close to punching the lights out on that prosecutor today. He was absolutely outrageous and out of line. But as you know, Emmett, witnesses don't have any power over how they're handled on the stand. I feel like I got slandered today, and there's not a darn thing I can do about it. Except talk to you."

"Yes, well, we should explain to people," Emmett says, "that you are an employee of DBS News—"

No, Emmett, we should not be wasting the time on that now! I scream in my mind.

"It doesn't matter who I am employed by," I say. "This is a major murder trial, being covered by every media outlet in the country, and the prosecutor this morning tried to paint a portrait of me as a woman who has sex, sex, sex and more sex with just about anybody who crosses her path."

So there! Just try and turn to another channel after that!

"It is true," Emmett says in a much more impressive voice, "that a witness is dependent upon the questions being asked by the attorneys. The redirect was rather effective, though, I thought. Lawrence Banks dispelled the image created by Prosecutor Perez that you are a—" He actually smiles.

"I have a great deal to say about Prosecutor Perez," I interrupt. "And also about the defense team, and what it's like to be in that courthouse, to be a part of that trial. And I assure you, it is unlike anything you've ever heard or seen before."

And so Emmett and I go, promising the world in our little promo interview, and, I think, why not? I am at liberty, finally, to say what I wish.

"Good job," Will Rafferty whispers to us on the little set when our four-minute-ten-second interview is over. "Don't move," he adds to Emmett, "you're on again in twelve minutes."

"I've got to go to the bathroom," he declares.

"Okay," Will concedes, helping him with his mike. When Emmett leaves, Will slides into his chair and leans toward me. "You got him through it, but don't screw around with the order of the questions on *Late Edition,* okay? Because we've got a lot of cutaways and tape to squeeze in."

"Will, he is immobilized. All those notes have him brain dead."

"I think he'll be okay on this. What he is to ask you is very straightforward." He grins. "We can't talk about your sex life forever."

"Everybody else is."

"Leave the air of mystery, then," Will says. "We need to talk about other things. *Legal* things."

"Yeah, yeah, yeah," I say, getting it. Make Emmett teach law in words people can understand.

"Tonight, you're the guest," Will whispers. "Tomorrow you're top billing on *DBS Late Edition.* Well, after Alexandra, I mean."

I smile.

Emmett returns to the set with water stains on his tie. I help him button his jacket to hide them, and then we have all of three minutes before we are on the air.

It's really cool.

CHAPTER | 25

After the debut of *DBS Late Edition*, I take a short nap in the car while Louis drives me across the valley to Encino where Paul has an apartment. The building is like countless Southern California complexes (and not unlike the one I myself lived in before moving back East): two floors of painted modular concrete and wood surrounding an inner courtyard of pretty gardens and a large pool where, at the moment, some sort of a makeshift luau is occurring. The mob of young people are wearing Hawaiian shirts and plastic leis—a couple of girls are wearing grass skirts and bikini tops—but there is no sand or food or ukuleles. They're listening to 'N Sync and drinking some sort of punch, which is currently being stirred in a large galvanized garbage can with a baseball bat.

I discreetly make my way on the edge of the party, smil-

ing politely as I struggle to get jostled on my relatively un-
injured side, but staring straight ahead to discourage anyone from talking to me. A short time later I'm in front of
apartment 21. I knock and the door quickly opens to reveal a smiling kid of about twenty-two (listen to me, like
I'm sixty-five), with startling blond hair, a rich tan and a
lot of very white teeth. He's wearing baggy denims and a
Buffalo Bills T-shirt. "You Sally?" he asks.

I smile, tempted to reply "Me Jane." But I say, "Yes, hi,"
instead and I show him my bandaged hand as a way of
apology for not extending it toward him.

"I'm Jack." He backs up quickly, pushing the door back
wider for me to come in. "Paul just got out of the bathtub. I
got him out of the hospital and all he wanted was to get clean,
so I had to wrap him up in plastic like a sandwich." He glances
at the hallway and adds in a whisper, "He's kind of a wreck.
And, like, he broke out of there? They wanted him to stay."

"I don't blame him," I say, walking in. "Hospitals are no
fun."

The living room is utter chaos. There is furniture here
somewhere, but clothes, magazines, books and sporting
equipment have clearly taken precedence. Jack flings a
beach towel, a couple of issues of *Sports Illustrated,* a
football and a dozen CD cases off a chair to make a space
for me. The TV is on, tuned to ESPN 2. A firefighter's com-
petition is going on, the one where they carry bags of sand
over their shoulders and run up six flights of stairs.

"You want a beer or something?" Jack asks, standing
there with his hands in his back pockets, rocking back
slightly on his bare heels.

"Oh, I couldn't possibly," I say. "I'm just barely upright
as it is."

He squints a little. "That accident really fucked you guys up."

"Hmm," I say in agreement, sitting on the chair and looking around. This place really is a mess. Not dirty, though, just messy. (A tremendous distinction in my book.)

Jack disappears into the kitchen and comes back, popping the top on a can of Budweiser. He sits on the arm of the other chair—buried under what looks to be piles of unfolded clean laundry—and smiles again. "So you're like a news—like a news *person*," he says, sipping his beer.

"Yeah," I acknowledge. "What kind of work do you do?"

"Oh, I'm a bum," he says good-naturedly. "I mean I work and everything—I'm doing construction right now. But my dad says I'm a bum." He sips his beer again and shrugs. "I've got an architecture degree from Cornell, but like—" He shrugs again. "Designing ventilating shafts in office buildings doesn't get me off, you know?"

"Might you do residential work?"

"Might," he says, grinning, "but I better start out somewhere other than L.A., you know? It's like the toughest market."

I smile. "You're not from here, are you?" *If you were,* I would add, *your parents would have found you something, somewhere.*

"Hell, no. I'm from Watertown. New York. You know, the place that disappears under the snow for four months and then reappears magically in the spring?"

I laugh. It's true, what he says.

"Sally?" Paul's voice asks. A moment later his head appears around the corner of the hallway.

"It's me," I tell him.

He smiles, eyes tired but warm. "Hi." He looks at Jack. "You could have told me she was here."

Jack's eyes are on the TV show now. "I was going to."

"I'm not dressed," he says with a slight flush. He steps out to reveal he is wrapped in a towel, and, as Jack said, his right side is wrapped up like a sandwich in plastic wrap. He has a nice body. Very nice. Fit. Muscular. Of course, most active twenty-five-year-old men do. Nice shoulders, not a lot of hair on his chest—but enough—and great thighs (I wonder if he skis). He makes an apologetic face. "I can't get out of this," he says, looking down at the plastic stuff. "Jack."

I sneak a look at Paul again while he's trying to get his roommate's attention. He is *so* appealing. He is also very banged up. His elbows and shoulder and side of his face are all scraped up and must hurt terribly, to say nothing of his arm.

Paul looks back at me and I swiftly bring my eyes up. "It's all packaging tape," he explains, gesturing to his arm. "I'm ready to be mailed." He looks at his roommate again. "Jack!"

"Coming," he mutters, taking a swig of his beer and finding a space on the coffee table to put it down.

"Give me five minutes," Paul says.

"You guys are kinda like a matched set," Jack observes, glancing at my sling and cast.

"It's all his crap," Paul says later, referring to the living room, as we sit at the table for two in the surprisingly orderly kitchen. "But he pays seven hundred and I pay five, so I let him throw his stuff all over in there."

I snip his hospital band off his wrist with scissors. "So you're an orderly kind of guy?"

"I'm the kind of guy who doesn't want to scare a girl away the first time she comes over," he says easily, smiling. Earlier I assisted in cutting up an old shirt to accommodate his cast.

My heart feels warm and I feel wonderful. I'm beginning to think Paul is for real and I should pay attention to how this might work. Of course, I am in shock and on drugs, as he is as well.

A cop. Me and a cop. Huh. He doesn't look like a cop. He looks like the president of an Ivy League frat house.

I hold up the band. "Do you want this?"

"Hell, no," he says, sounding like Jack. (I wonder which one picked it up from the other.) He plucks the band out of my hand and tries to toss it to the garbage, but freezes midaction, gasping for breath.

"Oh, no, I'm sorry," I say, feeling useless.

He grimaces, lowering his head and sucking in his breath between his teeth. "Man, how could this be so painful?" His eyes sweep miserably over to me. "I've got enough painkillers in me to knock out a horse."

"It was major surgery," I remind him. "I'm surprised they let you out."

"They didn't want to, but I was climbing the walls." His eyes settle onto mine and he smiles a little, moving his hand to touch mine for a moment. "I can't believe you're here. You've got to be wiped out."

"I am," I say softly, smiling back.

"So you were on TV tonight?"

"Uh-huh." I smile. "I don't usually wear this much makeup."

"You look beautiful. You always do," he says. His eyes trail down to my mouth for a moment and linger there. They come back up. "Would you like some more coffee?" he says quietly, reaching over to touch the back of my bandaged hand.

I meet his eyes, smiling, wanting him to read my mind. His eyes are gentle brown, with flecks of, what, green or hazel? He shaved today, but he has a five-o'clock shadow. I have the overwhelming urge to run my hand over his face, to see just how scratchy it is. I glance down at his mouth a moment and then back up. "No, thanks."

"Jack!" Paul suddenly calls out, startling me. In a moment, Jack appears. "I know it's a pain, but do you think you could go get that prescription for me?"

Jack looks at me. "He gets one night of me being nice to him," he explains. But then he frowns at Paul, suppressing a burp and tapping his diaphragm with his hand, as if debating whether or not this request is too much. He glances at me again, has an idea of something, because he says, "Yeah, I get it, all right," and shoves off into the living room. There is the jangle of car keys.

"Do you need some money?" Paul calls.

"It's just the ten dollars co-pay, right?"

"Yeah."

"No, I've got that money left over from today."

We hear the door close and I smile to myself, looking down at the table at my coffee mug. Paul scoots his chair closer, trying to hold my hand. It's awkward. So he just looks at me, and I look at him, and he looks down at my mouth and leans forward to kiss me softly. Very softly. He drops his face to nuzzle my neck briefly, with his lips. I kiss his ear and he makes a quiet sound deep in his throat, maneuvering his ear closer to my mouth. So I kiss it again, rubbing my mouth over it lightly. He likes this and offers quiet sighs of satisfaction. Then, suddenly, he pulls back. "I want you so much," he whispers.

I smile, swallowing.

He brings his hand up to touch my lips, the side of my face. And then he holds the side of my face in his warm palm, simply looking at me, his thumb gently stroking my cheek. He lowers his eyes, shaking his head. Then he lowers his hand to his lap. "I'm not rushing it, damn it. I'm not doing what every part of my body is screaming to do." He glances up, his expression tense, as if in pain.

He might well be in pain, for he is sitting on the edge of his chair, his newly operated elbow twisted to the side, his lower body caved in around my chair, as if he is trying to take me and the chair into his possession.

I am, down below, frankly a mess. This guy just looks at me now and something happens. I wish Paul hadn't said what he just did, because it only makes my mind frantic with speculative directives, like, *Right here, Right now. On my back on this table in about ten seconds.*

I take a deep breath and let it out.

"No," Paul whispers to himself, hoarse, heaving himself out of the chair—swearing at the pain it causes as he pivots and moves into the living room. I look at those hard buttocks outlined in those khakis and have no trouble at all imagining...

I can talk him out of this virtuous state of mind. Easily. All I have to do is go in there and press myself against him in a certain way to let him know that he will not only be forgiven for his lapse in gentlemanly conduct, but will be most enthusiastically and lasciviously rewarded—if he would only lapse right now, quickly, before Jack returns.

There is no future with a twenty-five-year-old cop who lives in L.A., I tell myself. *So why not just do it! Let's just do it in every blessed room!* I stand up and follow him into the living room, where he has taken refuge behind the laundry-laden chair. He keeps the chair between us, either as a blockade or as a screen for the state of his pants, which he doesn't realize was already noted in the kitchen.

"I can't do this," he says with such force and earnestness, I am stopped in my tracks.

"You don't want to?"

"No, no, that's not it," he says, absently touching his cast.

"You can't do this because I'm broken and you're cut in half?" I joke.

He's not buying it. He looks pretty upset, as a matter of fact. "Sally," he begins, struggling for the words. Then he shakes his head, looking away.

I walk over and turn off the TV set. Then I come over to stand on the other side of the chair, to be nearer to him without violating his space.

"If I try to have sex with you now," he tells me, "it means I believe what's been said about you. And I don't," he hastens to add.

He's got my attention. I feel my back stiffening. "You don't believe what?"

"The stories," he says.

I meet his eyes. What was, only a moment ago, warmth between my legs, now is only a damp, uncomfortable nuisance. "And what exactly is it that you don't believe? Or don't want to believe?"

If he could shrug, I'm sure he would. "I don't know," he says vaguely, looking around. Then his eyes come back to mine. "You know, that you're—" He looks miserably around the room. "I don't know, they made it sound like you, you know, enjoy sex."

"I do," I say clearly.

Now he looks afraid of me.

"But no," I say over my shoulder while I walk back to the kitchen, "I'm not an indiscriminate whore. Or maybe you think men like you are a dime a dozen, Paul. Bright, educated, has work that is meaningful to him, good-looking, *straight* and single." I rinse out my coffee cup, fill it with water and take a painkiller. I drink some more water and walk back into the living room. Paul hasn't moved. I feel overwhelmingly depressed now. Hopeless. "What happened when I met you is not a habit," I say.

He doesn't answer, but bites his lip and nods.

God. Look at what I nearly did with him at the hotel. A cop in uniform. Look at what I wanted to do right there on the kitchen table moments ago.

"The trial today," he finally says.

I wait, but he doesn't say anything more. Clearly he is upset, but just as clearly it is evident that talking about things like this is not his strong point. Of course, he is twenty-five.

I scratch my forehead with my bandages and wish I could just die right here and now. Or kill him. Because I hate Paul now, I really hate him. Kid. Jerk. Nearly killed me on a motorcycle. Screw him.

"So let me get this straight," I say icily. "You don't want to make love with me because if you do, you'll know for sure I'm a whore?"

"Sally," he begins.

"Forget it," I say, walking toward the door. "Just forget it, Paul. Let's call it a day and count our blessings it turned out the way it did."

"Sally," he says more loudly. "Wait." He comes over to stand next to me by the door. We are a pair, all right, with these casts, bandages and injuries. "Be in my shoes for a minute," he pleads. "I meet this sensational woman and when I felt something between us, I thought, well okay, this is a once-in-a-lifetime opportunity— But in your hotel room I knew it was wrong, almost immediately. Don't you remember?"

I don't say anything.

"Because I already knew it was a lot more than just the sexual thing. And I'm not minimizing that, God no. You are the most attractive woman I've ever met."

If he says it was love at first sight I'm leaving.

"That's why I stopped and I asked you to have dinner with me." When I only stare at him stonily he adds, "I wanted to know you."

"Right," I say

"Yes!" he declares. "That is right. I know you have to go back to New York. The easiest thing in the world would have been to just— You know, just do it and split."

So romantic.

"After that one dinner we had," he continues, "I finally broke up with my girlfriend once and for all. Because— well, it was the right thing to do." He points to himself with his good hand. "I knew, already, Sally, that something special was happening between us. I don't care if you have to go back to New York. Somehow or some way, I have to follow this through, to find out what this is between us." He moves forward, touching my good arm. "After meeting you, I knew something was happening. I've never felt this way about a woman I just met."

I look at him doubtfully. This all sounds pretty good. One wonders, though, how much practice he's had in patching up arguments like this. Pretty smooth for twenty-five.

"Let me ask you something, Paul," I say in a confidential tone of voice. "Are you going to try and tell me I am the first woman you've seduced while wearing your uniform?" I pause, watching his face carefully, and his reaction pretty much confirms what I suspected.

"I was off duty when I came up to your room," he says.

"An important distinction in your mind, I'm sure."

A glint of anger appears in his eyes. "What are you accusing me of?"

"I'm not accusing you of anything. I'm just admiring your style, which to me seems very well practiced. The ride in the squad car, your attentiveness—"

"That's not—"

"Oh, Paul, don't give me that bull," I say angrily. "I know a swordsman when I see one. You've probably used that uniform to seduce half the women in the county."

"Sally!" he protests, but if you could see his expression, I think you'd agree with me that I'm right, I've guessed correctly. This could be the Don Juan of the Santa Monica Police Department. The term "swordsman" has pleased him in some way, I know, for the anger has vanished from his eyes. (Paul needn't know I used to be stupid about such things—like swordsmen—until I met Spencer Hawes and learned firsthand how easily he could seduce women and how sincere he always was in an effort to please while he did. All of them.)

"I'm thirty-one years old," I tell him, "and I have slept with three men in my entire life. I dare you to tell me how many women you've slept with in just the last two years."

He blinks, unsure of how to respond. Finally he says, "The trial today, the testimony."

"What about it?"

"It just makes it harder to bring you home to my mother, you know?"

I do know.

"So that's why it came up, Sally. I just don't—didn't—see how we could go on if I didn't know what I needed to pave the way for." He looks at me. "It's none of my business what you've done in your past. It's the public part, the statements made in court today." He pauses, swallowing. "I don't want to hurt your feelings, Sally. I don't want to wreck my chances. But I had to ask so I could satisfy people's questions without compromising you. Or us," he adds in a rush, looking vaguely panicked.

"Well," I say, "I don't know what else to tell you than what I have already."

He is waiting for something else, but I don't know what. And then I remember, of course, Lilliana Martin, that whole thing today. "Oh," I say. "I know what you're wondering about. Well, not to worry, I'm not that way. No, I didn't do anything with Lilliana Martin."

He looks at me.

"I didn't," I say.

"It wouldn't matter to me if you did," he says. "And it's none of my business."

"I know how it sounded," I say, "and that's why the prosecutor made sure to present it the way he did."

Paul sighs. "I'm sorry. This is just awful. I've really messed this up."

"The trial's messed this up," I say. I raise one eyebrow. "But since I've told you about the three men in my life, I think you should answer my question. How many women have you slept with in the past two years?"

Paul drops his head, shaking it. "Don't do this, Sally."

"I've already done it, Paul," I say. "I told you the truth. And now you can tell me the truth. So I have some idea of what I'm getting into."

He doesn't say anything.

"Okay, just one year," I say. "In the last year. Since last November. Let's see, there's the girlfriend."

"Ex."

"The ex-girlfriend."

He looks at me, sighing. He looks off to the living room and then looks back at me. "Three." He blinks. "Four."

"Four," I repeat.

He nods.

"You've slept with four women in one year and you're worried about my sexual past?"

He sighs heavily, shifting his weight to one leg and looking at me gunslinger style, as if to size me up before shooting me.

"I'm sorry," I say, meaning it. Doug used to complain about this, my insistence on talking about things, but then how I would lose my temper, take whatever he had just told me and use it as a weapon against him in the next breath. "Truly," I say, edging a little closer to Paul as a means of apology.

"Oh, man, Sally," he sighs, trying to put an arm around me, "we're not going to be easy, are we?"

I let my head sink down to rest on his good shoulder. "Four women," I murmur admiringly.

"You're not going to hammer me with that forevermore, are you?"

"Well, I don't know," I say, raising my head to look at him. I do know we need to have a long and thorough discussion about sexually transmitted diseases and the fact that I do not have any. And don't want any.

Paul and I end up kissing, and while I feel pleasured, I no longer feel that sexual urge. Interesting...

I am tired suddenly and feeling a little light-headed. I pull away gently, murmuring that I've got to go, I have Alexandra's car and driver.

"Can I see you tomorrow?" he asks.

"I start covering the trial tomorrow, and then I have a half-hour program I have to do tomorrow night." I shake my head. "I don't think it's a good idea, Paul."

"Does that mean a definite no? Or does that mean if I can get a ride to the station, we could have an ice-cream cone or something after? I'd give you a ride home, but I'm not supposed to drive for a week."

"No one's supposed to know where I'm staying," I remind him.

"Hmm." His eyes are studying my injured cheek. "They're tracking that car down, you know."

"The one that hit us?"

"Yeah."

"Good." His eyes come back to me. "It wasn't an accident, was it?" I ask him.

He shakes his head. "Doesn't look like it."

"I'm sorry, Paul, to have dragged you into this."

"I just want you to be careful," he says, moving closer.

We kiss again and this time it feels terrific. We kiss like we've known each other a lot longer. (Of course, with all his practice! *Stop it!*)

"I'll walk you to the car," he says when we finally stop. He opens the door and we find Louis standing in the doorway.

"Hi," he says, looking back and forth between us and then settling on me. "Sorry, but I'm supposed to keep an eye on you."

I turn to Paul. "You don't have to come out. I think you really need to get to bed."

"Sleep well," he says, kissing me briefly. Then he whispers in my ear, "Be careful." And with a soft, quiet kiss on my ear, backs away.

Four women in one year, I think.

CHAPTER | 26

Nobody is around when I get up the next morning, which is to say, most important, my friend Hazel. I take the bandages off of my right hand and limp along, washing my own hair in the tub. My hand is tender and I spend half my time freezing in place, wincing as I've done something wrong, but I persevere and get somewhat clean.

I'm tired and achy but very excited, for today I go back to that courthouse as an observer, not a witness. Today I am a professional again. I choose slacks, a loose blouse and a blazer that can hang over my shoulders as if I'm sort of a 1940s movie star.

I walk into the kitchen, looking nervously about this eerily quiet house. I'm pretty sure no one is here, but hell if I'm going upstairs to make sure. It's eight o'clock, they should be up. I pour myself a glass of fresh squeezed orange juice and walk to the front door to look out. No car. Nobody.

I feel the urge to do something bad, like I did the very first time my mother trusted me to be home alone. (I helped myself to a cookie and practiced cartwheels in the living room.)

I retrieve my cell phone, attach the headset and stick the phone in my slacks pocket to free up my one useful hand. "Will cell," I tell the phone, letting it select and dial Will's cell phone number from the roster. In a minute he picks up. "Hi, it's your slighted folded, spindled and mutilated co-anchor of *DBS Late Edition* calling," I tell him, finding a box of raisin-bran-banana-crunch cereal that appeals to me.

"It wasn't too bad," Will says generously.

"Emmett needs a little—something," I say. "Maybe Xanax laced with Valium."

Will chuckles. "Well, he was a little uptight, but it looked good on camera. He's supposed to balance your, shall we say, more bohemian appearance."

"You don't know the half of it. You should see me this morning. Nobody's around to pull me together, so tell the boys on the courthouse camera not to close in too tight."

"Did you get your press pass?"

"Yes," I say, fingering the large plastic badge dangling from a string around my neck. It has my picture on it and my name in bold type. "I'm just not sure how I'm supposed to get to the courthouse. I can take a cab—"

Yawning, Will says, "Where is herself?" he asks, referring to Alexandra.

"I don't know."

He yawns again.

"Are you still in bed?"

"Uh-huh."

"Shouldn't you be up and slaving away at something?"

"Soon enough, soon enough."

I find a bowl and look for milk in the refrigerator. It's 1%. Okay. "Listen, Will, Alexandra told me about—well, about your very happy news. About you and Jessica."

"Thank you. We're pretty excited."

I bring the milk to the counter, not pouring it yet. "And she told me about your idea, about me trying to substitute."

Pause. "She did?"

"Yes. And I just wanted to thank you for thinking of me," and as I say that, I think, *Thank him for wanting me out of the news division?*

"There's a distinct personality type that does well in talk shows," Will says. "And Jessica thinks you could be good. I tend to agree with her. That's not to say," he hastens to add, "you're not doing a fine job for us in the news division. We just thought you should have a stab at it. I mean," he quickly adds, "not that Alexandra doesn't want you to."

"She doesn't," I say flatly. We both laugh.

"She has sort of blocked you from even trying," Will confesses. A moment of silence. Then Will says, "Unless you felt very strongly. I think if the request came from you directly, Sally, she'd let you do it."

Oh, yeah, she'd let me do it. Nine chances out of ten, though, it wouldn't work and I would be out of a job. Still, the appeal of a talk show is vast. There are long hours, but at least they're regular, and the bulk of the host's job is preparation and simply educating oneself on the topic and the larger American landscape as a whole, which is what I've done all my life, anyway.

Jessica Wright is a most distinct on-air personality, though. Make no bones about it, she is why people watch. They know what she's up to, about her marriage, her past problems with drinking, her struggle to get pregnant, who her family and friends are. When Jessica strides out on stage in her trademark cowgirl boots and skirt, people's faces light up with recognition and affection. She belongs to them.

Could I play such a role?

I don't know.

But think of it! Regular hours. A kazillion-dollar raise. The power to talk to just about anyone in the world. But what would be my trademark? Every host has something physical about them that is a trademark of sorts. Perhaps my boarding school do? Do you suppose I could transform America's women into wearing their hair like mine? (Like never!)

I think my first guest would have to be Mother, because she would convince everyone that I'm lovable. And then I guess we could do a bunch of shows about ill-fated romantic relationships or something and I could carry on about my exes. And then we could do childhood traumas, death of a parent, and I could just boo-hoo in front of four million people about Daddy.

Hmm. I don't know.

"Is that why she gave me this assignment, to cover the trial on the *Late Edition?*"

"I gave you this assignment," he tells me.

I consider this, pulling kitchen drawers out in search of a spoon. "Well, thanks."

"You're welcome," he says. "Look, Sally, Alexandra and I have a few things we need to work out and you're one of them. The news division has grown so much, so fast, we desperately need restructuring, we both agree on that."

"I've been going over the organizational charts. She gave them to me and asked me to prepare a report of recommendations."

"Have you done it?"

"I need to fine-tune it before I let it go." Which is my fallback line meaning, No, I haven't, give me some guidelines, Will.

"Understand, Sally, that you're a central player in it. The question is, are you production, on-air or executive administration?"

"Executive administration?" I say, openly astonished. "Who the hell would want to be that?"

He laughs. "Well, you might. I need two of me and Alexandra is way overextended, so there's a whole executive position there. Our guys like you, Sally, and they respect you. You've only been here a short while, but you've demonstrated a real talent in motivating people we haven't seen move in months." He pauses. "And I shouldn't be telling you this, but your contract is up in May and I'm personally afraid we might lose you. That's why I pushed for the talk show. We might as well find out how you'd do before you move on."

I am frowning, looking out the window at the ocean. "Move on to where?"

He laughs. "Sally, when was the last time you talked to your agent?"

"I don't know, a while."

"I think you better talk to him. Things in the marketplace concerning you have changed a lot in the past few days."

"Oh, yeah?" I say, feeling pleased.

"Oh, yeah," he confirms.

"Okay, well, I hear you," I say, looking at the clock. "I've got to get moving." I pause. "Will? Thanks for thinking of me. You and Jessica. The thing is, a move like that would pretty much shut me out of hard news forever."

"That's a major point to consider," he agrees. "It's just—well, it's hard not to think of you in this circumstance. Jessica's instincts are pretty good, and, uh, well, I've been pretty pissed off at Alexandra for not at least giving you the option of trying. But at least she told you about it, that's something."

"And she told me she blocked it."

"Okay then, we're all on the same page. That's all I've asked of her."

"Will? Is this why you and I have been, well, kind of funny lately?"

"Sally, I've been not so funny with everybody for months," he confesses. "I've been worried sick about Jessica and I want her out of there as soon as possible. It's not going to be an easy pregnancy, and it will just crush her if she loses the baby." Pause. "Again."

So that's it. Miscarriage. Well, this is clearing up a lot of confusion for me.

I hear the front door open. "Sally?" Georgiana Hamilton-Ayres's voice calls out.

"I'm in the kitchen! Will? I gotta go."

"Good luck today," he tells me.

"Oh, look, you're all dressed," Georgiana says as I disconnect the phone and take the earphone off. "Do you want me to do your makeup?"

"No thanks, I'm not on camera today. Not until tonight. So where's Alexandra?"

"I just took her to the airport. She's flying back to New York." She gestures toward the front door. "Louis is waiting to take you to the courthouse."

We stand there awkwardly for a moment. "Is everything okay?" I venture to ask.

"Yes, I suppose so," the actress says unconvincingly, turning away.

"Can I help?" I blurt out.

She turns around, a slight flush in her high cheekbones. She smiles a sad smile. "I wish you could." She turns away, trudging dejectedly down the stairs into the great room. She turns around. "I have this house, she has her farm, we both have apartments in Manhattan, we don't own a blessed thing together. Damn this world," she says, walking over to fling open the French doors.

I look at my watch. I have GOT to go. But—

I follow Georgiana outside. The wind has picked up, blowing Georgiana's hair everywhere. I wonder *What is wrong with Alexandra? Why is she making this woman so unhappy?*

Georgiana glances back at me. "Sorry, Sally."

Sawrry.

"This is what broke us up in the first place, this inability to have some kind of home that is *ours.*

"It is the whole DBS dependency on her." She swallows, looking out at the water. "And now Jessica—" She looks over at me.

"I know about Jessica."

"*She's* going to be free, so Alexandra feels more bound than ever. That damnable network is going to drive me mad." Georgiana turns around, resting her hands back on the railing. "I'm open for suggestions."

Since I don't really know what she is talking about, it's kind of hard for me to say anything. "Do you want to live together? Is that the problem?"

"She wants me at the farm," Georgiana says, "which is fine, I suppose, if you enjoy talking to animals and tenant farmers—which as it happens I do, but—" She smiles a little. "I mean, honestly, Sally, if you love someone, and you want to live with them, who the bloody hell cares what anyone thinks?"

"The network cares," I say honestly. "And movie producers care."

"I want to have a child," she suddenly declares. "There, I said it. A child, a baby—as if no one has ever heard of one before—and Alexandra's brother agreed to be the father. But Cassy, Cassy, dear Cassy, of course Cassy was terribly upset and so Alexandra backed off." She looks at me. "That's why I left her." She shoves off the railing. "For God's sake, we'll be seventy years old when she's ready." She paces a little and turns to me. "I did not intend on broadcasting this child's existence. All I ask is that we have a proper home for this child. And the farm would be fine and New York, I don't care—Alexandra can tell everyone she's taken me in off the streets from some dastardly villain who beat me and she is sheltering me and my child, I don't care." She looks up at the sky and yells, "I want a life for us! I want a home! I want us to have a family!" She looks at me. "Is that really asking too much?"

I shake my head and a moment later, ask, "Which brother?"

"David."

David Waring. He is the second youngest of five of former Congressman Waring and his wife. He is about five years older than Alexandra, making him around forty-three. As far as I know, he is married and has children and is living somewhere around San Francisco.

"I remember once," I tell Georgiana, "my mother told me a story about a woman at a train station. A train pulled in and announced it was going to Chicago, the woman said she wanted to go to New York. And when the conductor said, I'm sorry, but we're going to Chicago, the woman lay down in front of the train and refused to move until the conductor would tell her the train would take her to New York. So of course the conductor told her that the train would take her to New York and as soon as she got off the track the train left for Chicago. Happily, the woman did not run after that first train, but instead waited at the station and lo and behold, the next train that pulled in *was* going to New York, and so the woman eventually got where she was going, only it took her longer because she insisted on trying to change the destination of the first train."

The actress turns her head to the side, showing her magnificent profile, and looks at me out of the corner of her eye. "I don't much care for that story, Sally."

"Who does?" I ask her. "The point is, there are some things about people we love that we can do nothing about." I bite my lower lip a moment. "I think you have to make a choice about what is more important to you. Having it all your way, or giving Alexandra a chance to accommodate you on her journey. If you choose to travel with her, in many ways the destination wouldn't matter, would it? Since you would always be together." I pause, watching as she slowly turns to face me. "I think you have to trust her. And if you don't trust her, I think you should move on."

"Come along," she mutters, quickly moving past me into the house, "Louis is waiting."

I follow her, unsure if I've insulted her, or embarrassed her, or both.

Why don't I keep my mouth shut? I think, following Louis out to the car. He is carrying my briefcase as I balance my bowl of cereal without spilling the milk. Once settled in the car, I eat my cereal and try to clear my head of the domestic difficulties of my boss.

"The Mafia Boss Murder" trial, Sally Harrington reporting.

Get with the program, girl.

IV
Media Girl

CHAPTER | 27

"Look, I can let you into the courtroom," my old friend Sheriff McDuff says, examining the pass that has been given to me by DBS, "but he can't go in." The latter is said about Louis.

"He can come into the courthouse, though," I say.

"He can come into the courthouse," Sheriff McDuff says irritably, "I'm just telling you he can't go into the courtroom. There's no space."

"That's fine," I say, wondering why he's so angry. Maybe he's just sick of the chaos. It's got to be a strain.

"I don't suppose," I say a few minutes later to Louis, as I buy us both a cup of coffee at the stand, "you could take some notes on what you hear around the courthouse today?"

He looks at me. "Sure."

I hold out my bag to him and instruct him to take out several three-by-four index cards and a pen. "I'm interested in what is interesting everybody else. What they're talking about in connection with the trial. I don't care if it's the dress a juror is wearing or new views on the Bill of Rights."

"I understand," he says.

We are not allowed in the courtroom yet. I use the time to find another sheriff, Sheriff Jones, who, I quickly ascertain, is a fairly weak link in the courthouse order. "So what's going on?" I ask him.

He looks at me. "McDuff says you're trouble."

I smile. "McDuff just wants to keep me to himself." I sip my coffee. "I've got Laker tickets, you know. Did he tell you that?"

An eyebrow inches higher. "Maybe yes, maybe no." I know Sheriff McDuff hasn't mentioned it to him because I never said any such thing to McDuff. I actually don't have any Laker tickets, but am floating a proposition, fairly certain somebody at Darenbrook Communications can back me up with tickets if I need them.

The sheriff looks around and then back at me out of the corner of his eye. "The guy from Fox offered me five thousand bucks."

I make a sound of disapproval. "Tacky. I think you need to hang out with a better class of people, go to Lakers games and meet a movie star like Georgiana Hamilton-Ayres. You could have dinner with her, you know, I could arrange that. Georgiana Hamilton-Ayres." The look he gives me is appalling; I simply smile and say, "Just keep me in mind if you hear anything worth writing home about, will you?"

They have opened the doors of the courtroom and I wait in line to file in and take the DBS News seat. I'm almost in the back, sort of to the side, but I can still see pretty much everything. The people around me all say hello (between my newsworthiness and my tenure on the witness stand, they understandably feel as though they know me), and I formally introduce myself to the freelance guy sitting next to me, who is covering the trial for *Expectations* magazine.

"Clyde James," he says, offering a hand.

I show him the injuries on my one good hand.

"Gingerly then," he says, barely touching my hand, how-do-you-do.

He is a dark-skinned, nice-looking man who originally came from, I can tell already from the four words he has uttered, Jamaica.

"How are you feeling?"

"A lot better sitting out here, I can tell you," I say, prompting people around me to laugh.

"You've written for *Expectations*," he says next.

I nod. "Once."

"Verity Rhodes says she knows you."

"Yes." I take out my steno pad.

"She told me, 'Whatever you do, don't use my name, Clyde, or she will never talk to you.'"

I smile, looking over at him. "I'll talk to you." I look around the courtroom. "As long as you talk to me."

"I hear you." His is a deep, rich voice, highly educated.

I look down at his notebook. "Do you have a list of all the witnesses the prosecution called?"

He nods, pulling out a couple of sheets for me to peruse. I check them against the ones Alexandra passed to me. They're a fairly close match.

Prior to the defense's witnesses, the prosecution had called sixteen witnesses to lay out their scenario: Jonathan Small killed Nick Arlenetta in cold blood. It was premeditated.

Nick Arlenetta's personal secretary testified. She said that the executive in charge of production at Monarch Studios, Jonathan Small, had personally invited Nick Arlenetta to come to his office that fateful day, to discuss existing union contracts with the AFTW—the American Federation of Technology Workers. That was the meeting where Nick Arlenetta was shot dead. The defense then cross-examined the witness, asking if she hadn't previously been Cliff Yarlen's secretary. The answer was yes. Questioned, she talked about how terrific her first boss had been. When asked what had happened to him, she testified he was found shot through the head in a cargo hangar at JFK airport. Perez then came back for the prosecution to ask one more question of his witness: how had her most recent boss, Nick Arlenetta, died? Shot through the head at the meeting in Mr. Small's office.

The first police officer on the scene was called. He showed a diagram of the office where the shooting took place, and detailed the scene as he found it, and the dazed condition of the defendant. The defense, on cross, had him admit the police had not looked in the bathroom of the office when they arrived, and that someone else could have been concealed in there.

There was a police detective called, who detailed the

logging of evidence from the scene, including the finger-prints of the defendant on the gun. On cross, the defense pointed out the defendant's fingerprints were only the last set on the gun, that there were several other fingerprints, blurred beyond recognition.

The police coroner was called, who had detailed the nature of the gunshot wounds, how Nick Arlenetta had died, and that the gun in evidence was the murder weapon. The defense pointed out that death was instantaneous.

Jonathan Small's secretary testified that after hearing the gunshot, she ran into Jonathan Small's office and saw her boss standing there with the gun. The defense pointed out the defendant never said he shot the victim and that in the three years of working with him, she had never seen him do anything remotely violent.

Then the studio secretary who had applied CPR to the murder victim in an effort to revive him was called to the stand. Again, the defense pointed out the defendant never said he shot the victim. The prosecutor, conversely, pointed out the defendant had not tried to help resuscitate the victim.

A studio executive who ran in and saw the murder scene testified next. The defense pointed out that in the six years he'd known Small, the colleague had never even seen Jonathan raise his voice, much less commit an act of violence.

Another police detective had testified. He had taken Jonathan Small downtown to the police station. He related how Small had talked about how evil Nick Arlenetta was. Defense then highlighted, in the cross, the long list of murders and crimes Small had told the officer about.

A ballistics expert confirmed that the gunpowder stains

on both of Small's hands matched those of the murder weapon. Perez illustrated how Small would have held a gun police-style, or, as he said, execution style, to make sure he hadn't missed. Defense argued that it was possible Small could have been struggling for the gun, with his hands over the hands that actually shot the gun. The witness said if Banks was trying to prove Arlenetta had been shot in a struggle, the answer was no. What about if the struggle was with a third person? Was it not possible the defendant's hands were on top of the shooter's? Maybe a thousand-to-one chance, the witness said. But it is possible? the defense pointed out. At the odds of a thousand to one, the witness said, yes.

An FBI agent had testified about Small's fears that the authorities could not protect his family against Arlenetta. The defense underscored the years of FBI interest in Arlenetta and his organized-crime activities.

And finally a pistol range instructor testified he had worked with Small on sharpening his skills, saying that Small had complained of threats to his life and his family. Defense on the cross highlighted how many entertainment industry figures the instructor helped, all worried about threats to their lives and families. Perez countered by accentuating how Small had talked of one specific person.

All in all, the prosecution had presented a very strong case against Small, and despite the case the defense was making, that Jonathan Small shot Nick Arlenetta in self-defense, it still appeared that it was premeditated murder.

"This is what I've got for the defense list," I murmur to Clyde, opening my notebook so he can see.

The psychiatrist who testified before me, who said it

would be virtually impossible for Jonathan Small to commit murder, that because of the murder of his mother as a young boy he abhorred murder and violence in all its forms. The prosecution had fallen into the trap on that one. Perez asked the witness if his use of the word *virtually* implied that it *was* possible, after all? The answer came back, "Only if some extraordinary circumstance had occurred that caused a psychotic break in the defendant." Which, of course, opened another avenue for appeal if the verdict went against the defense.

Then there was me, whose meandering testimony revealed the murderous nature of Nick Arlenetta and the obvious threat to anyone who opposed the Arlenetta crime family.

Lucas Johnson was scheduled for today. He was a witness to the firebombing of the Presario mansion in Bel Air Frederick Small, aka Frank Presario, the defendant's father, was also scheduled today. Sky Preston, special federal prosecutor, was listed to testify after Frank Presario. Agent John Alfonso, Federal Bureau of Investigation, was to testify as his schedule permitted. And Lilliana Martin, aka Lise Presario, the defendant's sister, was due before the court next. Then, finally, the defendant, Jonathan Small, aka Taylor Presario, was scheduled last.

I look at my watch. It is now ten-twenty, and I think smugly to myself that even when I was about to drop dead while testifying, court still started on time. Still, the clerk has not come out.

The clerk has been a rather interesting person to watch over the course of the trial. She is a woman of about forty, I would guess, who, at the beginning of the trial, favored bulky black, navy or dark brown pantsuits to cover the fifty or so extra pounds she carries on her frame. She also, at the start of the trial, wore heavily framed glasses and her long auburn hair pulled back, but with bangs coming down to obscure a lot of her face. I'm not sure who has gotten to the clerk, but they have done an excellent job. Somebody, somewhere, coaxed her out of those pantsuits and into skirts that reveal nice legs. The flats have turned into pumps. The bulky jackets into sleek blazers, and the jersey tops to silk tops that, on occasion, drew admiring looks from the men when they revealed a discreet but admirable bust. The heavy glasses are thinly framed now, and her hair, for a while, was pinned up on the back of her head, but as of last week, had been stylishly cut to shoulder length.

The long and the short of it is, somebody has been doing a makeover on the clerk, and she's gone from being dowdy to a very attractive gal who carries her weight well.

I consider doing a little sidebar on her, you know, showing clips of her at various intervals of the trial to show the changes. But then I think forget it, why would I embarrass her. But then I think, now *there* is an interview to be had at the trial's conclusion. Forget the judge and the lawyers, I want to talk to *her,* she who is always at the judge's side, she who is there for everything, in the courtroom and in chambers.

And how convenient it is she's looking great.

I make a note to see what we have on her.

Speak of the devil, the door to judge's chambers opens and the clerk emerges. A sheriff stands on the other side of the door and says, "All rise," which we do. Judge Kahn comes out, his robes trailing, and takes his place on the bench. We sit down. "One of the jurors has had a dental emer-

gency this morning and cannot be here until two o'clock.
Court will resume at two. Thank you for your patience."

"All rise," the sheriff says, as Judge Kahn gets up again
and floats out of the courtroom.

"Well that was an exercise in futility," Clyde James says
to me.

"Thanks for comparing notes," I tell him.

We wait our turn to get out of the courtroom. We really
are packed in.

"Thank God you were a witness," Clyde says under his
breath, standing behind me. "You gave me a lot of color."

"You're welcome," I say over my shoulder.

He moves up to stand next to me as we emerge from the
courtroom. The hall is almost as crowded and we maneu-
ver to get outside, to a relatively private spot near the driveway. I have purposely led him to a place where the corner
of the building shields us from a direct view of the media
towers. I don't know about other networks, but I know our
cameras are constantly zooming in for close-ups of people talking outside, and in New York we have lip-readers
watching it.

"We were all asleep until you got on the stand," he tells
me. "Everybody just droned on and on."

I smile. I sense a valuable ally in this man. I've got to
come up with news every day; he needs a tremendous story
and a fresh, in-depth angle, but with a lead time of, at the
very best, three months. We can work together, he and I.

"Everything, until you, was scripted. And then you arrived, very pretty and outgoing and unruly—"

I am about to protest, but decide not to.

"And then there you were the other morning, all beat up

and half fainting and trying to deck the prosecutor with a broken arm. Very good stuff. I commend you."

I have to laugh. "I'm glad you enjoyed it."

"How's the cop?"

"Which one?" I ask him.

"Your boyfriend."

"He's not my boyfriend."

He smiles. "Sorry. The gentleman, then, who took you on the back of a motorcycle for a romantic dinner in Pacific Palisades. That police officer, Paul Fitzwilliam."

"He's good, he's coming along," I say.

"Have you seen him since the accident?"

I study Clyde's face carefully.

"I would like very much to talk with him," he says. "Very much."

I think about this. Clyde James is a good writer—he'd have to be to get this assignment with *Expectations*. I know his name; he's written about celebrity murder before.

"It's an interesting sideline to the trial," he adds. "I would like to follow it."

Would this or would this not endanger the possibility of a relationship with Paul? And do I care?

"I believe I have a trade that would be of great interest to you," he says. "Someone I'm sure Ms. Waring would like to interview."

I smile, slightly. "And this would be...?"

"Michael Arlenetta."

I am openly surprised. "You can deliver him?"

"I believe I can."

"What's your connection to him?"

"I know he wants his side of the story to be known."

"I see." My eyes travel over the gardens, settling on a bee crawling in a hibiscus blossom. I'm trying to figure this out, how he could have this kind of access.

Clyde James, *Expectations* magazine, Verity Rhodes—Verity Rhodes and Spencer Hawes. My Spencer Hawes, in the old days, executive editor of Bennett, Fitzallen & Coe.

My eyes come back to meet Clyde's. "Off the record, are you doing a book with Michael Arlenetta?"

Now it is his turn to look surprised.

"Off the record, I mean it," I say, "it will go no further, I swear."

He nods. "I'm ghosting. I've got a son going to college," he adds.

"What happens if there's a bad review or something?" I say with a hint of a smile. "Is he going to kill you, or what?"

He smiles. "I don't think he's like that."

I shrug. "I hope not. For your sake."

"The book is an answer to your series, *The Family*," he explains. "The Arlenettas' side of things."

"Don't tell me he's going to stick up for Nick."

"I don't think so. He's more concerned with the family in general."

"You mean the Genovese crime family?"

He gives me a vaguely disgusted look. "Will you hook me up with Fitzwilliam or not?"

"Sure. Give me Michael and you can have Paul."

His eyes crinkle up slightly. "He is your boyfriend, isn't he?" He raises a hand. "Don't answer that, I'll get what I need from him."

"Yeah, okay, whatever," I say, looking at my watch. "Meet you back here at ten of? To see if we have a deal?"

"Excellent," he says.

"Now, I'm telling you point blank, Paul," I say over the pay phone, "and this is highly confidential. I'm using you to get DBS an interview with Michael Arlenetta."

Silence. "You want DBS to interview the guy who tried to kill you?"

"Well, I don't know if it was him, exactly."

"You just finished testifying that he was there at the fire-bombing!"

"Well, yeah."

"Are you aware of the likelihood that he might also be behind whoever tried to kill us Sunday night?"

"We don't know they were trying to kill us, Paul. Hurt us, yes, but kill us? They should have hit us while we were moving, you know that."

A sigh. "I know I'm tired and sore and cranky and not wild about you having anything to do with this sophisticated scumbag."

"You don't have to talk to Clyde right away," I say. "In fact, I think it will probably be a little bit over time. He wants to follow the story out, about the accident."

Pause. "This is what you do for a living?"

"Yes," I tell him.

Silence. Finally, "What am I supposed to say when he asks about us?"

"Say whatever you want."

"You want me to tell him that I'm falling head over heels for you?"

I smile, feeling a little surge of adrenaline. "Paul, you don't have to talk to him. I'm just trying to be honest with you. This is a complete trade. I deliver you, he delivers Michael Arlenetta to DBS News. Up until now, Arlenetta has refused to talk."

A sigh. "Okay."

"What?"

"I said okay, tell him to call me."

"Thank you."

"And Sally? About tonight? I don't think I can do it. I don't feel so hot. I think maybe I should have stayed in the hospital another day and now I'm paying the price."

"Would you like me to bring you some ice cream?" I ask him. "After the broadcast?"

"I'd love it," he says. "But I know how much you've got on your plate."

"I'd love it, too, though," I tell him.

Clyde is waiting for me. "Deal?"

"Deal," I tell him. "He's not feeling well, but you might even be able to see him tomorrow if you want. Here's his number, he wants you to call him."

"Great," he says, delighted, pocketing the number. "I might be able to get Arlenetta for you tomorrow night, too."

I blink. "Really?"

"Really." He looks at his watch.

"Yeah, we should be going in," I agree.

"You know," Clyde says, escorting me back to the courthouse entrance, "I would be extremely interested in talking to you, too, at some length. When the trial's over and I have a lot of my material in place."

"You just say the word, Clyde," I tell him. "And presuming, of course, your employer doesn't decide to knock me off first."

CHAPTER | 28

"The defense calls Lucas Johnson," Lawrence J. Banks says.

I remember him well. The tall, thin black man of about fifty five years old, now making his way through the courtroom, was there the day of the firebombing in Bel Air. I am impressed by his calm assurance.

They swear Lucas Johnson in and he steps up into the witness box.

"Mr. Johnson, what do you do for a living?" Banks begins.

"I have a livery business here in the Los Angeles area."

"Livery meaning limousines?"

"I have a Lincoln Town Car." A twitch of a smile. "I'm not one of the ostentatious guys."

Polite chuckles.

"And Mr. Johnson, could you tell the jury about the afternoon of March 7 of this year?"

"Um, sure." He shifts in his seat slightly, absently smoothing his conservatively striped tie. "I received a dispatch call from Regal—"

"I'm sorry, Mr. Johnson, could you explain what that is?"

"It means I was free that afternoon and called into Regal. They sometimes refer fares to me, and I give them a percentage."

"Fine, thank you."

"So Regal gave me a pickup in Torrance. Sally Harrington. At the Taco Bell. I was to take her to Skyview Drive in Bel Air."

"Did you find this request odd in any way?"

"Well, yes. Ms. Harrington was very nice, but I knew there was something weird going on."

"Why do you say that?"

"Well, she said she was staying in Century City, but left her rental car at the Taco Bell all the way down in Torrance. That's a hike."

"Did she explain why?"

"No."

"Was there anything else?"

"She was upset, nervous. She made a call on her cell phone that seemed to upset her further."

"Do you know to whom?"

He shakes his head. "Somebody named Buddy. I only remember because that's the name of my dog."

"Did you hear any of her conversation?"

"She said something about somebody was pretty banged up and was being taken back to New York. Then she said something about a videotape and *Expectations* magazine. And then she said something about some woman being somebody's girlfriend, and how her first husband beat the hell out of her—"

"Objection, Your Honor," Perez says, standing up. "The people would like to know where this is going, and what its relevance is to the case?"

"Attorney Banks?"

"I will refocus the questioning, Your Honor."

"Objection sustained, then."

"Mr. Johnson, did you take Sally Harrington to Skyview Drive in Bel Air?"

"Yes, sir, I did."

"What happened there?"

"Well, there was a fence and a security gate at this house, which is normal, but there was a guy—a big guy— at the gate, which seemed odd to me."

"What happened then?"

"I rolled down the window and said Sally Harrington was here and he said Ms. Martin wasn't having any visitors today. Ms. Harrington asked that the guy check with Ms. Martin about that. He refused to."

"What happened then?"

"Ms. Harrington got out of the car and demanded the guy tell Ms. Martin she was there. He refused again, said she wasn't seeing anyone."

"What happened then?"

"Ms. Harrington said fine, she was calling 911, and tried to get back in the car but the guy grabbed her by the wrist. I opened my door and was ready to take him on—I was afraid he was hurting her—but Ms. Harrington wasn't in pain."

"And then?"

"The guy had this walkie-talkie and told somebody that he had a woman jumping up and down out here threatening to call 911. The other guy asked who it was. And he said Sally Harrington."

"What happened then?"

"They still refused to see her, but Ms. Harrington yelled that Ms. Martin could either see her now or wait until she testified for Sky Preston." Pause. "They let her in after that."

"And what about you?"

"The big guy told me to park across the street and keep all the windows rolled down."

"Did he say why he wanted you to do this?"

"He said he wanted to be able to see me."

"Mr. Johnson, did you have any idea what was going on?"

"I knew something was up, and a whole lot of people were scared. Nobody has that kind of muscle around their house."

"Was there anyone else you could see, other than the man at the gate?"

"Oh, yeah, I saw at least two other huge guys up in the driveway."

"And where did Sally Harrington go?"

"Up the driveway, with the big guy from the gate. He handed her off to the others and she went up to the house."

"So you parked across the street?"

"Yeah. I called in, though, to Regal, and told them I was on a weird fare, something was up."

"What happened then?"

"Another guy came out of the gate and came over to the car and told me to get off the radio or he would pull it out."

"Why did he say that?"

"I think he must have been listening. You know, on a scanner."

"Okay, so let's get this scene down," Banks says, starting to walk. "You picked up a scared young woman in Torrance and drove her to Ms. Martin's home in Bel Air. They wouldn't let her in until she threatened to call 911 and testify for...?"

"Sky Preston."

"Who is Sky Preston, Mr. Johnson, if you know?"

"Later, yeah, I heard them talking about him. He's some sort of federal official."

"All right, so you're parked across the street from this house in Bel Air, there are strange men guarding it, one of whom comes out to tell you to stop using your radio?"

"Yes, sir."

"Why didn't you leave?"

"I wanted to, believe me," he says, eyes wide. "But I was worried about Ms. Harrington. She was kind of upset to begin with and I didn't like the look of things."

"So what happened?"

"She was in there for maybe forty-five minutes?" He looks at the ceiling and back down. "Yeah, forty-five minutes, and then, I swear to God, it seemed like judgment day."

"What do you mean?"

"I heard a helicopter and I was thinking, man, that's flying pretty low, and I wondered if maybe there was a lost child, or a manhunt or something. And then I thought maybe the police are looking for one of these guys across the street, because the helicopter came straight down the mountaintop at us. And then the next thing I see is something pointing out of the side of this thing and this rocket takes off and blows up part of the house. This huge fireball." He sits forward in his seat, gesturing with his hands. "And no sooner does that blow up than the helicopter veers over me—my car—and another rocket is fired into the house!"

"What did you do?"

"Well first I jumped out of the car and looked for that damn helicopter—"

A few people laugh nervously in sympathy.

"No, it was really bad," Johnson tells the gallery. He turns back to Banks. "The side of the house was a ball of fire and the other side—well, it wasn't there anymore. And then this car—this black Caddie—you know, one of the Escalades, the four-wheel-drive truck? It had this crash bar on the front and it came tearing up the road—it rammed the gate in and went flying up to the house. And I thought, 'This isn't good.'"

"What did you do?"

"I ran across the street, through the gate and then circled through the woods around to the back of the house."

"Could you see anything?"

"Oh, yeah, I could see these guys, there were three of them, running around the house with guns."

"Did they say anything?"

"Yeah. They kept saying, 'She's not here. Look in the back.' At one point, this shorter guy said, 'With any luck, she was upstairs.'"

"And what were you doing?"

"I was lying on the ground. I didn't want to get shot."

"You were scared?"

"Hell yeah!" People laugh.

Banks doesn't smile. "Why were you scared?"

"It was clear to me they were looking for somebody, I thought it might be Ms. Harrington, but then this one guy started yelling, 'Lilliana!'"

"Could you describe the scene?"

"Sure. Um, there was a body lying in the side yard that had been decapitated. It was a man. There was a ton of smoke. And steam and stuff. Black soot, pieces of carbon. The back of the house was caved in and there was all this steam coming out with the smoke, because there was a water pipe that had burst. And the fire had spread. It was just a disaster, the whole house."

"What happened then?"

"The guys were in the back—"

"The guys with the guns?"

"Yes."

"And what happened?"

"One of them yelled that the basement doors were open—they were like cyclone doors. He yelled, 'She's gone!' And the short guy said, 'Check the pool house,' and one guy ran off, but the other two kept looking in the basement doors, coughing and stuff, 'cause there was all this fire and smoke."

"Did they say anything?"

He looks at the judge. "There was an expletive, Your Honor."

He nods. "That's all right, just tell the court what was said."

"The short guy yelled, 'Fuck, where is she?'"

"And then what happened?"

"You could hear a siren and the short guy said it was time for them to get out of there, and so they ran back around to the front—what was left of the front—and they got in the Caddie and split."

"What did you do?"

"I ran to the back of the house and started yelling Sally Harrington's name, hoping she might still be alive in there somewhere. And after maybe a half a minute, I saw her and someone else stumbling out of the cellar doors. So I ran over and helped her out into the yard. She had Ms. Martin by the arm and was helping her, and the three of us managed to get out on the grass, where it was safe."

"What happened then?"

"They were sick. They were suffering from smoke inhalation, but the fire department had arrived and the firefighters gave them both oxygen. And then police and the EMTs were there."

"What happened then?"

"Ms. Harrington begged me to get her and Ms. Martin out of there."

"Did she say why?"

"No. But I knew she was scared to death and so was I, so I took them down to the car."

"No one stopped you?"

"I think Ms. Harrington told one cop that she was a neighbor and had to protect her house or something. Anyway, we ran, and I drove the women away."

"Could you describe the condition of the women?" Banks asks.

"Well, they were very sooty. Ms. Martin only had on sweatpants and a bra. Ms. Harrington was all scratched up. I don't know, they just looked like what people who come out of a horrible fire look like."

"Did they say who it was who attacked the house?"

"That's what Ms. Harrington kept asking Ms. Martin, who had been responsible, but Ms. Martin wasn't talking, she kept saying, later, later, I'll explain later."

Banks takes a walk. "Could you describe for the jury the emotional state of Lilliana Martin after the attack?"

"She was clearly shaken and scared, but if I had to describe her..." He compresses his lips a moment, thinking. "I'd say angry and scared. Definitely scared, but definitely mad, too. I remember thinking, gosh, for an actress she's kind of tough. You know, I drive a lot of actresses, but this one—" He shakes his head.

"This one what?"

"I definitely got the feeling she wasn't all that surprised by what had happened. Like she'd been in something like this before."

"Very good, Mr. Johnson," Banks says, walking back to his table to look at some notes. He comes back. "Where did you take the women?"

"To a Mobil station near the airport. One with a convenience shop."

"Why there?"

"Ms. Harrington told me to go there. She said to head for the airport and then saw this station and told me to stop."

"Why?"

"Well, they were covered with soot, as I said, so they needed to wash up. Also, Ms. Martin didn't have a shirt on. So Ms. Harrington got her a shirt and sunglasses and food and water and stuff."

"Where did you drive them then?"

"Ms. Martin said she wanted to go home, to Larkensburg. So we drove back up 495 to take 10 East, toward Palm Springs. We drove into the desert."

"What else happened?"

"There was a news bulletin on the radio about the fire-bombing. Ms. Harrington made me pull over and she ran to a pay phone and Ms. Martin nearly had a fit. She was yelling at Ms. Harrington that she couldn't keep her mouth shut."

"Why did she say that?"

"Because Ms. Harrington had called into DBS News—she worked for them—and told them she had been there, at the firebombing. So a few minutes later that came over the news, too. Ms. Martin was pissed!" He looks at the judge. "Sorry."

"Now, with all this that had gone on, Mr. Johnson," Banks says, "you must have been feeling scared yourself."

He nods. "Yes. And then when the two of them started talking about the feds, and Ms. Martin said the firebombing was the failure of the feds to protect her, I really got nervous. Ms. Harrington asked Ms. Martin what the feds were supposed to be protecting her against, but she wouldn't say. And then Ms. Harrington said the feds were looking for her, too, and that she was in trouble with the New York City police department. So I finally had to say something. I said I didn't mind helping them out, but that I wasn't sure I wanted to get mixed up with antagonizing the federal authorities and the police."

"So what happened?"

A slight smile. "Ms. Harrington talked me out of my own car."

Light laughter.

"You let her take your Lincoln Town Car?"

"She said she couldn't rent a car without being caught and she certainly wasn't going to steal one, she said, and she didn't want to compromise me—that's what she said, 'I don't want to compromise your life or your integrity, Lucas.'"

A few laughs.

He shrugs. "So they took my car. And I gave Ms. Harrington my credit card for gas."

"Did you ever get your car back?"

"Oh, yeah," he says cheerfully. "Two days later. And a check for five thousand bucks."

"Who was that check from?"

"The defendant," he says, nodding in his direction. "Jonathan Small. He wrote a note, too, saying how much he appreciated my help in saving the life of Lilliana Martin."

"Did you know that the defendant was the brother of Lilliana Martin?"

"No, sir." He shakes his head. The note was on Monarch Studios stationery, so I just figured it was a business thing.

"Thank you, Mr. Johnson," Banks says graciously. "You are, in my book, a hero, and I thank you for your actions." He walks back to the defense table.

The judge looks to Perez. "The People may cross-examine this witness."

"Thank you, Your Honor."

Perez walks over. "I would like to echo the sentiments of Attorney Banks, Mr. Johnson, you are a good and courageous individual and we thank you."

Lucas nods slightly, looking embarrassed.

"I just have one question about the day you have testified about. Did you, at any time, hear the name Arlenetta mentioned?"

"No, sir."

"Ms. Harrington, Ms. Martin—no one mentioned the name Arlenetta?"

"No, sir."

"Thank you, Mr. Johnson, that will be all."

"You may step down, Mr. Johnson," Judge Kahn says. While Lucas is led out of the courtroom by a sheriff, the judge looks at his watch and confers with his clerk. Then he addresses the court, "We have time to call the next witness for the defense, Mr. Banks."

Banks stands up. "The defense calls Frederick Small."

A murmur through the courtroom. The door opens and the father of the defendant makes his way to the bench, where he is sworn in. He is not a tall man, only five-six at best, but he is squarely built and impeccably groomed. He is wearing a navy blue suit, white shirt and red tie. He could be running for president.

He climbs onto the stand and sits down, waiting expectantly.

"Good afternoon," Banks says.

"Good afternoon," Frank says.

"Your legal name is Frederick Small?"

"Frederick Jonathan Small."

"And your birth name was?"

"Frank Joseph Presario Jr."

"And who changed your name?"

"The Federal Bureau of Investigation, the division that handles the witness protection program."

"By which name would you prefer to be addressed, sir?"

"I would prefer to be called Frank Presario," he says. He looks up at the judge. "I am in the process of legally changing my name back."

"As long as it is clear in the record," Judge Kahn says, "and you, Mr. Presario, understand that you are under oath, regardless of what name you prefer to be called on the stand."

"Yes, sir, I do."

"Mr. Perez? Do the People have any objection?"

Perez stands up. "None whatsoever, Your Honor."

The judge nods. "Very well, Mr. Banks, you may proceed."

"Thank you, Your Honor." Banks takes a cruise around the jury box. "Mr. Presario, is the defendant, Jonathan Small, your son?"

"Yes." He looks at him with sad fondness.

"Who is his mother?"

"My wife, the former Celia Bruno."

"Is Mrs. Presario still alive?"

"No, sir, she's deceased."

"How did she die?"

"She was murdered by Nick Arlenetta."

Perez is out of his seat. "Objection, Your Honor, there is nothing on the record that indicates that what the witness says is true."

Frank stares at the prosecutor coldly for a moment and then looks at Banks.

"Your Honor, the witness is in a unique position to testify as to Nick Arlenetta's involvement in his wife's murder."

"Mr. Banks, such a connection is not on the record and so I will sustain the objection." Judge Kahn looks at the jury. "The jury will disregard the witness's statement."

An old lady on the jury nods. Of course, she's been nodding at everything that is said since I've been here.

"Your wife was murdered?"

"Yes."

"How?"

"A car bomb was installed under my car. It was meant to kill me. And my wife and I happened to switch cars that day, so she was murdered instead."

"Why did you think Nick Arlenetta placed that bomb under your car?"

"Because he had threatened to kill me."

"He told you he was going to kill you?"

"Yes. He said, 'Uncle Frank, get out of my way, or I will get you out of the way permanently.'"

"Let's step back, Mr. Presario, so that you may explain to the jury your relationship with the deceased, Nick Arlenetta."

He nods.

"Were you related to Nick Arlenetta?"

"Yes, sir. My older sister, Gina, was married to his father."

"And Nick Arlenetta's father's name was?"

"Joe."

"And what line of work was he in?"

"He was a front man for the Genovese crime family. He was in restaurant and hotel unions."

Banks turns to theatrically look at the prosecutor. "No objection to these facts on the record, Mr. Perez?"

"Objection," Perez yells, jumping up.

"Withdrawn," Banks says, holding a hand up and physically retreating.

"Mr. Banks, you'll refrain from comment, please," Judge Kahn says.

"Yes, Your Honor," he says. Coming back, he says, "So your brother-in-law was an established organized-crime figure?"

"Yes."

"Operating where?"

"Primarily Manhattan, Queens and Brooklyn."

"Now, you were working in some capacity with union organizations, were you not?"

"Yes. At the time I was president of the United Building & Construction Workers of America, Eastern Seaboard Branch."

Banks stops to look at him. "Was the United Building & Construction Workers of America ever implicated in organized-crime activities?"

"Yes, sir, it was. That was why I was elected, to clean it up."

"And did you?"

"Most people would agree that I did, yes."

"What was the reaction of your brother-in-law, Joe Arlenetta, when you cleaned up that union?"

"He said he thought my days on this earth were numbered."

"He thought you would be killed?"

"Eventually, yes."

"Why?"

"Because I was preventing crime families from siphoning money out of my union. Until I was president, it had been a relatively easy procedure for crime families—and a very lucrative one, I might add."

"How do you know how organized-crime families siphoned money from the unions, Mr. Presario?"

"My father was in the union business before me."

"Was he an organized-crime figure?"

"He was never convicted of any crime," he says, casting a meaningful glance at the prosecutor.

"Was he ever arrested?"

"No, sir."

"But he understood the ins and outs of organized crime in unions, is that correct?"

"Yes, sir. And he taught me about it, that's why I could be effective. I knew the players and the ways and means. More important, I knew ways of forcing members of crime families out."

"Why did you bother? Why didn't you just play along with the system?"

"Because I knew you didn't have to cheat and steal and terrorize workers to make money," he says, taking a sip of water. "There is plenty of money for everyone if good workers are treated well and organized effectively."

"Did you go to college, Mr. Presario?"

"Yes. I received a business degree from Georgetown University."

Banks walks over to look at his notes. "Was your nephew, Nicholas Arlenetta, ever arrested?"

"Objection, Your Honor," Perez says.

There is a significant silence.

"Sustained," Judge Kahn says.

Banks pauses and then says, "Mr. Presario, were you estranged from your nephew?"

"Yes."

"Why?"

"He murdered my wife," he says simply.

"Objection, Your Honor!" Perez cries.

"Sustained. The jury will disregard the witness's last statement." To the stenographer, "That statement will be stricken from the record."

Bank tries again. "Did your nephew ever engage a defense attorney?"

"Yes. Cocky Calhoun," Presario says. "Charles Calhoun."

The courtroom starts to buzz. Calhoun, now in his seventies, was for decades one of the top defense lawyers in the country.

"To your knowledge, Mr. Presario, had Charles Calhoun ever represented a member of an organized-crime family before?"

"No, sir, I believe it was the first and last time."

"Do you know of any particular reason why Mr. Calhoun would have chosen to represent Nick Arlenetta?"

"Nick was marrying Mr. Calhoun's daughter."

Banks stops in his tracks, looking shocked. "How and why would Nick Arlenetta, a member of the Genovese crime family, come to be married to Mr. Calhoun's daughter?"

"Nick had fathered her child."

Banks lets this sink in with the jury. "And did they get married?"

"Yes, sir."

"Did you attend the wedding?"

"No."

"Why not?"

"By that time my sister—"

"Gina?"

He nods. "Gina. She was estranged from Nick, her son. She wouldn't have anything to do with him, so we didn't, either."

"What about Nick's father, Joe?"

"They continued to work together."

Banks walks away, stops and turns around. "Did the marriage last?"

"For three years," Frank answers. "Until she died."

There is a gasp in the courtroom.

"How did Nick Arlenetta's young wife die, Mr. Presario?"

"She jumped off the roof of their apartment building. It was ruled a suicide."

Banks leaves that whole subject hanging, the courtroom abuzz and Judge Kahn hammering away until there is order.

"We will stop here for today," Judge Kahn says gravely. He confers with his clerk. "Court will reconvene tomorrow morning at nine-thirty."

CHAPTER | 29

"No, Emmett, I think Nick Arlenetta was a psychopath from day one," I say on national television. "You can make all the excuses you want, but I don't think Prozac would have stopped him from murdering people, stealing innocent families blind, and going into business with drug dealers, terrorists and other charming vermin of society that the court won't let the jury hear about."

Emmett stares at me with open astonishment.

"I know," I say. "It doesn't sound like a very objective viewpoint for a reporter, but I think our viewers understand where I'm coming from, that I am not so much a reporter on 'The Mafia Boss Murder' trial as I am a witness and a victim."

"Well, Sally, that's understandable," he says a bit woodenly, "but in matters of the law, the court must deal only in fact, and much of what was testified to today is essentially irrelevant to the issue of whether or not Jonathan Small murdered another man."

And so on it goes, our *Late Edition* (taping live at eight, Pacific Standard Time, to air live in the East at eleven), and I find that I've enjoyed myself immensely, carefully saying all I was supposed to, certain to meet our cues on time to run tape and allowing myself to opine only at the very end. When our gig is over, and the show is thrown back to Alexandra in New York for the closing, I feel pretty good.

"Alexandra for you on line two," Will Rafferty calls to me as I step down from the set.

I look at him. "My opening remarks? About being a victim?"

He laughs. "I should think so."

I take the phone in the control room. "Hello?"

"What, are you Shana Alexander now, doing *Point/Counter Point?*"

She's referring to the popular journalist who appeared on *60 Minutes* thirty years ago to debate issues. "Sorry," I say.

"You're not the least bit sorry," she tells me. "But you're not going to do it again. Understood? I know what you were trying to do, but it is not up to you to voice what *you* think viewers are thinking. It's tempting, because tonight I'm sure about five million people said, 'Exactly! Why hasn't anyone else just said what Sally Harrington just said? That Jonathan Small did the world a favor by killing that psycho!'"

I laugh.

"So from now on, you will leave your opinions out, all right? I know it's hard to shake the interviewee role, but now you're one of us again. Emmett is to give his opinion of legal issues, your role is simply to question him." Pause. "So how are you otherwise?"

"I miss my dog," I say.

"He misses you, too, I hear."

I bring the phone down to look at it a moment, wondering if I've heard this correctly, and bring it back up to my ear. "How would you know about my dog?"

"I talked to your mother. Actually, I talk to her just about every day, just to let her know that you're all right."

"You talk to my *mother?*"

"She called me Monday. She was worried and wanted to know what the real story on your arm was."

"And so now you talk to her all the time?"

A quiet laugh. "Not all the time. But I do feel responsible. You keep getting beat up and stuff," she says matter-of-factly. "I can at least let her know when times are good."

I smile a little. "I guess I should call her more."

"I wish you would. She worries." Pause.

I pick up the hesitation. "Uh-oh, what else?"

"Nothing. I just — well, your mother told me about Marion O'Hearn."

"My mother told you about Mrs. O'Hearn?" I nearly cry in disbelief.

"I told you, she's worried about you," the anchorwoman says. "She wanted me to know that you've been under severe emotional strain."

"Severe emotional strain? I haven't even thought about it until you just brought it up!"

"Well, it's safe to say it's very big on your mother's mind and she assumes it is on yours, too."

I don't say anything.

"I'm really not trying to get into your business," she tells me.

I wonder what Alexandra would think if she knew all that I know about her private life from Georgiana Hamilton-Ayres.

"I don't believe you, but that's okay," I tell her. "Mother really likes you. And if it made her feel better to talk to you, then thank you."

We hang up and Will is waiting for me outside the control room. "Everything okay?"

"Yeah. No more opinions, though."

He smiles, giving my arm a pat. "Good program, kid. Listen, I'm taking off tonight. Anything you need before I go?"

"No," I tell him. "Not a thing."

"Is there really a chance we can get that interview with Arlenetta tomorrow night?" I ask Clyde James on my cell phone, standing with the driver, peering in at the barrels of fresh ice cream at the Encino Creamery. "Chocolate chip," I whisper to the clerk.

"After you just called his brother a psychopath on national television?" Clyde wants to know.

"Yeah, but that's me, Alexandra won't say any of that stuff." I bend to look closer through the glass.

"He absolutely refuses to talk to Alexandra Waring," he says. "He says she already broadsided him once in New Jersey."

She did. I was there.

I whisper to the clerk, "A quart of cookie dough, too, please."

"Where are you?" Clyde says.

"Encino, at an ice-cream place, why?"

"Because I'm trying to set up an interview for you with

Michael Arlenetta and you're talking chocolate chips and cookie dough."

I smile, glancing over at Louis, in whose hand a cone looks like a dollhouse prop. "So if he won't talk to Alexandra, who will he talk to?"

"You. At least until you called his brother a psycho a half an hour ago."

I am stunned. "He wants to talk to *me?*"

"Yep."

"He should talk to someone in New York—"

"He's not on the East Coast. He's here."

"He's *here?*" Suddenly I feel a little chilly. Could Michael Arlenetta have had something to do with hitting me and Paul on Route 1?

"Why on earth does he want to talk to me?"

"Because you put the series together and he thinks it will play better if he talks to you, point by point of what you presented in the series."

I nod to myself. Makes sense. On the other hand, he might want to knock me off. It could be a family trait. "Okay," I say. "So call him and see what he says. If he still wants to do it, I'm game. Tomorrow night would be great."

Louis unlocks the doors of the limo and we get in. He turns around in his seat to talk to me while he finishes his cone. "Ms. Waring wants you back at the house by midnight."

"Oh, she does, does she?" I reach for my bottle of water.

"Yep." Lick, lick, lick, *crunch.* Chew, swallow. He glances at me. "And you're not to bring anyone home with you."

I frown, taking a swig.

"I have to turn over a log every day where I take you," he says apologetically. "Who you see and everything."

"Might be fun to make something up," I dare him.

He looks scandalized. "Nope," he says, shaking his head, "will never happen. Not on my watch."

"You actually brought it," Paul says, eyes twinkling in delight. He kisses me on the cheek and says over his shoulder, "Jack, Sally's got ice cream from the Creamery."

"Cool," says Jack, who is lying across the couch in pajama bottoms and nothing else.

Paul, on the other hand, is in blue jeans and a flannel shirt.

"Hi," I say to Jack, following Paul across the living room to the kitchen.

"Hey, Sally, we watched your show last night when it came on. It was cool."

"Thank you."

"So like, people try to kill you all the time?"

I laugh. "Lately," I say lightly.

"So like are you on tonight, too?"

"Yes. We just finished taping."

"Cool."

Now that I have received the public's approval, in the form of half-naked Jack, I continue to the kitchen where Paul is waiting for me. He steps close, sliding his left hand around my waist, looking into my eyes. "You were great," he murmurs, kissing me.

When we part, I murmur, "You are great."

He laughs, moving away to unpack the ice cream. "I wish you'd go back and look at my room, then come back and tell me where you would prefer to sit—here, in the living room with Jack, or in there. It's just down the hall."

I walk down the hall, pass the bathroom and a room that looks like Armageddon (clearly Jack's room) and find

Paul's. It is very neat. Wood floors and a cotton rug, a standard double with a beige comforter and four pillows, and in the corner, an easy chair and ottoman, small TV set and a desk. On one wall are nothing but photographs, which draw me. Paul and friends skiing. Paul filthy on an oil rig. Paul and friends fishing. Paul and friends on the beach. Paul and a pretty girl on a Ferris wheel. A family photograph. (He looks like his dad.) Photos of people I don't know, children who belong to who knows who.

I smile. A photograph of his graduation from the police academy. His BA degree from University of Southern California. A photo of him shooting hoops with street kids.

"Inviting you in here may or may not be considered a pass," he says from the door.

I turn around, smiling. "You look so much better today, Paul."

"I feel much better," he says, coming in. He's balancing a small tray with two bowls of ice cream, spoons and napkins. "But I'm still a little out of it. I don't like how those pills make me feel, but the pain—"

"I know," I say.

He places the tray on the side table. "Here, Sally, you take the chair, I'll take the ottoman."

We take our places and start eating. "I love women who like to eat," he says.

Catching my reaction to this, he adds, "I'm sorry, did I say something bad?"

He hasn't. It's just that someone told me that before when I first met him, Spencer Hawes, and ever since then I've taken it as some kind of sex thing. And heaven knows, it's not upsetting to me if Paul finds me sexually attractive, but I really don't feel like thinking about Spencer right now. And certainly not comparing Paul's and my early days to the ones with Spencer (although, admittedly, there are similarities, which is why I am upset).

I would like to give this a chance.

On the way over from the Creamery, I even developed a half-baked proposal in my mind that DBS transfer me out here for six months to overhaul the L.A. affiliate. That would be enough time, wouldn't it? To get to know Paul well?

Four women in a year, Sally! I remind myself.

He's drawn the side table between us and I watch him enjoy his ice cream. He's given us both a big scoop of each flavor. We talk ice cream, ice-cream headaches as kids, whether or not that fake soft stuff is really ice cream, and then both admit we like that stuff, too.

Paul finishes first, dropping his spoon with a clatter and wiping his mouth with his napkin. I notice the deep circles under his eyes and how pale he has gotten only the last minute or so. "You look better, but you still don't feel well, do you?"

He smiles weakly. "Not great," he admits. "It's really great to see you, though."

I slide forward. "I'm exhausted myself. I just wanted to say hi, see how you're doing."

"I might be doing better tomorrow," he says hopefully. But the signal is clear, he is still feeling weak and tired and I should leave.

He reaches for my hand. "I'm sorry about last night. It sucked, you know?"

He's twenty-five, all right. Lapses in his smooth method of operation still.

I smile slightly.

"I don't know what's going on, Sally," he says. "But I'm..." He searches my eyes. "I'm so into you. Already." He closes his eyes for a second. "I just wish I didn't feel so sick."

"You need rest," I tell him, getting up. "And so do I."

"Hey, you leaving?" Jack says as we come into the living room. "Aren't you going to watch your show with us?"

"I've got to get some rest," I explain. I notice that Jack has acquired the carton of chocolate chip ice cream and is eating out of it with a tablespoon. "I've got a big day tomorrow and I'm not running on all cylinders yet."

Jack swallows some ice cream and nods toward Paul. "It's my last day of being nice to him. Let's hope he feels better tomorrow."

"I will, I will," Paul says, opening the door for me. He looks out. "That driver guy's down the way." He draws close to briefly, but firmly, kiss me. "Good night. Thank you for coming over." He holds on to my hand as I walk out the door and then, finally, reluctantly, lets go.

I turn around to see Louis. We walk to the car in silence and he holds the door open for me. I climb in and then he does, too. Once he's inside he turns around, "Did you happen to see the girl in the lounge chair by the pool?"

I remember someone vaguely and tell him so.

"She was around last night, too."

"There were like a hundred kids here last night," I point out.

"Yeah, but this one was watching you."

I shrug.

"Look," he says, turning on the ignition of the car, "here she comes."

I can see a figure on the edge of the gardens, looking

around the corner of the building at us. It's a woman, I can see that, with long hair, but that's about it.

"I'm famous now, you know," I say, trying to get a better look at her.

"Hey," he says quickly, whipping his head around at me. "I didn't even think of that. Like the people at the ice-cream parlor, they didn't know who you were, but they knew they knew you from somewhere."

"Yes," I say, sinking back into the seat. I look out the window, smiling a little, thinking about the money that is coming my way, thinking about the new turn of my career. I can buy Mother's house now without having a nervous breakdown. I can do a lot of things.

The only question, I think, looking at the apartment house again as we drive away, is the young police officer who had four women last year.

It's crazy, but I think I'm falling a little in love. Or at least very much in like.

C H A P T E R | 30

I awaken Friday morning to realize I am moving without acute pain for the first time. I also slept very well last night. A magnificent day is unfolding over the Pacific. As I pad barefoot into the kitchen I spot a note from Georgiana. She's left already, she tells me, and highlights the breakfast possibilities. She also points out that the coffee is made and that the newspapers and remote control to the TV are on the table. I smile, pouring myself some coffee, and check my voice mail on my cell phone. One message is from Clyde James, saying despite me, the Arlenetta interview is a go.

I quickly call him back.

"He only wants to be interviewed by you," Clyde tells me.

"Fine," I say.

"And it's tonight or not at all," Clyde says.

"Tonight it is, then," I say, and we hammer out some details. I pour a second cup of coffee and call New York.

"Alexandra Waring's office," answers Benjamin Kim, Alexandra's assistant.

"Hi, it's Sally."

"*The* Mustang Sally?" Benjamin asks.

Ouch. "Mustang Sally," of course, is a song about a madam and her whorehouse.

"When Alexandra gets in—"

"Alexandra *is* in," he tells me.

"Oh, good." I look at the kitchen clock. It's early for her.

"But she's in conference. With the big bosses." That means Cassy Cochran, the president of the network, and Langley Peterson, the CEO of the electronics division.

"In whose office?"

"Cassy's."

"Switch me over, will you?"

Cassy's secretary picks up and I ask to speak to Chi Chi, her administrative assistant. (One can spend all day being bounced around this place.) "I think Jonathan Small did everyone a favor by killing that psycho, too," Chi Chi immediately says when she comes on the phone.

"Well, the psycho's baby brother is coming on the *Late Edition* tonight," I tell her. "I wish you would slip a note to Alexandra."

"What's his name?"

"Michael Arlenetta. Write down he will only do the interview with me and it has to be tonight."

"Fine. Hold on."

I sit down to the table, leisurely sip my coffee and review the sports scores.

I hear a click, then, "Michael Arlenetta wants to be interviewed by *you*?" Alexandra says.

"Yes, I know. He says it will be more effective to answer questions about *The Family* series with me. Besides, he's still ticked off with you about broadsiding him in Fort Lee that day."

"He does realize, doesn't he, that your testimony this week places him at the scene of a murder? And that he may be indicted because of it?"

"I guess," I say, eating a spoonful of yogurt.

Pause. "Do *you* have any objection to interviewing him?"

"None whatsoever."

"And it has to be tonight."

"That's what he wants."

"Then set it up," she tells me. "And we'll start running promos within the hour."

"Mr. Presario," Attorney Banks says to the defendant's father when court resumes at nine-thirty. "Would you please explain to the jury the circumstances leading up to the death of your wife?"

"Certainly. I was running the eastern seaboard branch of the United Building & Construction Workers of America and our members were heavily involved in the revitalization of Atlantic City. This was after gambling had been approved. It was a struggle to keep the operation clean, but we did—at least our guys. Joe Arlenetta approached me again, pressuring me to let the Genovese family have a piece of the action in the hotels. I told him it had nothing to do with us, it was Philadelphia who controlled it. I talked to Angelo Bruno about it—"

"And who was Angelo Bruno?"

"He was—well, he was the Don of Philadelphia."

"He was the head of an organized-crime family?"

"Yes. But to be fair to Angelo, he was well respected by many people. The feds, for example, didn't even bother investigating him for years because he had attempted to—well, keep order in a relatively legal way."

"Wasn't Angelo Bruno called 'The Gentle Don'?" Banks asks.

A flash of a smile. "Yes."

"Were you in any way related to Angelo Bruno?"

"Yes. He was my wife's cousin."

"And you spoke to Angelo Bruno about Joe Arlenetta?"

"Yes. And he had no intention of letting him in. The Genoveses were—" He shakes his head. "He thought they were despicable."

"So what happened?"

"Angelo told Joe to take a hike and right after that a bomb was placed under my car. My wife and I had switched cars that day, because I was taking my son and some of his teammates to a soccer game and I needed the station wagon. So when Celia started my car—" He blinks at the memory, looking down for a moment. He looks back up. "She was killed."

"What happened then?"

"I learned that it was Nick, my nephew, who had set the bomb."

"Objection, Your Honor," Perez says, standing up. "There was no proof the victim participated in this criminal act."

"Your Honor, Mr. Presario was in a unique position, with insider's knowledge of organized crime, which includes accurate information about who carried out this assassination."

There is a sidebar and then the judge sustains the objection.

"All right, Mr. Presario," Banks says, resuming his examination, "what happened after your wife was murdered?"

"I went to Angelo Bruno, told him it was Nick Arlenetta that had killed my wife." He looks down. "I told him I had no objection if something happened to Nick."

"What happened then?"

Presario looks up, blinks once and says, "Angelo was gunned down, murdered. A shotgun blast to the head."

"Was anyone ever arrested for murder?"

He shakes his head. "No."

"Do you know who killed him? Oh!" he suddenly cries, throwing his hands up in mock protest. "Don't answer that, Mr. Presario, because you might not have documented proof on who also murdered Angelo Bruno!"

"*Objection,* Your Honor! This is—" Perez sputters, so indignant he can't get the words out.

"Mr. Banks," Judge Kahn says, sounding tired, "you will refrain from innuendo. Objection is sustained."

Banks cruises around, all eyes on him. Finally he stops near the jury box and leans on it. "Please tell the jury what you did then, after Angelo Bruno was murdered."

"I contacted the FBI and told them I was willing to help them gather evidence against members of the Genovese crime family. I knew they were building a case against Funzi Tieri, who ran it—and I wanted to make sure Joe and Nick Arlenetta went down with him."

"And did they?"

"Joe was put away. Nick wriggled out of it."

"And what about you and your children, Mr. Presario?"

"We went into the witness protection program."

"And you changed your name?"

"*I* didn't pick the name," he says quickly. He smiles sheepishly. "When you're short, you don't pick a name like Small."

People laugh.

"And where did you go?"

"Illinois. With my son. My daughter, Lise—you know her as Lilliana—was placed over the state line in Ohio."

"Why wasn't Lise with you?"

"It made us too identifiable. And, to be honest, I wanted Lise to have a mother and I just wasn't—" He shakes his head, looking down.

"What did you do for a living?"

"I started a computer-chip manufacturing firm. I knew a bit about it from working with the union. My father gave me a stake when I left. I used it to start this company."

"You did very well."

"Eventually, yes, very well. And I relocated to Silicon Valley, here in California. Lise was acting in Los Angeles by then. Jonathan was at Harvard."

"Did you stay in touch with Lise all those years?"

"Jonathan and I saw her at least twice a month, every month. Until she went to college. We had a scare that year. We thought someone might have recognized me at a trade show in Chicago. After that, we didn't see each other very much. Not for a while."

"Did anyone else know about your relationship with Lise?"

"No. No one knew who Lise was."

"Your father didn't?"

He is silent for a moment. Then he bites his lip and nods.

"My father knew, but not until Lise was twenty. When my mother died. My father was inconsolable and so I—well, I took him to see Lise. And they have been very close ever since."

"Okay now, so we have you in Silicon Valley, Jonathan at Harvard, Lise, who is now Lilliana Martin, living and working in Los Angeles."

"Yes."

"Jonathan graduated?"

"Yes. And went to Los Angeles. He got a job right away as a production assistant at Monarch Studios."

"And people knew you were his father, correct?"

He nods. "Yes. It had been nearly fifteen years since we went into the program."

"Did you wear disguises or anything?"

"Well, I lost a lot of my hair," he says, prompting laughter. "Seriously, I had a nose job. And I got my teeth capped, a different shape. And then everyone thought we were Jewish, although we never went to temple, which was good, I guess, since I still had my rosary."

More laughter.

The judge hammers his gavel for order.

Frank looks more serious again.

"Were you related to Cliff Yarlen?"

"Yes. He was my nephew. Cliff was the second of my sister Gina's five children."

"Were you ever in touch with him? After you went into the witness protection program?"

"Yes."

"How did that happen?"

"After I went into the witness program, my father had a lot of trouble with the Genoveses. They were pretty mad.

After all, I had given a lot of evidence to the feds against them. As part of a peace gesture, Dad took Cliff into our unions in Jersey. Cliff was a financial guy."

"Your father is Rocky Presario?"

"Yes."

"Do you know what Cliff's relationship was like with his father, Joe, and with his brother Nick?"

"With Nick it was terrible. Cliff abhorred just about everything Nick did and Nick knew it. Nick always said Cliff had airs, thought he was better than his family, that kind of thing. And Nick resented him. A lot. For a long time we all thought he might do something to Cliff."

"What was Cliff like?"

"Very, very intelligent. Kind, patient, but tough when he needed to be. But, you know, Nick was a high school dropout, Cliff had gone to NYU and gotten a master's and carried himself well, had nice manners. He was a gentleman and his older brother was a thug."

"Objection!" Perez cries.

"Sustained," Judge Kahn says. "The jury shall disregard the witness's last statement."

"Who asked your father to take Cliff in?" Banks resumes.

"Joe. Cliff's father. He figured Cliff would become a door into Atlantic City."

"I thought you said the unions your family did business with were clean."

"They were, but that didn't mean Joe didn't see them as ripe for the picking."

"What happened to Joe?"

"He went to prison after his trial. And he died there."

"And Nick?"

"Nick took his father's place."

"Did Nick and Cliff cross paths then, professionally?"

"Not really. My father used Cliff to create a completely new union, one to represent technical workers."

"The American Federation of Technical Workers?"

"Yes."

"Did you have anything to do with that union?"

"I brought the idea to my father. I saw a growing need for some kind of organized front for computer technicians. Not just for salaries and benefits, but to create standards of expertise. Things change so quickly in our industry, and there needed to be a formalized system of constant reeducation."

"Was the union successful?"

"Extremely. Employers were as anxious for it as were employees."

"And what was the role of your nephew, Cliff Yarlen?"

"He became the first president of the AFTW."

"And the union was run honestly?"

"Yes, sir."

"How did your nephew, Cliff Yarlen, come to live in Los Angeles?"

"Well, I saw Cliff. We met. Several times, actually, over the course of creating the union. My father thought the world of him and I came to believe in Cliff, too. What happened was, there was an explosion of special-effects movies coming out of Hollywood, and the AFTW needed to be in there. In terms of unions for the tech workers, there was only a loose affiliation with a truckers union. So Cliff moved out here to bring in the AFTW."

"What studio was the first to sign an agreement with the AFTW?"

"Monarch Studios, where my son Jonathan worked."

"Was that by accident, that the AFTW would get into the studio where Jonathan worked?"

"No. Jonathan, at that point, had been promoted several times. He was an executive and he strongly advised the studio to do it. It was a case where the union actually saved the studio a great deal of money, in ascertaining the true special-effects costs needed and costs of each movie. Before, the sky was the limit because no one in management knew what the technical people were talking about."

"And so the AFTW was successful in Hollywood?"

"It is still working to establish itself. It is not a completely done deal."

"Why not?"

"Well, it's an honest union, let's start with that. And there are a lot of dishonest people who would like to attach themselves to it and siphon money out of it."

"For example?"

"For example, Nick Arlenetta."

"He wanted to be involved with the AFTW?"

"Oh, yes. He came to see my father about it and my father taped the meeting. The authorities have the tape now." He directs this last statement to the prosecutor, as a kind of FYI note.

Banks takes a walk, comes back. "Why did your father tape that conversation with Nick?"

"Because we had all decided to work together, for the feds, in building a case to take Nick down."

"Who is we?"

"Cliff, Dad, me, Jonathan and eventually Lise—Lilliana."

"What were you planning to do?"

"Set Nick up, catch him in the act. Racketeering, violence, bribery, murder, coercion, you name it. He did it."

"Earlier in the week, Mr. Presario," Banks begins, walking over to the defense table to take some papers from Cecelie, "a witness, Sally Harrington, testified about a night in February of this year. She said she and a friend had driven Lilliana Martin to a house in Cold Water Canyon where her alleged boyfriend, Cliff Yarlen, was moving out." He looks up from the papers. "Can you add anything to that? About what was happening?"

"Sure. Cliff and Lilliana had been pretending to be a couple. It was a way for Jonathan—who by now was production head of Monarch—Cliff and Lilliana to spend time together without raising suspicion."

"You did not worry that Nick Arlenetta would realize Lilliana Martin was his cousin Lise, or that Jonathan Small was, in fact, his cousin Taylor Presario?"

"No. The last time he saw them, Lise was eight. Taylor was maybe six."

"And what was going on that night? The night of the party?"

"The feds alerted us that Nick had become suspicious of Cliff, that he had been making inquiries."

"About?"

"If Cliff was setting him up. So that day I told Cliff to get away from Lilliana, leave her out of it. They pretended to break up. And he left the house."

"Now, this house they were in, did any of you have any connection to it?"

"No. Jonathan would find these houses. The owners would be away and they'd stay there, meet with the feds and move on."

"So the night Ms. Harrington testified about being at the Cold Water Canyon house, Cliff was pretending to break up with Lilliana."

"Yes."

"What else happened that night?"

"Jonathan called me. He said the house was being watched by one of Nick Arlenetta's thugs, and he was concerned about Lilliana's safety. He thought maybe they were going to kidnap her, to use as leverage on Cliff."

"So what did you do?"

"I went over and got Lilliana and took her into hiding."

"For how long?"

"Just a day, because her agent spread the alarm and the next thing we knew, the police were looking for her and it was calling a whole lot more attention to her than we wanted."

Banks looks through the papers. "Ms. Harrington also testified that her friend, Spencer Hawes, returned to the Cold Water Canyon house the next day and disappeared. Do you know what happened to him?"

He nods. "Nick Arlenetta's people picked him up."

"How do you know this?"

"Jonathan, my son," he nods to him. "He told me."

"I see," Banks says. He shuffles some of his papers. "Mr. Presario, Sally Harrington testified that Cliff Yarlen appeared the next day at her home, the day after you picked up your daughter. She said Cliff Yarlen had flown all the way to Connecticut, to come to her home, looking for Lilliana."

"I heard that."

"Why didn't Cliff know where Lilliana was?"

"No one was in contact with Cliff at that point. We

knew Nick was after him, we didn't dare expose ourselves. The feds promised us they were keeping an eye on him. But they weren't in touch with Cliff, either, it turned out."

"The feds promised they were keeping an eye on him," Banks repeats, looking at the jury. He turns around. "What happened to Cliff?"

"He was murdered, shot through the head."

"Yes, he was," Banks says quietly, walking back to his table.

After a long silence, Judge Kahn speaks up. "Mr. Banks, perhaps this is a good place to break for lunch."

CHAPTER | 31

"Okay, we're all set," Clyde tells me. "Michael will be at the studio at seven forty-five."

"I still would like him there earlier," I complain. "That's barely enough time to do a sound check."

He smiles. "Those are the rules. And hey, you can ask him whatever you want. He says he has nothing to hide."

I burst out laughing. "Right. What's a little arms dealing, stolen-car fencing and murder among friends?"

Clyde shoots me a warning look and I hold up my hand. "I won't say a word about it tonight," I promise.

We're sitting outside, in the sun, on the curb of the far side of the building. Security has shooed us away from everywhere else. I'm eating a sandwich; Clyde is having a salad. Of course, he's got two hands to work with.

After we finish eating, I go back inside to the land

phones to check my voice mail and return calls. The last is to Paul.

"I just wanted to apologize for last night," he says. "I was so tired suddenly."

"Oh, I know, that's why I said something."

"But you came all the way out here, and brought the ice cream and everything."

I turn away a little from the guy at the next phone. "I was just glad to see you."

"So that writer guy wants to come over," he says next.

"I just had lunch with that writer guy," I tell him.

"He's okay?"

"Very okay," I say. "Self-made man, went to Oxford and writes very, very well." I pause while Prosecutor Perez slowly walks by, his eyes on me. "Can I help you with something?" I ask him.

He shakes his head and moves on, looking back at me again over his shoulder.

Creepy.

"Sorry, Paul, somebody just walked by. Anyway, I did some checking on Clyde. I think you'll like him. He wants more color for his piece, so make sure to be vivid and dramatic, Officer Fitzwilliam."

Paul laughs. After a moment, he asks, "Should I tell him how I feel about you?"

I smile. "I don't know. That's up to you. How public you'd like to be."

My heart rate has picked up.

Pause. "Sally, has this happened to you before?"

"What?"

"I mean, isn't this unusual? To feel this way? When we don't know each other very well?"

My heart is pounding, all right. "I don't quite know what to say." Because what am I going to say? *Yes, Paul, I've felt this way before, I fell head over heels in love and it all turned out to be a terrible mess, with a whole lot of passion involved and not much enduring love.*

"Say you'll see me tonight."

"I have the *Late Edition* to do."

"I saw something on DBS," he said. "Michael Arlenetta's being interviewed?"

"Yes, he is."

"Who's interviewing him?"

"I am."

"*You?* From three thousand miles away, I hope."

"No, actually he's coming to the studio."

"Michael Arlenetta's *here?* In California?"

"Yes."

Pause. "You know, Sally, he very well may have been the one who arranged for us to be run down the other night."

"Well, if he did, after the interview the cops will know where to find him, won't they?"

Pause. "Oh, Sally, I wish you would stay away from that scumbag. Can't someone else do the interview?"

"I don't want anyone else to do the interview."

He sighs heavily. "I'm coming down to the studio then."

"Paul, *don't.*"

"I don't like it, Sally."

"Paul, this is what I do for a living. You've got to get used to it, just as I have to get used to what you do."

He doesn't say anything. And then, finally, "Can we meet after?"

I smile. "Sure. I'll tell Louis. We'll come over."

"I won't fall asleep on you this time, I promise."

"It's quite all right if you do," I tell him.

"I'd like that," he says after a moment. "I'd like to drift off to sleep with you. Having you close to me, drawing you closer." A laugh. "So speaks Officer Hallmark Card," he jokes.

I stand in the line for the courtroom, humming under my breath. Sheriff Jones catches my attention, flicking a finger for me to come over to him. "Hi, what's up?"

"The next witness, the prosecutor guy?" he says. "The fed?"

"Sky Preston?"

"Yeah. He's not coming. Defense is bullshit."

"Why isn't he testifying?"

"Can't testify," he says, "without compromising an ongoing investigation."

"What about FBI Agent Alfonso?"

He shakes his head. "He's not testifying, either."

"Son of a bitch," I say under my breath. "They're hanging Jonathan out to dry." I look at him. "This is on the level?"

He nods.

"You've got your tickets," I tell him before tearing for the telephone. I am put through to Will and he carefully takes down what I have to say. Within the hour, I am confident, Alexandra will break the news as a bulletin. Then I'm switched up to Jackson Darenbrook's office, where I plead my case—I need Laker tickets for opening day.

Then I hurry down the corridor to make the very end of the line into the courtroom. A bit breathless, I slip by the other people in our pew and sit down heavily next to Clyde, banging my cast on the bench as I do, making me cry out in pain. I lower my head, biting down, trying to wait out the bone-deep pain that is zinging and zanging up and down my arm.

"All rise."

Bending slightly, I do.

"Can I get you something?" Clyde whispers.

"New body," I whisper back.

Judge Kahn moves up to the bench. "We will resume with the testimony of Frederick Small," he reads. As Frank Presario makes his way up through the gate to the witness box, the judge adds, "For the sake of clarification, I remind the jury that the witness has asked to be called by his birth name, Frank Presario." To Presario, he says, "Sir, you are reminded that you are still under oath."

"Yes, Your Honor."

"Mr. Banks, you may proceed."

"Mr. Presario, before we broke for lunch, you had recounted for the jury the events leading up to the murder of your nephew, Cliff Yarlen, and your fear that Nick Arlenetta might harm your daughter, Lilliana Martin."

He nods. "If he found out who she was."

"At the time of Cliff Yarlen's murder, did you think Nick Arlenetta knew the true identity of your daughter?"

"No, I did not."

"So you let your daughter return to her home?"

"Actually it was my home," he says. "I owned it. But Lilliana was living there, yes."

"And where were you living at this time?"

"Larkensburg, in the desert. I had built a retreat for us: Jonathan, Lilliana and myself. A safe place where we could visit. We often spent weekends there together. My father used to come there as well."

"Is that where your daughter was when she disappeared?"

"Yes. She was with me."

"And when the FBI told you it was safe, she needn't worry, she could return to Los Angeles, she did?"

"Yes."

"Ms. Harrington testified that your daughter called her and told her where she could find her in Bel Air. Do you know why?"

"No."

"Did your daughter mention anything to you about Sally Harrington?"

"Up until that time?"

"Yes."

"No, she didn't."

"When was the first time you heard Sally Harrington's name?"

"The day the Bel Air house was firebombed, March 7. I heard on the news that she had been there and had survived."

"Let's back up to after your daughter returned to the Bel Air house. What did you tell her to do after Cliff Yarlen was murdered?"

"To act as normally as possible. And since she was supposedly involved with Cliff, it was normal for her to grieve."

"When did you perceive that your daughter was in danger?"

"The morning the house was attacked."

"The Bel Air house."

"Yes."

"What happened?"

"I got a call from Sky Preston that morning."

"Who is he?"

"A federal prosecutor we had been working with on the case."

"And what did Special Prosecutor Preston say?"

"He said he had reason to believe Nick had found out who Lilliana really was."

"So what did you do?"

"I called my father and he sent a group of bodyguards to the house. Sky was arranging to move her that afternoon. We argued. I wanted her with me in Larkensburg, but Sky Preston didn't want Nick to track me down through her."

"What happened then?"

He shrugs, sighing. "The house was firebombed, Lise was nearly killed. Sally Harrington helped get her out and they came to Larkensburg."

"What happened then?"

"The FBI took Sally away that night. Jonathan had come down, but he left to get back to L.A."

"What did your daughter do?"

"She stayed with me. I wouldn't leave Larkensburg. Until the threat was over."

"Mr. Presario, did you have any doubt in your mind about who was responsible for the firebombing?"

"None. Nor did the FBI."

"Objection, Your Honor," Perez says, standing up. "How could the witness know what the FBI thought?"

"They told me," Frank says flatly.

Banks smiles slightly at the judge. "Overruled," Judge Kahn says.

"Mr. Presario, were you aware of your son's plans to meet with Nick Arlenetta?"

"Yes."

"Would you care to explain to the jury how you felt about it?"

"I was very much against it. The FBI wanted Jonathan to continue with the charade, to recognize Nick as the union executive in charge of the AFTW and begin negotiations with him."

"And your son was willing to do this?"

"Yes. He believed it was the only way of getting rid of Nick, once and for all."

"Getting rid of Nick, once and for all, how?"

"Putting him away in a federal penitentiary. With any luck, he'd die there like his father."

Banks let the comment sink in.

"When you heard that Nick Arlenetta had been shot dead in your son's office at Monarch Studios, what was your re-action?"

"Disbelief."

"You were told that Jonathan shot him?"

"Yes. And I didn't believe it."

"What did you believe?"

He takes a breath, thinking a moment. He nods a little and says, "I thought the feds did it and had Jonathan take the rap."

"Why would you think that?"

"Because they had screwed it up. But they knew Jonathan certainly had good reason to stop this psychopath and they figured he would get off."

"Do you still believe that?"

"Objection, Your Honor!" Perez cries. "This is all pure speculation, it is not based on any facts."

"The witness is capable of reasonable conclusions, Your Honor. He has been collaborating with the federal authorities for over twenty years. His opinion as to what happened is certainly relevant to this case."

Judge Kahn thinks it over. "I'll allow it. You may answer the question, Mr. Presario."

"I think the federal agents set up Nick Arlenetta to be murdered. I don't think my son was responsible."

Murmurs in the courtroom.

"Those are all the questions I have for this witness, Your Honor," Banks says, returning to his table.

Perez stands up and moves over. "Good afternoon."

"Good afternoon," Frank says pleasantly, sipping his water.

"This has been a long and arduous ordeal for you," Perez remarks.

"Yes, it has been."

"I won't keep you long, Mr. Presario." He walks over to his table to look at some notes and then comes back. "Mr. Presario, your father, Rocky Presario, was a major figure in the Gambino crime family, yes or no?"

"I don't understand the question," he says smoothly.

"Was your father a boss for the Gambino crime family, yes or no?"

He doesn't answer right away. Finally, "At one time he worked for them, yes."

"The question was, Mr. Presario, was your father, Rocky Presario, a boss for the Gambino crime family?"

When he doesn't answer, the judge coughs a little and says, "You must answer the question."

Frank looks at Perez. "Yes."

A murmur in the courtroom.

"Mr. Presario, did you ever work for the Gambino crime family?"

"Not knowingly" comes the reply.

"Did you ever work for the Gambino crime family?"

He nods. "Yes."

Perez strolls over to the jury. "Mr. Presario, have you ever broken the law?"

"Yes."

"Have you ever lied to the authorities?"

Pause. "Yes."

"Have you lied in your testimony today?"

"No."

"No?" Perez says.

"No."

Perez walks over to get a pad. "You testified today that you saw a tape of Spencer Hawes being picked up at the Cold Water Canyon house by Nick Arlenetta's people."

"Yes."

He drops the pad. "Isn't it true that you ordered Spencer Hawes to be taken away?"

Presario looks puzzled, looks to the judge.

"Mr. Presario," Perez says sharply. "Isn't it true that you ordered Spencer Hawes to be picked up?"

He shakes his head. "No."

"Didn't you send him out on the barge, where he was beaten?"

He shakes his head again. "No."

"Then let me ask you this, did your daughter, Lilliana Martin, ever call you about the disappearance of Spencer Hawes?"

"Yes."

"What did she say?"

"She said he was a book editor and had nothing to do with Nick and somebody had to do something."

"So you saw that he was released, didn't you?"

"I made some calls, but—"

"Were you or were you not responsible for seeing that Spencer Hawes was freed from his captivity? Yes or no?"

Frank looks to the judge for help.

"You must answer the question, Mr. Presario," Judge Kahn says.

Frank sighs. "Yes."

Murmurs in the courtroom.

Perez walks over to the defense table, looks at a piece of paper and comes back. "Did you ever hear your son threaten to kill Nick Arlenetta?"

Frank pauses. "He may have made a reference to it."

"Did you ever hear your son threaten to kill Nick Arlenetta?"

"Yes."

"More than once?"

"Yes."

"Does your son know how to shoot a gun?"

"Yes."

"Did you teach him how to shoot?"

"Yes."

"Did you ever hear your son threaten to shoot Nick Arlenetta?"

A sigh. "Yes."

"For how many years did your son cooperate with the FBI in setting Nick Arlenetta up?"

"Three."

"Was your son close to Cliff Yarlen?"

"Yes."

"Was your son upset by his murder?"

"Yes."

"Was your son upset when his sister was nearly killed in the firebombing of the mansion?"

"Yes."

"Did he, at that time, threaten to kill Nick Arlenetta?"

"We all did."

There is a murmur and the judge raps the gavel for order.

"After Lilliana Martin, his sister, was nearly killed, did your son say he was going to kill Nick Arlenetta?"

"Only if the feds didn't get him," he says.

"Yes or no, Mr. Presario, after he learned how close his sister had come to being murdered, did Jonathan Small say he was going to murder Nick Arlenetta?"

"Yes."

"No further questions, Your Honor." He sits down.

"Mr. Banks?"

"Thank you, Your Honor," he says, stepping forward. "Mr. Presario, how old were you when you found out the Gambino crime family had something to do with your place of employment?"

He thinks a minute. "I was twenty-four."

"And what were you doing?"

"I was a unit manager in the finance department of the United Building & Construction Workers of America union. I had found some discrepancies in the records and I went to tell my supervisor about it."

"And what did he or she say?"

"He told me to leave it alone. I talked to my father about it that night and he said I had to leave it alone, too."

"Did he say why?"

"He said the Gambino crime family had corrupted the union and I would be in a great deal of danger if I persisted in my inquiries."

"What was your reaction when he told you this?"

"I was outraged. And disgusted and angry."

"So what did you do?"

"I started badgering my father about it. Asking why did the union have to be crooked."

"Could you give the jury an example of what upset you?"

"Sure. Phantom workers, that was the biggest thing. They used to bill companies for workers that didn't exist. Even made them pay them overtime."

"Did you have any effect on your father?"

"Yes, over the years, I certainly did. He, in fact, was the one who told me, and showed me, how to bide my time, build up my power in the union and how he and I together, could gradually over the years clean the union up."

"And how did the Gambino crime family take this?"

"Not well. They tried to get rid of my father, but he had friends. We weren't the only ones who were interested in clean, well-run unions. Eventually they left us alone and moved on to more vulnerable operations."

"But the Arlenettas came after you."

"Yes. The Arlenettas led Mario Tiezzi—he headed the Genovese crime family—to believe they could take us over and use the UBCWA to roll into Atlantic City."

"Is this the same Mario Tiezzi you helped the FBI to put behind bars?"

Blink. "Yes."

"Very good." Banks takes a turn around the jury box. "Mr. Presario, could you clarify for the jury exactly what your role was in the release of Spencer Hawes?"

"Yes." He clears his throat and looks at the jury. "Lise— Lilliana—called me and told me about this Spencer Hawes, the book editor, who was missing. As I testified, I saw a surveillance tape that showed Mr. Hawes being picked up by one of Nick Arlenetta's men. Until Lilliana called me, I thought Mr. Hawes was in collusion with Nick Arlenetta. So after Lilliana called me, I called my father and told him that Spencer Hawes wasn't anybody to anything, he was simply a bystander, and my father contacted people who worked for Nick Arlenetta and told them. Until then, they thought Spencer Hawes was connected to me. So they released him."

"Very good, thank you," Banks says, walking back to his table to look at his notes. He turns around again. "Mr. Presario, you stated to Prosecutor Perez a short while ago that 'all of us' had threatened to kill Nick Arlenetta. Could you explain that statement for the jury, starting with who you meant when you said 'us'?"

"Me, Jonathan, Lise, my father and FBI Agent Alfonso."

"FBI Agent Alfonso threatened to kill Nick Arlenetta?"

"Yes."

The courtroom breaks out in murmurs.

"When did he make this threat?"

"After Lise was nearly killed in the firebombing, the night of March 7."

"Where were you?"

"In the living room of my home in Larkensburg."

"And what was the context of this threat?"

"I was angry about the lack of protection of Lise, about what had happened, and Agent Alfonso said, 'I will kill Nick Arlenetta myself before he ever lays a finger on your daughter.'"

The courtroom explodes and I'm up and out of my seat, struggling to get out of our row.

Judge Kahn is hammering away with his gavel as I run to the land phones, the guy from Fox and the gal from ABC right behind me.

Within seconds I am connected with Will and Alexandra, relaying from my shorthand notes of what has just been said in the courtroom. Within a minute, all six phones are busy with reporters doing the same thing.

Sometimes it's good to be seated near the back.

CHAPTER | 32

Judge Kahn calls a short recess to bring some order back to his courtroom. I use it to search for Burton Kott and I finally find him as he emerges from the corridor leading to the witness holding room. I shoulder in close to him to ask, "Why aren't Preston and Alfonso testifying?"

He looks at me, dumbstruck. "I only found that out two seconds ago," he says. "How the hell do you know?"

"Banks only just told you?" I say incredulously.

He nods.

"Is Lilliana here? Waiting to testify?"

"I'm not telling you anything," Burton says, frowning.

That means yes. "Did Banks tell her that Preston and Alfonso have bailed out?"

"I told you, I'm not telling you anything," Burton insists.

Another yes. "That puts an awful lot of pressure on Lilliana," I say. "She's the last witness on the defense's list." Burton doesn't say anything. I look at him squarely in the eye. "But it's going well, isn't it? I don't think there's a person on the jury who wouldn't have killed Nick Arlenetta, too."

Still he doesn't say anything.

My smile fades. "Still the issue of premeditated murder, though. Right? Sky's testimony could have helped. Alfonso's, too. But then," I think out loud, "Frank's testified he thinks that the feds did it, they murdered Arlenetta." I squint slightly. "Is that what's going on? You're trying to create reasonable doubt by setting up the possibility the feds had something to do with it?"

Burton shakes his head. "I can't help you, Sally." He moves around me and continues down the corridor.

"We need facts, Sally," Alexandra is saying to me moments later over the land phone, "we have to be sure about this."

"Okay, the facts are these. Frank Presario testified he believes the federal authorities had something to do with the killing of Nick Arlenetta. Special Federal Prosecutor, Sky Preston, was scheduled as the next witness for the defense. He has canceled, he won't appear. FBI Agent Alfonso was scheduled as the following witness for the defense and he has canceled and won't appear. The only witness left is Lilliana Martin, who spent the time between the firebombing and the murder of Nick Arlenetta with her father, so no doubt she is going to support his story, or more than likely, is in some way going to advance the validity of the theory that the feds are somehow responsible for this mess and now they've baled."

"Hmm," my boss says, mulling this over. "Pity you have

the Michael Arlenetta interview tonight. This would be a good topic of discussion with Emmett."

"If the interview is bull, which we all know it will be," I say, "I can wrap it up by the second commercial break, and we can come back for the last eight minutes with Emmett."

"Hmm," she says again. "No, I think maybe you should switch the order around. Yes," she adds with more enthusiasm, "open the program with you and Emmett and this latest development. Take it right up to the first break and then promise Arlenetta. Come back, do him for the two segments, close out the show, but then, if he'll stay, keep interviewing him for as long as he'll sit there. I would like as much tape on him as we can get to use for the newscasts and the magazine."

"Great, I think that's great," I declare, excited.

"The only thing is..." Her voice trails off and I can visualize her turning in her office chair at West End to look out at the park while she's thinking. (She always does this.) "I just don't get why Arlenetta's out there, in California."

"Paul thinks he's the one who had us run down the other night."

"That's what I mean," Alexandra says. "There are all these pending indictments out there for him, and yet... There he is, wanting to come to the studio tonight. It's bizarre." Pause. "How well do you know this Clyde fellow?"

"Fairly well. Spencer knows him, I could talk to him." I won't tell her about his ghosting a book for Arlenetta because I swore I wouldn't tell anyone.

"It smells like a setup to me," Alexandra says.

"It will be fine," I tell her. "And whatever it turns out to be, we'll have a whole lot of people watching, and that's good, right?"

"Yes," she says softly. "Look, be careful and keep Louis close, all right? Will talked to Glen at the studio—there's going to be extra security there tonight. And at Georgiana's. Just make sure nobody follows you guys home tonight, all right?" She's worried. I suppose I should be, too, but then, I'm the one everybody says needs to be in therapy.

We have been waiting outside the courtroom. The so-called short recess has lasted over an hour, and I wonder, as it is approaching four o'clock, if court might be postponed altogether until tomorrow morning.

Something's up. But nobody's telling us out here.

Finally, at two minutes after four, we are led into the courtroom. When Judge Kahn enters, he looks tired and drawn. "Call your next witness, Mr. Banks," he says.

Banks stands up. "The defense calls Lilliana Martin."

A quiet hubbub begins in the courtroom as Lilliana dramatically enters the courtroom. She is dressed in black, in mourning for heaven only knows who, with a tiny black hat and veil that looks French. You know, Chanel-like. She is not tall, but makes up for it with a kind of squaring of her shoulders and graceful walk. Lilliana has an incredible body, but it is discreetly subdued in this suit, although nothing can hide those legs.

She raises her right hand and takes the oath in a clear voice. I suppress a smile, for this reminds me of a courtroom episode from her old daytime drama that's rerunning on the SoapNetwork.

"Please state your name for the record."

"Lilliana Martin, formerly Lise Anne Presario."

A murmur through the courtroom. It is very dramatic. But then, Lilliana was nominated for an Oscar.

It's funny. I wondered what they would do about Lilliana's hair for the trial. You see, it's this fake platinum-blond color that screams "bad girl." Lilliana has overtly dark eyebrows, so she is very clearly a bottle blonde, and yet the defense has instructed her to keep this look. Her makeup has softened her, though. And she is a beauty, with large brown eyes and olive skin, and so the hair thing is, well, interesting. But it works.

Funny, despite the hair color, today I can see her Italian heritage more than I ever did before.

Gracefully she takes her place on the witness stand, settling in, blinking several times in what is supposed to be nervousness. (Who could ever know for sure with Lilliana what is real?)

"Good afternoon," Banks says. "Would you prefer to be called Ms. Martin or Ms. Presario?"

"I wish you would just call me Lilliana," she says in a hushed voice.

"Lilliana," Banks repeats. "Lilliana, could you tell the jury what your relationship is to the defendant?"

"He's my baby brother," she says, sneaking a look of fondness at him.

"You have the same biological parents?"

"Had. My mother was murdered when we were children."

Everybody knows this, for heaven's sake, and yet the

way she says this provokes sympathetic murmurs in the courtroom.

"Lilliana, could you please describe for the jury what kind of child your brother was?"

"Objection, Your Honor," Perez says. "The People fail to see the relevance."

Judge Kahn looks at the defense. "Attorney Banks?"

(I make a note this is the first time I can remember the judge addressing Banks as "Attorney" and not "Mr." To finally gain this address of respect, Banks must be making more headway than I realize.)

"The defense believes it's important to present a balanced portrait of the defendant's character, Your Honor. Certainly the child that grew up into the man who is on trial is relevant."

"Objection overruled, you may continue," the judge says.

Lilliana hesitates.

Judge Kahn cranes his neck a bit, to look at the actress. "You may answer the question, Ms. Martin, about what your brother was like."

(*Good grief,* I think, *the judge is sweet on her.*)

"Taylor was very young when Mama was murdered," she says.

"Just to clarify for the jury," Banks interrupts her, "could you explain who Taylor is?"

"Taylor is Jonathan," she says, pointing to the defendant. "They changed his name in the witness protection program." She looks at the jury and offers a warm smile. "It's confusing, I know. You can imagine how we felt about it."

The jury smiles back.

"For the sake of clarity, then," Banks says, "perhaps we could simply refer to your brother, the defendant, as Jonathan?"

Lilliana nods. "Fine."

Banks walks over to stand near the jury box. "So what was your brother like?"

"Oh, he was a little sweetie," she says, smiling. "Of course, he was a little brother, so he could be a pain, always tagging along, but he was truly a sweet little boy."

"He was close to your mother?"

"Very close," she says, nodding, eyes widening. "They had a lot in common."

"Like what?"

"Music. Jonathan was very musical—Dad and I weren't, that's for sure—but Mama was. Jonathan liked opera, which I always thought was bizarre for a little kid, but he did."

"Why did you think that was bizarre?"

"Because he was like, six or something, and could sing all these arias—*in Italian.* He started taking the violin, and then he and Mama started making videos—of course I would star in them...."

The jury and gallery laugh lightly. They love her.

"He was a remarkable little boy. While other boys were dropping water balloons and being pests, Jonathan was dreaming of producing full-fledge operas in the backyard."

"Did your brother have friends?"

"He had jock friends—kids he played sports with." She lowers her voice. "There weren't a whole lot of little boys who fancied opera in Short Hills, New Jersey."

A courtroom chuckle.

"He was small for his age—he was short like Dad's side of the family—but he was a terrific soccer player. So he had friends from that. And he played baseball pretty well. And then he was in this G and T class—"

"What is G and T?"

"Gifted and Talented," she explains. "And he had a couple of friends from that. They would write books and plays." She smiles. "He was a most remarkable little boy, my little brother." Again she shoots him a look of love.

"Lilliana, did you ever see your brother be violent?"

She looks incredulous. "Taylor? I mean, Jonathan? Never. Just the opposite. He was a softhearted kid, to the point that kids sometimes took advantage of him."

"How so? Could you give the jury an example?"

"Sure." She looks at the jury. "One time, an older boy in the neighborhood found this wounded bunny. It was a baby bunny and a cat or something had gotten to it. Anyway, this kid was teasing it, poking it with a stick, and it made this horrible high-pitched screaming sound, and I was crying and yelling at the boy to stop it and then Jonathan came running over—he was maybe six—and he threw himself down in front of the bunny and told the boy he'd pay him to stop it."

"What happened then?"

"The bully said, 'How much?' And Jonathan said he'd give him everything in his piggy bank, he would just hand it over. And then he told me to run to the house and get his bank." Suddenly she starts to cry, dropping her head in her hand.

Banks looks surprised, glancing up at the judge.

"I'm sorry," she says, raising her head. Her face is splotched with red now, her nose is red. "I'm sorry," she says again, "does somebody have a Kleenex?"

Banks gives her his clean handkerchief, for which she thanks him, and proceeds to collect herself.

The judge looks at his watch and whispers something to the glamorous clerk.

"This story upsets you?" Banks asks.

"It happened just before Mama was killed," she says, tears threatening again, "so it's just the whole memory is linked to so much sadness."

"Did you go and get your little brother's bank?"

She nods, wiping her eyes. "Yes. And when I came back, the bully was poking Jonathan with the stick, but Jonathan wouldn't budge, and that poor bunny was lying there behind him."

"What happened?"

"I gave him—"

"The bully?"

"Yes. I gave him the bank, he smashed it against a tree and money went everywhere and he started picking it up. Jonathan took off his shirt and moved the bunny onto it and ran home with it."

"What happened then?"

She blinks, looking miserable. "I went home and Jonathan was sobbing his heart out, because the bunny was dead. Mama was there and she tried to tell him the bunny was in heaven and he had done a good thing—" She bursts into tears and I have no doubt but many of them are real. Lilliana has lost control.

"Perhaps this is where we should stop for the day,"

Judge Kahn says, clearing his throat. "Court will resume at nine-thirty tomorrow morning."

I hurry out of the courthouse to find Louis. I've got to get to the Burbank studio and rush hour has begun.

CHAPTER | 33

"So what happened to her?" Emmett Phelps asks as we step up onto the set.

"It was just one of those childhood memories that got to her." I pull my blouse out from my skirt band to allow the soundman to run the microphone wire up. With one arm in a cast, there's no way I can do it myself. I glance over at the monitor to see Gary Plains doing the weather. It's ten thirty-five in New York; seven thirty-five here in Burbank, *DBS News America Tonight with Alexandra Waring* is on the air on the East Coast.

"For real, though?" Emmett says. "After all, she is an actress."

"I don't know," I say truthfully, looking back at him. "She misses her mother a great deal. Those memories can be tough." The local news producer catches my eye. "Glen! I thought you were outside waiting for Arlenetta."

"I've got Becky out there."

"No!" I protest. "Come on, this is Michael Arlenetta—*hello*—like the biggest interview of the trial?" I look at my watch. "He's going to be here any second. *You* should be out there."

Glen gives me a look like, *bitch,* and leaves the studio. I say into my mike, "Can you guys hear me?"

"We're here, Sally," a voice in my earphone says. It is Zigs, the director in the control room.

"Can somebody make sure Glen gets out there? Arlenetta thinks he's first up—somebody needs to explain the format, check his makeup and get him prepped. We also need a sound level on him. He doesn't have the timbre Emmett does."

"This isn't New York," Zigs says.

I'm about to say *I'll* say, but refrain. I have a list a mile long outlining what's wrong with this affiliate. My vote is for DBS to buy the darn station and revamp the operation from stem to stern. It is too important a location to keep staggering along with this happy-hands-at-home operation. Take the news director, for example, whose nickname comes from a particular kind of rolling paper.

Emmett and I review our opening segment on the federal officials canceling their testimony. I keep an eye on the time. I want to change the order of my index cards, but have to hold some of them in my mouth to do so.

"You have pretty teeth," Emmett tells me. "You must never have smoked."

Where his mind is at, I have no idea. I for one am preparing for the broadcast.

Seven-forty. I glance at the studio door, next to which Louis is quietly standing. "Somebody let me know when Arlenetta gets here?" I say into the mike.

"Will do," Zigs answers.

I look at the monitor. Alexandra's doing a plug for the interview on the newscast; I can see a little picture of Michael Arlenetta up in the corner.

Seven forty-two.

Where is he?

Seven forty-three.

Clyde said seven forty-five, don't worry.

The floor manager turns the monitor away from us so the camera guys can see it.

Seven forty-five.

"Is he here?" I ask.

"Not yet," the reply comes. "And Glen *is* outside."

"I don't know, Sally," Emmett says warningly, looking at his watch. "What happens if he doesn't show?"

"We keep talking," I tell him. I sigh. "Heaven knows, we've got all the Presario testimony to recap."

"But I don't have that!" Emmett cries, panicking suddenly and tearing through his papers.

"All you have to do is ask me what happened today," I say irritably. "I was there, remember? Just—be a lawyer, okay? Emmett! Are you listening?"

Emmett stops fussing with his papers for a moment, eyes wild behind his glasses, his chest heaving with short gasps. He's losing it, great.

"Relax," I whisper. I smile. "You are very, very good on your feet," I say. "In fact, if worse comes to worse and he doesn't show, you'll be much more effective in this format. You'll just follow your own curiosity."

He stares at me a moment longer, his breathing coming under control, and he shuts his parted mouth to swallow.

I nervously check my watch. Seven fifty-one. *Damn. Where is he?*

"What happened at the trial today, Sally?" Emmett says under his breath, taking a pen out of his breast pocket to write this question down.

Live, from Burbank, it's the Happy-Hands-at-Home Late Edition!

Seven fifty-three.

"Shit!" somebody yells in the control room, making all of us clutch our ears—me, Emmett, the cameramen and the floor manager.

"Harry," Zigs barks, "we need a live camera outside, on the double."

The man behind camera three rips off his headset and starts running across the studio.

"Sally, you better get out there," the director says next. "All hell's breaking loose."

I tear out my earphone, rip the microphone out of the floor socket and jam it in my skirt band as I hurry out of the studio.

"Come back!" Emmett yells. "We're on in seven minutes!"

"Six," the floor manager says, correcting him.

I run through the studio and down the back hallway to the back entrance. When I turn the corner I see a cascade of pulsating lights playing over the walls, yellow and red. I open the glass door and see a gray limousine surrounded by California state trooper cars. The cameraman is coming up behind me; the floodlight of the remote camera on his shoulder coming on. I hold the door for him, urging him ahead and following him through the people.

Seven fifty-six.

Michael Arlenetta is leaning over the end of the limo, his wrists are being handcuffed behind his back. He sees me and smiles, straightening up. "This is quite a reception, Ms. Harrington."

"What are you doing?" I cry to the troopers. "He's doing an interview on DBS News in four minutes!"

"He's under arrest," the trooper closest to me says.

"Can't you arrest him *after* the interview?" I say sensibly. "Just give us ten minutes? He can do the interview right in handcuffs."

"Only if you wear handcuffs, too," Arlenetta jokes. He looks into the camera. "She invites me to an interview and sets me up to be arrested. I don't even know what for. I haven't done anything."

I lean over the trunk of the car. "I didn't do this," I tell Arlenetta.

"Somebody did," he says, looking mildly amused.

"Michael Arlenetta," the trooper says, reading from his notebook, "you are under arrest for the murder of Mario Cantano, and the attempted murder of Lilliana Martin. You have the right to remain silent..."

"Michael? Did you want to say anything?" I plead, aware of the camera over my shoulder.

"I'd appreciate it if you would get out of my face, Ms. Harrington," an officer tells me firmly, pulling me away from the car by my good arm.

I look at my watch. One forty-five to air. I run inside the building, down the corridor and back into the studio. "Go out to the parking lot, Emmett," I say, yanking out his earphone and microphone and dropping them on the floor. "Arlenetta's being arrested. Interview the cops." I squat down to plug my microphone into the stage outlet, stand back up and pick up my note cards before plunking down in my chair. "Can you hear me? One, two, three, hello, hello, hello," I say into the mike. "Emmett!" I bark. "Get out there, *move!*" I point to an intern, "*You,* take him out there! *Go! Move!*" Emmett seems to wake up and hurries out of the studio.

Into my mike, I say, "Zigs, I'll open and then see if you can cut to a live picture outside and I'll do a voice-over." Aloud to the studio, "I need a monitor!"

"Can do," the director says in my earphone.

"Fifteen seconds," the floor manager says calmly, rolling the monitor back into my view, where I can see a commercial is giving over to the opening graphics of the *Late Edition.* "Sally, your collar," he whispers, gesturing.

I straightened it, smooth my hair, lick my lips and take a deep breath.

Show time.

The red light on camera one comes on. "Good evening, and welcome to *DBS Late Edition.* I'm Sally Harrington and we're coming to you live from KWRK in Burbank, California, where just moments ago Michael Arlenetta, younger brother of slain New Jersey mobster Nick Arlenetta, was arrested." Out of the corner of my eye I can see that Zigs has switched to the outside camera. I smile—it looks great. Arlenetta is still out there in handcuffs, the lights are flashing, the troopers looking grave. I refocus my attention on the monitor to narrate. "Mr. Arlenetta was scheduled for an interview tonight, but California state troopers intercepted him outside the studio and have arrested him for the murder of Mario Cantano, and the attempted murder of actress Lilliana Martin."

I swallow, trying to think fast. "These charges stem from the firebombing incident viewers will remember that occurred on March 7 in Bel Air, California, which is part of the Los Angeles area. A helicopter attacked the Presario mansion, firing two grenade rockets. Mario Cantano, a bodyguard for the Presario family, was killed—he was decapitated in the first blast—and Lilliana Martin was very nearly killed, as well.

"At this time it is not known how or why the authorities chose to intercept and arrest Michael Arlenetta outside our studio—"

"We've got a headset and mike on Emmett," Zigs is telling me in my earphone.

"But one would assume it is linked to the testimony given this week at 'The Mafia Boss Murder' trial unfolding in nearby Santa Monica, where Jonathan Small is on trial for the murder of Michael Arlenetta's brother, Nick. But right now we're going to go live, outside, to where our legal expert, Emmett Phelps, professor of criminal law at USC, is standing. Emmett?"

"Hi," Emmett manages to say. He is not on camera, but standing next to the camera, which is enabling us to watch a man in a suit arguing with state troopers, while Arlenetta continues to stand there behind the car, in handcuffs.

"Emmett, what's happening out there? Why haven't the state police taken Michael Arlenetta away?"

"His lawyer's here."

I wait a full second. "Was his lawyer in the car with him when he arrived?"

"I'm sorry, Sally. It's hard to hear."

"Just tell us what happened," I half plead, ready to run out there myself.

"Just tell her what happened!" Glen's voice is heard to rasp in the background.

"Yes, okay," Emmett is heard saying. "Yes, uh, Sally."

I think I'm going to have a heart attack.

"Evidently Michael Arlenetta drove up to the back door of the KWRK studios at seven fifty-three," he begins.

I can't believe it. Emmett's starting to thaw, to speak rationally, smoothly—

"Fully intending on being interviewed by you on the *Late Edition*. As soon as the limousine stopped, however, five—six California state trooper cars surrounded the limousine. In the car with Michael Arlenetta was his legal adviser, Marvin Delacroix, who you can see talking to state troopers. He is the gentleman on the right, in the blue suit and gray tie."

Now I'm smiling. Emmett's doing great. Professor Phelps is acting like a reporter now.

CHAPTER | 34

"Where are you now?" Will Rafferty wants to know.

"I'm with Louis, going to Encino, why?" I say, peering out the car window to see where on 101 we are.

"The air force shot down an unidentified helicopter near the Bennington Reserve in New Jersey less than an hour ago."

"Oh, my God," I say. To Louis in the front seat, "Turn on news radio, will you?"

"It's not a terrorist attack, is it?"

"Nobody knows. Homeland Security picked up a warning from Newark about a helicopter that refused to identify itself, heading down through Bergen County. The air force intercepted it over Bennington Reserve, tried to force it down, it refused, so they shot it down. That's right near Alexandra's farm so she's called people to try to get to the scene and find out something. But she thinks—we think—there's a good chance this was going to be a rerun of the firebombing in Bel Air. But at Rocky Presario's compound."

"Oh, boy," I say, sighing.

"I know," Will says. "It's creepy."

"It would explain why Michael Arlenetta is out here on national TV, wouldn't it?" I say quietly. "*Who me? I couldn't have done it. I was being arrested for the other firebombing I had nothing to do with.*"

I hang up, thinking this over and praying it was simply another incident in the long battle between the Presarios and the Arlenettas, and not another terrorist attack. I don't know why, but I feel better about sick-and-twisted Americans than I do about sick-and-twisted foreigners here in America.

By the time we pull up to Paul's complex, I feel a tremor starting in my right hand. My nerves are shot. Still, I need to see Paul, I need to hear what he has to say. When he opens the door, he immediately asks me if I'm all right, to sit down, to let him get me something. "Anything that has alcohol in it, please," I tell him.

"I have beer."

"Great." I start to move a laundry pile but then say forget it and simply fall down on top of it, rubbing my eyes.

"How did the interview go?" he asks, coming back in with a glass.

I look at him, "We didn't have it."

"Why not?" He hands me the glass of beer.

I take a large swallow. "He was arrested when he arrived at the studio."

"You didn't do the interview?"

"No," I tell him. I take another drink and watch him as he walks away, sitting down on the arm of the chair opposite me.

"Sally," he begins.

"Yes," I tell him, "I'm upset. Very upset."

He looks up, his face flushing slightly.

"I know you tipped off the police, Paul, you're the only one who could have. Everyone else thought the interview was taking place in New York."

"I knew you'd be upset," he says. "But I didn't care, Sally. It was much more important that you remain safe." He pauses, swallowing. "And I don't know any better deterrent for someone who might be trying to kill you than to have him arrested."

I don't say anything.

"I know it doesn't help much, but they were supposed to pick him up *after* the interview. You were supposed to interview him and then they were supposed to pick him up."

"That does help," I tell him.

"Hi, Sal," Jack says, walking by with only a towel around his waist to the kitchen.

"Hi," I say.

"How are you?" he calls.

"Fine," I say, looking at Paul.

"You guys want to shoot some pool?" he asks, coming out with an open milk carton in his hand. He drinks out of the carton, looks at my cast, and then at Paul's, and laughs. "Guess not, unless we use both of you on one stick." He drinks some milk and holds up the carton. "Gotta coat my stomach. They drink a lotta beer in this league." And off he trundles back down the hall.

"I told you about the interview in confidence, Paul, that's why I'm upset."

"I'm a law enforcement officer," he tells me. "And this guy may have nearly killed us both on Sunday."

My anger temporarily ebbs. "Any evidence?"

"Not yet. But ten to one—"

"Paul," I say putting the beer down and hauling myself out of the chair, "it's my career, you know?"

"It's your *life*, you know?" he counters, rising also.

"That's not it, Paul," I say as I move toward the door. "If you don't understand what I'm saying, there's no point in trying to talk about it."

"I'm sorry, Sally, truly I'm sorry," he says, following me. "But I gotta tell you, I'd do it again if I thought you were at risk."

I look at him. "So I can't tell you things, I can't trust you. Is that what you're telling me?"

He comes over to me. "You can't put yourself in the line of fire. Not without me wanting to put myself in front of you." He pauses, searching my eyes. "I'm really serious about us, Sally. Really serious."

"We've known each other for a week, for Pete's sake," I say, moving away.

"Come here," he says, walking toward the hall. He turns around. "Come on, I want to show you something."

"Paul."

"Please. Just come and see this and then you can go."

I sigh and acquiesce, following him down the hall to his bedroom. He steps aside, gesturing for me to go in first. I walk in and stand there, waiting. He reaches for a folder on the ottoman and brings it to me, trying to open it. He puts it back down on the ottoman and pulls out a letter and hands it to me.

I scan it. It says something about LSAT exams. "Law boards," he translates. "I'm going to take the law boards."

I look at him, not understanding.

"I'm going to go to law school," he says. "And I can go back East."

I bring a hand up to my face. "Paul—"

"Do you get it? Don't you understand?" he says. "I've never met anyone like you, Sally. I don't know what this is between us, but I do know I feel goofy and scared and excited and nervous and—" He grabs my good arm firmly. "I don't want to see you in harm's way, so sue me, okay? I want you alive. I want you for me."

My heart is pounding, but my head is telling me this is ridiculous, what am I doing here with this kid cop who's screwed up my interview.

"I won't do it again," he says quietly, drawing close. "Because I won't ever be sidelined like this again."

I look at him, frowning. "You have a career. You don't need to go to law school."

"I want to go to law school," he says seriously.

I raise my eyebrows. "It's not as active a career—"

"Sally."

I look at him.

"I'm falling in love with you," he says.

I shake my head. "It's impossible."

"It's not," he whispers, moving close. He puts his hand on my waist and softly kisses my cheek. He kisses my neck. "I will be there to protect you myself."

"I don't need protecting," I say, closing my eyes, feeling the magic.

"Maybe you need protecting from me," he whispers, gently pressing his lower body against my hip.

I know what that is down there, there is no mistaking it. And this time it is not a long gun in a leather holster.

I swallow, slipping a bit away. "I'm exhausted, Paul. And I need to think."

He looks earnestly at me. "I am sorry. I just want you to understand why I did it."

"I know why," I murmur. I look at his mouth briefly, smile slightly and move away, willing my body to march out of this bedroom and to the front door before it is too late. "Tonight's program didn't turn out too badly," I admit to him over my shoulder. "You should watch. Eleven o'clock."

"I wouldn't dream of missing you," he says.

"Bye, Jack," I call as I pass his bedroom door.

The door opens a crack. "Leaving, Sally? I was just going to ask if you guys want to be alone."

"Another time," I say.

At the front door, I turn awkwardly to Paul and he is not awkward in the least as he proceeds to kiss me deeply. Clearly he is feeling better, stronger. After a bit, I reach around to open the door behind me. We are murmuring good-nights when Louis suddenly steps out of the bushes. "Oh, my," I gasp, covering my heart with my hand.

"Sorry," Louis says. "Officer Fitzwilliam, there's somebody who's been looking in your window. I think maybe it's your bedroom window? In the back?"

I look at Paul over my shoulder.

"Who was it?" Paul says gruffly. "Could you see?"

"Oh, yeah, I could see. It was a girl, a young woman, blond. She was pressed against the glass, practically." He looks at me. "It's the same girl we saw before."

Paul moves around to my side. "It's Mindy," he sighs.

"Is that your girlfriend?" I ask.

"Ex," he says.

"She's still around," Louis says, kicking his head to the left. "She was over by the pool a minute ago, hiding behind the soda machine."

I'm getting a decidedly creepy feeling.

Paul closes the apartment door behind him. "I'll talk to her. You guys go on ahead. Take Sally to wherever she's going, will you?"

"Maybe we should stay," I say.

"Sometimes it's better to have witnesses," Louis adds. We both look at him. "If it's an ex-girlfriend, sometimes it's tricky. They get mad and make all kinds of accusations."

Paul thinks about this a moment and then shakes his head. "Mindy wouldn't do that."

"She's spying on you," I point out. "Sneaking around, looking in your bedroom window."

"Well, she knows there's somebody," he said. "I don't particularly want her to know who."

"I think she already knows," I say. "She was staring at me last night when I was here."

Louis confirms this.

"I'll wait here," I suggest, "and Louis can go with you to talk to her."

Paul looks at Louis. "I should do something, say something, right now before this gets out of hand."

Off they go. As soon as they're out of sight, I double back the other way so I can watch them. I sneak across the pool area and see Paul approaching, softly calling, "Mindy? I know you're out here. I want to talk to you."

Suddenly, she appears. She is a tall, leggy blonde. I

can't really see her features in the dim lighting, but her body is certainly terrific. Wow. "Paulie?" she says, and instantly I cringe because it sounds like the classic little-girl bimbo voice.

"What are you doing, Mindy?" Paul asks, sounding tired.

"Who is that woman, Paulie? Are you fucking her?"

"Mindy, I'm not sleeping with her."

"You've been kissing her, I've seen you. You've been cheating on me."

"But, Mindy, we agreed—"

"I didn't agree to anything!" she shrieks. "You just started running around with her! You're fucking her, I know you are!"

All I can visualize is this girl in front of news cameras. This is all I need for my reputation to become complete.

Paul steps forward to put a consoling arm around her. Immediately she starts sobbing on his shoulder. "I love you, Paulie, I love you with all my heart."

He doesn't say anything, but pats her on the back and looks at Louis as much as to say, *Now what?* Finally he says, "You're tired and upset, Mindy, you need some rest."

Suddenly, her grasp turns sexual and she grinds herself into him, shooting a hand down to rub his crotch.

"Mindy," he says, trying to get her hand. She drops down to her knees and tries to unzip Paul's pants.

"Mindy, no," he says quietly but firmly, stepping back.

"You love it," she says, moving forward on her knees. "You liked it in the hospital."

I'm learning a lot more about Paul than I think I wish to know.

"Miss," Louis says in a loud voice, startling the girl,

"Officer Fitzwilliam and I have a meeting. And unless you wish to be arrested for lewd and lascivious behavior, I suggest you go home now."

She looks around at Louis, then up at Paul, and slowly rises to her feet, self-consciously tugging down her shift.

"Go. I'll call you later," Paul tells her.

"You promise?"

"I promise."

She walks over to kiss him on the mouth and then, staring at Louis again, mumbles, "What are you, the fucking president or something?" and makes her way across the pool area. She turns around, walking backward, "You promise to call?"

"I promise."

"I love you," she calls softly.

This girl is like off the charts, I decide, ducking into the shadows to watch her. In the parking lot she walks over to a black Mustang convertible and gets in. A moment later, she gets out again and starts walking around to the other side of the building. I'll be damned, she's going back to spy on him again. I follow her and see her sneak around to the pool area.

I hurry back to the parking lot. I open the door of the Mustang and slide in, quickly opening the glove box and finding the registration.

Bramson K. Carl, 346 Forsythia Drive, Pasadena.

Huh. Her father, maybe?

Also in the glove compartment is a long wooden box. I think I know what it is, and when I open it—to confirm my suspicions—I discover that it *is* a gleaming fishing knife. She doesn't look like the fishing type, I think.

Quickly I replace the knife and registration and get out

of the car. I walk casually back toward the apartment, bumping into Louis on the way. "We were worried about you," he whispers.

"She's back spying on him, you know. She went around the other side of the building."

"She's hopped up, I think," Louis says, looking over his shoulder. "Look, I better get you out of here. He can handle it himself. Besides, his roommate's there."

"I suppose." We walk back to the Town Car. "That's her car over there, the Mustang. She lives in Pasadena."

Louis unlocks the limo and holds the door open for me to climb in. He opens the driver's door, climbs in to get something and tells me, "I'll be just a minute," and he gets out again. I watch Louis walk over to the Mustang and see a flashlight come on. The light plays slowly over the Mustang, hesitates, moves back to a certain spot. Then it goes off and Louis comes back to the car, rocking it as he gets in. "So much for Michael Arlenetta," he says. "There's your hit-and-run vehicle right over there."

CHAPTER | 3 5

When I climb out of the car at the courthouse the next morning, I find Clyde James blocking my path. "That was a nice broadside last night," he says.

"I didn't set him up, Clyde," I say wearily. I've had about three hours' sleep, my arm is killing me and all I want is a cup of coffee.

"It really stinks, Sally," Clyde continues, following me.

"He's already been released, Clyde."

"That's not the point."

I turn around. "Listen, Clyde, I didn't set him up, okay? I appreciate the opportunity, really, I do. But let me tell you something else," I add, starting to wag my finger at him. I move slightly, however, so that Clyde's body will block the view of the cameras on the media tower. "Your *colleague*— or whatever you want to call him—is not upset. He's thrilled. And let me tell you why. He wanted everybody in America to know that he was here in California last night, not in New Jersey, where, you may have heard, an unidentified helicopter was shot down near Rocky Presario's compound."

Clyde frowns, his eyebrows knitting.

"Yeah," I tell him. "Smart money says it was a failed attempt at firebombing Rocky Presario's compound. So you tell me, what could be better for Michael Arlenetta than to be arrested on national television three thousand miles away?"

Instead of being upset, Clyde seemed energized, his eyes dancing with excitement. "No shit," he says.

"So ask him about that," I say, turning to walk into the courthouse. I can hear the dollar signs ringing in Clyde's head with sales of Arlenetta's book. I get in line to go through the metal detectors.

"Did they get anybody?" I hear Clyde whisper in my ear. "Anybody survive the crash?"

I look at him. "It was more like they were blown up in midair. But they're tracing the remains." I don't mention that the son of Alexandra's tenant farmer had reached the wreckage—pieces were all over the woods—and found a piece of an arm, which he dutifully turned in.

This gang-and-mob stuff is a grisly business. I wonder when I'll get to work on something a little more lighthearted, say, systematic fraud and embezzlement of the entire country by Enron or something.

I hand my bag to the searcher.

* * *

As I sit here in the courtroom, getting my notes in order, waiting for this day to begin, I think over what Paul called to tell me this morning, that Michael Arlenetta was released and the charges of murder were dropped. While my testimony placed him at the scene of the firebombing in Bel Air and Mario Cantano's murder, his fingerprints did not match any of the fingerprints found on the physical evidence.

And so, he was, once again, a free man.

"And now with Mindy," Paul said, sounding very upset (and well he should be!), "we know Arlenetta didn't have anything to do with the accident."

Oh, great, now he's calling it an accident. Before it was attempted murder, but now that he knows it was his bimbo girlfriend who gave him a blow job in the hospital this week, it's "an accident."

Yes. It was Mindy who hit us. She followed Paul to my hotel Sunday night, followed us to the restaurant—where, it turned out, he had taken her, too, in the past—spied on us, followed us home, and seeing us stopped at the light with my arms wrapped around him, she lost it and decided to give us a scare. So she hit us and drove away.

We are told to rise and Judge Kahn enters the courtroom. He settles on the bench. The jury is brought in. Judge Kahn calls Lilliana to retake the stand.

Lilliana is wearing a muted red suit today. Her blouse is black. She is wearing pearls. Her makeup is subdued.

She looks different today. Glamorous, yes, dyed blond, obviously, but faded, somehow, almost—vulnerable. Certainly she is shorter than yesterday because the high heels have been replaced with black flats. Maybe that is what's

bothering me, the shoes. I've never seen Lilliana allo~
herself to appear at the five-feet-four height she is. Eve
her sneakers have lifts.

"Ms. Martin, I must remind you that you are still und
oath," Judge Kahn says gently.

He's got it bad, I decide.

"Attorney Banks?" Judge Kahn says. "You may procee
with your examination of this witness."

"Thank you, Your Honor," Banks says, rising from hi
table and moving forward.

"Good morning, Lilliana."

"Good morning." Her voice is subdued today, too. Sh
appears almost fearful.

Interesting.

"Yesterday you shared with the jury an example fron
your childhood to illustrate the kind of young boy the de
fendant was."

"Yes," she says softly, looking even more fearful, a
though Banks might strike out and hit her.

"Can you remember a time your brother was ever vio
lent?"

She shakes her head. "No."

"Have you ever seen him defend himself?"

"Oh, yes. You mean, as a boy, right?"

"Yes."

"Yes. He was pretty good boxer, a phantom weight. I
saw him box, that was defensive."

Mr. Banks smiles. "You never saw your brother in a
plain old fistfight?"

"No."

"What about as an adult? Did you ever see your brother
be violent in any way?"

She shakes her head. "No."

"Could you describe what your brother was—is—like as an adult?"

"Well, he is very successful at what he does, making movies. And he should be, because he's been messing around with film and video and audio-visual things and computers, animation, all of that, since he was little." She thinks a moment. "He's kind of—" She sends an apologetic look to her brother. "He's kind of a nerd, you know?"

A little laughter.

"Because he's such a technical geek," she adds, further provoking laughter.

She's got them. They understand.

"But your brother, Lilliana," Banks says loudly, beginning to pace, "was part of an extremely important and dangerous federal racketeering case."

"Oh, yes," she says, nodding. "It was the right thing to do. For all of us."

Banks pauses, but doesn't pursue this line of questioning. Instead, he comes back to his table to look at his notes. "Lilliana, how were you related to the deceased, Nick Arlenetta?"

"His father, Joe, married my father's oldest sister, Aunt Gina."

"And what provoked your father into testifying against your uncle Joe and cousin Nick in the 1970s?"

"Because Nick murdered my mother."

"Objection," Perez says. "The victim was never convicted of the crime, Your Honor."

Lilliana shoots a somewhat poisonous look at Perez and moves her eyes back to Banks.

"The prosecutor has a point, Mr. Banks," Judge Kahn says. "The objection is sustained."

"Lilliana, how was your mother murdered?"

"A bomb was placed under my father's car," she says. "Dad took Mama's car that day, because Taylor—" swallow "—Jonathan, had a big soccer game. And so when Mama went grocery shopping—" Her voice breaks and she lowers her head.

"The bomb went off and she was killed?"

She nods, looking down. "Yes." It is a whisper.

"Where were you when it happened?"

"At school."

"And what happened to you afterward?"

"Dad picked us up at school and he took us to Poppy's, my grandfather's. He told us what happened."

"What happened then?"

"We had a wake, the funeral." She is frowning, eyes creased, trying to think without breaking down.

"Did any of the Arlenetta family come to that funeral?"

She nods. "Aunt Gina. My cousins Rose, Theresa, Cliff and Mike. They came."

"But Joe and Nick did not come?"

"No."

Banks walks over to the jury box, giving her a minute. "How old were you?"

"Nine." She is wringing her hands, looking down at them in her lap.

Banks gives her a minute and then says, "It must have been very traumatic for you."

She nods, sniffing, wiping under her eyes with the back of her hand.

"And after your mother was murdered," Banks resumes, pushing off toward the stand again, "that's when your father started working with the FBI?"

"Yes, sir."

"And what happened to you?"

"I was taken to Ohio, to John Martin, and, um, they told me my name was Lilliana Martin now, and I was going to live with him."

"What did you know about John Martin?"

She shrugs. "They just told me we were to pretend he was my father, and that we had just lost my mother, and had moved to get a fresh start."

"So you went to school as Lilliana Martin?"

She nods. "Yes."

"And pretended this stranger was your father?"

"Yes."

"You didn't have a pretend mother?"

"Not right away," she said. "But John got married, maybe five months later, and she was my stepmother. She was very nice," she adds, "she was and is very good to me. Both of them. I owe them a great deal."

"Did you ever see your father, Frank Presario?"

"Yes. Twice a month. We'd meet for a weekend, somewhere different every time."

"Why couldn't you live with your father and brother?"

"They were afraid we'd be too easy to find."

"Who were the authorities afraid would find you?"

"Members of the Genovese crime family."

"Did you ever hear of any specific names?"

"Well, I knew Dad had helped put the head guy in prison, Tiezzi. And he put Uncle Joe away."

"What about your cousin Nick?"

"Nick? They were scared of Nick finding us," she confirms. She frowns slightly. "There were pictures—John had them—and he would show them to me. Make me study them, because if I ever saw any of these people, was to run."

"Would you have recognized Nick Arlenetta had yo seen him?"

"Oh, my God, yes," she says loudly.

"Would he have recognized you, though?" Banks asks "Had you changed at all since he last saw you?"

"Yes. I was a redhead, for years they made me dye m hair. Until I was seventeen, I think, when I went to college And then I went platinum. I also—" She stops, looks down smiles sheepishly but looks at the jury. "I had a nose op eration, rhinoplasty. When I was thirteen." A smile. "I ha Daddy's nose."

The jury smiles understandingly. The old lady nods, a she always does.

"So Nick Arlenetta would not recognize you."

"No one recognized me as an adult," she said. "No even Aunt Gina."

"Did you ever see your aunt Gina?"

"Yes," she said, nodding. "When I had just started or daytime TV. They sent me to a shopping mall opening ir Fort Lauderdale, you know, to promote the show and me, and Aunt Gina was there with my cousin Terry. I even signed a picture for them." She lifts her eyebrows. "I was scared to death, but they didn't know it was me."

"How did you feel after that?"

"Better. Confident I was going to be okay. The public-ity machine in my business was working in my favor. The feds do a good job in the witness protection program. My foster parents had played the role of my parents for so long we were all beginning to believe it ourselves."

"If you were safe from detection, Lilliana, why did you

agree to work with your father and brother and your cousin Cliff Yarlen and the FBI to build a case against your cousin Nick Arlenetta?"

"Because I hated him." This is said with such dead seriousness, we're all brought up a little short.

"Because he murdered your—" Banks stops himself, looking over at the prosecutor. "Withdrawn." He walks over to the table, looks at a note and comes back to Lilliana. "When did you start hating Nick Arlenetta?"

When she doesn't answer, he moves closer. "Lilliana, you said you hated your cousin Nick Arlenetta. When did you start hating him?"

After a moment, she says, "I was eight."

"Eight years old," he repeats. "How old were you when your mother was murdered?"

"Nine."

Banks looks surprised. "So did something happen the year before your mother was murdered? That made you hate your cousin?"

She doesn't answer. Her eyes are looking past Banks, to the floor somewhere around the bar to the gallery.

"Ms. Martin?" the judge says gently. She turns her large brown eyes to him, blinking. "You need to answer the question."

She nods, looking oddly detached suddenly, dazed maybe. She turns slowly to Banks and whispers something.

"You need to speak up Ms. Martin," Judge Kahn tells her.

She takes a breath. "What was the question?"

"Did something happen the year before your mother was murdered? Something that made you hate your cousin Nick Arlenetta?"

She nods. "Yes."

"Could you please tell the jury what happened?"

She does not want to tell this. Reluctantly she turns to the jury. "He was evil" is all she says.

Banks looks baffled. "Lilliana?" She looks at him. "Could you please tell the jury what happened?"

She doesn't say anything, her eyes sinking miserably to the floor again.

"When was the first time you thought your cousin Nick Arlenetta was evil, Lilliana?" Banks says loudly, pushing her.

"At my cousin Rose's wedding," she finally says.

"Rose? Was that Nick Arlenetta's sister?"

"Yes."

"How old were you?"

"Eight."

"What happened?"

"We went to Rose's wedding in Queens," she says quietly. "I was a flower girl. After, they had a reception at this big place in Long Island."

"And what happened?"

"Nick came over to me and said he had this present for me, for being the flower girl. He said it was out in his car, in the parking lot, so I went with him to get it." She swallows, eyes vacant. "There wasn't one, though."

"What do you mean?"

She drops her head, shaking it slowly.

"Could you tell the jury what happened?"

She sighs, her head hanging. "He exposed himself."

"Is that all?"

She shakes her head, still looking down. "No."

"Could you tell the jury what happened, Lilliana?"

Pause. "He started masturbating."

Silence in the courtroom.

"Did he ask you to touch him?" Banks asks gently.

She shakes her head. "No."

"Did he touch you?"

She shakes her head. "No." Pause. "He wanted me to watch."

"What did you do?"

No answer.

"Lilliana? What did you do?"

Still, the actress's head is down and she does not answer.

"Lilliana?" Banks says again.

Finally, she looks up. Tears are silently streaming down her face. "I watched him."

Banks looks at her. "How old was he? When he did this?"

She mumbles something, lowering her head.

"The jury couldn't hear you, Lilliana. How old was Nick Arlenetta when he did this?"

"Twenty-two."

"And how old were you?"

"Eight." It is scarcely a whisper.

"What happened next?"

"Um," she says, hesitating. "After he—you know—"

"Ejaculated?"

"Yes." Her voice sounds dead, void of emotion, as if she is on some sort of automatic drive. "Suddenly my aunt Gina was there, and she pushed me aside and she threw herself at Nick. And she started screaming and crying and clawing at his face."

"This was Nick Arlenetta's mother?"

"Yes?"

"Screaming and crying and clawing at his face?"

"Yes."

"So she knew what had happened?"

Lilliana nods solemnly. "Yes. She knew."

"What happened then?"

"My cousin Cliff came running over."

"And was he related to Nick?"

"He was Nick's younger brother."

"And what did he do?"

"He pulled Aunt Gina away."

"And what did Nick Arlenetta do?"

"He ran away, across the parking lot."

"And what did your cousin Cliff do?"

"He took Aunt Gina inside."

"And what did you do?"

She sighs, eyes down again. "I just stood there, for a while. And then I went inside."

"And what did your aunt Gina do then?"

Slowly Lilliana raises her head to look at him. "Nothing."

"What did she say to you?"

"Nothing."

"Did you say anything to her?"

"No."

Banks blinks a second. "Did your cousin Cliff talk to you?"

"No."

"Lilliana, did you tell your parents what happened?"

She shakes her head again. "No." She drops her head.

"Why not?"

"I was afraid. I thought I had done something really bad."

"You thought *you* had done something really bad?"

She nods. Slowly she brings her tearstained face up. "I knew I should have run away from him or something. But I didn't. And I didn't want to get into trouble."

There is a strangled sob in the front row of the gallery. I think it must have come from Frank Presario.

Banks glances over and then back to Lilliana. "Did you ever see Nick Arlenetta again?"

"As a child, no," she says.

"As an adult?"

She hesitates, looking to her brother.

Banks frowns, looking concerned. If I were to guess, I would say she was expected to say no. He looks up at the judge. "Your Honor, I respectfully request a recess. I believe the witness needs some time to collect herself."

Judge Kahn nods gravely, looking at his watch. "We'll break for lunch now. However, we'll resume at one-thirty." To the jurors, "Not two o'clock."

I simply shove my way through the crowd to get outside the courtroom and call New York on my cell. To hell with the land phone, everyone's calling in the same sensational testimony I am, of the Oscar-nominated actress being sexually abused as a child by Nick Arlenetta. "He's beginning to take on monstrous proportions," Alexandra observes, listening in with Will and a news writer. "How can the jury help but think Jonathan Small did the right thing by killing him?"

"It's the nature of the charges that's the problem," I explain. "It doesn't matter if the jury thinks Jonathan should have killed him—the question is, did Jonathan plan in advance to murder Nick Arlenetta and then carry his plan out? If he did, that's premeditated murder and they have to convict him."

"What about sentencing? Can't the judge show leniency?" Will wants to know.

"Check with Emmett, but from what I understand, California has very strict sentencing requirements for premeditated murder."

"But they will appeal."

"Undoubtedly."

"Okay," Alexandra says, "let's get Emmett and then get on the air with this. Thanks, Sally."

And they are gone.

I walk down the hall to the snack bar and get a grilled cheese sandwich. They're good when your stomach hurts. And mine does.

Poor Lilliana.

CHAPTER | 36

After eating my sandwich, I hang around the door to the witness holding room, hoping to see Burton or Cecelie. I am balancing my pad on my cast, writing some notes for tonight's *Late Edition* when Frank Presario appears at my side. "'Scuse me," he says gruffly, reaching for the doorknob.

"It's locked," I tell him just as he finds this out for himself.

He starts pounding on the door with his fist.

I want to say something to him, like how sorry I am about all this painful stuff in the trial, but realize nothing could possibly sound right, or help, and so I simply stand there, watching him.

Sheriff Jones comes over to us. "I want to see my daughter," Frank tells him.

"I can't let you in there," Jones tells him.

Frank starts pounding on the door again, attracting on-lookers from down the corridor. Abruptly the door swings open. Cecelie. "I want to see my daughter," Frank tells her.

"That's not a good idea, Frank," she says.

With a grunt, Frank simply shoves her and pushes forward. Sheriff Jones moves quickly, grabbing him from behind. Frank Presario has been trained, it seems, for after a vicious jab with his elbow in the sheriff's diaphragm, leaving him doubled over, he tries to move forward again, but by now the female sheriff has arrived, making a flying leap and bringing Frank Presario, Sheriff Jones and Cecelie Blake crashing down to the ground. As the sheriffs struggle to subdue Frank, Cecelie has the presence of mind to push me back and slam the door in my face.

"What's going on?" the guy from Fox asks breathlessly.

"Don't know exactly," I say, hedging.

The Fox guy puts his ear to the door and grimaces when someone on the other side kicks it. Moments later, it swings open and Frank Presario is wrestled out in handcuffs, yelling, "I want to see my daughter!" all the way down the hall and through another door leading to heaven only knows where.

Then Sheriff McDuff emerges from the same room and begins shooing us down the hall, saying court is going to begin shortly. Dutifully we move along, me on my cell phone, whispering the latest to New York.

When Lilliana Martin retakes the stand, she is visibly pale and obviously shaken. I couldn't make out Jonathan's expression when he was brought in. Frank Presario is obviously not here. Something is definitely up.

"Lilliana, before court broke for lunch, you told the

jury about the incident with Nick Arlenetta, at your cousin's wedding reception, that occurred when you were eight years old."

"Yes."

"I want to move ahead now, to the day you were nearly killed in Bel Air, when a helicopter sent two rockets into the house where you were living."

She nods.

"Sally Harrington has testified about that attack."

She shifts slightly in her seat, waiting.

"After the attack, you and Ms. Harrington drove to Larkensburg?"

"Yes."

"Where your father was? At the compound?"

"Yes."

"Who else was there?"

"My brother, Jonathan, and, um, several five or six men who worked for Dad. I don't know their names. And there was a housekeeper, Catalina. And I think that was it."

"These men worked for your father in what capacity?"

"Security."

"Did anyone visit the compound after you and Sally Harrington arrived?"

"Yes. Federal Prosecutor Sky Preston and FBI Agent Alfonso."

"Had you met them before?"

"Yes."

"Where?"

"Once in Larkensburg, once in a house on Summitridge in Beverly Hills and once in Palm Springs."

"Who else was present at those meetings with Prosecutor Preston and Agent Alfonso?"

"My brother, Jonathan, my cousin Cliff Yarlen and Dad."

"And why did you meet with them?"

"We were gathering evidence to make a case against Nick and his, uh, gang, I guess you would call them."

"And what was your role?"

She offers a thin smile. "I wasn't supposed to have one. But I went to Palm Springs to see Dad, and Cliff was there, and this photographer from the *Inquiring Eye* got a picture of us, me and Cliff, and so we just pretended to be boyfriend and girlfriend. As a cover. We didn't know how else to explain what he was doing with me."

"So you were never really supposed to be involved with this case?"

"I wasn't, no. I wanted to, and Sky Preston—the federal prosecutor—wanted me to, but Jonathan and Dad were very much against it."

"So you became a part of it, over the protests of your brother and father."

"Yes."

"To your knowledge, is that investigation still ongoing?"

She nods. "Yes."

"Are you still a part of it?"

"No."

Banks goes to look at his notes. "Lilliana, when you and Sally Harrington went to Larkensburg, how long did she stay?"

"Until after dinner. Then FBI Agent Alfonso took her back to Los Angeles."

"And where did Prosecutor Preston go?"

"He stayed for a long time, talking to Dad."

"Did you hear their conversation?"

"No. They were behind a closed door in his study."

"And what about your brother? How long did he stay?"

"He left right after Sally left with Agent Alfonso."

"And where did he go?"

"Back to Los Angeles. He needed to be back at work the next day."

"Did anybody know the real identity of your brother at that point? Besides you and the federal people working on the case?"

"No. No, wait—Sally did. Because Jonathan was there when we arrived in Larkensburg and we told her who he was."

"But for all intents and purposes, your brother's true identity was still a secret?"

"Yes."

"What was your brother's role supposed to be in building a case against Nick Arlenetta?"

"Sky wanted him to make nice with Nick, demonstrate his support, Monarch Studios' support, in his bid to run the AFTW."

"And what would this involve?"

"Tape recordings, video surveillance, that kind of thing."

"So despite the fact that Cliff Yarlen had been discovered cooperating with the feds and had been murdered because of it—"

"Objection, Your Honor, no such determination was officially ever made," Perez says.

"I'll withdraw the question, Your Honor," Banks says, acquiescing. He clears his throat. "Your cousin, Cliff Yarlen, was working with the federal government to build a case against his brother, Nick Arlenetta, who was a suspected mobster. Is that correct?"

"Suspected mobster and murderer," Lilliana adds. "And a child molester." She glares defiantly at Perez, as if daring him to object.

"And Cliff Yarlen was murdered?"

"Executed, yes."

"Your father called you and warned you that Nick Arlenetta's people suspected your true identity, is that correct?"

"Yes."

"And on March 7, you were nearly killed in the firebombing of the Bel Air mansion, is that correct?"

"Yes."

"Your father was in fear of his life?"

"Yes."

"And yet the federal authorities wanted your brother to continue building a case against Nick Arlenetta?"

"Yes."

"All right," he says, looking at his notes. "The day after the firebombing, Lilliana, what did you do?"

"I rested."

"At the compound in Larkensburg?"

"Yes."

"And the next day?"

"I was still there."

"How long did you stay in Larkensburg?"

"Six days."

"And did you talk to your brother?"

"No, but my father did."

"Did your father tell you about any of his conversation with Jonathan?"

"Yes. He said Jonathan said he thought it would be over soon—"

"Objection," Perez says. "This is hearsay, Your Honor. None of this was in Mr. Presario's testimony."

"Your Honor, the witness is simply telling the jury what it was her father said."

"I'll allow it. You may continue, Ms. Martin."

She hesitates, seemingly unsure of where she was.

"Your father said, Jonathan told him he thought it would be over soon," Banks prompts.

She nods. "Yes. And he said Nick was coming to see him. The next day. In his office. And Jonathan told him he already had some stuff on tape about a new arrangement between the AFTW and Monarch."

"Do you know what this new arrangement would entail?"

"A ten-percent increase in the union members' pay. Nick was to offer this as an incentive for the union to back his leadership."

"Was Jonathan to gain anything by this deal?"

"You mean in reality? Or for the sake of setting Nick up?"

"In the context of your brother setting up Nick Arlenetta," Banks says.

"A kickback. A payment equal to five percent of the dues of every new union worker hired by Monarch."

"And do you know how it was going to be paid?"

"It was going to be laundered through a bank in the Cayman Islands."

"And when your father told you this, about his conversation with Jonathan, was he happy that Jonathan said it was almost all over?"

"No."

"Why not?"

She sighs. "He didn't want Jonathan to meet with Nick.

He thought it could be a setup. Dad didn't trust the feds anymore. They hadn't protected Cliff. He was dead. And they had certainly messed up with me. It was only by a merciful act of God I hadn't been killed." Her voice has grown stronger, anger starting to show itself.

"What did your father want Jonathan to do?"

"To pull out, call the whole thing off."

"But Jonathan wouldn't?"

She shakes her head. "No."

"So what did you do, Lilliana? The night before your brother was to meet with Nick Arlenetta?"

"I drove back to Los Angeles."

"Did your father know?"

"Only after I left. When he couldn't stop me."

"Why did you go?"

"To talk Jonathan out of it. I was scared. I knew Nick was up to something. Even if he didn't know who Jonathan really was, there was no question in my mind that after doing the deal with Jonathan, getting things signed and in place, Nick would probably just knock him off."

"Why did you think that?"

"That's what he did with Cliff. As soon as Cliff brought Nick into contact with the AFTW—" She cuts the air with her hand. "He killed him."

"Objection," Perez says, sounding weary, standing up. "That's speculation, Your Honor. There's no evidence."

"Sustained. The jury will disregard the witness's last statement."

"The night you drove up to Los Angeles, did you see your brother?"

"No."

"Why not?"

"I couldn't find him. He wasn't home."

"What did you do?"

"I stayed over at a motel near his house."

"Did you find him in the morning?"

"No. He never came back to the house."

"So what did you do?"

"I went to Monarch, to the studio."

"And what time was this?"

"Ten o'clock."

"Did you see your brother?"

"Not right away."

"Why not?"

"The guard let me through reception, because he knew me. I had just finished a picture there. I went up to Jonathan's office. Nobody was around, so I just went in there and waited for him."

"And did you see your brother?"

She nods. "Yes. After about a half hour. He came in. He freaked out when he saw me, though, closed and locked his door."

"So you never saw his secretary?"

"No. Just the guard downstairs."

"And what did your brother say?"

"He was very angry I was there. Said Nick was coming and if he saw me there, the whole thing would be blown. I tried to talk him into calling it off, but he said it was too late, that Nick was coming any minute."

"What did you say?"

"I asked him if the office was wired. And he said no, it wasn't. The conference room down the hall was, and the feds were set up in one of the old bungalows next to the building. To watch and listen."

"Did your brother appear frightened?"

"Yes. He was scared because the feds were supposed to be watching the building, but they couldn't have seen me because they'd just let me walk into the middle of it. And so I said to Jonathan, that's what I mean, that's why I'm scared, they're going to mess this whole thing up again."

"What happened then?"

"Jonathan's intercom buzzed. His secretary told him Nick had arrived and was out in reception."

"What did your brother do?"

"He told me to go into his bathroom and stay there until he came and got me."

"The private bathroom connected to his office?"

"Yes, the door right behind his desk."

"What happened then?"

"I went in there and waited."

"What happened then?"

"I heard voices, Jonathan's and someone else's. I leaned close to the door—it wasn't closed all the way—and I heard another man say, 'I prefer to do business in a man's office. I don't like conference rooms. Gives me no insight into a man's character.' And then my brother said, 'Whatever you prefer, Nick, have a seat.'"

"So Nick Arlenetta had come into your brother's office?"

"Yes."

"But your brother and the federal authorities had set up the conference room to be bugged?"

"Yes."

"So coming into your brother's office was a surprise to him?"

"Yes."

"What did you do?"

"I sat on the john, in the dark, and listened."

"And what did you hear?"

"Nick gave my brother some papers to look at."

"Where was your brother sitting?"

"In front of his desk, in the chair opposite Nick's."

"You could see this?"

"Through the crack, yes. I could see Jonathan, but I couldn't see Nick."

"What happened then?"

"Nick got up and was moving around. He said, 'You've made some good movies,' and Jonathan thanked him." She swallows. "And then he said, 'Isn't this Lilliana Martin?' and Jonathan got up and I couldn't see him, but I heard him say, 'Yes' And then Nick said, 'Is it true what they say, you know? She's a whore?'"

"What did your brother say?"

"He said, 'No, I don't think she is.' But Nick kept at it. He said, 'Oh, I know it for a fact.' And my brother said, 'Oh? How do you know that?' and Nick said—"

She is breathing heavily now, eyes fierce. "Nick said, 'I could have fucked her once, but I turned her down.'"

"What happened then?" Banks says quickly.

"I walked out of the bathroom, aimed the gun and pulled the trigger."

There is a stunned silence. Nobody is sure they've heard this correctly. Banks looks openly astonished. Finally he says, "You were holding a gun?"

"Yes. I brought it with me from Larkensburg. Jonathan used to use it for target practice."

The courtroom erupts. The judge bangs the gavel, calling for order.

"Ms. Martin," he says, having trouble keeping his voice level, "are you confessing to the murder of Nick Arlenetta?"

"Yes, Your Honor, I am." She looks across to her brother. "I brought the gun in my bag. I walked out there and I looked Nick in the eye and I told him he was a murdering, lying son of a bitch, and I pointed that gun and Jonathan tried to stop me. But I shot him." She turns to the jury. "I killed him. Goddamn it," she says, voice breaking, "somebody had to stop him."

I am up, stumbling over the people in my row, and running out of the courtroom. I burst through the front doors of the courthouse and run as fast as I can across the parking lot to the DBS cameras.

CHAPTER | 37

"That's a shot of him right there," I point out to viewers as I watch the studio monitor.

"Walking out of the Santa Monica courthouse," Emmett adds, "a free man. The first time Jonathan Small has been outside the county jail in seven months."

We watch—and hopefully a lot of America is watching with us—as Jonathan solemnly ducks his head to slip into the back seat of an unmarked state vehicle.

"Coming back to you on one, Sally," Zigs says in my earphone.

I shift slightly, looking into the camera as the red light comes on. "The breaking news again, in case you're just joining us—in surprise testimony today, the actress Lilliana Martin, sister of the man on trial for murder, Jonathan Small, confessed to shooting and killing Nick Arlenetta.

According to Ms. Martin, she had arrived shortly before Arlenetta at her brother's office at Monarch Studios, was hiding in the private bathroom attached to the office when she heard Arlenetta make lewd sexual comments regarding herself. As you may recall from her earlier testimony, as an eight-year-old child Ms. Martin was a victim of sexual abuse at the hands of Nick Arlenetta. When Ms. Martin heard Arlenetta's lewd comments in her brother's office, she ran out of the bathroom and shot him. Her brother, Ms. Martin said, tried to stop her, placing his hands over hers, but it was too late."

I sigh dramatically, turning to Emmett as I hear Zigs say, "Take two."

"It was just extraordinary, Emmett," I say. "I am probably more familiar with this case than anyone, and yet—" I shake my head. "I didn't see this coming."

"No one did, Sally," Emmett says.

"The question is, what happens to Lilliana Martin now?"

"Well, Sally, as you know, Lilliana Martin has already been arraigned and tonight is out on bail. Unlike the charges of premeditated murder that had been brought against her brother, the charges against Ms. Martin are simple manslaughter. Clearly, at least according to her testimony, Ms. Martin was provoked into shooting him. As you mentioned, only earlier today she had testified to the sexual abuse she had suffered from Arlenetta when she was a child. She also believed Nick Arlenetta had murdered her mother, had murdered her cousin Cliff Yarlen, and tried to have her killed in the firebombing of the Presario mansion in Bel Air." Emmett shakes his head. "For the prosecution to even consider anything but manslaughter would be setting themselves up for disaster. There's not a jury in this land that wouldn't understand why she did what she did. And when she did it."

"She did bring a gun with her to Monarch Studios," I point out. "That could indicate premeditation."

He shakes his head. "She carried the gun for protection. Who wouldn't believe that after everything she had been through?"

"So you think she'll get off."

"Not completely, no. But I do think she'll get a suspended sentence."

"Which gives me pause for thought, Emmett," I say slowly. I squint a little. "Who is to say that any of what Lilliana Martin said today really happened? According to her testimony, no one other than her brother and Nick Arlenetta saw her in the building."

"There was the security guard who let her in," Emmett says.

"That nobody seems to know anything about. And her name wasn't in the log. This was a major murder investigation—one would think the police would have found someone before now who would have mentioned that such a famous person as Lilliana Martin was there the day of the murder."

Emmett smiles. "That's why we have trials, Sally. To carefully weigh and consider all the evidence before rendering a verdict."

"Yes," I say, looking directly into the camera. "And that is the big news coming out of Santa Monica, California, tonight, ladies and gentlemen. Jonathan Small has been released, and his sister, actress Lilliana Martin, is out on bail, after being arraigned on charges of manslaughter. While on the stand today in her brother's trial, she confessed that it was she, in fact, who shot and killed mobster Nick Arlenetta at Monarch Studios on March 13.

Glen hands me a piece of paper as I come down off the set. "What's this?"

"It ran in tonight's *Post*," he says. "Alexandra faxed it through."

I scan the piece, which reads, in part:

Harrington's mildly manic-depressive career at DBS News is growing on us. On one program she's nearly hysterical, a beat-up, slightly bug-eyed interviewee, confiding in viewers how she was nearly killed. On the next program, she suddenly has all the calm brilliance and regal restraint of her mentor at DBS News, Alexandra Waring. Somewhere between the two lies the real Sally Harrington. We are anxiously waiting to see exactly where she will emerge. In the meantime, however, we will enjoy watching her, for Harrington is incapable of being boring. She makes for good TV. The question is, does she make for a good TV journalist?

I walk into the control room, feeling tired and depressed. Manic depressive, right. "Alexandra for you," Zigs says, pointing to the phone.

I snap up the telephone. "Thanks," I say. "I wouldn't have wanted to miss this review for the world."

She laughs a little. "I didn't send it to upset you."

"No, you just wanted to spread around that part about your calm brilliance and regal restraint."

"No," she insists, sounding amused. "I want you to think about what they said."

"Why?"

"It's made me stop and think about Jessica's show," she says. "Maybe she and Will are right, maybe you should give it a shot."

I feel scared suddenly.

And my mind reels. Me doing a talk show. Regular hours. The money, good Lord, think of the money.

But I love news. I've always worked in news. So what if I'm slightly loony?

"Why don't we just both think about it for a few days," Alexandra says. "What's most important about the piece is that everyone agrees, you make great TV, Sally. But you're going to have to make up your mind about what kind of TV you want to do."

I swallow. "Do I still get to do *Late Edition?*"

"Of course you will. For as long as it's appropriate, anyway. It sounds as though the situation with Lilliana Martin could be wrapped up very quickly." Pause. "Do you think she really shot him?"

"I don't know," I say honestly. "It wouldn't surprise me if she did—on the other hand, I wish I could stop thinking that Banks might have convinced her to confess to the murder."

"That's a very serious allegation," the anchorwoman says.

I sigh, smiling slightly. "That's why we have trials, Alexandra. To carefully weigh and consider all the evidence before rendering a verdict."

"I knew you'd warm up to Emmett," she says.

Louis and I walk out to the car. I am beat.

Paul's waiting outside, standing by our car. "Hi," he says.

"Hi." I feel shy, suddenly. (*Manic depressive,* I think.)

He smiles. "Quite a day."

I nod. "Quite a day and quite a night, last night."

He averts his eyes, nodding, mouth pressed into a line. "I'm so sorry."

"Why? It wasn't your fault," I say. "You didn't know she would run us down."

He makes a sound of agreement. "I'm just sorry about her altogether, believe me."

I look down a moment. "It was the hospital crack that got me, you know. I heard what she said."

"I know it was," he says quietly.

I look at him. "It really happened?"

He nods with a painful expression. "I'm afraid so. It wasn't like I was in my right mind. I actually didn't even think it really happened, until she said that. I thought it was a dream. Oh, man," he sighs, running a hand through his hair. "How embarrassing is this?" He looks over at the car. "It was about as embarrassing as the recovery room nurse walking in on her doing it."

"The recovery room?" I ask, amazed.

His face is turning red. "I was just coming out of the anesthesia and found her— Oh, God," he says, and wheels around.

I start to laugh a little and he whirls around. "I'm sorry," I say, "but it is kind of funny."

"As long as you think so," he says, sounding relieved.

"I do think so," I say. "Stuff happens."

He moves a little closer, careful not to bump casts. "I just don't want to mess this up, Sally. And yet everything seems to be making this harder."

I look at this twenty-five-year-old's face and I wonder,

how can this possibly work? "I'm going to be here at least another week," I tell him.

A light comes into his eyes. "What are you doing this weekend?"

"I've got to work."

He nods. And then, "You need some help?"

Now I smile. "Yes, as a matter of fact, I do. I'm in need of a left hand."

He reaches with his left hand to take my right in his. He squeezes it. "I'm your man," he tells me.

I wonder. But happily so. This is just one of those roads I'm going to have to explore.

Mira Books
Proudly presents
THE KILL FEE
by
Laura Van Wormer

Available in hardcover
November 2003

Turn the page for an exciting preview of
Sally Harrington's newest escapade!

The road winding up to Castle Kerry is almost two miles long. The castle is actually a turn-of-the-century stone tower built on the highest point in central Connecticut. While Roderick Reynolds, a feature writer for *Expectations* magazine, finishes his cupcakes (the Twinkies are long gone) and guzzles his decaffeinated Diet Tea (what is the *point?*) in the car, I explain what it is he is about to see. It's going to be cold up in the tower and I might as well keep him warm now. The wind is blowing the flag the Castleford Lions Club put up here very hard, and it is a cold, whipping wind from the north.

We will see Long Island Sound in New Haven to the south, I explain, and we will see Hartford to the north. We will look over two thousand magnificent acres of Castleford park land; he will see reservoirs and traprock ridges; in the city he will be able to see our one hundred-year-old former city library—domed in copper, built with white marble, skylights and soaring windows—that has been renovated into a cultural center; he will see our new state-of-the-art hospital, rated one of America's finest; and he will then, I tell him, see the housing projects in their true context. "People come to Castleford when they need help, but we are, by nature, a generous community. Always have been." I, Sally Harrington, am determined that Roderick will see my hometown through my eyes.

"Yeah-yeah-yeah," Roderick says, tossing his sticky wrappers and napkins on the floor of the back seat. "You're going to make me climb that thing?"

"Yes," I tell him, getting out. Whoooo boy, it is cold, and I turn up the collar of my coat, jam my hands into my pockets and start walking. I take a quick look back to make sure Roderick is following me and then walk up to the stone wall that marks the edge of the landing to wait for him.

Golly, it's beautiful, even in this naked time of the year. While we climb the circular stairs up to the top of the tower, I tell him about the festival of lights we have in the park from Thanksgiving through New Year's. I hear him puffing ahead and I back off a little, allowing him to slow down if he wants. He makes it, though, kind of pulling himself up the railing at the end, hand over hand.

What he sees at the top makes him involuntarily straighten to attention. And then smile slightly. Huffing and puffing still, he takes a few steps out, rests his hands on the stone wall and squints into the horizon, first looking south—"New Haven?" I nod, yes—then north, to Hartford, the state capital.

"Jesus, I wouldn't have believed it," he says, looking west and east, marveling at the cliffs and peaks and endless acres of woods and streams and reservoirs that stretch from Middletown to Middlefield to Castleford to Southington (although the latter has desecrated their peaks with a mess of transmission towers just around the corner). "This is really beautiful."

I smile. Maybe he will be kind to my town after all. I start telling him about how Castleford is regenerating and reinventing itself, of the progress and plans, and of the slow and steady improvement.

"Yeah, okay," he says without taking a note and heading for the stairs, "but I gotta take a piss."

I sigh, rubbing my eyes. Then I take one last look out, take a deep breath of clean fresh air and follow him down the stairs, reminding myself why this article will be important. What the point of this whole nightmare of a day is. "There's no bathroom up here, Roderick. I'll take you down to—"

"No, I gotta go *now*," he informs me, reaching the bottom of the stairs. "Wait for me in the car."

I stop on the last step. "You can't do it in here," I tell him, horrified.

"Why not?" He's already got his hands on his zipper.

"Because this isn't skid row." I grab his arm and push him toward the doorway. "Go piss on the view."

"It's cold out there."

"So help me God, Roderick," I tell him, shoving him outside, "if one molecule of you lands on this tower, I will throw you off it myself."

"All right, all right," he says, turning away. "Just go away and let me do my business."

I stomp back to the car, calling back, "I'm going to check, you know!"

I climb into the Jeep and start the engine. I turn on the radio, scanning stations for a weather report, find one and glance back across the parking lot, wondering what to do with this idiot now.

After a minute, I look around for him again.

Where is he? He's got to be freezing in that wind.

After another minute goes by, I start to worry that he's sick or something. Maybe he has the trots. Heaven knows, with what he's eaten today that could be a possibility. That or sugar shock.

I decide to wait a little longer.

This is ridiculous, I think after two minutes, grabbing some Kleenex out of the glove compartment and climbing out of the car. I walk tentatively toward the tower. "Roderick?" I call. Nothing. "Roderick? Are you okay? I've got some Kleenex if you need it."

Nothing. Well, the wind is blowing—maybe he can't hear me. I step next to the tower and yell, "Roderick? Are you okay?"

Now I have a queasy feeling. Something is really wrong. I can't stand the guy, but I don't want to embarrass him. But—

I walk into the tower. And then through to the other side. "Roderick?"

All I hear is the wind, and the flag rope banging against the aluminum pole. I look around. No sign of him.

I walk all the way around the tower calling his name. Now I'm getting scared. He couldn't have—

I try to look over the stone wall, but I can't see over the cliff. "Roderick!" I call.

I run up the stairs to the top of the tower. He's not there, either.

I run over to the south side and look down. Rocks, shale, bushes, traprock. Where *is* he? I scan the horizon, noticing the clouds that have rolled in, and that my breath is coming out in puffs of frost now, and quickly being taken by the wind.

Dear God, where is he? I think, looking. Looking. No movement but the flag waving wildly, no sound but the wind in my ears and the flag rope banging.

And then I see something. Way down.

It's a leg. I can't see anything more. Not from here. Except that the leg is not moving.